REGENCY

SECRETS AND
SCANDALS

REGENCY

SECRETS AND SCANDALS

Louise
ALLEN

MILLS & BOON

REGENCY SECRETS & SCANDALS © 2023 by Harlequin Books S.A.

The publisher acknowledges the copyright holders of the individual works as follows:
THE EARL'S RELUCTANT PROPOSAL
© 2021 by Melanie Hilton   First Published 2021
Philippine Copyright 2021   Second Australian Paperback Edition 2023
Australian Copyright 2021   ISBN 978 1 867 29451 1
New Zealand Copyright 2021

RUMORS
© 2013 by Melanie Hilton   First Published 2013
Philippine Copyright 2013   Second Australian Paperback Edition 2023
Australian Copyright 2013   ISBN 978 1 867 29451 1
New Zealand Copyright 2013

® and ™ (apart from those relating to FSC®) are trademarks of Harlequin Enterprises
(Australia) Pty Limited or its corporate affiliates. Trademarks indicated with ® are
registered in Australia, New Zealand and in other countries.
Contact admin_legal@Harlequin.ca for details.

MIX
Paper | Supporting
responsible forestry
FSC® C001695

Published by
Harlequin Mills & Boon
An imprint of Harlequin Enterprises (Australia) Pty Limited
(ABN 47 001 180 918), a subsidiary of HarperCollins
Publishers Australia Pty Limited
(ABN 36 009 913 517)
Level 19, 201 Elizabeth Street
SYDNEY NSW 2000 AUSTRALIA

Printed and bound in Australia by McPherson's Printing Group

CONTENTS

Louise Allen has been immersing herself in history for as long as she can remember, finding that landscapes and places evoke powerful images of the past. Venice, Burgundy and the Greek islands are favorites. Louise lives on the Norfolk coast and spends her spare time gardening, researching family history or travelling. Please visit Louise's website, www.louiseallenregency.com, her blog, www.janeaustenslondon.com, or find her on Twitter @louiseregency and on Facebook.

The Earl's Reluctant Proposal

Author Note

Lucy, the fourth of my Liberated Ladies, was more than happy to stay single. But then her music was snatched from her and, it seemed, so was all the joy and magic in life. I wondered how she was ever going to get it back, but then Max arrived—too perfect, too cold, too aristocratic for her—and he knew how.

Reluctantly, it seemed, Max found himself giving Lucy the magic back and, in the process, shattering the ice that had imprisoned him for years. What happened then surprised them both...

I hope you enjoy following Lucy and Max's journey together as much as I did writing it.

DEDICATION

For the Quayistas for restoring
lockdown sanity via Zoom.

CHAPTER ONE

July 19th, 1815—London

Thump.

Lucy woke with the scream lodged in her throat, yet, when she looked down at her hands cradled defensively against her chest, there was no pain, no blood. A dream? But the sound had been real, she realised when it came again. This time she recognised it for what it was: a fist hitting the door panels, not a keyboard cover slamming down on her unwary fingers.

She scrambled off the sofa, confused and oddly dizzy. Where was she? It came back as she stumbled to the door, turned the key. Lady Sophia's piano lesson... That was what she was here for, she recalled as the door opened and she backed unsteadily away.

'Sophia, what the devil do you think you're about, locking yourself in here for half the day?' The speaker stopped dead, three strides into the room. 'Who are you and where is my sister?'

'Lucy Lambert and I do not know.' Lucy sat down with an inelegant bump on the sofa and stared at the man. *What is wrong with me?*

'She said, um... She said she had received an urgent message to go to her old governess. She said she would return in two or three hours and that I should make myself comfortable, take refreshments, read a book. It was ten o'clock when she left.'

The clock on the mantelshelf chimed four thin notes. 'But that's impossible.' Lucy blinked it into focus and as she did so the louder, deeper, strokes of the hall clock echoed the time. 'We spoke for a moment or two. Lady Sophia was in great haste, but she pointed out the refreshments on the table and showed me the bookcase for entertainment. Then she left. That way.' She pointed to the second door. 'I was thirsty, so I drank a glass of lemonade and sat down to go over my notes for the lesson and… That is all I recall.'

The man stooped and picked up something from the carpet. 'Yours?'

'Yes.' She reached out and took the little notebook, her thoughts coming into focus as her vision cleared. 'The lemonade. That is why I feel so strange. She drugged me.' Then, indignant as it sank in, '*Drugged* me!'

The man went to the table, picked up her glass, sniffed it, then poured some liquid from the jug and sipped. 'You drank this?'

'It wasn't very nice.' Rather bitter, she remembered. 'But I was thirsty. It is hot outside. I did not like to ring and disturb the staff.'

'Who are you?'

Lucy could guess who *he* was because she had looked up Lady Sophia Harker in the *Peerage* before accepting the invitation to come to her home. Single women with any sense did not enter the private homes of complete strangers, not without taking some basic precautions. Lady Sophia Harker lived in Cavendish Square with her stepbrother, Lord Burnham, the son of her mother's second husband.

'Miss Lambert, music teacher.' She produced one of her newly printed cards from her reticule. 'My lord,' she added as an afterthought.

He took it, and Lucy got the better of her indignation, nagging headache and confusion and looked at him properly for the first time. Max Fenton was what her friend Melissa—never bashful—would describe as a fine example of his sex, she supposed. Not a massive specimen thankfully, because being of only medium height herself she disliked being loomed over. Even so, he had more than enough presence to fill the room and was possessed of an aura of chilly authority that, as he was clearly displeased, was uncomfortable.

Another friend, Jane, Lady Kendall, who was an artist, might not want to draw him, Lucy decided. He was too predictable—tidily just under six foot, she guessed. Lean and fit, but not overly muscular. Regular features—strong, straight nose, firm jaw, dark grey eyes and modishly cut light brown hair that looked as though it might bleach blonder if exposed to the sun.

Thirty, possibly. No scars, freckles, imperfections and just the hint of a dip in his chin that he would no doubt hate to have called a dimple. Yes, Jane would dismiss him as not interesting enough to be a challenge for a portraitist.

'Will you be able to describe me adequately later, do you think?' he enquired, and Lucy realised she had been staring.

'Yes, I think so. When confronted by an angry male it is always prudent to be able to describe him afterwards to the authorities,' she said and had the satisfaction of seeing him blink.

Mousy, skinny, brown-haired music teachers did not normally bite back when sneered at by earls, but recently Lucy had found her teeth and something that was not so much courage as a sense of frustrated irritation with the ways of the world. It was, she had discovered, a perfectly good substitute for bravery.

'You think I might become violent?' He spoke as he walked away from her to throw open the other door, the one his stepsister had left by.

'I have no way of telling, my lord. You appear to be labouring under a strong emotion and I have noted that some gentlemen, in the absence of the real cause of their anger, will lash out at whoever is nearest. Verbally or otherwise.'

He opened the door, looked through, sighed, closed it again and walked back. 'I do not *lash out* at women, children, servants or animals, Miss Lambert. You are quite safe.'

However, you, My Lordship, are very much on edge, despite your veneer of calm.

'Excellent. I am much reassured that all those you consider your inferiors are safe from your ire.' She stood up and looked around for her bonnet. 'In that case, if you will be so good as to pay me, I will be on my way.'

'Pay you? For what?' Lord Burnham enquired. His eyebrows had drawn together into a straight line that echoed the lips that had tightened when she had answered back.

'For the waste of a day. I was engaged to give Lady Sophia a morning's lesson in the pianoforte, not to be drugged and rendered unconscious for the best part of six hours. In addition to which I will have the expense of a hackney to return home from this wasted journey. I certainly have no intention of walking, not after this experience.'

'How much are you owed?'

Lucy did a rapid calculation, added in the cab fare, a weighting for the effects of the lemonade and five shillings for aggravation by the earl and told him the result.

The eyebrows did not relax, the vertical line between them growing a little deeper.

'The labourer is worthy of her hire, my lord.'

'Of course. But before I do pay you and you leave, Miss Lambert, tell me exactly what happened today. My sister, you see, does not have a governess, retired or otherwise, closer than Northumberland.'

That explained his grim expression, at least. 'You think she has eloped?'

'I *think* I would like to know what happened.' She was not quite certain, but she thought he grew tenser at her suggestion.

This was definitely a man used to getting his own way without an argument. 'I was recommended to Lady Sophia by a friend of mine, the Duchess of Aylsham.'

There, that's given you pause, my lord.

Lucy did not give him time to express any doubts about a duchess being the friend of a spinster who earned her living as a humble music teacher. 'Lady Sophia wrote to me expressing an interest in learning the pianoforte and engaged me to come and give her a preliminary lesson for two hours this morning. You appear surprised, my lord.'

'Exceedingly. Sophia has been proficient on the pianoforte and the harp since childhood.'

'She implied she was a complete beginner which, I must admit, struck me as unusual for a young lady of her background. I suppose I thought she had struggled with it as a child.'

Lied to and *drugged. I would like a word with you, my lady.*

Lucy refrained from saying what she felt and continued to report as concisely as possible. The man had some excuse for both anger and concern, she could understand that.

'I arrived as requested at half past nine and Lady Sophia

told the butler that she did not wish us to be disturbed. But that cannot be right—if he was expecting me to be teaching her to play, why was he not concerned when there was no music and no one emerged for hours?'

'Because when I came in just now he informed me that my stepsister was engaged all day with a teacher of French and that as she found the language so difficult—another untruth, I regret to say—she needed to immerse herself without distraction. Hence the refreshments to cover luncheon. As this is her sitting room and that door leads to her dressing room and bedchamber, there would be no need for either of you to emerge to use the…facilities.'

'And there is a back stair to the ground floor, I suppose?' Lady Sophia appeared to be an excellent strategist as well as an accomplished liar.

'A branch of the servants' stairs, yes.' The Earl had the air of a man concentrating on not grinding his teeth. 'You arrived. Then what happened?'

'I was shown in, but Lady Sophia immediately put on her bonnet—I had not even untied the ribbons of mine—and said, in an agitated manner, that she had received an urgent message and that she must go to her frail governess, but would return in a while. She begged me to stay so that we could begin her lesson when she returned, promised to pay me extra for my trouble and pointed out the refreshments. She also locked the door and left the key so that I would feel secure, being in a strange house, so she said. Then she rushed out that way.'

The headache was clearing now and she could remember more. 'It was peculiar, now I reflect upon it. She appeared animated, but not upset. More excited, I would say.'

'I have no doubt of that.' At least Lord Burnham no longer sounded as though she was a dishonest housemaid about to be sacked for stealing the silver. He was clearly more exasperated with his stepsister than with her.

'So it *is* an elopement?'

To her surprise Lord Burnham stopped pacing and sat down opposite her. 'Not yet,' he said cryptically. 'Or so I hope.' He raked his fingers through his hair, looking considerably more human. 'You say you are a friend of Aylsham's wife?'

'We have been friends for years, since before Verity married Will.' She ignored the way his expression changed when she used their first names. Lucy reminded herself that antagonising members of the aristocracy was not the way to begin a successful career teaching their families. 'I choose to make my own living, but that does not make me unfit for polite society,' she added mildly.

'No, it does not,' Lord Burnham said slowly. Those cold grey eyes were surveying her much as he might have sized up a horse he was being offered for sale, one he suspected of being unsound in some way he could not quite detect. 'But have you the gowns for it?'

Lucy knew she was gaping and closed her mouth with a snap. 'What has my wardrobe to do with anything, my lord?'

'Humour me, Miss Lambert.'

He did not *appear* to be completely deranged. Lucy decided to indulge him. 'My wardrobe is adequate for dining with a duke, attending a garden party or dancing in select company, yes.' She did not add that it had been considerably boosted by gifts from her married friends discarding their pre-wedding gowns for outfits more suitable to married ladies of rank.

'Mmm.' The Earl, elbows on the arms of his chair, steepled his fingers and began thoughtfully tapping them against his lips. Lucy waited patiently for him to finish whatever the thought was. 'You say Sophia left almost immediately after you arrived, before you had the chance to remove your bonnet. Had you raised your veil?'

Lucy eyed the door, rapidly revising her assessment of Lord Burnham's mental stability. It was closed, but not locked. If she scooped up reticule and bonnet and ran—

'Well? Had you?'

She walked her fingers along the sofa to her right, hooked the cord of her reticule and began to pull. It hurt, but she was becoming used to the strain on the injured tendons now. The cord slid over her wrist and she stretched to pick up the bonnet as though prompted by his question. 'The veil?' She folded it back. 'Let me think. I was just lifting it, then I let it drop, I think—she took me by surprise—and then she had gone.'

'In that case,' said Lord Burnham, 'what would you charge for an entire week?'

'An entire week of what?' Lucy relaxed a little. 'Music lessons?'

'Your time, Miss Lambert. I wish to hire you for a week to attend a house party.'

'You... You *libertine*.' She found she was on her feet and halfway to the door. No, not deranged at all, merely a rake. Poor Lady Sophia, having to live with a stepbrother like this!

'Really, Miss Lambert, I am asking to pay for your time and your assistance, not your bod—your *person*.' He was on his feet, too. 'Hear me out.'

The old Lucy, before her injury, would either have hardly noticed an improper suggestion or would have been cast into confusion at having to deal with it. She realised just how much she had changed when she found herself sliding the long hatpin from her bonnet and holding it beneath the veil as she stopped and turned back, one step from the door.

'Very well. But I should warn you, Lord Burnham, that so far I have formed the impression that you are either a rake or unhinged. Possibly both.'

'*You* would be unhinged if you found yourself responsible for a pretty, well-dowered eighteen-year-old with as much common sense as a bank vole, the town bronze of a cloistered nun and a disposition for parties, shopping and romance. Especially *romance*,' he added bitterly.

When she stayed where she was he walked away to the window seat at the far end of the room. 'Please, sit again. Move that small chair to the door, if you must. You can always hit me with it if I become a ravening beast and sticking that hatpin into me does not stop me in my tracks.'

There was nothing wrong with his eyesight, however unstable he might be in either mind or morals. 'I am listening.' Lucy perched on the arm of the sofa, the hatpin still in her hand.

'A little family history may help. My mother died when I was ten and my father remarried late in life, for companionship, I believe. His choice was Amanda Harker, the Earl of Longdale's widow. She had a daughter—Sophia— who was ten years old at that time. I was twenty by then, so the arrival of a stepsister who was a mere child hardly impinged on my life.

'When my father died four years ago I gave my stepmother the full use of all the family homes. I am unmarried, so I had no reason to unseat her and she had her own social circle. Then three years ago she became ill—or fancied herself so. She installed a distant cousin as a chaperon for Sophia and took herself off to Bath where she has fallen under the influence of some quack healer. She alternates between sending Sophia ridiculous tracts on inner healing, inappropriately large sums of money and letters expressing a fervent desire that she marry.'

'And the cousin is an inadequate chaperon?'

'Miss Hathaway is a *romantic*.' His tone might have been appropriate for pronouncing her to be a dead rat.

'Replace her.' It seemed an obvious solution. 'There are any number of single ladies of excellent breeding, firm will and much reduced circumstances who would be delighted with the position.'

'She is employed by my stepmother. I am, as head of the family, Sophia's guardian. I do my best to influence her, protect her, but I can hardly compel her into prudent behaviour by force.'

In the absence of anything more constructive to say than *Oh, dear,* Lucy made encouraging noises.

'Her godmother has invited her to a house party, I refused to provide her either maid or carriage—it appears she has found a way around that and has set out on her own. I encountered Miss Hathaway returning from the pharmacist as I came in.'

'Her godmother is not a suitable hostess for an unmarried girl! That seems... Whereabouts does she live?'

'Staning Waterless in Dorset. Her name is—'

'Ah, it must be Lady Hopewell.'

'You know her?'

'I spent some time in Great Staning, which is ten miles away.' Lucy had grown up near there, to be more accurate, and had left only three weeks ago, just as soon as her hands were healed sufficiently to manage with just the help of a seventeen-year-old maid-of-all-work promoted to personal maid.

Her friends had wanted her to stay with them, of course, but that was too much like running away from home. She had left—on her own terms—although she was not so proud, or so foolish, as to refuse the help of her friends the Duchess of Aylsham, the Countess of Kendall and the Marchioness of Cranford in finding respectable lodgings and making introductions to potential clients. She wanted to make a success of her new life, not have to pocket her pride and go crawling back home a failure.

'I have never met Lady Hopewell,' she added. 'But surely, if all Lady Sophia has done is to run away to her godmother, then it will be a simple matter to go after her and bring her back.'

Her own family was perfectly respectable gentry and they did not mix in aristocratic circles. But she had heard her mother and the other more upright members of the congregation holding forth on the sins of the widow in a way that was decidedly uncharitable, given that she merely appeared to be highly sociable and fond of parties. But obeying the outward rules was what her parents were obsessed with. Apparently, bitchy gossip about the sinful was not covered by the dictates of godly behaviour. Lucy had thought that the frivolous widow had sounded rather fun.

'There is no reason why she should not visit Lady Hopewell, if it were not for the fact that she was so very anxious to do so and that her interest did not seem usual. When I suggested that we accept a different invitation to a house party in Northamptonshire she became so upset that I was suspicious.

'I believe the silly chit fancies herself in love and her urgent desire to attend the house party is driven more by the wish to be with this wretched man than it is by the desire to gratify her godmother.'

'Who is he?' Lucy asked, not expecting to be told.

Lord Burnham did not tell her, although not for the reason she had been expecting—discretion. 'I have no idea, Miss Lambert. He could be some callow youth or a hardened rake for all I know. All I do know is that one of her more sensible friends was concerned enough to speak to Miss Hathaway about hints that Sophia had dropped. Then Miss Hathaway told me.

'I have nothing to go on other than the belief that a man who an eighteen-year-old girl cannot admit to knowing is no fit suitor. Which, to come to the point, is why, if I cannot keep her away from him and she will not confide in me, I need to find out who he is.'

He paused and Lucy found herself trying to read the expression in grey eyes that seemed all too effective at hiding his thoughts.

'I can arrive at Waterless Manor and expect a warm welcome from Dorothea Hopewell and glares and sulks from Sophia—but she is far too cunning to be easily caught with the object of her affections or be tricked by me into revealing his name. But another young lady should be able to observe unsuspected, discover who he is and inform me.'

'You want me to spy on your stepsister? But that is—'

'In her best interests,' Lord Burnham interrupted impatiently. 'She is innocent, wealthy and impetuous. Do you wish to see her ruined or, at best, making some utterly inappropriate match because you are too nice to watch her?'

'It is not my business to watch her,' Lucy said indignantly. But his words had hit home. Her friend Prudence had fallen for an unscrupulous rake, lost her virginity to him and, as a consequence, had to make a very hasty marriage to another man. The fact that it had turned into a love match was the purest good luck. 'But I do understand your concern...'

'I will pay you five guineas a day for however long this takes. You will travel in comfort and be entertained lavishly. I believe Lady Hopewell has a very fine new pianoforte, one of concert standard.'

And he thinks that is an inducement? It would be torture. Lucy doubted she'd be able to stay in the same room with it.

'I no longer play, my lord. I cannot.'

'How so? You teach.'

She stood up, held out her hands in their thin black kid gloves so he could see the twisted fingers on her left hand, the shortened middle finger on the right. 'I can demonstrate, with discomfort, enough to guide a pupil. I cannot play.'

'What happened?' Lord Burnham got up and moved closer.

'The keyboard lid slammed down and I was not fast enough to move my hands away. It is not something I choose to discuss, my lord.'

Not something she could bear to.

CHAPTER TWO

Max looked at the long-fingered hands. A keyboard cover might fall, but would that be heavy enough to inflict broken bones, to crush a fingertip? *Slammed down*, she said. A person had done this to her, deliberately.

The thought that Miss Lambert was someone who had attracted violence made him uneasy, but on the other hand, if she was a friend of the Duchess of Aylsham—wife of the man known as the Perfect Duke—then he could be certain she had not been at fault.

He could have a word with Aylsham before they left… No, no time for that. He must take the risk. This would not be like last time. This time he would save an innocent, however much she resented it.

Max shrugged. There was no reason to make Miss Lambert any more uncomfortable than she already was by speculating aloud about her injury. 'A great pity,' he said. 'Now, what do you have to say to my proposition?'

'You wish to employ me as a spy?'

'I wish to employ you to assist me in protecting my stepsister,' Max said. 'I realise that as a single lady you may not be fully aware of the dangers Sophia may encounter if she puts her trust in a man of unsteady character—'

'Yes, I am,' Miss Lambert said without a blush for such a shocking admission.

Really, for such an insignificant drab of a female she was remarkably self-assured. Nothing to look at, of course, which made him decide that, however she had acquired her knowledge of the dangers to young ladies, it was not by personal experience. Libertines had far prettier and richer prey to pick from.

Miss Lambert had soft brown hair, no figure to speak of, nondescript features and brown eyes, possibly her best feature, narrowed now in what looked remarkably like irritation.

Being lured here under false pretences and then drugged would be sufficient reason for anyone to be annoyed, but young ladies were trained from birth to be sweet and accommodating. Something else was adding acid to Miss Lambert's tongue and he wondered suddenly if she was still in pain from her injured fingers.

'Your hands—do they hurt you?'

She raised her eyebrows at the sudden personal question, but answered readily enough. 'Not particularly, until I stretch my fingers or try to grip hard. Or knock them. It has been eight weeks since it happened.'

He watched her as she spoke, but the anger he sensed in her did not appear to be related to the injury. Not directly, at any rate.

It was not that he was particularly interested in the workings of Miss Lambert's mind, but he wanted to be certain that whoever he employed for a task was fit for it. Inefficiency was unacceptable, but it was his responsibility to choose wisely in the first place and the threat to Sophia made his usually iron-hard stomach churn.

'Five guineas a day including today and my expenses?' Miss Lambert said.

'Yes,' Max said, impatient now. He would have paid double that. He knew that if he turned up on Dorothea's doorstep and began to probe into Sophia's behaviour, his infuriating stepsister would become a pattern card of virtue and the man dangling after her would go to ground.

'In that case I would like ten guineas now.' He was not sure what had shown in his expression, but she said, 'I presume you have never had to pay rent in advance to secure your rooms, or worried that you would not have sufficient funds to continue to employ the maid on whom your respectability depends.'

'No,' Max admitted. To be honest, he had never given the finances of the genteelly poor a second thought. 'Here.' He handed over the coins. 'I will collect you at six tomorrow morning from the address on your card. Please bring with you everything appropriate for two weeks.'

There was no point in setting out now. Sophia, the little wretch, had too long a start on him and it occurred to him that stopping her en route would give him no chance of identifying the man involved.

'Thank you, Lord Burnham. I will be ready.' Miss Lambert put the money in her reticule, her bonnet on her head and let herself out of the door before Max had a chance to say anything else.

He had a momentary qualm, almost a feeling of foreboding. This ordinary young woman was unimportant, useful only as a way of protecting Sophia, so why did he feel as though he had started something in motion? He had a sudden mental image of a huge boulder rolling unchecked down a hillside, flattening everything in its path, and gave himself a sharp mental shake. *Nonsense.*

A long and doubtlessly tedious journey down to Dorset is all that lies ahead, he told himself.

He wondered just where his wretched sister had found the money to hire a post chaise, because headstrong she might be, but Sophia liked her comforts. He was not going to find that she had endured hours on the common stage, thank heavens.

The anger that had sustained him for the past half-hour ebbed like a retreating wave and he sat down abruptly, all too aware that underlying his show of irritation at Sophia had been a fear that cut like acid on raw skin.

Julia. Laughing blue eyes closed for ever. Long dark lashes sticking to wet skin as pale as porcelain, the lush black hair she had been so vain about tangled with the foul water that made her sodden shift cling to every revealing curve of her young body...

No.

He was not seventeen and powerless now and he would not let the nightmare have power over him. Besides, the heedless young woman he was anxious for today was as cunning as a basketful of monkeys. He would find his cash box empty, he had no doubt, and her ladyship would have hired a chaise and four and two postilions to see her safely to her godmother. It was once inside that house that she would be in danger.

He, on the other hand, had the prospect of ten hours with the prickly Miss Lambert. Or perhaps not... Max tugged the bell pull. Time to make preparations for the morning.

EARLY RISING WAS a matter of habit for Lucy. Mama and Papa considered lounging in bed—which meant staying there a moment beyond six-thirty—virtually a sin, so breakfast had always been at seven-thirty sharp.

Lucy had risen at five, having decided at three o'clock that she would definitely go with Lord Burnham. The money was just too tempting. The prospect of possibly as much as seventy guineas, as well as two weeks with no expenses for her, or for Amy, her maid, would give her a very comfortable reserve to live on until she had established her business on firmer foundations.

At the moment she had a bank account with fifty pounds in it—a legacy from her grandmother—and just over ten pounds split between her reticule and her corsets.

She had left home just as soon as she was sure she could manage to travel to her friends in London and, when her parents had flatly forbidden her departure, she had told them that if they did not pay her legacy and her quarter's allowance, then she would tell the entire parish what had caused her injuries.

'It was an accident!' her father had spluttered. 'And caused by your own outrageous behaviour on the Sabbath.' When she had simply waited, silent, he had narrowed his eyes. 'You can prove nothing.'

'Do you wish to risk the gossip and speculation?' Lucy had asked and had received her money. Then she had been told that she was a disobedient and immoral disgrace, shown the door, and warned never to darken it again.

At least I am not pregnant and it wasn't snowing.

With the help of her friends she now had a very pleasant, though modest, lodging, a wide-eyed maid and a talent that could earn her a living without risking her virtue. At least, she hoped so. Lord Burnham had behaved in a most gentlemanly manner so far. Although that could just be his low cunning, of course. She had no experience of rakes, or of many men either, come to that. Her friend Prue had fallen for a cold-hearted seducer and it was only outstanding good fortune that had saved her from utter disgrace.

She stared critically at her reflection as Amy—much better with a needle than the curling tongs—rather inexpertly twisted up her mistress's hair and pinned it, something she could no longer manage easily herself.

Or it could be that Lord Burnham *was* a libertine, but

that plain music teachers were of no interest to handsome, eligible earls. He doubtless had a beautiful mistress who possessed sophisticated erotic skills, whatever they might be, and any number of eager and pretty young ladies hoping for a proposal of marriage: she couldn't be safer.

Lucy and Amy were waiting on the pavement in Little Windmill Street, wrapped up against the cool morning air, when not one, but two sleek black travelling carriages drew up, both with the same crest on the door panels. A groom jumped down and took their modest luggage—a small trunk and two valises between them—and loaded it on to the back of the second carriage as Lord Burnham descended from the first vehicle.

'Good morning, Miss Lambert.' He raised his hat and gestured to the carriage with their luggage. 'I trust you will be comfortable in here. Grenley will look after you and there is a refreshment hamper.'

'Good morning, Lord—'

But he was already getting back into his coach and the groom was standing with the door held open. Lucy climbed in with a tight smile for the man, Amy scrambling behind her. The only other occupant was a young woman in a plain black travelling dress and bonnet sitting with her back to the driver. A maid, she guessed.

'Good morning, miss.' The young woman half rose and bobbed as much of a curtsy as was possible in the space. 'I'm Grenley, miss. Lady Sophia's maid.'

'Miss—' What had Lord Burnham told the maid about her? Had he given her name or not? She feigned a stumble, muttered something and then added more clearly as she sat down, 'This is my maid, A—Pringle.' She remembered just in time that, for the sake of both her own status and Amy's within the household they were visiting, calling a servant by her first name would be considered very bourgeois.

Grenley moved to one side to make room for Amy and then sat silently looking down at her hands.

Naturally shy—or does Lady Sophia insist on her being a meek dogsbody, I wonder?

'You did not travel with Lady Sophia, then?'

'No, miss.' She shifted uncomfortably. 'I packed for her and then I overheard Lord Burnham telling her that she was not to go, so I started to unpack and she said to leave everything because she would make him change his mind. That was the day before yesterday. Yesterday she gave me the whole day off and when I got back she had gone and His Lordship was not best pleased, I can tell you.'

'And Lady Sophia's chaperon? Miss Hemmingway, was it?'

'Hathaway. His Lordship dismissed her and gave her the money to go down to Lady Sophia's mama in Bath. She was in floods of tears, but he'd gone all icy. Ever so polite and no shouting, but— You know?'

'Fortunately not.' Although she could imagine all too well. 'Poor lady. I do not imagine she had much control over Lady Sophia's actions.'

'No, miss. But she was a bit of a wet duck, if you know what I mean. Always drooping about and reading novels and sighing.' She seemed to realise that these revelations, which were fascinating Lucy, were indiscreet and subsided into awkward silence.

The carriage moved off and Lucy smiled at her own maid who was staring round at the passing scene with eager curiosity. No one could accuse Amy of being either silent or a dogsbody. She must remember to warn her not to discuss her mistress's business when they arrived.

A sudden thought had her sitting up with a jerk. Her

reticule landed on the floor of the carriage and the maids bumped heads as they both scrabbled to retrieve it. Of all the things that had run through her agitated brain last night, this, the most important, had been absent.

What was Lord Burnham going to tell Lady Hopewell about her? Who would he say that this uninvited guest was? He could hardly introduce her as a music teacher brought along to spy on his sister and a single gentleman could have no respectable reason to be escorting a young lady who was completely unrelated to him. There was only one conclusion that their hostess could come to—even someone as inexperienced as Lucy was perfectly aware of that.

And what if it was the correct conclusion? What if the Earl had lured her to this house party on completely false pretences and had every intention of seducing her? Was there even a house party? It might all be a cunning plot to abduct her.

Then she looked at her own reflection in the glass and common sense reasserted itself. A handsome, eligible, rich, humourless, domineering earl did not need to go around seducing boring and irritable music teachers by means of elaborate deceptions. He only had to lift a finger and women threw themselves at him, she was sure of that.

But even so, she could hardly arrive with Lord Burnham and offer no explanation, nor could she use her own name. Lambert was not at all unusual, but her parents lived quite close to Lady Hopewell's house, even if they never mingled in such circles. Someone—staff or guests—might know of a local Lambert family. She must ask Lord Burnham what they were to do about it at the first change of horses.

The two maids were looking out of the windows. Lucy did the same. This was going to be a long journey and she hadn't thought to bring a book or a travelling chess set.

Before, on a lengthy carriage ride, she had just allowed the music in her head to sweep through her. Her friend Miranda had told her that her fingers would be in constant motion, playing the notes.

Now the music was still there, of course: she could hardly forget it. But she could not play it and the loss made her want to weep. When she was able to play, it would flood through her, taking over her body, flowing from her fingers. Now, listening to the music in her head was like having someone describe a scent or a colour rather than being able to smell or see it for herself.

It had taken her several weeks to understand. At first there had been pain and shock, then the void where the music had been was filled with the world and all the people and things in it that she had always been able to ignore before, all clamouring for her attention. There was no escape from it now and, somehow, she had to learn to live like this, totally focused on the here and now, on other people.

Her friends were different and always had been. They were all creative, tolerant and supportive. They had never minded her abstraction. She loved them dearly, but only now was she coming to understand how tolerant they had been, how willing to accept her as she was—only half attending, not quite engaging. It had been selfish, she acknowledged with new-found insight.

But accepting that was no real help in dealing with a world that she had to learn to navigate, tolerate, conform to—not when her music had been torn from her. A butterfly without its wings was just another creeping insect.

She was feeling sorry for herself again, she realised. No wonder she was so irritable. There was this whole intrusive, half-strange world to deal with and the knowledge that she should be managing better. She should be thankful that her injuries had not been worse, that she had good friends and a skill that should enable her to earn her own living.

Somehow she had to learn how to be less abrasive, more accepting, without becoming just another meek little mouse of a spinster.

And that is quite enough self-examination and good resolutions, Lucy thought as the carriage began to slow. If this was a stop to change horses she would tackle Lord Burnham now.

'My lord!'

Now what? The confounded female was making her way across the cobbled yard towards him with the air of a brig going into battle against the entire French fleet. Max had provided her with a comfortable carriage, refreshments *and* she had two maids to chaperon her. On top of which he was paying her a great deal of money.

'Miss Lambert?'

'We have not discussed how my presence is to be explained to Lady Hopewell and the other guests.'

Which was true. Max had intended to puzzle out that tricky point somewhere between London and Staning Waterless and inspiration had yet to strike. 'There is no need to worry about that.'

'Of course there is. And do not stand there looking so ineffably superior—I can assure you that it does not fill me with confidence.'

As Max had been aiming at projecting reassurance stemming from trustworthy masculine superiority, this was not the response he was hoping for. He fixed her with the look that normally reduced people to uneasy silence. 'Tell me, Miss Lambert, are you always so irritable?'

'If you had as much to be annoyed about as I have, Lord Burnham, I can assure you that you, too, would be irritable.' She glared at him from under a plain coffee-coloured bonnet that ought to have been drab, but somehow managed to set off those indignant brown eyes and the colour in her cheeks. It suited her, that flush of annoyance. In fact, a state of irritation seemed to bring out the best in her looks.

Which is not saying much, Max thought regretfully.

Feminine beauty was a constant source of pleasure that he was as happy to admire from a distance as he was to enjoy intimately: he did not have to possess it to enjoy it. Although all his mistresses had been very lovely, naturally. He felt a passing pang of regret for Hortense, the latest. Not that he missed her throwing Meissen figurines when provoked, but still…

'We have to think of something, otherwise everyone will assume I am your mistress,' Miss Lambert said flatly, erasing the fleeting memory of Hortense's delicious skills at making up a quarrel.

'I very much doubt it,' Max retorted without choosing his words.

Miss Lambert's chin jerked up, the flattering colour vanishing from her cheeks. 'I am quite well aware that I am plain, Lord Burnham. A gentleman would refrain from pointing it out quite so bluntly.'

Protesting that she was not plain was futile—the woman had a mirror, he was sure. Max had the presence of mind not to make things worse. 'That is not what I meant. Anyone who knows me would be aware that I would not dream of bringing a…a partner of an irregular kind to a gathering where ladies would be present.' Which made it sound as though wild bachelor parties were another matter altogether, he realised, as Miss Lambert curled a lip.

'A very fitting guardian for a young sister, I am sure. Discretion coupled with hypocrisy. Even so, however convinced your acquaintance may be of that discretion, we still need a reason for you to be escorting me.'

'And I told you, I will think of one. Now, the fresh horses are harnessed, so if you will take your place we can be off.'

'In a moment.'

The provoking female turned on her heel and marched into the inn, presumably in search of the privy. Ladies were supposed to slink discreetly out of the carriage and slip inside, not make it quite clear what they were about while leaving a gentleman to kick his heels.

Max signalled to the coachmen to wait and began to pace, wondering if he had suffered a brainstorm the day before when he suggested this scheme. He could hardly get in his own carriage, let alone drive off leaving Miss Lambert to make her own way back across a crowded inn yard.

She emerged five minutes later, characteristically unappreciative of his chivalry. 'There is no need to march up and down, I was as quick as I could be.'

Max closed the carriage door behind her and strode back to his own vehicle. He had thought her gently reared—now he was beginning to wonder. *As quick as I could be*, indeed! Had the female no shame?

Max sank back against the squabs with a muttered curse that made Hobson, his valet, jump and applied his mind to the question of finding a plausible and respectable reason why he was turning up at the house party uninvited and with the addition of an unknown female. At least it gave him some relief from brooding on Sophia.

But he had definitely experienced a brainstorm the day before.

CHAPTER THREE

Miss Lambert refrained from pestering him for two more stages and, by the time they arrived at The Ship in Farnborough, Max had what he thought was a convincing explanation for both his own arrival on Dorothea Hopewell's doorstep—and hers.

'Would you care to take a stroll, Miss Lambert?'

He held out a hand to steady her as she stepped out and, to his surprise, she took it. He remembered in time not to put any pressure on it for fear of hurting her.

'Thank you.' She sounded subdued, which was a relief, of course, given that he had no plate armour to protect him from any further prickliness, but she removed her hand the moment she was on the ground.

They walked to where a patch of rather worn turf and an old apple tree gave shelter to a pair of benches, but Miss Lambert ignored them, apparently preferring to pace up and down.

'I shall tell Lady Hopewell that I was concerned to see that Sophia had arrived safely,' Max said. 'She knows how headstrong my stepsister is, so it will come as no surprise that she took herself off without waiting for me to organise transport and an escort. Sophia will not have told her she did not have my permission.'

'But what about me?'

'You, Miss Lambert, are the daughter of an acquaintance who finds himself in difficulties—which I will be far too discreet to tell anyone about and Lady Hopewell will not ask. I discovered that your father was not in London to meet you from Harrogate—'

'Harrogate?'

'Where you had been companion to an elderly relative. We need you to have arrived in London expecting to be met and with nowhere to go when you were not. I was in receipt of an urgent message from your father and went to the inn where the stage had deposited you. I racked my brains for a solution to finding respectable accommodation for you and then discovered that Sophia has gone rushing off without me. Solution: cast myself on the mercy of my dear friend Dorothea Hopewell.'

Silence. Max braced himself for a list of criticisms, but Miss Lambert was merely considering his suggestion.

'Excellent, provided one has no objection to telling falsehoods—under the circumstances, I cannot see how we can avoid them. But there is one problem.'

Max, who had relaxed, tensed again.

'I will have to change my name or your sister will recognise it.' She looked around, clearly in search of inspiration.

Max followed the direction of her gaze to a shop front across the road. 'Rumpole and Marsh: Cabinet Makers, Undertakers and Funeral Furnishers?'

'Miss Rumpole sounds most strange, but Marsh will do nicely. I will retain my first name. At the next stop I will remove my maid from the carriage and instruct her on all of this. I assume you do not wish your stepsister's maid to know our purpose?'

'Absolutely not.' Max did not know whether Grenley would obey him if he told her to be silent about his plan. In any case, he was not at all certain he wanted someone in his employ who would be disloyal to Sophia. 'Very well, Miss Marsh. Shall we proceed?'

LUCY HAD NOT given Amy any reason for the journey down to Dorset. At the next change of horses she asked the maid to accompany her as she stretched her legs around the yard while Grenley hopped down and scuttled off into the inn, presumably in search of the necessary.

'Amy, can you be very discreet? Good. I am helping Lord Burnham because he is concerned that Lady Sophia, his stepsister, may have made an undesirable acquaintance.'

'A man, you mean, Miss Lambert?'

'Yes, and I am to try to discover who he is. Now, we must be as careful as possible—poor Lady Sophia is quite under the influence of this person and there is no saying what indiscretion she may commit if she discovers my purpose. No one can know who I am, so I am using a different name and I am not telling anyone I teach music. You must call me Miss Marsh.'

Amy listened wide-eyed to the story of how Miss Marsh had found herself stranded in London. 'I've been to Harrogate, Miss L—Miss Marsh. My auntie keeps a boarding house up there and I helped out for a month when her daughter had her baby. So if anyone asks, I can sound as though I know what I'm talking about. Miss Marsh,' she repeated, nodding firmly. 'I'll keep saying it, then it will stick.'

'Thank you, Amy, that is very helpful. And I must get used to calling you by your surname so you do not feel out of place with all the other ladies' maids.'

Lucy wished she could afford to pay the girl more—she was clearly bright and loyal. Then she realised that, with Lord Burnham's fee, she could.

They took their seats again and Lucy discovered she was feeling better than she had for weeks. This was an adventure quite outside her experience, and now she felt more secure about her disguise as Miss Marsh, she was almost relaxed. Even the infuriatingly superior Lord Burnham was proving to be reasonable.

Of course, when they arrived at Lady Hopewell's house there could be any manner of snares awaiting her. She had to hope there was no one from the neighbourhood who might recognise her—her parents lived only ten miles away. Then, in addition to that and watching for clues as to Lady Sophia's love, she had to remember her supposed reason for being there *and* make conversation.

Lucy had always sailed quietly through life, her head full of music and her abstraction from everything and everybody explained as shyness. Now she had to be sociable, which was worrying.

Still, she consoled herself, she would be a very insignificant guest among far more prominent people. She could be a quiet wallflower, make herself agreeable to Lady Sophia if possible, and watch and listen. She felt a little unease about spying, but surely, if the man intriguing with Lady Sophia had good intentions, he would be open about his feelings and seek Lord Burnham's permission to court her.

No, with this secrecy he would prove to be a rake: either a subtle rogue or a seemingly well-meaning suitor like the wretch who had seduced her friend Prue. He would certainly not be some humble but worthy swain daring to aspire to a lady, because otherwise he would hardly be a guest at an aristocratic house party.

Thinking of Prue was reassuring. Yes, this was the right thing to do and, by some miracle, it was the profitable thing as well. Her cynical friend Melissa would say that anything too good to be true probably was just that, but on the other hand, this adventure also contained Lord Burnham's chilly presence and the prospect of small talk, so that dire warning probably did not apply, the negative aspects being already obvious.

Lucy sat back, closed her eyes and set about inventing a plausible elderly relative in Harrogate, a father who had been called away on urgent family business and a thoroughly dull personal existence that no one would want to bother to quiz her about. She exercised her fingers as she plotted, stretching and curling them as Dr Horncastle had instructed her, trying to ignore the ache and the pull, the occasional sharp twinge when her fingers cramped without warning. They were not getting much better now, but at least she might stop them becoming worse.

IT WAS PAST five o'clock when the carriages finally pulled up outside Waterless Manor. At least the name of the place was a possible talking point, Lucy thought, adding it to her painfully short list of safe topics of polite conversation.

Footmen came out, a black-suited butler descended the front steps and bowed gravely to Lord Burnham and went back inside. By the time a footman was handing her down from the carriage a short, plump lady with a startlingly high crown of blond curls on her head was surging down the steps.

'Burnham! What a delightful surprise! Dear Sophia never mentioned that you were coming—such a *pretty* head full of fashions and flirtations and no common sense, the sweet child. No, no, never apologise for arriving unannounced, you are always welcome under this roof. Now, who might this be?' She turned beady blue eyes on Lucy and smiled, which was a relief.

'Miss Marsh, the daughter of an old friend of mine. She found herself stranded in London and I am hoping we can cast ourselves upon your mercy.' He bent to murmur something in Lady Hopewell's ear and she nodded, patted his arm and turned to her butler.

'Formby, I believe the Rose Bedchamber is free.'

'My lady.'

'Then please see that Miss Marsh's luggage is taken up and her maid is accommodated. I hope to get to know you better when you have refreshed yourself, my dear. We are gathering in the drawing room before dinner,' she added kindly.

The bedchamber proved to be small but charming, although exceedingly pink, and the butler informed Amy that he would have hot water sent up immediately. 'Come to the Hall when you have finished, Pringle, and you will be directed to your room.'

'It's all very nice, Miss… Miss Marsh. I just hope the servants' hall isn't too stuffy,' Amy observed, peering into cupboards once Formby had left. 'Oh, here's the dressing room, miss. I'll lay your things out for when the water arrives. Which gown for this evening?'

Thank heavens for Verity and Jane's kindness, Lucy thought, mentally reviewing the gowns they had insisted she accept.

'The cream silk with the amber ribbons and the brown and gold Paisley shawl and my amber set,' she decided. The amber necklace and earrings were, with Grandmama's pearls, virtually all her good jewellery. Mr and Mrs Lambert were firmly of the opinion that all a young lady required in the way of adornment was her own pristine virtue. Clearly she was not virtuous enough, Lucy decided as she studied her reflection in the mirror, because she certainly felt her appearance *would* be helped by additional adornment.

She peeled off her gloves while Amy took the hot ewer

from the maid at the door and then sighed with relief as she plunged her hands into the warmth. The scars stood out starkly across her knuckles, but at least the missing fingertip had healed now. If it was not for those ugly red lines she might have risked leaving off her gloves during the day, but for evening they were, in any case, *de rigueur*.

Had Lady Hopewell accepted Lord Burnham's explanations? She had seemed a pleasant person and, of course, it would be highly insulting to doubt a gentleman's word. The thought gave her pause: Lord Burnham was telling untruths on her behalf, which was not honourable behaviour.

But was it? She pondered the point as Amy tightened her corset strings. He was attempting to safeguard his stepsister which was definitely what a gentleman should do and to do so he needed Lucy's help and he could not compromise her—so, logically, not telling the truth was the correct thing to do.

She was making excuses for him, Lucy realised, and wondered if that was because it would make her feel safer if she believed that he was a man who would take care not to damage her reputation by carelessness. Or action, she thought with a renewed qualm.

'Are you cold, Miss Marsh?' Amy almost spoilt the effect by grinning with triumph at remembering the right name to use. 'You shivered.'

'No, just a little tired, I expect.' Even so, she was glad of the soft folds of the Paisley shawl and resisted the urge to wrap it round herself to cover her modest neckline. Lord Burnham was not a rake—he had behaved impeccably.

Objectionably as well, she added, as she pulled on her cream silk evening gloves and took the reticule that Amy handed her. Frosty, emotionless and always right. Still, that was better than being all hands…

With that somewhat unnerving image on her mind,

Lucy ventured out and found that she could locate the main staircase easily enough. The footman on duty in the hall escorted her to a pair of tall double doors which stood ajar, allowing a loud buzz of conversation to escape. He opened them fully for her and, taking a deep breath and straightening her back, Lucy ventured into the room full of strangers.

Lady Hopewell, thankfully, was an attentive hostess and came over immediately. 'Now come along in, Miss Marsh. I trust you found your room to be comfortable? Yes? Excellent. Now, let me see.' She raised an eyeglass on a stick and scanned the room through it. 'Who shall I introduce you to first? Ah, yes, Miss Thomas and Miss Moss, this is Miss Marsh who is all alone, so I am relying on you to make her feel quite at home.' She beamed and swept off to greet a middle-aged couple who appeared in the doorway.

Lucy smiled. The two young ladies, both she guessed about nineteen, a few years younger than she was, smiled back politely. They did not have quite the experience to survey her without it being obvious, Lucy thought with inward amusement. Probably they were confused by the excellence of her gown and shawl contrasting with the simplicity of her jewellery and hairstyle. She sensed a certain relief that she was not a rival to their prettiness.

'You are from Dorset, Miss Marsh?' That was Miss Moss, a petite brunette with very pink lips, a pointed chin and a very good set of pearls.

'I have been in Harrogate for some time as companion to an elderly relative,' Lucy said. 'But I have visited Dorset before. Are you and Miss Thomas from the locality?'

She rather doubted it, because she did not recognise the names.

'Hampshire, both of us,' Miss Thomas said, then her gaze shifted towards the door. 'Oh, who is that gentleman?'

'Lord Burnham,' Lucy said without thinking. Then she realised that she would have to admit to some acquaintance with the Earl, otherwise, if she had been seen alighting from one of his carriages, it would seem most strange.

'He escorted me here when I found myself in difficulties, stranded in London. My father had been called away and there was a misunderstanding over dates—a complete muddle, in fact. I arrived on the stage from Harrogate to find the house was shut up, Papa somewhere between London and Brussels and no one to turn to. Fortunately, Papa was able to contact Lord Burnham, who rescued me.'

The story was flowing now—she just had to recall all the details for the next time someone asked. 'He very kindly secured an invitation for me to attend the house party and gave me the loan of one of his carriages for myself and my maid,' she concluded, slightly breathless.

'Oh.' Miss Thomas looked disappointed. 'So you and he are not...' Her voice trailed away suggestively.

The old Lucy, the one with her head full of music, would never have noticed that tone of voice, nor the avid look in Miss Thomas's eyes. This Lucy most certainly did.

'Whatever can you mean, Miss Thomas? Not what, exactly?'

The girl backed down immediately. 'Oh, betrothed, of course. Goodness, what else might I have meant?'

'No, I am not betrothed to Lord Burnham,' Lucy said decisively. 'Nor anything else that you might imagine. His Lordship, although infinitely obliging in this matter, is also authoritarian, arrogant, cold and ruthless. One cannot imagine anyone less amiable to be...' She realised, far too late, what had caused the wide-eyed expressions on the faces of the two young woman as they looked past her.

There was a moment of sheer panic as she heard in her mind just what she had said. It took only a second to reach a decision: she would not turn around, she would not let anyone see she knew he was there—it was surely imagination that she felt the flames of furious hot breath fanning the nape of her neck—she would simply keep talking.

'…associated with. But most decisive and helpful.' No, she was not imagining that the heat of His Lordship's regard was diminishing—the two faces opposite her were proof of that.

'Oh, Miss Marsh—Lord Burnham was right behind you, what if he overheard?' Miss Thomas whispered.

'He cannot have done,' her friend objected. 'His expression did not change. He is rather alarming, is he not? I was reminded of that painting of a great white bear on an ice flow that we saw at the Academy last year.'

'White and shaggy?' Lucy asked, bemused.

'No, not the bear, the ice—smooth and frozen and implacable.'

Yes, that was Lord Burnham. But he would have heard her unflattering comments—Lucy had no doubt his hearing would be inconveniently excellent. Now what would he do?

CHAPTER FOUR

'We should circulate,' Miss Moss said with a glance at the doorway. 'More people are arriving.'

Lucy half turned and saw a group of four young men, a middle-aged couple and, just behind them, Lady Sophia. The sight steadied her nerves a little. She had been employed to undertake a task and, unless her employer was so affronted by her tactless pronouncements that he sent her home with a flea in her ear and an empty purse, then she was going to do it.

Lady Hopewell moved to greet them as Lady Sophia, without a glance at the gentlemen, strolled across and began to talk to Miss Thomas.

'I will introduce you to my parents.' Miss Moss led the way to the couple and waited while they finished speaking to their hostess. 'Mama, Papa, this is Miss Marsh who arrived late this afternoon. Miss Marsh, my parents, Sir George and Lady Moss.'

Lucy bobbed a curtsy, forestalling anyone offering a hand to shake, and listened while Miss Moss recounted the tale of her arrival at the house party and Lord Burnham's rescue. 'Which was very kind of him, of course, but I have to say he seems a very cold sort of gentleman,' she said rather breathlessly.

'He is an earl, Clara,' her mother said with gentle reproof. 'Naturally he shows a proper distance in his manner.' She glanced around the room. 'And his sister is here, of course,' she added vaguely. 'So naturally he—' She broke off. 'So naturally he would think this a proper place to bring a young lady in difficulties.'

In other words she has worked out that Lord Burnham is highly unlikely to bring his chère amie *to stay in the same house as his sister, therefore I am probably as respectable as I appear.*

Lucy managed a smile. 'So thoughtful of him. Of course, it is a trifle awkward, but everyone has been most kind.'

'I am sure they have. Now, let me see, who else I can introduce you to.' Lady Moss cast a disapproving eye over the young men. They had been joined by some others and were gathered together at one end of the room, talking rather too loudly. 'Lady Hermione, I think.' She began to shepherd Lucy towards an angular lady of middling years wearing a startlingly vivid blue gown and an expression of equally vivid interest in what was going on around her.

'Daughter of the late Marquis of Fotheringhall, you know. Very much a bluestocking, but such an entertaining observer of the social scene,' Lady Moss murmured, then raised her voice to normal conversational levels. 'Hermione, dear, do allow me to present Miss Marsh who has only just reached safe haven here after quite an adventurous few days. Miss Marsh, Lady Hermione Felix.'

She went back to her family, leaving Lucy to be inspected by Lady Hermione through blue eyes for which her gown was a perfect match.

'Are you wearied to death of recounting your adventures or would you find another telling therapeutic?'

'I would much rather talk of other things, ma'am,' Lucy admitted gratefully.

'Excellent. Who here are you not acquainted with? I will not drag you about making introductions, but thorough character assassination does require a knowledge of whom one is discussing, does it not?'

'Most certainly,' Lucy agreed. Provided it was not her own character under scrutiny she was more than happy to hear Lady Hermione's opinion of the other guests. Particularly the young gentlemen, of course. 'As yet I only know the Moss family and Miss Thomas. Oh, and Lord Burnham, of course. I believe that is his stepsister over there in the primrose gown?'

Lady Sophia had posed herself prettily against the dark green wall and the young men began to drift in her direction, despite the fact she was ignoring them. Or perhaps because of it, Lucy speculated.

'It is. A pretty chit with more brains in her head than she allows to be seen, most of the time. One can understand why—most men flee in the face of feminine intelligence: a depressing fact of life.'

'Indeed. I have four close friends, all of them intelligent and skilled. Three have found husbands who appreciate them for what and who they are. They are men who are confident enough not to be intimidated by their wives' attainments, which seems like a small miracle when one considers how empty-headed young ladies are expected to be. The fourth maintains that she has no wish to wed, so they are all happy.'

'And you?' Lady Hermione raised one perfectly plucked eyebrow.

'I am very content to be single.' She had seen the happiness true love brought and she was practical enough to know that the chances of it happening to her were nonexistent and wise enough to have learned to ignore the little spark of envy. Time to change the subject from herself—those blue eyes were far too intense. 'Who are the young gentlemen?'

'The very tall black-haired one with the large nose is Viscount St Giles. Next to him, on his right, with the red hair and the deplorably shiny waistcoat, is Benedict, Lord Easton. The good-looking blond youth with the Brutus cut is Philip Doncaster. The one attempting to simultaneously toss his hair and look languid is Lord Tobias Jerman—someone was once foolish enough to tell him that he resembled Byron. The somewhat rotund young man being strangled by his neckcloth is Algernon Tredgold and, finally, the intelligent one with the brown hair and the green and brown waistcoat is my nephew Terence, Viscount Overdene. The best of the bunch, but then, I am prejudiced.'

Which of those had caught Lady Sophia's fancy? Lucy wondered. Viscount Overdene certainly looked both intelligent and handsome. Mr Doncaster was even better looking. Viscount St Giles might have a personality that counteracted the nose and perhaps Lord Tobias had good qualities, despite the posturing. A poor taste in waistcoats and a degree of plumpness moved Lord Easton and Mr Tredgold down the list of probabilities, but one could never tell what might appeal to another woman. There were doubtless those for whom Lord Burnham's frosty demeanour was highly attractive.

'And are those the only single gentlemen?' she asked, creating a list in her head and ranking them within it.

'The only young ones whose antics might amuse us. There is Lord Burnham, of course. He is single, but twenty-eight and, therefore, one hopes, has reached an age of discretion. The Marquis of Petersbridge is just out of mourning. A very eligible catch, of course, if one does not mind a husband in his forties, so there may be some entertainment to be had in watching the girls batting their eyelashes at him.'

There was a small flurry at the doorway and Lady Hermione turned. 'Ah, more young ladies. The brunette in pink—oh, Lord Burnham, good evening.'

The man moved far too quietly for comfort, Lucy thought, arranging her expression into one of modest insipidity. She had good practice with that expression because it was the one she used most of the time at home. It usually deceived her parents into assuming only correct and ladylike thoughts were passing through her head.

'Lady Hermione, a pleasure to see you again. Miss Marsh, I hope you are comfortably settled?'

'Yes, indeed, thank you.'

'Do excuse me, I have just recalled something I must say to Terence. I hope to further our acquaintance later, Miss Marsh.' Lady Hermione drifted off across the room like a bright blue dragonfly—she was far too angular to be a butterfly, Lucy decided.

She turned back to Lord Burnham, expecting some cutting remark about her indiscreet comments earlier.

'You may wish to inspect the conservatory, Miss Marsh. It is a particularly fine one, and usually unoccupied at this hour.' He gestured towards an archway in the far corner of the room. 'Through there.' And then, just as she was on the point of telling him that she would look at it later, he strolled off in the opposite direction.

Lucy narrowed her eyes at his back. It was, she had to admit, a fine one—broad shoulders apparently in no need of buckram or padding on the part of his tailor, a trim waist, which certainly was not due to corsetry, and long legs. It did not make him any less infuriating, of course, but at least he was *decoratively* maddening.

And then she realised that his remark about the conservatory had not been a suggestion, it had been a direction. An order from her employer.

She meandered across to the archway, smiling at anyone who smiled or bowed to her, but not stopping. The opening led to a short passageway with a glass door at the end. It creaked as she pushed it wide and she found herself in warm heat, the air filled with the smell of greenery, moist earth and a drift of heavy, exotic scent. From the far side there was a tinkle of water. The sound of voices from the room behind her disappeared as she let the door swing closed. The hinges really did need oiling.

What am I supposed to do now? Wait for His Lordship to arrive and deliver a lecture, I suppose.

Lucy wandered through the glasshouse, ducked under drooping palm fronds, found the source of the exotic perfume in a white-flowered creeper and finally discovered the source of the water, a fountain trickling into a large raised pool against the far wall. She perched on the rim of the basin, quite content to watch the little gold and silver fish that darted among the water weeds. It was peaceful here and she did not have to make any small talk.

The door creaked again and footsteps sounded on the tiled floor. She watched warily until Lord Burnham came into view, ducking around a large fern in a Chinese vase.

He would be angry with her, of course. But Lucy had found that being constantly considered to be in the wrong at home had given her an admirably thick skin when dealing with disapproval. She should apologise, though. It had been wrong to let her tongue run away with her like that.

She got to her feet as he approached, rather glad of the solid marble rim at the back of her thighs for support. 'Lord Burnham, I—'

'That was an excellent tactic, Miss Marsh, I congratulate you. Word will get back to my stepsister that you find me unsympathetic and that will make her far more willing to confide in you,' he said with the nearest thing to a smile she had yet seen on his face.

'Er…yes,' Lucy said, amazed. He thought that had been deliberate? She tried to look like a woman who was a mistress of cunning. 'I am glad you understand and did not take offence,' she said.

Oh. Goodness. That *was* a smile, a real smile. And it transformed a conventionally handsome face into something far more interesting, because the left side of his mouth quirked up slightly more than the right. The effect was somehow quizzical and…and charming.

'Is something wrong, Miss Marsh?'

Lucy realised she was staring. Probably her mouth was open. 'No, nothing, it is just that you have some fallen flowers from that white climbing plant on your shoulder.' She reached out a hand to brush them off, he stepped closer and the far door creaked.

Lord Burnham shifted, half turning as though to shield her from the view of whoever had just come in. As he moved, Lucy tried to step behind him, found she could not because of the fountain basin and, off balance, toppled helplessly backwards.

The basin was about the size of a half-barrel and her head was above water as her bottom hit the base. With a splutter she scrabbled to sit up.

'Shh! Stay down.'

'What!'

A ruthless hand descended on the top of her head, pushing her down as Lord Burnham sat firmly on the basin rim, his back to her. A man's laugh, deep and warm, and the trill of feminine amusement came from quite close. They must be behind the fern in the Chinese pot, she thought, trying not to move abruptly when the little fish darted against her skin.

'Oh, Philip, how you do make me laugh!' The speaker was young—too young to be unchaperoned in a conservatory with a man.

As am I, Lucy thought. A fish nibbled delicately at her fingertip and she pushed it away.

'And how you make my heart beat faster, Elizabeth, you know you do. May I beg just one kiss?'

'Ooh, I shouldn't really…but, Philip—oh!'

'Miss Gainford. Doncaster.' Lord Burnham stood up, squarely in front of the fountain.

Lucy slid down until the water almost reached her nose, took a deep breath and prepared to submerge. Were there snails? She really did hope there were no snails.

'Might I suggest that Miss Gainford's chaperon might not wish for her to be in here alone with a gentleman?' Lord Burnham said reprovingly. The footsteps halted.

'Er…yes. Quite right, sir. We got talking, didn't notice we were in here all alone, if you know what I mean. Then the heat of the moment… Come along, Eliz—Miss Gainford. Back we go…'

There was the sound of retreating footsteps, the creak of the door. Lucy sat up and plucked at the waterlily leaf that had attached itself to her cleavage.

'They have gone.' Lord Burnham turned and held out his hands, then reached down farther and took her arms just above the elbow.

He didn't want to hurt her hands, Lucy realised, allowing herself to be pulled upright. How thoughtful of him to remember and take care.

And then she was aware that she was soaking wet and dressed in light fabric that clung as though glued to every curve of her body. Water dripped down her forehead and off the end of her nose and, as she pushed back her hair, a fish dropped in a flash of silver into the water.

Lord Burnham was still holding her upper arms, his gaze fixed tactfully on her face. He was smiling, just a little.

If it had not been for his grip she would probably have ended up sitting in the water again, she realised. 'This is not amusing, my lord.'

It most certainly is not. I am alone with a man, in a compromising position, soaking wet and I appear to have lost my wits, simply because he almost smiled.

'No, it is not, you are quite correct. Forgive me, Lucy.'

That smile had vanished, but the memory of it lingered and so did the warmth of his hands on her bare, wet arms. He had called her Lucy and she was within an inch of losing her head over a man, she realised, belatedly discovering why she felt dizzy.

It was ridiculous: she, Lucy Lambert, ordinary, unimportant, awkward and independent, did not even *like* men, let alone take leave of her senses over one. And she was standing up to mid-thigh in cool water.

'Of course, *Max*,' she said with enough of a sarcastic edge to bring both of them to their senses, she would have hoped. Although, of course, he was still in full possession of his and was simply teasing her. Or toying with her, or whatever sophisticated men of the world did with music teachers who had found themselves thoroughly out of their depth.

'Let us get you out of there,' was all he said as his hands left her arms, fastened around her waist and lifted her right out of the pool, over the rim and set her, with a regrettable squelch, on the tiled floor.

He is strong, she thought, all those unruly senses scattering again.

'Now what are we going to do with you?'

His hands were still on her waist, unmoving. Lucy thought he had forgotten he was holding her like that.

'You are going to let go of me, give me your coat and I am going to drip my way out of that door over there, which hopefully leads to the staff quarters, where I will climb the back stairs and ring for my maid,' she said firmly.

Then his gaze flickered down, fixed, and she saw him turn white.

OF COURSE, SHE must be wet through. Max looked down. Down at the soaking cloth clinging to the slender body, the trails of water weed. The warmth and the scents and the sounds of the conservatory faded, leaving the slap of Thames water on stinking mud, the creak of oars, the bone-chill of winter. He felt once more the shock of seeing death for the first time, the sheer horror of recognising the sheet-white, mud-smeared face.

He felt the blood draining from his head, heard a high-pitched keening sound in his ears—and then the woman in front of him moved, spoke, and he realised that he was still clasping Lucy Lambert around the waist. Max released her abruptly.

Lucy, not Julia. Alive, not dead.

'I beg your pardon, Lucy.' Damnation, he had done it again, used her name. This was ridiculous. He did not knock young ladies into pools, he did not use their given names, he did not have nightmare hallucinations of drowned girls or of scrawled words blotched with tears.

I love him, but not enough. He says this is all my fault. I cannot live without him...

He was the Earl of Burnham and a man and he should behave like it.

'You will have to help me off with my coat,' he admitted. It had taken Hobson a good ten minutes to ease him into it and it was new, one of Weston's best. Thinking about what contact with wet skin would do to the burgundy silk lining was another lifeline back to reality.

Max glanced around, but there were no convenient throws on the marble benches, not even a pile of sacking left by the gardeners. He would have to endure Hobson's silent displeasure.

He would also have to endure the expression of disdain for such foppish tailoring—he had no doubt that was how Lucy would categorise it. He turned his back on her and began to ease it off his shoulders. The shuddering nerves so close to the surface of his skin had almost calmed now. He took a steadying breath.

Cold, damp fingers hooked into the collar and pulled and then, as the coat began to slide off, seized the cuffs and tugged. By the time he turned back Lucy was enveloped in it, her hands hidden by the length of the sleeves.

'I hope it did not hurt you, pulling like that.' That was certainly no laughing matter, even if the sight of her swamped in his coat, the swallow tails almost touching the floor, was ludicrous.

'The doctor encourages me to exercise my hands daily, past the point of discomfort,' she said, chin up.

It occurred to Max that since he had reached adulthood, no one had ever answered back to him like this. Sophia wheedled and coaxed or threw tantrums, but in-his-face defiance like this was a novelty. And, curse the woman, it was an intriguing one.

'I will go and make certain that door goes to the back stairs and that the way is clear.' The squeak and squelch of wet shoes followed him across the tiles. 'In fact, I had best come with you and go to my own chamber—I can hardly appear in the dining room in my shirt sleeves.'

Lucy's instinct had been correct. The door, which was much plainer than the one by which she had entered, opened on to an uncarpeted corridor. Max strode along it, found the foot of the stairs and called back, 'Come on, there is no one in sight.'

They went up swiftly. When he glanced down there was a trail of moisture behind them, but it was a warm evening and hopefully it would evaporate before anyone came and wondered about it. A careless maid with the water cans, perhaps, would explain it.

Two floors up he opened a door and looked out. 'The coast is clear.' Then he realised that while he had at least half a dozen coats with him, a music teacher was unlikely to have a supply of evening gowns. 'Have you anything to change into?'

'Thank you, yes. I will contrive to appear downstairs shortly adequately dressed for the occasion.' Lucy stalked off down the corridor. He could not see her face, of course, but he strongly suspected that her nose was in the air.

With a sigh, Max opened the door to his own room and braced himself for Hobson's reaction. The man was a perfectionist and Max was all too aware that his appearance was seen by the valet as a direct reflection on his own skills and, by extension, his reputation.

'My lord?' Hobson stopped, clothes brush poised over the riding coat Max had travelled in. *'My lord.'*

'A damsel in distress and an encounter with a body of water, Hobson. I regret to say that the new Weston coat may return somewhat the worse for wear.'

CHAPTER FIVE

Max arrived downstairs just as the butler entered the drawing room to announce that dinner was served. As Lady Hopewell began to usher her guests into order he glanced around. No sign of Lu—of Miss Marsh.

Then, as Dorothea bore down on him, making little shooing gestures to urge him towards Lady Hermione, he saw her slip through the door. Her hair was still dark with moisture and had been pulled back into a severe knot to disguise the fact that it was wet, but her gown of pale fawn muslin was unexceptional for an unmarried lady and she looked remarkably composed.

'Burnham?' Lady Hermione tapped lightly on his arm with her fan. 'Are you quite well? I declare you are positively pale.' When he forced a smile and a rueful shake of his head she laughed. 'No, do not dissemble, it is the prospect of sitting next to me, I know it is. Why, I have even routed Wellington before now!'

'I am sure you are quite capable of it, but the explanation for my seeming a little out of sorts is quite prosaic. I had an accident and spilt something on a brand-new coat and my valet was, to put it mildly, displeased. I would wager he is someone else who could overcome the Duke. Not that he says anything, but he can sigh like a disapproving dowager.'

He steered her round to her place next to the Marquis of Petersbridge who was seated at the foot of the table.

Max settled himself and discovered to his horror that his hands were not quite steady as he shook out his napkin. He dropped it into his lap and spread them palm-down on his thighs, willing them to stillness. Shaking hands, pale skin—the effect of seeing Lucy soaking wet was worse than he had realised. The image of the dead girl's body on the Thames foreshore had been buried as deep as will-power could make it and yet it had taken only that moment to bring it all back.

Guilt, he supposed. He should not have taken the risk, should not have allowed himself to be convinced by Julia's talk of love. The sense of failure stuck like a burr in the soul even though he was an adult now, not a child to be frightened by phantoms.

Max took a deep breath, nodded to the footman who was offering wine and set himself to make conversation. At least with Hermione Felix one had to engage all your wits, which left no room for old nightmares he had thought himself long since hardened to. He reached for his glass, his hand steady now.

LUCY STUDIED THE other guests while she recovered her breath. A benefit of being the least important guest meant she was placed halfway along the table with an excellent view of everyone else. She was seated between a Mr West, who introduced himself as the Vicar of the parish and Mr Tredgold, who blushed every time she ventured a remark.

The Vicar seemed rather young for his position and she was not certain he had even attained thirty years. He was also gravely serious and darkly handsome which must, she supposed, make him the target for every hopeful spinster in the parish. That might account for his reserved manner.

She did a rapid count of the company and saw the number at table had been made up to twenty by two young ladies she had not encountered before. Her last-minute arrival had unbalanced the numbers and, she suspected, the Vicar had been invited at short notice to make up the number of men. Probably being summoned to dinner at short notice, and having to look appreciative of the honour, was an occupational hazard of holding a living in a country parish when one's patron resided close at hand.

But for now Mr Tredgold had escorted her in and it was to him that she must address her conversation.

'I have not yet been introduced to everyone,' she told him. 'Who is the lady on Lord Burnham's left?' She gestured discreetly towards a pale-faced blonde who was looking shyly down at her plate.

'Lady Georgiana FitzRichard.' He shifted slightly for the footman to serve the soup, then must have realised his reply had been somewhat abrupt. 'Her family lives somewhat to the north of here, I believe. Distant neighbours of Lady Hopewell.'

'And almost opposite us?' Lucy lowered her voice, although the auburn-haired girl in question was prattling so animatedly to her dinner partner that she was highly unlikely to hear.

'Anne Easton, Easton's sister.'

So this was everyone and, if Max was correct, Sophia's unsuitable swain must be among this company.

She should stop thinking of him as Max, although it seemed to make him less imposing, more of a human being. The name suited him, she thought, letting her gaze halt for a moment on his profile at the end of the opposite side of the table. Strong and to the point. He didn't look quite himself, but perhaps that was the candlelight.

Or he might not be feeling well: he had certainly reacted strangely when she had emerged from the pool.

Then Lady Sophia laughed, a bright trill of amusement, and his head came round, just for a quick, frowning glance. That was it, of course. He was worried about his stepsister. It was time to begin earning her wages.

'Lady Sophia seems a delightful, light-hearted person,' she remarked to Algernon Tredgold.

He swallowed a mouthful of *potage de la reine* and nodded. 'Yes, very jolly girl. Sporting, game for everything. Archery, dancing, parlour games. No airs and graces.' He buttered a fragment of bread roll. 'Doesn't expect a chap to do the pretty all the time. You know, flirt and pretend to be dying of love.' He snorted.

That was interesting. Or perhaps Lady Sophia was tactful and knew that kind of behaviour would embarrass Mr Tredgold. She decided she could most definitely cross him off the list, unless he was a consummate actor.

Sir George Moss was married and did not look at all the kind of man who would indulge in an illicit flirtation with an unmarried girl—or anyone but his wife, come to that. The Marquis was possible, if Sophia found a brooding, older man attractive, and she supposed that after a year in mourning he might welcome the attentions of a pretty, lively young lady.

But if he *was* the man, then why the secrecy? A marquis, middle-aged or not, was a staggeringly good match, even for the daughter of an earl, and her mother and stepbrother might be expected to greet the courtship with heartfelt approval.

The remaining five young men were far more likely, although what was wrong with any of them that would cause Lady Sophia to keep her feelings a deep, dark secret, Lucy could not determine. Not yet.

The soup was cleared and Lucy turned to her other neighbour. The Vicar turned sloe-dark eyes on her. 'You have only just arrived, I understand, Miss Marsh.'

Yes, that confirmed it—a note must have been sent to the vicarage urgently requesting his attendance at dinner. She hoped he did not object, but young clergymen rarely earned much and the food was very good, so perhaps he regarded an evening of making conversation a fair exchange.

'Yes, I have. Very late this afternoon, in fact. I know no one present except Lord Burnham who was good enough to rescue me when my father was called away unexpectedly. But no doubt you are acquainted with all the regular guests here.'

'I am new to the parish so this is the first large gathering I have attended at the Manor,' he said gravely.

'Where were you before? In another parish?'

'I was a curate at Walcot for three years. This is my first appointment as Vicar.'

Walcot? The name was vaguely familiar, but Lucy could not place it and she didn't like to ask, so she made an encouraging sound and listened to his description of this parish and its challenges.

'Do tell me about the village's unusual name,' she prompted as she watched Lady Sophia, trying to catch her exchanging a lingering look with someone, or watching one of the gentlemen too intently.

'Waterless, I believe, derives from the frequent failure of the wells in the Middle Ages. They are deeper now, but there is only a very small stream at the extreme southern edge of the parish, which makes things hard for the farmers,' Mr West explained.

Lucy listened with half her attention. Either Sophia was being extraordinarily discreet or Max—*Lord Burnham*—

had been misled. Or possibly the object of her affections lived locally and was not at the house party.

She was pondering that thought, while simultaneously responding to the Vicar's polite enquiries about her own home, when she caught Max's eye. Without thinking, she smiled and then bit her lip at the suddenly arrested expression on his face. What on earth was she doing smiling at the man? What had provoked that?

Look at him, all starched up and disapproving. Now what have I done wrong?

Max looked away—without, of course, returning her smile—and Lucy focused on the Vicar. 'I live in London now, but I was brought up in the country,' she explained. She was saved from having to invent somewhere by the arrival of the footmen to clear plates for the next course and turned back to Algernon Tredgold.

'Do tell me all the gossip, Mr Tredgold. Are any of the other single guests betrothed or courting?'

'Courting?' He seemed startled by the concept. 'Oh, no. Not to my knowledge. I wouldn't know anything about that. I'm just here to get out of London, don't you know?' He went pink again and lowered his voice. 'Repairing lease.'

'Cards or horses?' Lucy asked sympathetically. Yes, she could definitely eliminate Algernon from the field.

'Cards,' he muttered.

CROSSING ALGERNON TREDGOLD off the list was the sum total of her success so far that evening, Lucy thought as she followed her hostess out with the other ladies, leaving the gentlemen to their port. It was time to tackle Lady Sophia.

The old Lucy would have found a corner to hide in, but the new, independent Lucy, with a fee to earn, found herself rather bolder and, by careful manoeuvring, she was in position to take the seat next to Sophia on one of the sofas in the drawing room.

'Good evening. I am Miss Marsh and I believe you must be Lady Sophia Harker. You have probably heard how Lord Burnham very kindly rescued me.'

Lady Sophia turned with a look brimful of mischief. 'Whatever possessed him to do something so gallant? I would have thought dear Max had not a drop of romance in his soul. But to be quixotically scooping up young ladies and bearing them off to the depths of Dorset when he ought to be pursuing me with fire and brimstone—why, it is quite wonderful! I am very pleased to meet you, Miss Marsh.' She looked puzzled for a moment. 'Were you not wearing a different gown earlier this evening?'

'An accident—I trod on the hem and tore the flounce,' Lucy said airily, making a mental note to mention that to some of the other ladies if she had the chance. 'But as for my arrival here, I can assure you, there was no scooping up involved. I cast myself on his mercy because I had heard Papa speak of him as the best man in a crisis and, very fortunately for me, he happened to be coming here and he knew Lady Hopewell would take pity on me. But why fire and brimstone, Lady Sophia?'

'I am quite in disgrace.' Lady Sophia wriggled herself into the corner of the sofa with the air of making herself comfortable for a good gossip. 'Max had forbidden me to come, you see, so I tricked him and here I am and now he has to pretend there is nothing wrong in case that causes talk.'

'Oh. But… Surely Lady Hopewell is a perfectly… I mean, why on earth should he take exception to you coming here?'

'The foolish man thinks I am conducting a secret love

affair.' Lady Sophia dimpled a naughty smile and blushed a little.

'My goodness!' Lucy had no trouble sounding surprised. She was *admitting* it? 'You are?'

'Goodness, no.' The dimple vanished and with it Lucy's belief in the denial. Sophia was looking entirely too calculating, in her opinion. 'Max is such a stuffy old thing. I flirt a little, silly people gossip and the next thing I know he is planning to lock me up like some medieval maiden in a tower.'

Just for a moment Lucy had thought she was going to hear a name. But of course, it couldn't be that easy.

'How tiresome for you. But here you are, despite your stepbrother—I do admire your courage. Fancy travelling all the way from London by yourself. I would never contemplate such a thing myself.'

Lucy hoped some wide-eyed admiration might provoke more confidences. Although whether that *had* been a confidence or something Lady Sophia was happy to share with all the guests, she wasn't sure. The other woman merely smiled and wafted her fan.

'I must say, I do not blame you in the slightest for running away,' Lucy persisted. 'This seems to be a most delightful party. So many single young men,' she added, lowering her voice further.

'Fribbles, the lot of them,' Sophia said roundly. 'Algernon is a dullard, Tobias fancies himself to be a romantic hero—I can remember him when he had spots and his verse is execrable—Philip Doncaster is making sheep's eyes at Lizzie Gainford and the others are far too young to be interesting.

'But never mind the tiresome gentlemen, come and meet the other girls.' She jumped up and held out her hand to Lucy. 'Oh, what is wrong with your fingers?'

'An accident. Something heavy fell on them,' Lucy said shortly.

'Ghastly for you. What a good thing you didn't play the harp! Oh, goodness, so tactless of me—you didn't, did you?'

'No. I never played the harp.'

'Well, that's a mercy. And really, with gloves on, one can hardly tell. Now, here's Lizzie and Georgie. Darlings, this is Miss Marsh who has been cast adrift among us. Be lovely to her, I have just been so tactless!'

LUCY EXCUSED HERSELF as the clocks struck half past ten. The group showed no signs of breaking up, but she was weary from the journey and the effort of keeping names and impressions straight in her head. There had been no sign of Max when she had extricated herself from the chattering group of young ladies and gone to wish her hostess goodnight. Perhaps he was playing billiards or cards. Or perhaps he, too, had retired. He had certainly not been looking particularly well at dinner time.

Which, on reflection, was odd, she mused as she reached the first landing. She would have thought he was as healthy as a horse and probably as strong as one. The memory of being lifted bodily out of the pool produced a both disturbing flutter of her pulse and a possible explanation—perhaps Max had wrenched a muscle in his back. It was easily done, even for the fittest person. Their local blacksmith had done it the previous year lifting a small bucket of coals when he was slightly off balance—and he was built like a barn door.

'Miss Marsh!'

Lucy jumped, then fanned herself with one hand. 'Ma— Lord Burnham. I thought you had gone to bed.'

'Clearly not,' he said. 'I was waiting to speak with you.'

He stepped on to the landing, looked over the banisters. 'Still early, the others will not be coming upstairs for a while.' He led the way along the corridor. 'Come in here.'

In here proved to be the little sitting room attached to his bedchamber. Lucy hesitated on the threshold. To step inside a gentleman's bedchamber—even an annexe to it— was, effectively, to court ruin, even if they spent the entire time playing piquet while fully clothed.

On the other hand, ruined for what, exactly? She had no expectation of ever marrying, she had no gimlet-eyed mother or chaperon waiting to sweep in and demand that Max Did The Decent Thing. She wasn't even here under her real name.

Nor had she the slightest fear any longer that he might make advances. A man who could knock a girl into a fountain, then fish her out and regard her body, revealed by clinging wet clothing, with total indifference—he was not going to pounce on her now.

She sat down on one of the two armchairs as a small, treacherous voice in her head whispered, *Unfortunately*.

'Are you all right, Miss Marsh? I am afraid I startled you.'

'No. I am quite all right.'

I startled myself.

'And you?' she added. 'I am sorry if you hurt your back lifting me from that pool.'

'No, I did not.' He was pacing on the other side of the room. Not so very far away, with only the other armchair between them.

'I thought… You were very pale afterwards. I thought you looked unwell.'

'A passing headache.' He certainly looked perfectly fit now and was certainly back to his intense, tight-lipped state. 'What have you discovered?'

'Not a great deal. I am sure we can eliminate Sir George. Algernon Tredgold is surely not the man. He is shy and, frankly, not the brightest candle in the box. If Lady Sophia had fallen for the Marquis, I cannot imagine you would consider him so unsuitable that she would be driven to underhand tactics to see him and there would surely be no reason for him to encourage such behaviour. But that still leaves five young men.' She hesitated, wondering if something that had occurred to her would provoke his anger.

'Out with it, Miss Marsh. What is making you bite your lip like that?'

'I suppose he could not be a servant of one of the guests? A groom or valet?'

Max narrowed his eyes at her, and she hurried on. 'Someone she might have met at another house party, perhaps?'

'I find it unlikely. Improbable. But not impossible— *hush!*'

But she had heard it, too—voices just outside the door, both male.

'…game of cards? Aye, that I would. I'll just straighten His Lordship's room so it is ready when he rings—'

'Hobson.' Max strode around the armchair, seized Lucy by the wrist and towed her into the next room, closing the door softly behind him as the door from the landing opened. 'My valet,' he breathed in her ear.

The soft light of an Argon lamp turned low burned on the dresser, revealing that this was his bedchamber.

'He'll come in here, surely,' she whispered back. 'Is there an exit from your dressing room?'

Max shook his head. 'He'll have the clothes press open, so that's no good either. He'll check the window, so not the curtains… Under the bed, *now.*'

Lucy scrabbled after him under the bedframe, pulling

the valance down as she did so. With it in place there was only a thin line of light showing. Max inched towards the farther side and she wriggled farther in, then froze as the door opened.

They lay flat on their backs, shoulder to shoulder, like effigies on a medieval chest tomb, she thought. Carefully, she lifted her hand and found that, fortunately, it was a high bed. There was perhaps eight inches of space above her body.

The valet was clearly someone who liked to talk to himself, because he kept up a low-voiced running commentary as he moved around.

'Window, just ajar. Fresh water on the night stand. Aha, there's that collar stud...' Mentally, she followed him around the room, heard the door of the clothes press creak open—thank heavens they hadn't hidden in there—the dressing room door open and close. Then, 'Chamber pot...'

Light flooded in as the valance at the foot of the bed was lifted. She raised her head and squinted down the length of her body, across over the upturned toes of Max's shoes, and saw a hand reach in. There was chink of porcelain, the utensil was pushed back and the valance dropped.

At which point Lucy realised that Lady Hopewell's housekeeping was not as perfect as it had seemed. Dust tickled her nose.

'Going to...sneeze,' she whispered in Max's ear, then clamped her hand over her nose and mouth in an heroic, futile effort to stifle it.

He twisted in the narrow space, grabbed her shoulder and pulled her tight in against his chest so her face was buried in his neckcloth.

'Atchoo.' It was a very muffled sneeze, but she heard the valet stop moving, stand still. He was listening.

CHAPTER SIX

Lucy knew she was going to have to start breathing in a moment, but the valet was still motionless, still silent. Listening. Right beside the bed.

'What the devil was that?' he muttered. Then outside, an owl hooted. 'Gawd, I'll be imagining ghosties next.' He chuckled. 'Best check the clothes for tomorrow, I suppose.'

Clasped against Max's chest, Lucy made herself relax, which was almost as impossible as holding back a sneeze. The Earl was lean and hard and should have been exceedingly uncomfortable to be half lying upon, but somehow she seemed to fit quite well. That meant she could feel his breathing, quiet and steady, hear the thump of his heart under her ear. That was steady, too, which was more than could be said for hers, which was pounding.

Fright, she told herself. That might have been the case, but intimate proximity to a man—this man—was contributing, too. And the smell of him. A hint of brandy from his coat, starch and white soap from his linen, a smoky, subtle tang that would be his cologne and under it a not displeasing muskiness that must be his skin.

A faint moan escaped her.

'*Shh.*' Max gathered her even closer. Now she was virtually lying on top of him, squashed between his body and the webbing and frame under the mattress. That had the effect, of course, of squashing her closer against his body.

He had noticed. He could hardly fail to, of course, but the noticing was more than intellectual. Lucy was a country girl and, however much society liked to think that young women knew nothing of such matters, she understood perfectly well what happened to the bodies of male animals during mating.

She noticed something else: Lord Burnham, the iceberg, was not at all icy. Not this close.

It was interesting and strange and stirred something inside her. She ought to be frightened, but she was quite certain that Max was not going to attack her. After all, he could have committed any number of indecencies with his hands if he had been inclined, but they had not strayed an inch. She found herself relaxing, safe.

THIS WAS TORTURE of the most refined sort. Goodness knew what it would be like if Lucy was a curvaceous, attractive young lady. Unfortunately, the message that she was a rather ordinary, sharp-tongued female with as few curves as she had graces did not appear to have reached his body.

Why the blazes hadn't he called out, stopped Hobson coming in before the man had the door open? He had been caught off guard, Max admitted to himself. And that was inexplicable, because normally he was quick-thinking in an emergency. He told himself it was worry about Sophia, but he knew that, in truth, Lucy had distracted him.

Now he was aroused—and that was an understatement. He was hard and aching and furious with himself for getting into this predicament and for responding to it like this. The confounded woman was virtually lying on top of him—which was his fault—he'd hauled her so close when she was about to sneeze. Surely even a respectable virgin could not fail to notice the state his body was in?

On the other hand, he discovered as he fought for control, she was as relaxed and limp now as a sleeping cat. Perhaps she really was that innocent.

At last, at the point when he was distracting himself by cursing the fates for wishing such a conscientious and thorough valet on him, Hobson left the room. Max heard him walk away, then the loud click of the outer door closing behind him.

'Has he gone?' Lucy whispered, her breath tickling his ear and adding another few twigs to the blaze.

'Yes.' Max managed to slide her off his body, then reached out for the side of the bed frame and pulled himself out. 'Can you manage?' He did not want to haul her out by the hand.

'If I wriggle.'

Max stood up and held the valance clear, eyes fixed on the bed head. There was only so much wriggling he could cope with. The thought was bad enough, to say nothing of the breathy little sounds she was making.

Lucy emerged and began to brush down her skirts.

'Another evening gown ruined?'

'Not at all.' She twisted round to check the back. 'It was only slightly dusty and I didn't feel anything catch or tear. Pringle will be able to brush it down. And the other one was not silk, thank goodness, so it will dry without watermarks, she says. The ribbons will probably need replacing, but that's all.'

Sophia would be furious at having one-tenth of the damage done to her own gowns, he knew. Lucy cheerfully brushed off the dust and carried on.

'You are not concerned that she will gossip with the other staff about this succession of mishaps to your clothing?'

'Of course not. Pringle is very loyal.' She began to stab hairpins back into her coiffure. 'This feels like a haystack.' She caught his slight huff of amusement. 'What is funny about that?'

'I was imagining Sophia under the same circumstances. She would be having a tantrum.'

'Your stepsister is a beauty, used to looking perfect at all times. It must be a great concern to her if she looks less than her best.' She shrugged. 'I am not a beauty, so I do not care.'

What was a gentleman supposed to say to that? *You are too modest?* But she was looking at him now with those clear brown eyes and he knew such flummery would be treated with the disdain it deserved.

'You are an original,' Max said, his tongue apparently several beats ahead of his brain.

That was received with a look that said, quite clearly, that he had disappointed her. Or possibly insulted her and she was trying to work out whether to be offended or dismissive.

At which point Max, who *always* thought before he spoke, plunged in, feet first. 'Hedge sparrows. Those little ones the country folk call dunnocks. They hide away under hedges and look small and brown and nondescript. But when you study them they are subtle and charming. And they have a beautiful song.'

What the devil was wrong with him? Dunnocks? Hedge birds? He was lucky that the chamber pot was empty because, when Lucy had taken in what he had called her, she was going to look for a blunt instrument.

'Oh,' she said softly. 'I know the birds you mean. They *are* charming. What a very kind thing to say. Thank you.' And she smiled up at him, transforming her irritated expression into something else entirely.

They stared at each other for a moment, then she said, 'What is it?'

Max, already in the hole, began to dig himself in deeper. He knew it, but he seemed dunnocks powerless to control his own words. 'I was thinking that I would like to kiss you.'

'You would?' She didn't scream or faint or slap him.

He was dreaming, of course. He, Max Fenton, Earl of Burnham, connoisseur of lovely women, renowned for his self-control, had apparently lost his head. 'I would,' he said simply.

Lucy tipped her head to one side, considering him. Blinked. 'Yes, please.'

So he kissed her. As his lips touched hers and her hands came up to rest against his chest, an inner, cynical Max thought fleetingly that perhaps she was not the innocent she appeared, or that this was a cunning ploy to entrap him.

The little gasp she gave as he drew her closer, sealed his mouth over hers, silenced the cynic. No one could feign this innocence, this curiosity with its endearing earnestness. She tasted of the tea served after dinner and, faintly, of tooth powder. Her skin smelt of Castile soap and her hair of rosemary.

She stood quite still, her hands flat against his lapels, and moved her mouth experimentally against his, making a little humming sound as she explored. When he ran the tip of his tongue along the seam of her lips she opened to him and the hum became a little gasp, but she did not recoil.

But he must, he knew that in the part of his brain that was not lost to all sense. Lucy had no idea what this would lead to, but he knew, only too well. Regretfully Max lifted his head, stepped back and sought for the right words.

Instead, Lucy found them. 'That was…interesting,' she said prosaically. Women had been known to feign a swoon at the intensity of his kisses. Not Miss Marsh. 'Rather nice, but very unexpected. I had wondered what all the fuss was about.'

All the fuss? Rather nice? 'I must apologise,' Max said stiffly. 'I do not know what came over me.'

A wicked dimple appeared at the corner of her mouth. 'You don't?'

'Are you unshockable, Miss Lambert? Miss Marsh, I mean.'

'No, of course not. All sorts of things shock me. Cruelty and unkindness—and tripe and onions. But I do understand the facts of life. From a purely practical standpoint, naturally,' she added seriously.

Max had a suspicion that she was teasing him. No one ever teased him. *Not since Julia.*

'Anyway,' the provoking woman said, walking back to the sitting room, 'where were we before your valet arrived?'

'You were suggesting that my stepsister might be engaging in a liaison with a servant.' That was as effective as a bucket of cold water over the head for subduing any lingering traces of arousal.

'It does happen.' Lucy perched on the arm of a chair and began to rub and stretch her fingers. He doubted she even realised she was doing it. 'Servants are people, too. And just like those who employ them, many are individuals with interesting minds, decent moral standards—and physical attractions.'

'Thank you, Miss Marsh. If I wanted a lecture on the rights of man I would read the works of Thomas Paine. However, we have no need to invoke the possibility of a misalliance between an earl's daughter and a groom. I am quite certain she would not have had the opportunity to encounter any of the staff of the guests here. No, she is secretive because none of that collection of young bloods is a suitable pretender for her hand and she knows it. Sophia is a considerable heiress.'

He stood by the fireplace, one foot on the fender, feeling a ridiculous urge to maintain a dignified pose, to keep control of the situation. In front of a woman who had been rolling around under a bed with him while his valet checked the chamber pot, for goodness sake? The woman who had driven his body into a state of aching arousal just by lying on him?

'Very well.' Lucy gave her fingers one last stretch and stood up, brushing her skirts down. 'I will take them one by one tomorrow and see what I can discover.'

'Miss Marsh… Lucy—'

'Yes, Max?' She turned, one hand on the door handle.

'What happened just now—I would not have you fearing that I would take advantage of the situation.'

The look she sent him was level and cool. 'You would certainly not get the opportunity to, Max, believe me.'

She eased the door open, peered cautiously around the edge and then was gone, leaving him staring at the blank panels.

Of all the confounded— Then he felt something very like laughter welling up inside him. *Pompous ass. She certainly told you what was what. And took what she desired from that situation, too.* If she had not wanted to kiss him he would have known about it in no uncertain terms, he was quite certain. And she was a good judge of character—she knew he would not presume on that kiss.

Much as he might want to. The certainty of that came as the final unsettling moment in a very long day.

'WOULD YOU BE so good as to pass me the cherry preserve, Lord St Giles?'

It had taken Lucy an uncomfortably long time to get to sleep the night before, but at least that had given her the opportunity to decide on her strategy. She would work systematically through the young gentlemen and make notes of conversations with them, what others said of them and how they and Lady Sophia behaved together. Finding the Viscount next to her at breakfast, she concluded that she might as well begin with him.

'The cherry? Certainly, Miss Marsh.' He passed the silver dish, looking rather like a very amiable heron with his height and beak of a nose. 'Do you have sufficient toast?'

'Ample, thank you.' So, polite to the least significant female guest. Neatly turned out for what would probably be a morning of walks or other recreation in the grounds, no objectionable habits apparent. So far, so amiable. His clothes were very good quality, of tasteful cut and appropriate colour. The sapphire in his cravat last night, the intricate links of his watch chain and the fine, but sombre, antique intaglio ring on his signet finger seemed to show he was not so short of funds that he needed to seduce an heiress.

That might signify a good tailor and large outstanding bills. And he might hold on to his last few pieces of jewellery to appear solvent, of course. She should not leap to conclusions.

Lucy wondered what Max had against him or whether it was simply that he was apparently friendly with the rather louche Lord Tobias and Lord Easton, he of the dubious waistcoat.

'The post, my lady.' Formby came in with a substantial pile on a silver salver.

'Excellent. Deliver it to those of our guests who are here, Formby. Everyone—do not stand on formality, feel free to read your letters.' She began to flip over her own pile.

There was nothing for Lucy, of course, but an envelope was placed beside Lord St Giles's plate.

'Do, please, open it,' she urged, seeing him glance at it, pick up his knife, then restrain himself. The handwriting was very feminine. 'Unless it is a beastly bill, of course!'

'If you do not mind, Miss Marsh. Thank you. I will just take a quick look in case it is something urgent.'

He slid his knife under the seal and opened out the folded page.

Reading someone else's letters was something no lady would ever contemplate, but, Lucy reminded herself, she was here as a spy, not a lady. She buttered her toast and slid her gaze sideways.

Yes, definitely a feminine hand and, at the bottom, a signature she could just make out.

Your Jane XXX

Lord St Giles stroked his fingertips over the words, sighed, then folded the letter again and slid it into the breast of his coat. There was the trace of a gentle smile on his lips and Lucy fixed her attention firmly on her toast.

It was the smile that convinced her that she could cross him off her list. It had not been the smirk of a man who had made a conquest, nor that of someone amused by an infatuated female. No, that had been as tender as the brush of his fingers over the signature.

The Marquis came in, said good morning to his hostess and went to the sideboard. When he came back he approached the seat next to Lucy. 'May I?'

'Certainly.' She moved the conserve dish aside for him and tried not to let her disappointment show. She had hoped for another member of The List, as she was beginning to think of the young men.

Sandwiched between a marquis and a viscount, she was glad that her friends' remarkably good marriages had at least left her comfortable with gentlemen of rank. Hopefully they would not realise they were making small talk with a humble pianoforte teacher.

A humble pianoforte teacher who had been kissing an earl in his bedchamber the night before.

Even as she thought it, the man in question strolled in, greeted the assembly and went to peruse the chafing dishes.

Was she blushing? Lucy touched her cheek, but it was difficult to detect heat through the fine cotton of the crocheted gloves she wore. No one was staring at her, anyway. She had woken that morning half convinced that the kiss had been a figment of her imagination. Now, she told herself that her imagination had never been that vivid. She could still feel the pressure of Max's lips down to her toes.

There had been the evidence of the gown, as well. Pringle was proving to be an absolute godsend. She had not turned a hair when she came to undress Lucy and was confronted with another distressed garment and, that morning, had announced that it was as good as new after a brushing and a light sponging.

'I don't think much of their housekeeping here, miss,' she'd said with a sniff. 'If you got that dusty tripping over in the corridor, I hate to think what it's like under the beds.'

Lucy hadn't known whether to laugh or hide her face. Now, catching Max's gaze across the fruit bowl as he sat down opposite her, she wished she could share that observation with him. But perhaps he didn't have a sense of humour.

I could never fall for a man with no sense of humour.

The thought shocked her so much that she dropped her teaspoon into the saucer with a clatter.

I am not—I couldn't be. I don't want to fall for any man and certainly not this one.

There was only one outcome of developing an attraction for an earl—heartbreak, or ruin followed closely by heartbreak. This was physical attraction, of course, nothing more.

She made herself look at Max again. He looked back from beneath heavy-lidded eyes. Either he hadn't slept well or he was plotting goodness knew what. It did not seem to bode well for whoever he was thinking about with that calculating expression.

You could freeze ice cream with it, she thought fancifully in an effort to distract herself from her own unruly imaginings. It would be a novel flavour at Gunter's in Berkeley Square. *Iced Earl: a tart and stimulating experience.*

The whimsy made her smile and Max's expression changed, lightened. Goodness, did he think she was smiling at him, attempting to flirt?

The arrival of the rest of the party in a flurry of chatter and greetings, dropped napkins and attentive footmen, distracted her. When she glanced back, Max was deep in conversation with Lady Hermione.

The lifting of his regard felt almost physical. Lucy buttered another piece of toast that she did not really want and cut it into small pieces while the other guests settled themselves around the table. Then she located Lady Sophia and set herself to watch the remaining men on The List while she nibbled at the toast.

Sophia smiled sweetly at her stepbrother and then applied herself to gossipy chatter with the young ladies nearest her. They were all clearly aware of the gentlemen and the effect they were having on them, but both sides kept up the pretence that no flirtation was happening. Lady Sophia seemed to be attracting no more, and no less, covert attention than her friends.

Were the lovers so very skilled at hiding their feelings— or was Max wrong in suspecting a serious liaison? Perhaps Sophia's eagerness to attend the party was simply a wilful girl's rebellion at having a treat refused and the hints her friend had given the chaperon merely troublemaking.

What would flush a lover out of hiding if one really did exist? Lucy recalled the intruders in the conservatory the evening before: perhaps she could eliminate at least one of the gentlemen, after all.

What she needed was half an hour of quiet thought to work out who to approach first. She abandoned the toast and got up with a murmured, 'Excuse me', to the gentlemen on either side before slipping from the room, unremarked, she hoped.

She should have known better. No sooner had Lucy found a window seat in the small Blue Salon to curl up on than the door opened. It was shielded from the window by an ornate Chinese screen so she hoped whoever it was would think the room empty and leave. But, no. The door closed and Max came around the screen.

'You wanted me?'

CHAPTER SEVEN

Did she want him? Well, yes, was the honest answer, although the rational, sensible part of her brain was jumping up and down and shouting, *Run!*

'Um?' It was hardly an intelligent response, but at least it was non-committal.

'You smiled at me rather secretively over breakfast. I thought you wanted a private word.' Max strolled across the floor and leaned one shoulder against the opposite end of the window embrasure.

'Oh. No, not at all. I was thinking about ice cream.'

She had discovered how to disconcert the Earl, it seemed. After a long moment during which he was almost visibly examining her words in his head, Max said, 'Ice cream? At breakfast?'

'Yes, I adore it, don't you? I like the unusual favours—parmesan cheese, burnt sugar and ginger.' It was a fib, she had never tasted any of those, although her friend Jane had once regaled her with mouth-watering descriptions of the delights to be sampled at Gunter's.

'But possibly not all at once,' Max murmured. 'How do you intend on spending your day?'

'I should report that we can rule out Lord St Giles: I saw his reaction to his morning correspondence and the man is in love. I hope to eliminate Mr Doncaster as well, this morning.'

'On the basis of his appearance in the conservatory with Miss Gainford?'

'Exactly. I was just considering how to find a way of raising the subject without appearing to pry, because, of course, he may be flirting with her as a cover for his interest in Lady Sophia.'

'Or he may simply be a rake and be leading both of them on,' Max observed. 'And have you decided how to approach the problem?'

'I shall begin by luring Miss Gainford into discussing Mr Doncaster's manifold charms and hope she will betray her feelings. I shall then try to find some opportunity to talk of her with him, although that may be more difficult to arrange. Perhaps I can manage it during dinner.'

Max nodded. 'That sounds the best way to go about it. You must be careful not to reveal that you saw them together.'

'I might have seen them entering or leaving. I can hint.'

'You appear to have a talent for this.' Max straightened up and wandered over to a side table where a mass of roses had been arranged. He extracted a half-open red one from the middle, snapped the stem short and slid the flower into his buttonhole.

'A talent for spying? I hope not, it sounds rather unsavoury as a general principle. But I am enjoying the puzzle, I find. I never… When I could play, when the music filled me, occupied my mind, I confess I did not pay a great deal of attention to the world around me. My friends, of course, but mysteries and puzzles—I do not think I noticed those before.'

'Your music was totally absorbing?'

She had bent her legs so she could clasp her hands

around her knees and Max sat down at the end of the window seat in the space that created.

'Yes.' She hesitated, wondering whether he was merely being polite or was actually interested. 'It made me selfish, I can see that now. I paid very little heed to anyone else. My friends were very understanding.'

'And your parents?'

'Hymns, sacred music, pure and sentimental ballads were all acceptable. Fortunately one of my friends, Verity, is the daughter of a bishop and was possessed of a good pianoforte. My parents were delighted that I spent so much time in such a worthy household.'

'Your friend Verity who is now the Duchess of Aylsham. I see.' No doubt he had been wondering how an ordinary person like herself was friendly with a duchess. Max rested his head against the folded-back shutter and looked out at the lawns. 'Miss Gainford has just wandered past clutching a slim volume and looking mournful. Or that may be lovelorn. Or perhaps she is attempting to show a romantically sensitive disposition.'

'Unkind,' Lucy chided as she twisted to see. 'No, you are quite correct, I do believe that is extreme sensibility—there, she has stopped to pick a rose and clasp it to her bosom. I do hope it is free from earwigs.'

Max snorted. When she looked at him he was grinning. It took quite five years off his apparent age.

Lucy smiled back, caught by another of the rare moments of charm.

'I have not seen you smile as much as I have today,' Max said. 'You are not feeling prickly?'

'Prickly? Oh. No. No, I am not. Perhaps the puzzle of Lady Sophia's lover is distracting me.'

'From the pain of your hands?'

'No,' she said shortly. The physical pain was manageable and improving. But Lucy doubted whether the anguish of losing her music was ever going to fade.

'I think I understand,' Max said, as though she had explained. Then he was expressionless again. 'This might be an ideal time to talk to Miss Gainford and see if she is in a mood to confide.'

'Yes. Could you open this window for me?'

Max pushed up the bottom part and Lucy was able to swing her legs over the low sill and hop down on to the terrace.

'Thank you!'

She ran across the flagstones until she reached the balustrade and saw Miss Gainford was already crossing the lawn towards the low-spreading branches of a great cedar of Lebanon. Lucy waited until she had disappeared under the shelter of the boughs and strolled after her, taking care to tread softly until she reached the tree.

'Oh! I am so sorry—have I disturbed you?' She did not wait for an answer, but crossed to the iron seat against the trunk and sat down at the other end to her quarry. 'It is so beautiful out here and away from all the shallow chatter about gossip and beaux, don't you think?'

Either Miss Gainford was too well mannered to tell her to go away or she actually welcomed some company, because she smiled wanly and laid down her book. She placed the rose carefully on top.

'Miss Marsh, is it not? Yes, when one's heart is full of genuine sentiment, one does not welcome idle chatter about flirtation.'

'I do so agree with you.' Lucy managed a sigh that she hoped conveyed yearning and fine feeling. None of her friends as they fell in love had drifted about speaking like this, but she should not be unfair—there might be genuine, deep emotion here. 'Forgive me asking, but are you separated from someone? It must be very hard if there is someone you would wish to be with, but you must hide that feeling.'

'Oh, no.' Miss Gainford had forgotten to be languid and her smile was eager now. 'No— Oh, can I trust you not to betray me, Miss Marsh? There is no one I can confide in here.'

'You may trust me, Miss Gainford,' Lucy assured her. After all, even if she was able to tell Max that Miss Gainford was indeed involved with Mr Doncaster, he would keep it to himself.

'My parents wish me to marry the eldest son of our neighbours in Hampshire, but he is the most stolid creature—good-natured enough, but a positive *block*. And I love another,' she added with a dramatic tremble in her voice.

'Someone unsuitable?'

'Oh, no. Well connected, financially secure and of such good character...'

Can we be talking about the same man who leads unmarried girls into the conservatory for a tête-à-tête, I wonder? But I am not going to spend the morning coaxing a name out of her.

'Might I guess? Mr Philip Doncaster?'

'Ah!' Miss Gainford's hands flew to her mouth. 'How did you know?'

'I guessed. I saw a glance between you, saw how he looks at you, and my judgement of his character, on very short acquaintance, made me wonder if it is he.'

Oh, Lord, now I am talking like a sensation novel myself!

Miss Gainford nodded shyly. 'Is he not wonderful?'

'I am sure he is. Are you promised to each other?'

'We are.' Miss Gainford tugged on the thin gold chain

around her neck and a ring threaded on it emerged from her bodice. 'This was Philip's grandmother's. He has great prospects in the legal profession,' she added in an awed voice. 'His prospects will soon be secure and then he will speak to Papa.'

'I wish you every happiness. But I disturbed your quiet contemplation and will go. Be assured, I will do nothing to harm your romance.'

'No, please stay and talk, Miss Marsh.' Sharing her own confidences seemed to give the other girl more assurance. 'Will you not call me Lizzie?'

'Thank you. I am Lucy.'

'And I think you, too, have a secret of the heart. Am I right?'

'Me?' It emerged as a squeak.

'Lord Burnham.'

'Oh, goodness, no. He merely took pity on me when I was stranded in London. He is an acquaintance of my father,' Lucy said with a casual air and sinking heart. 'That is all.'

'Really?' Lizzie sounded disappointed. 'But the two of you exchange such looks. And he watches you, when you are not looking. It is very romantic.'

What?

'I assure you, there is no such feeling between us,' Lucy said, trying to sound puzzled and not in the least defensive. 'I am concerned he will report to my father that my behaviour and deportment is unsatisfactory. I am unused to such elevated company so I suppose he feels some responsibility to keep a watchful eye on me. But my goodness—*romantic*? He is far above any aspirations a squire's daughter might have, believe me.'

Was she protesting too much? *That kiss. That look of understanding in the little salon just now...*

'Oh, how disappointing. I suppose, being in love myself, I want everyone else to be, too,' Lizzie said, laughing at herself, it seemed.

'A generous thought.' Lucy managed a smile as she stood up. 'I will leave you to your romantic musings.'

She was halfway across the lawn before she realised where she was going—to find Max. How foolish... But then, perhaps she ought to report the progress she had made. Unless Mr Doncaster was an expert deceiver he was highly unlikely to be the man in Sophia's heart, so that was one more to cross off The List.

The window into the Blue Salon was still open, so she ducked through and down on to the window seat, her feet in light sandals soundless on the cushioned surface. Before she could straighten her skirts and jump down the door opened. Lucy knelt quietly on the seat, hoping not to appear the kind of hoyden who scrambled in and out of windows.

But the newcomer did not come around the screen. 'Oh, there you are, Max. I have been looking everywhere for you, you really are the most provoking man.'

It was Sophia—and Max must be sitting on the other side of the screen. She could either try to climb back out without making a sound or she could stay where she was and hope Sophia did not come around the screen and find her, compromisingly alone with Lord Burnham.

'If I had any idea I was so urgently needed, my dear, I would have flown to your side,' Max drawled.

'Beast,' Sophia said amiably. 'I need you to frank some letters for me.'

'I do not know why I should do anything for you, except pack you straight off to your mama in Bath under the escort of two strapping footmen and the dourest chaperon I can find.'

'Oh, don't sulk, Max. What do you expect me to do when you virtually lock me up and forbid me such an innocent pleasure as a house party?'

Wisely, perhaps, her stepbrother did not answer. 'Bring me the letters, I will frank them for you when I have finished reading *The Times*.'

Sophia was clearly hoping for a stimulating argument. Lucy could hear her moving restlessly about the room, the swish of her skirts punctuated by the rustle of Max's newspaper. Could she tiptoe out unseen? Sophia sounded to be close to the door. Lucy settled back on to the window seat, then almost leapt to her feet when Sophia spoke again.

'And you should not be so high and mighty, Max, bringing your latest mistress with you. She seems very nice, I must say, but hardly up to your usual standard. Besides, I thought your *belle amies* were always married ladies or widows, not spinsters.'

'Miss Marsh is *not* my mistress.' There was the sound of a newspaper being folded with some emphasis. 'She is a young lady who found herself in a difficult situation and I did what I could to assist, given that I was distracted at the time by you running off like a petulant schoolgirl.'

Sophia muttered something. Then, 'I should have realised. She really isn't pretty, is she? And you always have beautiful mistresses, someone told me. And there's her hands, poor creature. But she is very pleasant, for all that.'

'There are times, Sophia, when I think the best thing would be for me to marry a lady of iron will and the utmost propriety who will teach you to behave as a young lady should.'

'Your Miss Marsh, for instance?'

'No. *Not* Miss Marsh. Pleasant ladies of genteel origins do not make suitable wives for earls. A lady of impeccable breeding will be required. In addition perhaps I should look for someone with a large dowry. It would be useful to save me from being bankrupted by your spending.'

'I knew it! You are going to propose to Lady Cynthia Probert, aren't you?'

'She is very suitable. I wish you could see the necessity for suitable marriages, Sophia. You have commonality of station, of wealth, of acquaintances and culture. There is clear understanding on both sides from the beginning and the assurance that your spouse is who they seem. Our parents had marriages that worked very well, did they not?'

'Well, yes, if all you want is monotony and blandness.'

'I would say tranquillity and stability—and for children, too. I was happy growing up and I have seen the awful consequences for everyone when there is no stability.'

'It sounds dull,' Sophia said petulantly. 'Max, Lady Cynthia is the crossest creature in creation. She'll turn you into even more of a stuffy old man than you are now! Oh, I despair of you—what you need is to fall in love and then you might be human!'

The echoes of the door slamming rattled the porcelain plates hanging on the wall. Lucy bolted out of the window again while the sound still rang.

Well, that would teach her to thinking yearningly of Max's—no, the *Earl's*—kisses, Lucy thought bitterly as she rounded the corner of the house and saw the young ladies of the party. Two were playing shuttlecock and battledore on the lower lawn, with a net slung between two posts, and the others were seated on rugs, watching.

She hesitated, reluctant to join them. She felt too sore and too cross with herself for being such a ninny as to imagine that one kiss meant anything to a man like the Earl of Burnham. Then Miss Moss saw her and waved and she changed her mind. It would be rude to turn and walk away and an hour or two spent in the company of the sort of young ladies who were ideal partners for a titled gentle-man would be salutary.

Miss Thomas and Lady Georgiana were playing very seriously, their faces fixed with concentration.

'Oh, well done, Mary!' Clara Moss called as Lucy sat down beside her and her friend's shot had the shuttlecock sailing over Lady Georgiana's head and into a bush. 'Do you play, Miss Marsh?'

'Lucy. And, no.' She lifted her hands. 'Not that I am sorry on such a warm day.'

'Oh, I forgot. Do forgive me.' Clara looked chagrined at her own tactlessness, then brightened, seeing a way to make amends. 'Have you not brought your parasol out? Here, use Mary's for the moment, it would be dreadful if you caught the sun.'

Clara settled down to the game again, calling encour-agement or uttering groans of sympathy when her friend lost a point.

Lucy tilted the parasol so that it shielded her face and tried to make sense of her feelings. Only there was no sense to be made. Had she lost her mind? To be thrown into a tizzy after being kissed by an earl—her first kiss—why, that was entirely to be expected. To be excited more than embarrassed when someone made utterly incorrect assumptions about the feelings the Earl in question might have for her—that was surely a danger signal? And to be utterly cast down when he made it clear to his sister that she, Lucy, was a *pleasant lady of genteel origins* and in no way fit to be the wife of an aristocrat? Now that reac-tion was more than dangerous.

She was, she hoped, pleasant. Her upbringing had cer-tainly been genteel and a day ago she would have agreed wholeheartedly with anyone stating that she was quite unfit to be the wife of the Earl of Burnham. Her head was still firmly of that opinion, but her heart, or possibly some demon of irrationality that had taken possession of her, was thoroughly miserable.

Perhaps it was some sort of delayed reaction to her injury? She pondered that for a moment, willing this feeling to be easily explained. She had heard that people who had a dreadful shock sometimes did not fully react to it until much later. Certainly before, when she could still play, when her music possessed her, it had never occurred to her that she might marry.

Mama and Papa, of course, expected their daughter to make a good match—by which they meant to a dull, respectable, God-fearing man. An attorney, perhaps, or a clergyman. Quite how they expected this to happen was not clear. Possibly, Lucy thought with a flash a bitter humour, they expected eyes to meet across a pile of hymn books. But, no, that would imply undesirable emotion, not rational choice.

Verity, Prue and Jane had not made rational choices— they had been pitchforked by emotion into happiness and it seemed to be the most wonderful of accidents. But without that, the prospect of becoming a spinster had seemed no hardship, not if she had her music. One day she would inherit everything and then she would live alone, quite happily, she had thought. *If I had my music...*

Some of the young men strolled down from the upper lawn to watch the game and the girls brightened, began to laugh and flirt. Perhaps, now the music had gone, she was making up for all those years of not flirting, of not looking yearningly at men and, by the most unfortunate timing, she happened to be kissed by Max.

It is like those goslings that hatched out in a basket by Mrs Philpot's range at the farm, she thought. *The first thing they saw was Toggle the cat and they decided he was*

their mother and followed him everywhere. I was kissed
by Max and now all I can see is him.

It was very unfortunate, but simply dealt with, she
decided, closing the parasol with a snap and sitting up
straight. She would ignore this…yearning, or whatever it
was. It would go away and Max would go away and everything would be just as it was before.

Or, if it were not, she could pretend until it was so.

CHAPTER EIGHT

Lucy told herself with fierce determination that there was no choice. She had accepted her changed life, now she must adapt to this, too. She was a single woman with damaged hands and without looks or dowry or family support. She would never marry and she was not going to attract any man as his mistress. Not that she would contemplate such a thing for a moment. All the business of dowries and settlements in marriage was bad enough with its overtones of the marketplace, but the thought of selling herself… No.

Someone sat down close by with a murmur of apology for disturbing her. Lucy smiled brightly, murmured, 'Not at all', and, 'Do you have sufficient space on the rug?' before she saw it was Philip Doncaster occupying the edge of the blanket.

'Oh, Mr Doncaster. I'm afraid Miss Gainford is not with this group.'

He turned so sharply to look at her that he had to put out a hand to stop himself sprawling on the grass. 'Miss Gainford?'

'I am sorry if I was tactless.' Lucy glanced around. 'Nobody can overhear us. It is just that I thought that you and Miss Gainford had an understanding. But perhaps I am wrong?'

No, she was not, judging by the way the tips of his ears

turned pink. 'Ah… Er… Well, I am dashed fond of Lizzie, you see. But…'

'But?'

'My father wants me to marry Miss—er…someone else. But I love Lizzie.' He glanced around, the picture of guilt. 'You won't tell anyone?'

She would have to, but it would go no further than Max. 'I do not gossip, Mr Doncaster. Your secret will not reach your father through me, I assure you. But how do you intend to carry on your courtship? You do not plan to elope, I hope.'

'Certainly not.' Suddenly the young man about town looked as sober as a judge. 'I have been working in my uncle's chambers at Lincoln's Inn as a clerk. My godfather is a barrister also and he has promised to take me into the practice with a partnership in a year—he is not far off wanting to retire from the Bar, you see. I plan to convince Mr Gainford that I can support his daughter as he would wish, with every good prospect for my future career. If I show Papa that I am truly dedicated to advancing myself and that I love Lizzie, I have hopes he will relent about my betrothal and continue my allowance.'

'But until then you must avoid every appearance of scandal, I can see that. No meetings in the conservatory, then,' Lucy said before she recalled that he could not know she'd been there. 'I saw you go in there the other evening.'

The blush spread down over his cheekbones.

'Miss Gainford is seated under that cedar of Lebanon on the top lawn. It is in full view from the house, should anyone choose to look hard enough—there can be no harm in you sitting with her, I'm sure.'

He scrambled to his feet, grinned at her. 'You are a sport, Miss Marsh.'

She smiled as she watched him walk away. Yes, definitely another one crossed off The List without any awkward encounters over dinner. Now she had to compose herself sufficiently to report to Max. To *Lord Burnham*, she reminded herself.

MAX LET HIMSELF out of the garden door and looked down the slope to the party playing at battledore and shuttlecock. There was no sign of Sophia, which was a concern, but all the young men were visible, so doubtless she was just sulking. Lucy was deep in conversation with young Doncaster, establishing his feelings for Miss Gainford, no doubt.

He turned away, followed the wall of the house to the corner and then struck off, crossing the carriage drive and making for the stable block. Dorothea had told him to take his pick of the saddle horses, should he wish to ride, and now, unsettled by that confrontation with Sophia, he was in the mood for exercise, the more physical the better.

It was typical of his stepsister to turn and attack when she was criticised, but he did not like the way she had fixed on Lucy, although he had not picked up a suggestion that any of the other house guests suspected a liaison. And what did the minx know about his mistresses? But she was correct, Lucy was as unsuitable for his *chère amie* as she was for a wife.

And why was he even thinking about her in either of those roles, damn it? He should be thinking about Lady Cynthia Probert, the ideal candidate to be the future Countess of Burnham. The problem was, Sophia was quite correct. Lady Cynthia was a pattern card of propriety and as dull as…as dull as that implied. She would not do.

Somehow he had to balance the need to find someone fitted for the role with the need for that person to be pleasant to live with. And that, he knew, was quite different from being in love with that person. His Uncle Robert had married for love, a merchant's daughter from a nearby town, and he recalled asking his father why they always seemed so cold with one another.

'She did not learn fast enough to fit into his position in society and her gaucheries began to embarrass him and she saw that and became angry and defiant. The love that had made him deny our father's prohibition was rubbed away and all that was left was resentment,' his father had explained.

It had puzzled him then: surely love was supposed to last and to be a true touchstone of the worth of the beloved? And then he saw Julia, bedazzled, betrayed and quite unfitted for the life she found herself in and, finally, despairing.

But it was time he stopped looking for another Julia, a wilful beauty with blue eyes and far more courage than sense. She would have made a most unsettling wife, unless, of course, she had loved him. Which she had not. He heard her voice in his memory as he walked through the great archway into the stable yard.

Oh, Max! You are far too young for me even if we are the same age. I want a grown man—the man I love. I am going to live happily ever after, you wait and see.

And he had waited and not betrayed her secret and Julia had died because of his misplaced sense of loyalty. Ruined, abandoned and desperate, she had found oblivion in the cold waters of the Thames and his punishment for sentimentality and muddled thinking had been to identify her and to open her final letter when it eventually reached him.

Surgeons could cut away diseased flesh, but no one had discovered how to cut away a memory, to keep it from returning in nightmares.

'My lord?' The groom's voice jerked him back to the present. 'May I show you around the stables? Or would you like to take a horse out now?'

'Thank you. I thought to ride at some point during my stay here. I prefer something with some character and a turn of speed.'

'I have just the thing for you, my lord. The grey in the centre box. Jerry!' A lad looked out of a nearby stall. 'Run out Windrift.'

The grey was a stallion with obvious Arab blood betrayed by the dished nose and the flowing tail carried so high. He took exception to the stable cat, the mounting block, the dung barrow and a passing blackbird, but when he was trotted up to Max he dipped a soft muzzle into his extended hand and did not try to bite.

'Very nice. Does Lady Hopewell intend to breed from him?'

'Not sure, my lord. He's a bit of a handful, to be honest. More than her ladyship bargained for, I reckon.'

Interesting. Max wondered if she might be willing to sell. If Windrift rode as well as he looked, he was a tempting proposition.

He thanked the man and strolled back to the house. Luncheon would be called soon and then he would have to spend the afternoon being a considerate guest, taking part in whatever Dorothea had planned. And tomorrow he would have accumulated sufficient credit to escape for a ride, he hoped. Get away from worrying about Sophia, fighting ghosts and guilt, fretting that he might have placed Lucy in a difficult situation and exposed her to insult. And escape, somehow, this nagging sense that something was missing in his well-ordered life.

Lucy spoke once to Max when she found him by her side entering the dining room for the midday meal. 'As we hoped, that name can be crossed off The List,' she murmured, then moved away to take a seat next to Lady Sophia.

She might want to tip the glass of lemonade that the footman poured for her all down Sophia's pretty sprig muslin but, if she wanted to gain her confidence, she had to forget what she had overheard her say to Max.

'Would you care for some salad?' she offered, taking care to wield the serving spoons without a fumble. It was humiliating to be pitied for her hands.

'Thank you.' Sophia looked slightly taken aback by the friendly tone. 'Yes, please. May I pass you the cold salmon?'

'Please.'

'There is to be an archery contest tomorrow,' Sophia said as she helped herself to the fish. 'I am so looking forward to it and I think the weather will stay fair, don't you?'

'It looks as though it will—there is hardly a cloud in the sky. You will be taking part? I imagine you have a very accurate eye.'

Sophia dimpled a smile. 'I have! I should not boast, but I do pride myself on being a good shot.'

'Then perhaps I should lay a wager on you.'

'That would be such fun! We could wager for pennies, or forfeits.' She raised her voice. 'Oh, do listen, everyone! Miss Marsh has had such a good idea. We are to wager on the archery tomorrow—just pin money or trifles or some such thing. Will that not be amusing?'

There was a buzz of agreement and the men immediately began to argue about the stakes and who should act as bookmaker.

'Tredgold for bookie,' Lord Overdene suggested. 'He's the only one of us who can add up straight.'

This was obviously an in joke among the younger men and there were roars of laughter in which Algernon Tredgold joined.

'So clever of you, Miss Marsh,' Sophia said. 'I am certain to win.'

'And what will you wager on yourself?' Lucy asked. 'Perhaps you will offer odds in kisses? Who do you favour to bet on you and win?'

Sophia laughed, a delicious trill of amusement that had the men turning to look at her. They all smiled.

She kept her voice low, but her smile was wicked. 'These gentlemen? Oh, come, Miss Marsh, you cannot believe that I would welcome a kiss from any of them? Dimwits, poseurs or just too ordinary for words, I assure you.'

Was she protesting too much? Somehow her opinions had the ring of truth, but as Lucy was all too well aware, Lady Sophia was skilled at deception. The archery match would be useful, she decided. Sophia would surely wish to impress a man she admired and her willpower would have to be extraordinary if she did not watch him to see his reaction to her prowess.

THE AFTERNOON WAS spent strolling in the gardens, reading and taking in the shade. The young men discovered the lake and its boathouse, wheedled the ancient gardener into finding them the key and then spent a noisy, wet, but apparently entertaining hour or so discovering which of the rowing boats and punts had holes in the bottom.

'Quite a few of them,' Lucy observed to Miss Easton as two very wet young men walked past on their way to the house to change.

'That is my brother under the pond weed,' Miss Easton remarked. 'Benedict! Make certain you have no newts in your unmentionables!'

The other young ladies either blushed or collapsed in giggles as Lord Easton turned as red as his hair and strode off without replying.

'Oh, dear,' Lady Hopewell lamented as she joined them under the shade of the rose arbour. 'I had meant to have the boats overhauled before you all arrived and it quite slipped my mind. I do hope some, at least, are sound.'

'Is it quite safe, Lady Hopewell?' Lady Georgiana enquired, averting her gaze from another pair of wet and laughing men.

'Perfectly—if one takes out a boat that isn't leaking, that is! I shall have the gardeners remove all the dubious ones and clean those that are sound. The lake is very shallow almost everywhere, which is why we have the punts. When the young gentlemen have had their fill of falling in, I expect they will be eager to show off their prowess with the punt pole. There are some little islands to explore as well, and a folly.'

That sounded amusing, if one could rely on the wilder spirits not to attempt water jousting or to try ramming each other, Lucy thought as she stood up, gathered up the blanket, strolled across into rather deeper shade where the sun would not be in her eyes and settled down again.

She had pleasant memories of islands in lakes after being a bridesmaid at Verity's unconventional wedding to Will, which had taken place on the tiny islet where they had been stranded and comprehensively compromised.

'Pleasant thoughts, Miss Marsh?' Max folded himself down elegantly on to the rug beside her.

She must have been smiling to herself, she supposed. Now she struggled to keep the curve on her lips and not freeze into rigidity. Lucy took several deep breaths and willed her shoulders to relax, reminding herself that she was *pleasant and genteel* and that she must not read anything into Lord Burnham choosing to sit beside her, other than good manners and amiability.

Amiability? Yes, he did appear rather less chilly than normal. It must be the sunshine.

She pulled herself together. 'Yes, very pleasant, thank you. I was recalling the Duke and Duchess of Aylsham's wedding.' She glanced around, but no one was very close to overhear.

'The one that set society on its ears, with the guests arriving by rowing boat?'

'Yes. I was a bridesmaid.'

'And the aquatic adventures of our fellow guests have not dissuaded you from setting sail here?'

'No. There is the archery tomorrow afternoon and that will give the staff the opportunity to remove any boats that are unsafe.'

'You will be taking part?'

'In the archery? No.' She managed a smile. 'I have never learned to shoot.'

'Your hands?' Max asked. She liked that he did not avoid the subject.

'No, the fact that I never learned. Although now I do not think I could manage it anyway. My parents do not approve of frivolous sports for girls. Any sports, in fact, because they draw attention. And besides, as my mama always observes in horror, archery so often gives the gentlemen the opportunity to come very close to demonstrate. It was declared quite indecent.'

All he said was, 'I see.' Lucy decided that it was quite clear that he did not. What would an aristocratic male know about the life of a girl growing up with parents obsessed with the idea that pleasure was ungodly and that appearing virtuous and unblemished was the best their daughter could aspire to in life?

'Excuse me, I must speak to our hostess about a

horse.' He stood up abruptly and walked away to Lady Hopewell's side.

Lucy watched him go. There was something about the ease with which he had risen, the muscles in those long rider's legs that made her feel warm all over. Far warmer than sitting in this shady spot could account for. She pulled her gaze away and met that of Miss Easton, who grinned and then fanned herself in an exaggerated manner.

Goodness, Miss Easton thought she had been... Well, she had been. Ogling, that is. It was disgraceful and she should be ashamed of herself. Melissa would say it was natural, human, merely a question of appreciating a fine physical specimen. But Max was not a *specimen*. He was a very attractive man, although when she had begun to think that, she could not quite recall. Before he kissed her? Afterwards? Certainly not *during*, because then she had been incapable of any thought at all.

'Tea is here, everyone!' Lady Hopewell called, and Lucy went to join the others, thankful for something else to think about. The footmen had carried down some hampers, jugs of lemonade and trestle tables with white cloths to set the food out on.

Lucy filled a plate and went to sit by shy Lady Georgiana who could be counted upon not to admire passing gentlemen, or their legs. Or, if she did, she kept it to herself.

DINNER WAS VERY PLEASANT. Lady Hopewell had changed the seating plan and Lucy found herself between Mr Doncaster, who appeared to regard her as already a friend, and Sir George, who made intelligent conversation about the local wildlife.

Lucy was feeling positively relaxed until the dessert was served. Lady Hopewell raised her voice and announced, 'I have a treat for after dinner. As you may know, I have recently purchased a really wonderful new pianoforte and I propose that we have a little concert. It is one of Broadwood's grands. I thought I would mention it now so that everyone could think what they might like to play.'

'Is that a good make of pianoforte, do you know?' Philip Doncaster asked.

'Yes. They make instruments of the highest quality,' Lucy said, her stomach tightening. Suddenly the confection of cream, strawberries and little almond biscuits in front of her seemed impossible to eat.

A Broadwood grand. Even the pianoforte at the Bishop's Palace, which Verity used to let her play, had not been as good as that. Piano students learning to play were tolerable for her to listen to now, but if one of the guests was a good player—and Max had said that Lady Sophia was—then listening was going to be a nightmare.

Lucy kept up the conversation with Mr Doncaster until Lady Hopewell rose to lead the ladies out. She would make herself invisible while they all discussed what they were going to play. That would lead to the usual polite squabble over who would perform first and nobody would notice her.

'Lady Sophia should play first, she is so accomplished,' Miss Moss said.

'Oh, no, she should play last so as not to show the rest of us up,' Miss Easton protested. 'I shall go first because everyone will sound better once I have played.'

Lucy found herself a corner and hoped that her dark cream gown against a beige silk sofa would render her invisible. It appeared to work, or at least the others were too tactful to suggest she play something.

BY THE TIME the gentlemen joined them it was agreed that Miss Easton would be first, Lady Sophia last, and Lady

Hopewell would decide the rest of the order, including any gentlemen who wished to play.

The men were polite enough not to linger over their brandy and the entire party trooped through to the ballroom where the pianoforte was installed on a low dais and chairs had been arranged for the audience.

Lucy managed to go in last and found an alcove to sit in. Probably it was a favourite trysting place when balls were in progress, just secluded enough for a flirtation, but not so cut off as to be shocking.

No one took any notice of her, they were all too occupied admiring the instrument, choosing seats and bickering gently over who was playing what.

She would be all right, she told herself. She could put her fingers in her ears and nobody would notice.

Anne Easton stepped up on the dais, settled herself at the keyboard and began to play.

CHAPTER NINE

Max looked around for Lucy, then saw just the hem of her gown showing beneath one of the draperies that framed a niche in the panelled walls. Of course, she would not want to make herself conspicuous by being the only one of the young ladies not able to perform.

He found a seat in an unoccupied row at the back of the audience and settled himself, wondering vaguely why, whatever their appearance or style, the gilt chairs provided at balls and receptions were, without exception, uncomfortable after ten minutes.

Miss Easton began with a lively country air. She was more than competent, he thought, and the pianoforte itself produced a beautiful sound. He normally endured, rather than enjoyed, musical interludes at house parties, but this evening might prove the exception.

Miss Easton was succeeded by Lady Georgiana, pink-cheeked and with the air of rushing to the dentist to get it over with. But, despite appearances, her playing was competent, if without the personality or vigour of Miss Easton's. She also kept to one short piece and retreated, blushing even harder, to friendly applause.

Next came Doncaster and young Overdene. Doncaster played and Overdene sang a comic song that stayed carefully on the right side of saucy. There was much laughter and calls for an encore, so they finished with a sea shanty and then bowed themselves off to be followed by Miss Thomas.

Now, she *was* good, Max decided, re-crossing his legs in an attempt to get comfortable. Not as good as Sophia, but quite delightful to listen to as she played her chosen piece of Mozart.

He glanced over to see what Lucy made of it. Surely she would appreciate such fine playing?

For a second he thought she had gone, then he saw the trailing hem of her skirts and realised that she must be sitting hunched up on the upholstered bench. He looked back at the stage, then back at the alcove. Young ladies did not sit in public with their feet up like that. Was she ill?

Max slid from his chair and padded quietly across. No one appeared to notice him.

Lucy was huddled on the bench, her arms around her knees, her face buried in her skirts. He realised that her arms were crossed so that she could put her fingers in her ears. Her shoulders were shaking.

'Lucy,' he whispered, going down on one knee beside her. 'Are you unwell?'

She started so violently that she almost pitched off the narrow seat into his arms. There were no tears on her face as he had feared, but it was white and strained and utterly miserable.

'Sorry.' She scrubbed a hand over her face and sat up.

'Come outside, you need some air.'

Max put one hand under her arm and guided her out, along the corridor and on to the terrace. The sound of music pursued them and he closed the door.

'Thank you.' She drew a deep, shuddering sigh. 'I am so sorry to have troubled you.'

'Nonsense. What is wrong? Should I fetch your maid? Or the housekeeper?'

'No. No, it was the music, that is all.'

'I thought it very good, although, obviously, I am no expert as you are.'

'It was beautiful,' Lucy said, her back half turned to him. 'Intolerable.'

'I do not understand.' There were still tremors running through her. Even in the moonlight he could see, even though she tensed slender shoulders against them. He wanted to hold her, but he had no idea whether his touch would make things worse. 'Can you explain?' Perhaps talking of it might help her.

'I will try. You will probably not understand. Even my close friends find it hard. When I play... When I *played*, the music possessed me, my mind and my body. It was... all enveloping, part of me. Now I can still listen to it, hear it, but it is not the same. It is like being suddenly blind or dumb, but I do not know how to explain it. How would you describe purple to someone who has never had sight?'

'I don't know.' He felt uncharacteristically helpless. This was not something he could make right, nor could he walk away and ignore her misery. Perhaps talking about it would help. 'Could you explain more?'

Lucy shrugged. 'Can you imagine a feeling that sweeps through you, body, mind, soul? Something that takes you over, something transcendental? Something that you have done, created with your body, your skill. And then it has gone and you are left with the memory of it and you need it again. Perhaps it is like a drug. Like opium.'

Max knew exactly what it sounded like to him—a truly wonderful orgasm. But you could hardly offer that as a suggestion to an innocent. Because that was what

Lucy was, even if she kissed with a sensuality that was surely instinctive.

He could not have closed the door properly because it swung open with a faint creak, allowing the music to float out, faint on the soft evening air. Lucy shivered, turned with a graceful swirl of skirts, and Max had an idea. She could no longer play, but—

'Lucy, can you dance?'

She looked back at him, puzzlement clear, even in the moonlight. 'Not very well. Mama and Papa rarely went to the assemblies and when my friends danced together I was the one who played for them.'

'Will you humour me and try?' Max held out his hands.

'Dance? Here? But why?'

'Because I would very much like to.'

She had that expression again, the one that told him she thought he was either all about in his head or planning something dubious, but to his surprise she stepped forward and let him take her hands.

'I warn you now, I will tread on your toes.' She said it lightly, but he could feel the tremor still running through her and the glance she gave towards the door was haunted.

At least it was a waltz tune, which meant he could hold her and the rhythm was strongly marked, which helped. Max put one hand on her waist and lifted her hand in his, feeling the stiffness in her fingers. Her other hand rested lightly on his shoulder.

'One two three,' he murmured, starting to move.

Lucy caught the beat immediately, as he guessed she would. They circled cautiously as he counted out loud, then he felt her catch hold of the steps and he stopped speaking, let the music talk. She had stopped trembling and when he looked down he saw her eyes were closed, her lips slightly parted.

Then the music ceased, they drifted to a halt and she stepped forward, as though instinctively, and rested her head on his shoulder. Max slid his arms around her and just stood, feeling the softness of the relaxed body, trusting against his, listening to the faint sound of her breathing.

He wanted to kiss her, he realised, just as he knew he must not. Kisses raised expectations and he could not do that again to his prickly music teacher. Lucy showed no obvious signs of developing a *tendre* for him, but then, she was a very private person. He knew what it was to love hopelessly, to hide it, to have his heart broken, and he was not going to risk hers by being thoughtless. This was bad enough, this intimacy here in the shadows, the owl hooting in the trees, moths floating white against the night-flowering plants.

Lucy murmured something and he bent his head to hear. 'I felt it,' she repeated, her face still pressed to his lapel, her breath warm over his shirt front. 'I felt it, right through me. It was different from playing, not so intense, but still wonderful. Oh, *thank you*, Max.'

She came up on tiptoe, so suddenly he was caught off guard, and kissed him on the mouth, her arms twined about his neck.

Yes. Then…*no.* He put up his hands and unlocked her grasp, stepped back. 'No. It is bad enough that we are out here. I am sorry if I gave you the impression that I wanted—'

Instantly, the soft, melting woman changed into something of fire. 'I was saying *thank you*, that is all. *Thank you* for a few moments of joy. I do not think for a moment that you *want* anything from me except what you hired me for. Or do you think I want to entrap myself an earl? Let me assure you, my lord, that if I *was* such a conniving female you are the last man I would set my sights on.'

Max let her rage at him. There was not much else a gentleman could do and explaining himself was only going to make everything very much worse. Joy? Was that what he had felt, too, as they had circled in the moonlight? Was it even an emotion that was safe to feel, to desire? Contentment was safer, not a fleeting emotion that left pain behind it when it was taken.

He watched Lucy stalk off towards the door, then she stopped and turned.

'But thank you for giving me my music back, even if it is in a different form. Thank you for listening and understanding.'

'Lucy—'

'But I still think you are a stiff-rumped authoritarian who looks down on the rest of us sadly genteel creatures from the lower ranks.'

He gave her full marks for not slamming the door.

LUCY RAN UPSTAIRS, not certain whether to float or stamp. That dance. The way the music had flowed through her… It had been different from playing, far less intense, but still marvellous. She had been immersed in the music, a part of it, responding to it, and Max had given her that, had cared enough to take her out of the ballroom, seek to comfort her.

And then he had reacted to a spontaneous kiss, a gesture of thanks, as though she was seeking to compromise him.

And it *had* been spontaneous, Lucy decided, searching her conscience. She certainly had not intended to do it. She hadn't even thought about it, she had just done it.

At least there was no danger of him getting close enough to her for either of them to do anything unwise ever again. She just wished that her nostrils were not full of the scent of Max, that her lips did not taste of him and her body did not ache to dance again. Dance in his arms.

Melissa was right, men were the devil.

THE NEXT MORNING Lucy kept well out of everyone's way in the library. She would observe Lady Sophia and the gentlemen during the archery contest that afternoon, but for now, with no clues to follow as to who might be Sophia's secret love, there was not a great deal she could do.

The only constructive idea she had was that a man willing to carry on a clandestine liaison with a respectable young lady might be the sort of person who was a menace to the female servants. While she was dressing she had asked Amy to find out if any of the maids had been accosted or harassed, but it was too soon to hear what she had discovered.

Lucy told herself now that she was thinking of more tactics to discover the man but, after half an hour of gazing blankly at the ranks of book spines, she had to admit that all she was doing was brooding on Max. Max and the miracle that had happened when she danced. Was it only with him or would the same magic be there with any partner? For the first time in her life Lucy was hoping her hostess would decide to arrange an informal dance.

Which just left Max for her to daydream about, she acknowledged ruefully. But that was what daydreams were all about. They were impossible fantasies and she was a working woman with no room in her life for those.

AFTER LUNCHEON THERE was an interval for everyone to change into whatever outfits they considered most suited to archery and then they assembled in the hall.

Lord Easton, who announced that he was a member of the Toxophilite Society of London, appeared in a green coat with a white waistcoat and breeches. His hat was black with a green feather and he had a leather belt around his waist supporting a quiver full of arrows. He had his own bow and began boring Lord Tobias with a lecture on how green was the only colour to be worn and how he had gone to great pains to find a glove-maker who could make archery gloves to the right specification. Lucy suspected he was also rather fond of the way the colour set off his red hair.

Lord Tobias tossed his long black locks and announced that it was all too exhausting and he would sit in the shade and compose verse on the subject.

'That's because he couldn't hit a barn door with a pitchfork,' Philip Doncaster murmured to Lucy. He was wearing riding clothes with gloves and a wide leather belt with a quiver. 'Borrowed this from Easton,' he confided. 'I *think* I could hit the barn door if I stood six feet from it. Beyond that… I wouldn't put your wager on me.' He grinned and strolled off down the slope.

Lord St Giles was also looking competent in green and Lord Overdene, although only in riding clothes, seemed equally at home handling a bow.

Lady Hopewell emerged from the house, deep in conversation with the Marquis and carrying a much larger bow, almost as tall as she was. Algernon Tredgold hurried along behind with a large schoolroom slate and chalk, clearly intending to take his bookmaking duties seriously.

Then the female guests appeared, all in a cluster. Lady Sophia was dressed in what was clearly the feminine equivalent of Lord Easton's club uniform. Her green gown was narrow skirted and tight-sleeved, with little Tudoresque puffs at the shoulder. Her hat, green with a black feather, was tilted provocatively to the left and she had a belt with a quiver, a leather wrist brace and gloves.

Lady Hermione was in a similar outfit, but the other women were all in walking dress. Whether that meant they were inexperienced archers or had simply not packed specialist clothing, Lucy was not sure. If she were to place a bet, she thought it would be on Lady Hermione who looked calm and very competent.

Three targets had been set up on the lawn, the pale straw clear against the dark green of the shrubbery, perhaps twenty yards behind them. White flags fluttered from stakes set between the targets and the shrubbery, presumably, Lucy deduced, to mark the edge of the danger area.

'Now, everyone, cluster around!' Lady Hopewell called. 'We are using light bows today, so if anyone wanders off, be sure to stay beyond the line of the flags and then you will be quite safe.'

'That is a very fine bow you have there, Lady Hopewell,' Lord Easton said. 'May I try the pull?'

'Of course. But we will not be using it in our little competition. I only brought it out to show Lord Petersbridge. It was my late husband's,' she explained as Easton took hold, drew back the string and gasped at the effort. 'He had it made as a replica of a medieval longbow and the range, in the hands of an expert, is almost four hundred yards.'

Easton, looking as though he had almost put his back out, handed it back hastily to the Marquis, then flushed when one of the other men sniggered.

Lucy looked around for Max as the group clustered round the bench where Algernon had set up his slate. But there was no sign of him. That was probably all for the best; she would not have to avoid him and could relax, but it did mean there was one fewer pair of eyes watching Sophia and the men.

Finally, it seemed, all the wagers had been placed. Lady Sophia was the clear favourite with Miss Easton second and Miss Thomas third. 'What are the stakes?' she asked Algernon Tredgold.

'One shilling. That was all Lady Hopewell would permit,' he told her.

'In that case, please put me down for one shilling on Lady Hermione.'

He raised his eyebrows, but made a note on a piece of paper and adjusted the odds on the slate.

The ladies took it in turns to shoot, dropping out if they missed the target twice in succession. That soon whittled the number down to Lady Sophia, Miss Easton and Lady Hermione, who was proving a more consistent shot than Miss Easton, Lucy thought.

'Neck and neck, Lady Sophia and Lady Hermione,' Lord Overdene, who was keeping score, announced. 'Three arrows in succession to decide the match. Lady Hermione first.'

Her first two arrows hit the gold, side by side in the centre. The third just missed gold and thudded into the red.

Sophia stepped forward with a modest smile that Lucy thought verged on smug. She scanned the audience, but it seemed the gentlemen were more concerned with their wagers and she could see no sign of a proud or possessive look.

Sophia took her stance, nocked her arrow and sent it straight into the centre of the target.

'Bullseye!' Miss Moss exclaimed, clapping. She was shushed as Sophia took aim with the second arrow. It landed squarely in the red.

Lips compressed, Sophia took out her third arrow, drew and hesitated for just a fraction too long. It hit the target side by side with her second shot.

To her credit, Lucy thought, Sophia was a good sport, smiling and congratulating her rival, with no excuses made.

Now that the ladies' match was over the gentlemen were clustered together, tossing a coin to establish the order in which they would shoot.

Having no opinion on who was likely to be the best shot Lucy decided to preserve her winnings on Lady Hermione and moved to a secluded spot in the shade of a chestnut tree to think what to do next about Lady Sophia's mystery lover. The man who had seduced and abandoned her friend Prudence had been a very plausible character, apparently. Prue was no fool and if she could be misled, then even the bright and apparently sophisticated Lady Sophia might be also.

A burst of cheers pulled her attention back to the match. Mr Doncaster had scored a bullseye and his backers were celebrating. Which marksman was Sophia watching? She scanned the excited faces under wide sun hats and scalloped parasols.

Sophia was missing.

CHAPTER TEN

Sophia might have gone up to the house for some reason, of course, but a glance showed nobody walking away on the long expanse of grass. A quick head count showed that all the gentlemen were present.

Where could she have gone? As Lucy looked around she realised that the curve of the shrubbery almost reached the lawn at this point. Sophia could have vanished into the greenery within seconds if she had chosen her moment carefully.

And at the other end of the arc of the planting were the stables and the yards leading to the servants' part of the house. Was she meeting a groom or a valet? Lucy edged back from her sheltering tree and sidled into the shrubbery. Nobody took any notice.

Once there she found herself on a gravelled path wide enough for two people to walk abreast. It wound off between the plantings, deliberately beckoning the visitor to explore, she supposed, as she hurried along it, her light shoes making little sound.

On the path in front of her was a flash of green and, when she stooped to pick it up, she saw it was an arrow with green feather flights. Sophia's arrows had been fletched in green and the little quiver she had carried them in had swung loose at her hip. If she had been hurrying it was possible that an arrow might have bounced out unnoticed.

Lucy picked it up and hurried on. The path wound around a number of wrought-iron seats, taking far longer than a direct line. She could hear the laughter and applause from the archery match and an occasional collective groan. From glimpses through the undergrowth she could see that she was now almost in a direct line behind the targets— and there was still no sign of Sophia.

'Bother the girl.' She could go and look around the stables, she supposed, walking towards the high wall that was visible at the end of a short side path.

The thud of hooves came just as she reached the track that lay between the edge of the shrubbery and the wall. 'Miss Marsh! Are you lost?' It was Lord Burnham astride a very handsome grey horse and looking dangerously fit, capable and masculine in a snuff-brown coat and low-crowned hat. 'Or are you playing the part of Cupid?'

'What?' Was he scrambling her thoughts again? 'Oh, you mean the arrow. I found it on the path.' Lucy kept her voice down. 'Max... My lord, I have lost track of Lady Sophia. She left the archery and, I think, came into the shrubbery.'

He swung down from the horse, tossed the reins over a branch and joined her. 'They are still shooting? Ah, yes, I can hear them.'

'And see them. But all the men are there and Sophia dropped this arrow from her quiver on to the path, so she must have been hurrying to meet someone else entirely.'

'The stables? I wonder.' Max took a step back towards the horse, then turned again and went to the edge of the planting, pushing back the low branches. 'Best to check she has not returned before I start taking the place apart, stall by stall.'

Why she was suddenly uneasy, Lucy did not stop to examine. 'Max, don't—'

She was too late.

MAX SHIELDED HIS eyes and studied the group, counting heads. Yes, Lucy was correct, everyone appeared to be there—except Sophia.

Behind him he heard Lucy stir. 'Max. Don't—'

A tall figure stepped up to the mark, drew and someone shouted, 'Stop!' just as the man loosed his arrow.

It was somewhat unnerving, being in the line of fire, but the distance from the targets— The thought, all thought, was lost in a sudden whistling sound and a blow to his left upper arm that sent him staggering back.

He hit the ground before the pain struck, shocking a gasp from his lips, then his head slammed back into something hard and the world went black.

MAX CAME SWIMMING back up into consciousness. Distantly there were the sounds of raised voices and he realised that Lucy was kneeling beside him.

'Lie still, I'll get help.' He heard her push through the bushes and then shout, 'Here! Help! Someone's shot!'

Someone's shot, he repeated to himself. *Hell, that is me.*

Through a mist of pain he lifted his right hand, groped towards his shoulder and found blood, but no arrow shaft.

'No, lie still or you'll make the bleeding worse. It was a hunting arrow, I think, and barbed, but it cut through the flesh of your upper arm, it has not stuck in. I'll pad it with your neckcloth—I took that off while you were unconscious. But you hit your head on a tree root when you went down and knocked yourself out. No! Lie still, you may be concussed.'

She did something that felt competent—and painful—

with a wad of fabric and then what must be his neckcloth. 'There. Now, I will feel underneath, make certain you aren't bleeding at the back.'

At least the thing wasn't in him and hadn't hit his chest. He had seen the arrows designed to take down a stag and a man would be lucky to survive that. He felt Lucy slide her hand under his shoulder, blinked and her face came into focus, intent and frowning. She winced and he realised this must be hurting her damaged fingers.

'Shh. Don't try to speak,' she said soothingly, slipping her hand free. 'There's virtually no bleeding, I cannot believe how lucky you were.'

'Lucky? Six inches to the other side and it would have missed me entirely,' he said with some bitterness.

He could hear running feet now, thudding across the lawn and, from the side, shrubs being pushed aside.

'Max!' That was Sophia's voice. He forced his eyes open and saw her white face and, behind her, the Vicar... West, that was the man's name.

'Don't need last rites yet, Vicar,' he said. It came out as a croak as his head spun.

Then they seemed to be surrounded. Bodies, voices, chaos. One voice cut through, clear and confident.

'Get hurdles or a door to use as a stretcher. Send a groom for the doctor. Someone run to the house, tell the staff to prepare a bed on the ground floor: he mustn't be tilted up the stairs. Bring clean soft padding. Hurry! And the rest of you get back, give him air.'

It was Lucy, he realised. She sounded urgent, angry and yet fully in control. *Lucky someone is*, he thought as darkness swept over him again.

'Max.' Sophia rushed forward, fell to her knees beside her stepbrother's sprawled body and seemed about to throw herself on his chest.

'For goodness sake, be careful!' Lucy pulled her back. 'I have bandaged the wound, but if you hurl yourself at him you will only dislodge the dressing and it needs to be tight.'

Sophia burst into tears and cast herself into the arms of Mr West, who appeared to be the only person prepared to pay her any attention.

Lucy became aware of a furious, low-voiced argument.

'If you hadn't shouted at me, I would have hit the target.' That was Lord Easton.

'You shouldn't have been using that bow at all—the range is far beyond the warning flags. Totally irresponsible behaviour.' When she spared them a glance she saw the other man was the Marquis, clearly angry, berating Easton who was white-faced and still clutching the powerful hunting bow.

'Oh, do be quiet,' she barked out.

Easton glowered at her, but Lord Petersbridge nodded. 'Quite right. Now is not the time for recriminations. Ah, here they come with the stretcher. Ladies, might I suggest that you all go back to the house?'

That reduced the crowd somewhat. Four footmen came running with a door, followed by a maid, her arms full of pillows.

Lucy arranged the pillows on the door then the men eased Max on to it, lifted it and began to walk back.

'The doctor has been sent for, Miss Marsh.' Lucy realised the maid who had brought the pillows was Amy. 'And they are making up a bed in the little parlour off the library.'

'Thank you,' Lucy said absently, her attention on watching the men to see the door was kept level, that Max wasn't stirring. It was a flesh wound, she told herself. There wasn't much bleeding, and the doctor would be here soon. Those positive thoughts, somehow, were not very soothing and he had hit his head with such force…

THE DOCTOR ARRIVED soon after they had managed to get Max on to the bed. Formby, the butler, pulled a screen around and Max's valet undressed, him, cutting away the clothes on his upper body with scant care for the expensive tailoring.

Lucy stayed on the far side of the screen, as much to stop Sophia from rushing to the bedside and weeping all over Max as out of maidenly modesty on her own part.

He must have come round, because they heard the doctor asking questions and Max's voice replying.

'Come along, we should leave.' Lucy put her hand on Sophia's arm.

'Leave him? How could you be so callous? My place is by his side.'

The doctor said something, and Max's reply was short, basic and very much to the point.

'Out.' Lucy dragged Sophia from the room. 'He does not want us listening to this. I am sure the ability to say just what he feels will be a great help.' She shut the door firmly on a sentence that she suspected was essentially Anglo-Saxon in origin. 'It is a flesh wound and it will need rather a lot of stitches, I expect.'

'You are hateful.'

'Possibly. But I know that when I hurt my hands it made it worse having everyone fussing round me and having to pretend to be brave and not cry out and upset them.'

Sophia shook off Lucy's light grip. 'What were you doing alone with Max in the shrubbery, anyway?'

'I became bored with sitting watching the archery so I took a walk. Your brother was riding back to the stables when I came out on to the path. He went to look and see if you were still with the archery contest.'

'A likely story.' There were tears spiking the ends of Sophia's lashes and her voice was shaking. 'You are trying to entrap him, don't think I cannot see what you are about. And to think I quite liked you.' She turned with a flounce. 'I shall tell everyone. I would leave at once, if I were you.'

Lucy stared at her retreating back, the skirts of Sophia's archery outfit twitching with every jerky stride. The attack, so sudden, so personal, took her breath and she sat down on one of the hallway chairs and stared blankly at the door of the room where Max lay.

'What a spiteful little madam.' Amy marched over and stood beside her. 'What has she got to hide, I wonder?'

'What do you mean?' Lucy blinked back tears and focused on her maid.

'If she was worried about His Lordship she'd be outside this door, like you are. She's carrying on like that because she's trying to distract you from something. My sister used to be just the same, cunning little minx.'

Startled, Lucy thought that over. Yes, in retrospect Sophia's tantrum did seem almost artificial, as though she was winding herself up to make a scene, not expressing her genuine emotions. But what could she be trying to hide? She could not have known that Lucy was following her, nor did she know that Max had asked Lucy to discover her secret lover. If one existed.

But Lady Sophia *had* sneaked away from the archery party…

The door opened and Mr West the Vicar came out. He looked up and down the hallway and seemed surprised to see them. 'Oh. Miss Marsh. I came out to reassure Lady Sophia that Lord Burnham's injury is far less severe than might have been feared. The bleeding has stopped, thanks to your prompt action. But is she not here?'

'She was very upset.' Lucy gestured towards the front of the house. 'She went that way.' He turned to leave, but she stood up. 'Can you tell me what the doctor says?'

'Oh, yes, of course. It appears to be a flesh wound through the muscle of the upper arm. No major blood vessel has been cut and no joints damaged. It was most—' He broke off, clearly searching for a word suitable for a lady's ears. '*Unpleasant*, stitching it. However, if infection can be prevented, then Lord Burnham should make a complete recovery. The doctor was able to remove all the fragments of cloth in the wound and, of course, they were very clean. The blow to the head, however, was forceful and there is always the danger of a concussion.'

'Thank you.'

Lucy watched as he strode off in the direction she had indicated. 'You know, I wonder—'

'He is very concerned about Lady Sophia, isn't he?' Amy said at the same moment. 'Oh, excuse me, Miss Marsh.'

They stared at each other.

'You know, if we put two and two together, it is not impossible that it makes four,' Lucy said slowly.

'Or even a pair,' Amy agreed with a grin.

'Come on.' There was no need to specify where or what for and any scruples about spying were more than smothered by Sophia's clumsy attempt at blackmail. 'Tread softly.'

They did not have far to go. Just around the corner, the Ladies' Small Drawing Room was a little chamber that no one seemed eager to use. It had a dull view of the lawn and was tucked away from the main reception rooms. Ideal for a tryst, in fact.

Amy crouched so she could peep through the keyhole. 'There's a screen just inside the door,' she whispered.

They eased the handle down and the door opened without a creak. From the far side of the room they could hear Sophia and Mr West in what sounded like urgent conversation. They squeezed through the narrowest possible gap, then pushed the door to again.

'...sure she suspects something. I can only hope I have frightened her into leaving.'

'Dearest, that was not well done.' The Reverend West sounded fond but stern. 'Threats are wrong and besides, you have probably only aroused Miss Marsh's suspicions.' There was a sound suspiciously like a sob. 'You know you should not have come here, Sophia. We must not meet alone again and we must put these feelings behind us.'

'How can we?' Sophia demanded. 'These feelings? It is not *feelings*, Anthony—I *love* you. You told me you loved me. That is not a feeling, that is...*everything*.'

'Oh, my darling—'

Lucy couldn't stand it any longer. She stepped out from behind the screen, gesturing to Amy to stay where she was.

Sophia gave a small scream as Mr West stepped protectively in front of her.

'Lady Sophia, I have no desire to cause you difficulties, but really, attempts at blackmail ill become you. Surely the Vicar here is a most respectable suitor to present to your stepbrother?'

Sophia burst into tears.

Mr West drew himself up like a man facing a firing squad and announced, 'I fear that my birth is irregular.'

Wild visions of gynaecological disorders flitted through Lucy's head, then she grasped what he meant. 'Your parents were not married? But clearly you are respectable and educated. You are in Holy Orders, your bishop considers you a fit and proper person to minister to a congregation.' She tried to remember what little she knew about the appointment of clergymen to parishes. 'You have, I imagine, a patron?'

'I have. Lady Hopewell holds the advowson of this parish and was kind enough to take an interest in my career. Even so,' Mr West continued, 'I am not a suitable match for the daughter of an earl.'

'Then it is a pity you allowed the attachment to develop this far, is it not?' Lucy enquired tartly.

'You are quite correct to reprove me. As you may have overheard, I was attempting to explain to Lady Sophia how impossible—'

'Oh, I hate you both!' Sophia burst out. 'Anthony, you should stand up and claim me, not hide behind this beastly propriety. What does it matter if you are dismissed from your post? I have *thousands* of pounds. And you...' she turned on Lucy as the Vicar spluttered and tried to interject '...you are a spy and a hypocrite.'

'Miss Marsh.' Amy put her head around the screen. 'Lady Hopewell and some of the ladies are coming and I think they heard Lady Sophia just now.'

'Come in, quickly, Pringle.' Lucy contemplated fleeing through the nearest window and scrabbled frantically for some explanation that she could offer for what was going on. 'Lady Sophia is upset because of Lord Burnham's injury. We are trying to soothe her—'

'Liar!' Sophia declaimed as Lady Hopewell, followed by Lady Moss and Lady Hermione, swept into the room.

'What on earth is going on? I thought someone screamed. There is not bad news of Burnham, is there? I thought it was only a flesh wound. And who is a liar?'

'She is.' Sophia, doing credit to leading actress Sarah Siddons at her most dramatic, flung out an accusing hand. 'Miss Marsh is Max's mistress and she is trying to blackmail me into keeping quiet about it.'

'I am no such thing,' Lucy protested hotly. 'Lady Sophia is distressed, she does not know what she is saying.'

'She is threatening to say that Mr West here and I are… are *involved*. In order to silence me.'

'I have no intention of saying any such thing.' *Not to anyone but Max, at least.* The Vicar was looking desperate. If he confirmed Sophia's story he would be corroborating a lie, to admit it was a fabrication would be to compromise his love and disgrace himself in front of his patron. To do him credit, she thought, it was probably the danger to Sophia that was most concerning him.

'I believe that Lady Sophia, anxious about Lord Burnham, misunderstood Miss Marsh who came across us as I attempted to calm Lady Sophia.'

'What the devil is going on? Sophia?' It was Max, barefooted, clad only in breeches with a bed robe thrown over his bare shoulders, revealing a considerable amount of muscled torso and a glimpse of white bandaging.

Lady Moss gave a faint shriek, Lady Hermione raised what Lucy, staring distractedly at the scene, could only describe as an appreciative eyebrow and Lady Hopewell rushed to his side.

'Burnham, you should not be out of your bed. Sit down, this moment. The doctor will be furious.'

'I will go to my bed when I discover what my stepsister is shrieking about, why Miss Marsh is as white as a sheet and why the Vicar is looking like an early Christian martyr.'

'The last is easy to answer,' Lucy said. Her nails dug into her palms and the damaged tendons sent a stab of pain through her hands that, somehow, steadied her. 'Mr West is attempting to calm your stepsister down and make her behave more rationally. It would appear to require the patience of a saint.'

She saw Max put out his right hand to steady himself against the door frame and resisted the urge to go to his side. He had his pride. After a moment he walked to the nearest upright chair and sat down, just as a chattering group—all the remaining guests, it seemed—flocked into the room, staring round with barely disguised curiosity.

Sophia drew herself up, clearly emboldened by an audience. 'I was trying to make your…your *paramour* realise that her presence is a disgrace and that she is most definitely not wanted here now.'

There was total silence, then Lady Hermione said brightly, 'What nonsense. The shock of Burnham's injury has disordered your mind, Sophia dear. What do you know about irregular relationships? Nothing, I should hope. You should go and lie down and take a composing draught and perhaps you will be more yourself in time for dinner.'

Lucy watched Max. He, very definitely, did not look at her.

'Sophia will apologise to Miss Marsh before she goes anywhere,' he said.

'I will not! I will *not*. She is hateful.' Sophia burst into tears and cast herself on the Vicar's chest. To his credit he held on to her and made soothing noises: Lucy would have been tempted to drop her on the floor.

She saw understanding dawn on Max's face and, finally, he looked at her. She tipped her head slightly towards the pair and nodded. His eyes widened.

There was, she realised with relief, another door out of this room. 'I think we are beyond apologies. Excuse me.' She was out and the door closed behind her before anyone reacted.

The next room was merely an antechamber off the hall, and she was halfway up the stairs before Amy caught up with her.

'That lying little madam! I could have boxed her ears for her,' the maid said indignantly. She was bristling like a mother hen confronted by a cat. 'I told them, I did. I said, "My lady's as virtuous as she could be and anyone who says different is a nasty liar." And that Lady Hermione, the bony one, she said, "Well said, young woman."

'But you tipped His Lordship the wink, so he'll know why the silly chit is telling those lies.'

'Yes,' Lucy agreed wearily. Her initial rush up the stairs had slowed to a trudge. No one had come hurrying after her with protestations of belief in her virtue, of course. 'Lord Burnham is not going to tell everyone why his step-sister is attacking me—he will not want people to know that she is entangled with a country vicar of irregular parentage.'

'I had better pack, don't you think, Miss Marsh?'

'Yes. I expect Lady Hopewell will be glad enough to get rid of me and will send us to the nearest town in the gig. But not until I am given what I am owed by Lord Burnham,' she said with sudden decision. 'This household may believe he is paying me for my body, but it is true he did employ me to find him an answer and I have done that.'

'Quite right, miss,' Amy said stoutly. 'Look, there's a footman. Hey, James, fetch my lady's valises down right away. We're leaving.'

CHAPTER ELEVEN

Max leaned back in the chair and concentrated on not slumping. He was damned if he was going to fall flat on his face in front of an audience on top of everything else. Lucy, at least, was out of this for the moment and he had to deal with this mess first before he could go to her, much as he wanted to. Through a sickening headache he could see clearly enough that to do so would only add credence to Sophia's tale.

I have to get rid of Sophia and her confounded clergyman before she says anything else and digs the hole we are all in any deeper.

'West, kindly take Lady Sophia to the room I am currently occupying. I will join you in a moment.' He waited until the door closed behind the white-faced Vicar. The man would be several shades paler before he'd finished with him.

'My sister is hysterical. Miss Marsh is not my mistress, but she is my agent: she reports to me on confidential matters that I am not going to discuss here.' Was that enough? He could hardly explain that Lucy was spying on Sophia or he risked her ruin, too.

Lucy's white, set face danced before his eyes like the after-image caused by staring at something too long in bright sunshine. She had discovered Sophia's secret for him and she had kept it to herself in the face of a vicious attack on her own reputation. He was not certain how he was going to be able to repay that. But his shoulder was throbbing as though someone was prodding the wound in rhythm with his pulse, he was dizzy and knew he was not going to be able to stay focused on more than one thing at a time: his stepsister had to come first.

His statement had produced a buzz of speculation. He could see mystification on several faces—mainly the young ladies—speculation on those of the older guests and intense interest among the younger men.

'I would appreciate your arm to get back to my bed,' he said to Petersbridge. The Marquis was possibly the most sensible, and certainly the most influential, of the guests.

'Of course.' Lord Petersbridge got him to his feet with minimal discomfort. Once they were outside and halfway along the hallway he added, 'Anything I can do?'

'Calm down the speculation. Sophia is…upset and saying things she does not mean. Miss Marsh is a thoroughly respectable young lady.'

'Of course.'

Petersbridge didn't exactly pat him on the hand, but the soothing tone set Max's teeth on edge. He believed Max was lying to protect Lucy—the lesser of two evils— and the Marquis approved of that. If he assured everyone else that it was all a hum, he would be about as convincing as the Prince Regent would be swearing off rich food and wine.

The Vicar was standing outside Max's temporary bedchamber door, which was closed. 'Lady Sophia is within, my lord.'

'Then you can relieve Lord Petersbridge of his burden and help me inside.'

He ignored Sophia until he was sitting propped up on the bed. 'Well?'

The response was a stifled sob. 'I wish I was *dead*.'

'Mr West? Might I hope for some sense from you?'

'My lord. Lady Sophia and I formed an attachment—of the utmost propriety, I assure you—when we met in Bath. I was the curate at St Swithin's where her mother attended, the Walcot parish being more convenient than walking to the Abbey. However as soon as I realised who she was, I knew that such feelings must not be acted upon, that I am an impossible husband for Lady Sophia and that we must forget that we ever met.'

'And yet here we are.'

'Indeed,' the Vicar said miserably. 'I have attempted to explain to Lady Sophia the impossibility of our situation, but in her innocence, she fails to grasp it.'

Max closed his eyes. The throbbing in his head was getting worse and the prospect of being left alone in a darkened room was enticing. He forced the lids open again. 'You appear to be a gentleman. Lady Hopewell is a fair judge of character. What seems to you to be the bar to you making an honourable proposal? The match would be very far from brilliant, of course.'

'My parents were not married,' West confessed. 'Not to each other, that is.'

'Ah. You know who your father was?'

'Yes. My mother was his daughter's governess.' West sounded bitter. 'He died some years ago.'

And there was a definitely unclerical satisfaction in that statement, Max thought.

'And your prospects?' Not that they were relevant—not now he knew West's background. It was no fault of the man. He seemed decent enough, but this was Sophia's future they were considering here.

'They are those of any country clergyman with no family connections. I work hard, I would seek advancement and I have a generous patron in Lady Hopewell. But even if I were to accept the allowance left to me by my father, I cannot support a wife.'

'But I am an heiress,' Sophia said. 'Max, I keep telling him that and he will not listen.'

'That only makes it worse,' West said.

An honourable man, it seemed. 'You appear to be intelligent. Tell me, what possesses you to think yourself in love with Sophia?'

'Max.'

He ignored her.

'Lady Sophia has been over-indulged, I know—'

'Anthony!'

'But she has a kind heart and a good mind and a warm, if impulsive nature. I cannot tell what makes anyone fall in love. Can you, my lord? All I can say is that I love her with all my heart and I will not see her ruined on my behalf.'

'In that at least you have my blessing,' Max said. 'Sophia, you know this is impossible. Do you want your children to be merely the offspring of some obscure country vicar?'

'I want them to be Anthony's children,' she retorted.

'You will lose your station in society, your friends, the way of life you are used to. And don't start reminding me about the size of your inheritance, I am perfectly well aware of it. Do you think this man is going to let you drag him off to London to be your lapdog?'

'Oh, Max!'

'Every feeling revolts, my lord.'

'There, Sophia. If you have any true affection for West, then you will not try to force him to do what his conscience very clearly tells him is wrong. And you will tell everyone that your accusations about Miss Marsh were a joke that misfired. Do you hear me?'

Sophia fled.

West looked at Max. 'I will do what I can, my lord.'

It was the right decision, even West admitted that. Sophia would not be happy as the wife of a humble country clergyman and he had to stop her throwing her life away. This was not like Julia, infatuated by a wicked rake, but even so, the results for Sophia of a marriage she would surely come to bitterly regret would be a long life of discontent. He had to protect her from that.

But even so, he could not shake off the memory of the look of blank unhappiness in West's eyes. The man genuinely loved her, Max realised. He was going to do the right thing, but it was stabbing him in the heart and Sophia was beside herself. *Lord, what fools these mortals be!* That was what Puck had said, watching the lovers in *A Midsummer Night's Dream.* Love was risk and pain and disorder.

An hour later, when Hobson had repaired the damage to his bandages caused by Sophia hurling herself on to his chest in an excess of emotion, there was a tap on the door.

'Unless that is someone ignoring the doctor's orders and bringing me brandy, send them away, Hobson.'

His valet came back. 'Miss Marsh's maidservant, my lord. She has a note.' He hesitated. 'She appears somewhat agitated.'

'Let her in.' He knew he should speak to Lucy, but if Sophia had done what she promised, the fuss should have died down by now.

'My lord.' Pringle thrust a folded note at him and Max unfolded it one-handed.

My Lord,
I would be obliged for the fee which we agreed for my
duties here. I will be leaving for London immediately.
L.M.

'Why is Miss Marsh returning to London, Pringle?'

'Because of what they are saying, of course.'

'I told my stepsister to explain her ridiculous accusation.'

'My lord! You really should not get up again!' Hobson was positively flapping, as though to shoo a flock of geese.

'I am trying to sit up, Hobson. Dealing with insanity while flat on my back is impossible. Another pillow—Thank you. Well, Pringle?'

'They don't believe her. Not the young gentlemen, nor most of the young ladies, anyhow. They think you've ordered Lady Sophia to change her story.' She bit her lip. 'And there's ever such a big pile of letters waiting to go to the post. I think some of them have been writing to tell friends the gossip.'

When it came to it and you were drowning, there was no point in struggling. He would do his best to make this work and he was certain that she would, too. They could be civilised about this, learn to live together somehow. It felt very...cool and, oddly, that no longer felt desirable.

'Please ask Miss Marsh to join me here, Pringle.'

'In your bedchamber, my lord?' Hobson protested.

'Hobson, either Miss Marsh is my mistress, in which case there is no further damage to be done, or she is not, in which case I am hardly in a fit state to leap from my bed and ravish her, now am I?'

Hobson stood guard just inside the door, as though to defend his master's virtue with a clothes brush.

TEN MINUTES LATER, Lucy sailed in, bonnet firmly on her head, lips tightly compressed.

'Thank you, Hobson. You and Pringle can wait outside.'

'At least you are conscious and sitting up in bed, not flat out and delirious, which is what I had expected after your appearance in the Small Drawing Room,' she observed tartly.

'This has got out of hand,' he countered. 'Oh, sit down, for heaven's sake.'

Why was he angry with her? Because she was stubborn, of course. Because she would not agree to what he... He almost thought, *wanted*. The word startled him and he tried to work out why. *Ought to do* was the correct phrase, not *wanted*.

'Yes, my lord,' Lucy said with a mock meekness that jerked him away from the disconcerting train of thought.

'And stop perching on the edge of the chair like a scullery maid in disgrace. We had best announce our betrothal.'

'Our... No.' She stood up.

'You are effectively ruined, Lucy.'

'Lucy Marsh may be, if she took any notice of such nonsense. Lucy Lambert, teacher of the pianoforte, is not.'

'You want to risk it? Before, when I came up with this insane scheme, I thought you could fade away again afterwards. Now you are the focus of all eyes. They have seen your hands, they have seen *you*. All it will take is for someone to say in the course of conversation that their daughter is doing so well with her new pianoforte teacher, despite the poor lady having injured her fingers, and it will be all over town.'

Yes, she had thought of that, he could see it in her face and, from the haunted look in her eyes, it would keep her awake at night now. 'I will take that chance.'

'You do not *want* to marry me? You would gain a title,

wealth—' Even as he said it he knew that those things would not weigh with her. Or perhaps they would weigh her down. You could not measure the things that seemed to matter to Lucy—friendship, music, independence…

'And the reputation of someone who entrapped an earl into marriage,' she stated, as though slamming down another brick into the scales against what was important.

'Lucy, come here.' Max held out his hand and, reluctantly, she stood and moved to the side of the bed. He caught her hand and felt her tense, but she did not pull away.

'I will tell them all that we were already secretly betrothed and you agreed to help me because we were concerned that Sophia had made an unwise connection. Now we know the man in question is the eminently virtuous Reverend West, who naturally refuses to presume on her unwise attachment, you were about to return to London to await the formal announcement of our betrothal.'

'No.' Under his fingertips her pulse was rapid, like a tiny creature caught in his hand.

'My honour demands—'

'The sacrifice of my self-respect? I doubt it. There is one reason I would marry and this is not it. This is the very opposite of it. I will not marry to observe the decencies, to make you feel better—not that you *would* feel much better once this had begun to sink in. I am going to leave now. If you do not give me the money you owe me, then we will have to walk to London, finding rides on farm carts where we can.'

Was that true or did she simply not wish to risk him having an excuse to see her again in London? Did he want an excuse? He would have expected to feel relieved and somehow he could not. She was trembling now, he could feel it, but could not tell whether it was anger or distress.

What did she mean about a reason to marry? Not love, surely, not sensible, prickly Lucy? Love was a burden, love deceived and bound you.

He wanted to pull her into his arms and kiss away her objection, whatever it was. He let his thumb trail lightly over the inside of her wrist, exposed by the short gloves, and a little gasp escaped her.

'Hobson!'

'My lord.' The valet appeared from his discreet retreat in the dressing room.

'I am getting up. Find me something that will go over these bandages and a sling.'

'You cannot!' Lucy jerked her hand free, sending painful shocks up his injured arm. 'What are you going to do? Have men no common sense at all?'

'Miss Marsh. I have a headache which you are making worse. I have a flesh wound that is aggravating, but which will be a mere nuisance in the morning and only mildly troublesome if I wear a sling. It appears that, if you are set upon ruin, then the only way I can prevent it is by exposing my stepsister to public humiliation. So be it. I gave her every opportunity to behave as a lady should. Now, I suggest that unless you wish to assist me in getting into my breeches, you leave.'

LUCY LEFT WITH as much dignity as she could muster.

'Miss? What's happening, Miss Marsh?' Amy was hanging over the banisters.

'I have to think. Stop packing while I do.'

She had to be logical about this because the emotions involved were simply too painful and destructive.

If Max told everyone about Sophia and the Vicar, then they would both be embarrassed and upset.

But... Nobody seeing Mr West would imagine for a moment that he would have done anything to actually ruin Sophia and she had been given every opportunity to say she had been mistaken about Lucy, so she deserved a little discomfiture. Lady Hopewell was not going to hold this against her choice of vicar, she imagined, and if he did lose his post she could trust Max to make certain he did not suffer for it.

And... *If I do leave now it would put Max in a difficult position. It would seem like an admission that I have been his mistress and that he could not manage his private life effectively and discreetly.*

What was more... *I could never be absolutely certain that I would not be recognised and exposed. I would have to move to some unfashionable place—Manchester or Norwich—where society ladies were unlikely to hire me.*

Finally... *None of this is my fault. Why do I have to suffer for it? I might have developed a ridiculous* tendre *for that man, but that did not cause any of this.*

No, not finally... *What is best for me is to stay and have Max set the record straight. But what is best for Max? That, too, I think. No more deception, no awkward pretences and lies that might be exposed.*

It was going to be unpleasant and she felt sorry for Sophia, not least because, if she really did love Mr West, then her heart would be breaking. But being unhappy was no excuse for making anyone else suffer, Lucy decided.

But there was that proposal of marriage... She made herself think about it when she reached the end of her very logical and dispassionate assessment. It had never, for a moment, occurred to her not to refuse and yet it had been as if she were two persons. One was the sensible, honourable woman who would not dream of presuming on a man's sense of obligation and forcing a marriage that was so unequal. A second knew that he made the offer out of duty and not love and that was why she'd refused. *If he loved me*... But she did not love Max, much as she might desire him and, increasingly, like him. She had seen the dream made real and she could never accept second best, or inflict it on someone else.

'Put out my evening gown, please, Amy. And ring for hot water. We are staying, at least for tonight.'

THE ATMOSPHERE IN the drawing room lifted the fine hairs on Lucy's arms as though a thunderstorm was about to break. The younger ladies were wide-eyed, the older guests were gathered together as if awaiting an artist to paint a group portrait and, in the centre of the room, Sophia was laughing, surrounded by the young men.

'It was very naughty of me,' she said with a gurgle of amusement that positively invited the chorus of denial. 'I only meant it as a joke because darling Max was so stuffy about me flirting with Mr West and now I have embarrassed the poor man and he has fled back to his vicarage and Max's headache is worse and as for poor little Miss Marsh—'

Lucy cleared her throat.

'Oh, there you are!' Sophia dashed over, ribbons fluttering, and seized Lucy by the hands. 'I was just telling everyone how dreadful that my silly little revenge on Max got so out of hand. I never dreamed for a moment that anyone would believe you were his mistress and it's so awful, I am having to apologise to *everyone*.' She beamed at Lucy, but her eyes were bleak. 'Say you forgive me, do.'

'Of course I forgive you,' Lucy said, smiling through gritted teeth. 'Just as long as you stop squeezing my hands,' she added quietly.

'How dreadful of me—I forgot. But we are friends again? Say we are.' She linked arms with Lucy and turned back to face the room. 'See, everyone, Miss Marsh forgives me. Isn't she wonderful?'

So, Sophia had seen the danger she was putting herself in and Max had not needed to publicly shame his stepsister to save Lucy's reputation. That was an enormous relief. 'Your brother was very anxious about you,' she said, slowing down before they reached the young men.

'There was no need and I do not forgive him. He had broken my heart and I will make him regret it. But I am sorry I picked on you, truly I am.'

She meant it, Lucy realised. Of course, Sophia had no idea that Max had engaged Lucy to spy on her and she still did not realise that she was Miss Lambert, the music teacher she had tricked in London. It was Lucy's guilty conscience about her own role in all this that had made it so easy to think that Sophia had acted out of personal spite.

'Come and talk to me,' she said, angling away towards a deserted part of the room.

'Really?' She was nervous, Lucy could tell. All the bright, brittle confidence was gone.

'Yes, really.' She sat on a little sofa with just room for the two of them. 'Now, tell me, are you truly in love with Mr West? Or is it a flirtation?'

'I love him and now he is being all noble about things I don't care about, and Max just doesn't understand.'

'Smile, or everyone will think we are arguing,' Lucy said with a laugh. 'But he could never rise much beyond this parish, unfair though it is. His birth is no fault of his, but he would be miserable thinking that he had torn you from the life you are used to, wouldn't he?'

Sophia nodded. 'It isn't even that Anthony *wants* to be a clergyman. Oh, I know he is a good one and he cares for people, but it was the only path open to him. His education was excellent because his mother insisted that he take his father's money for that and he agreed because he wanted to support her all her life. But if Lady Hopewell had not known her and offered this living once he had some experience in the church, I do not know what he would have done.'

Lucy suspected that more than half the Anglican clergymen were only clerics because it was one of the few respectable openings for younger sons of good family to earn a modest living. Was there any other occupation that might make Anthony West a more suitable husband for Sophia?

'Let us join the others and, with any luck, they will all have the tact to forget about this.'

'I hope so. I hate having to pretend that I don't love Anthony. You are kind after I have been so horrid.' Sophia stood up and shook out her skirts, then froze. 'Oh. Max has come down.'

Lucy was on her feet, too, staring. 'He shouldn't,' she said, but she was hardly aware of what she was saying, she was so focused on the man in the doorway.

Max was in full evening dress, his coat draped across the shoulder of his injured arm and Hobson had somehow fastened it to the black sling she could see against the deep crimson waistcoat. He was pale, which made him seemed icier and more aloof than ever, like a wounded hero facing his enemies, she thought fancifully.

'How romantic he looks,' Sophia said.

Lucy nodded.

'The beast,' Max's loving stepsister added.

CHAPTER TWELVE

There was a surge of people towards Max, led by Lord
Easton. 'I'm sorry, Burnham. I was reckless and I'm just
damn—apologies, ladies—I'm just relieved it wasn't any
worse.' He shuffled his feet, looking very young all of a
sudden. 'When you are better you are very welcome to
punch six bells out of me at Jackson's Salon.'

'I heal well,' Max said. 'I might get those punches in
before we leave here.'

There was laughter at what Lucy recognised as one of
those incompressible male remarks that, instead of actually promising bloody retribution, signalled forgiveness.

'Now, do not crowd the poor man, you will set his head
to aching again,' Lady Hopewell chided. 'Come and sit by
me, Burnham.'

'Delightful as the prospect is, Dorothea, I have been
flat on my back all afternoon and the prospect of a little
mild exercise is tempting.'

She laughed and let him go to saunter around the room,
exchanging a word here and there before stopping to talk
to Lord Overdene and his aunt, Lady Hermione.

Lucy and Sophia strolled in the other direction and
ended up with a group of the younger guests who were
debating what to do the next day.

'What will the weather be like, I wonder?' Miss Gainford said.

'It will remain fine, I asked one of the gardeners.' Mr Doncaster seemed pleased to have the answer for her. 'The other men assure me he is a local weather prophet and can be relied upon. The breeze will cease, the sun will shine and parasols will be on parade.'

'Then we will take to the boats and explore the lake,' Sophia announced. She sounded her usual lively self, but Lucy thought she could detect the strain under the rallying tone. Sophia was a good actress and she had enough pride not to show her feelings, now that the shock of having her dreams so abruptly crushed had lessened.

'Have you not been out on it before?' she asked. 'I thought you were very familiar with this house.'

'Not since I was quite a child. The weather has never been quite right, or we were doing something else or there was no one I trusted not to hand me a frog or tip me out into the water.'

There was general laughter and Miss Easton embarked on a lively account of how her beastly brother once put two newts down the front of her dress in church and she had screamed in the middle of the sermon.

'Lucy?'

'Hmm? Oh, sorry, I was thinking—I am not sure about what. It has been rather a long day.'

'You were gazing at…at Terence Overdene, I do declare,' Sophia said. 'He is dreadfully intellectual, you know,' she added. 'Perhaps, like me, you prefer a man with some thoughts in his head beyond race horses and the knot in his neckcloth.' That was said in a murmur with a nod towards Lord Easton.

'I haven't really noticed Lord Overdene,' Lucy said with perfect honesty. She had been looking at Max, she realised.

Thank goodness there was another personable male in the same direction. 'I was just letting my attention wander. Oh, good, dinner has been announced.' She had every intention of slipping away immediately afterwards. It had been a long, hot, fraught day.

THE WEATHER-FORECASTING GARDENER deserved his reputation, Lucy thought, as the guests gathered around the breakfast table. The sun was shining, not a whisper of a breeze stirred the flowers in the urns on the terrace and the staff had already set the windows open and were lowering blinds on those facing south.

'The boats and the punts are all clean and watertight,' Lady Hopewell announced. 'The estate carpenter has removed those that leaked and has had his lads rowing around to check the rest. I had thought we might have a picnic luncheon on the bigger island if everyone would like that.'

There was a chorus of approval and someone suggested boat races, which seemed a popular idea.

'I am punting,' Mr Tredgold announced. 'Someone else can keep the odds this time.'

The men, including the Marquis, Sir George and the languid Lord Tobias, announced that they would compete, which left Max to act as bookkeeper and referee. There were four punts and six rowing boats among eight competitors, so it was decided to have two heats of rowing and a final for the first and second in each, followed by two punt races on the same principle.

'Formby, please proceed to send over the rugs, chairs and trestle tables and so forth and advise Mrs Pettigrew that all the guests will be present at the picnic,' Lady Hopewell ordered. 'I shall have to think of trophies to present and one for the ladies' archery yesterday.'

An hour later Lucy was handed carefully into a punt by Sir George and the little flotilla of ten small craft set off for the island, laden with guests.

As they rounded a headland in the lake she saw that, unlike the island that had been the catalyst in Verity and Will's romance, this one was low and long with a little wood in the middle. There were spreading grassy banks that formed something very like a lawn and on it some of the groundsmen were erecting little striped tents. Maids were shaking out rugs while footmen set out trestle tables and chairs.

'Our hostess has clearly planned this well in advance,' Sir George said, handling the long pole with commendable grace as the rowing boats pulled ahead of the punts. 'There is quite a little garden party set up already.'

In fact, it was more like a fête on a village green. There was a flat area set aside for quoits and skittles, two shady awnings, a discreet tent for a ladies' retiring room, another tent for Mrs Pettigrew, the cook, and her little force of kitchen maids and the lads to fetch and carry. A wide plank swing was swaying gently beneath a sturdy horizontal bough and, as the first boat grounded gently on the shingle beach, Miss Easton and Miss Moss were helped out by one of the footmen and ran laughing towards it, already pulling off their wide sun hats so they could sit side by side.

As the punt scraped to a standstill two more footmen, bare-legged below their knee breeches, stood on the soggy margins of the grass to help the passengers alight.

Lucy wandered up the gentle slope. Max had set up a board and was pinning up what she assumed were the competitors and the running, or rather, rowing order for the races, and the older ladies were settling themselves in the shade.

'Do come and play quoits,' Mary Thomas said, skipping

down to the water's edge. 'Lizzie Gainford and I and Mr Tredgold, Mr Doncaster and Lord Overdene are playing and, if we had another lady, we would have three pairs.'

Lucy was uncertain how well she could toss the rope rings, but she was willing to try it and within a few minutes they were in the thick of a tightly contested match, shouting encouragement to their partners, booing the opposition and once or twice sending the rings rolling down the hill to be retrieved from the lake by the good-natured footmen.

'Thank you so much.' Lucy took a dripping quoit from James, who was grinning, and walked back to the game. 'I think they are enjoying themselves, too.'

The game was finally settled with Lizzie and Mr Doncaster first, Lucy and Lord Overdene second and Mr Tredgold and Mary third by a long way, owing mainly to his total inability to aim true.

Lord Overdene looked round at a call from the main tent. 'The boat race order has been settled by the look of it. Come on, let's see what the opposition is like.'

It was agreed to hold the rowing races first. Max was chalking up odds on a blackboard that was considerably larger than that used for the archery and must have been brought from the old schoolroom, as well.

As wagers were placed the Marquis emerged as the favourite for the punting and Lord St Giles for the rowing. Lucy hazarded sixpence on Sir George for the punting and sixpence on Algernon Tredgold in the hope of raising his morale after his quoits defeat.

He was with the first four rowers against Lord Overdene, Lord St Giles and Sir George and they all removed their coats, jammed their hats more firmly on their heads and marched off down to the boats.

'Miss Marsh?' Max was standing right beside her. It was the first words he had spoken to her since she had refused his offer. He looked outwardly composed, but his eyes were questioning.

Lucy swallowed and found her voice. 'Lord Burnham?'

'Would you start the race for me? You need to raise this handkerchief, then let it fall. I will stand at the finish line with a footman as a runner to bring back the results.'

'Yes, of course,' she agreed, deflated. What on earth had she expected him to say? 'But why me?'

'Because I can rely on you to get them in a straight line first,' he said and walked off towards the far end of the island where a flag had been erected as the finish post.

So that was the answer! Foolish, romantic creature that you are, she scolded herself.

Was it even a compliment? Perhaps. Lucy shrugged and went down to the water's edge. 'Get straight, gentlemen!' She waited while there was some backing and splashing, then raised the handkerchief and they were off.

To everyone's surprise, but, she suspected, not his, Algernon Tredgold won by half a length with Lord St Giles second. The next four were won by Lord Easton with Mr Doncaster second. By now the betting on Mr Tredgold was increasing and Lucy risked another sixpence before the rowers lined up for the final. Their blood was up and she had some trouble getting them in order, but they were finally off, the younger men and several of the ladies running along the shore to cheer on their favourites.

'Mr Tredgold,' the panting footman announced when he arrived back, closely followed by the rowers on the water and the runners on land.

After a rest and considerable back-slapping and teasing of Mr Tredgold the first four punters lined up: the Marquis, Mr Doncaster, Lord Tobias, languid as ever, and Lord Overdene.

Mr Doncaster fell in after six yards, Lord Overdene

spun round in a circle and ran ashore before pushing off and giving chase to the Marquis, who was clearly an experienced punter, and Lord Tobias who, to Lucy's amazement, was staying level with him. It was, the panting footman announced, a dead heat.

The second race was won by Sir George with Lord St Giles second.

'Would you like to start the final, Lady Hermione?' Lucy passed her the handkerchief without waiting for a reply and walked along until she was halfway to the finish line. The start was all very well, but she wanted the excitement of the finish of at least one race.

It was clear from the start that punting needed skill and experience and more than a young man's fitness. Lord St Giles fell behind from the start, but Lord Tobias, his hat discarded, his hair rippling in the breeze, full shirt sleeves billowing, was holding his own with his two seniors. As they came level she began to run to follow them and, at the last moment, the Marquis bent his knees, pushed hard, and his punt slid ahead of Sir George to pass the flag first.

Laughing, Lucy cannoned straight into a solid obstacle that grunted and then held her upright.

'Oh! Max—I am sorry!'

MAX KEPT HIS BALANCE, but he staggered sideways. 'Lucy. I should have known.'

She was still laughing, despite the collision. Her cheeks were pink, her eyes were bright and her bosom was rising and falling with the exertion.

Max was conscious of a sudden stab of anger, largely at himself and his own doubts and worries. All that drama and emotion the day before and now Lucy was laughing, happy. It seemed that her refusal had been genuine and she was deeply relieved not to be betrothed to him. He had agonised over that in long sleepless hours last night. It appeared he had wasted the time and emotional energy.

'Miss Marsh.' He was suddenly acutely aware of James, the footman, just a yard away. 'James, run back with the result, will you? Lord Petersbridge, Sir George and Lord Tobias.'

The man took off at a brisk trot. He should have followed but, somehow, his feet were staying firmly rooted to the slightly muddy turf.

'Did I hurt you?' Lucy asked. 'I'm so sorry. No? Oh, I'm glad. That was exciting, wasn't it? I would never have imagined that Lord Tobias would be so good.'

'I suspect that he has spent a good deal of time in a punt with his notebook, drifting around looking romantic with a capital R,' Max said. 'That young man is not such an aesthete as he would like us to believe.' No, she hadn't jarred his shoulder, but there was something decidedly odd with his breathing and he realised that he was still holding Lucy by the upper arm.

'Let us walk back.' It came out more abruptly than he meant.

'Yes, of course. You should go and rest in the shade. Shall I take your arm?'

'*No*. No, thank you.' What the devil was the matter with him? The arrow wound had settled down and was showing no sign of infection, and he always healed well, anyway. It wasn't fever. Perhaps he was suffering concussion from that blow to the head after all. That and a sleepless night. 'We do not want to miss the prize-giving,' he said more moderately and offered his arm, making it quite clear he had absolutely no need to lean on her.

They began to stroll back. He really did feel decidedly strange. Reckless, almost rebellious, not that he had anything to rebel against. There was a faint breeze whisper-

ing in from the water now, bringing with it the scent of cut
grass, a hint of jasmine and warm woman.

'Is everything all right? Have the others accepted that
there really is nothing to Sophia's ridiculous tale?'

'I believe so, now that they see she and I appear to be
firm friends and they have had time to digest the fact that
she really is enamoured of someone of whom you do not
approve. And quite how ridiculous it would be for me to
be your mistress, as you said.'

Perhaps that had not been the most tactful way of putting it. Max found himself hoping that there would be
dancing that evening. That would cheer her up. He wanted
to see Lucy dance, see her face light up as it had just now.
And then he could take her in his arms and feel that thrill
of happiness shiver through her again. Just to calm his
anxieties about her, of course.

Before he could explore that desire any further she said,
'Lady Sophia is throwing herself into the spirit of the day.'

'You say that as though it is a bad thing. Personally I am
delighted that she isn't sulking. And, if she is happy, then it
just goes to show that it was a whim, a foolish infatuation.'

'Of course it doesn't,' Lucy retorted, the old, prickly female back again. 'If it had been that, then she would sulk
at being caught out and told off. If she loves Mr West, then
she will try to hide it. She will not give up. Why should
she, if he is the man to make her happy?'

'Love in poverty to a man with a disreputable ancestry?
How long would that last? I have had more experience of
the world than you, Lucy. I have seen the effect of reckless marriages for love, or what passes for it.'

'His parentage may be disreputable—and I would wager
that any fault was his father's—but Mr West is not. He is
too proud and honourable to live off Sophia's money—
why don't you find him a better position? He has no reli-

gious calling to be a clergyman. You could discover his strengths and help him to find something that would earn more and which would suit him. Thousands of people live very happily outside the orbit of those who would turn their noses up at a man for something that happened before he was born.'

'How do you know what he feels about the clergy?' Max demanded, feeling attacked. Dammit, he *was* being attacked. And lectured.

'I took the trouble to find out, which is more than you did,' Lucy retorted. 'This is Sophia's happiness at stake, her whole life. Don't you care?'

They had almost reached the rest of the party. Max slowed down. 'And I know what happens when a girl is blinded by what she thinks is love, when she puts her trust in a man who is not a suitable husband for her. A broken heart—if such a thing exists outside fairy tales—is a small price to pay for her life.'

He had said too much and either shocked or intrigued Lucy, he could tell by the jerk on his arm as she took a beat before she matched his pace again. The group surrounding the victors of both the races swallowed them up and he made himself smile and clap the two men on the back, join in the laughter as Philip Doncaster emerged from a tent attempting to dry himself with a small towel while fully clothed and tease Lucy when the extent of her winnings on Algernon Tredgold were revealed.

Under cover of the banter and the arrival of Doncaster's valet with dry clothes and an armful of towels, Max watched Sophia and Lucy. They were both good actresses, he realised. If you did not know his stepsister well, you would believe the smile, the laughter, the flirtatious little games she played. You would not see how brittle that smile was, how bleak her eyes became when she was quiet for a moment.

As for Lucy, she had been exasperated with him, he knew, but now she was smiling and defending Tredgold against accusations of employing whatever methods race-horse trainers used to give their beasts an advantage. Only days before she had been reserved, almost shy with ev-eryone—and cross as crabs with him. That, at least, had not changed.

He saw Sophia was watching him intently. He raised an eyebrow and she pursed her lips as though he had done something wrong. His conscience was clear, he told him-self. Making hard decisions was what being head of a family was so often about. It was his duty. So why did he feel guilty? No, this was not guilt—it was as though he had lost something.

CHAPTER THIRTEEN

Max took a seat in Lady Hopewell's boat for the return to shore and allowed her to fuss over him. Dorothea was an old friend and her gentle nagging was almost soothing. She was quite correct—he had spent a long day, mainly on his feet, and it was only yesterday that he had been injured.

'I cannot imagine why you are not flat on your face on the turf, Burnham,' she scolded as he stepped ashore and handed her out of the rowing boat. 'You must have the constitution of a horse and it is a miracle that you are not throwing a fever.'

'It is only a flesh wound,' he said as they walked up the long slope towards the house.

'Well, I think you should change into something very comfortable and spend a peaceful evening in your room. I will have them send up the decanters—although doubtless the doctor would say that alcohol will only raise your temperature—and a good dinner. And a pile of all the latest books that have arrived from Hatchard's.'

'That sounds very tempting.' It made him feel eighty to admit it, but everything ached now, including his brain.

'I am sure you will feel much better for it. Certainly more rested than if you spend the evening with this collection of sad romps, dancing.'

'Dancing?' Just what he had hoped. Max's vision of

a cosy evening by the fireside being pampered began to sound less tempting.

'Yes. I engaged the excellent little string band that plays at the local Assembly Rooms. But do not worry, you will not hear a thing from your bedchamber.'

And no doubt, if I ask, they will find me a gout stool, a nice rug for my knees and an ear trumpet.

'Dancing? Oh, I think I can manage to sit and enjoy watching that,' Max said. A good dose of the willow bark powder that the doctor had left would see him through the evening.

'Well…if you are certain. I don't know what Dr Williams would say.'

'He would have said I could not manage today's picnic, I imagine. Doctors make their money with doomladen prognoses from which only their skill can rescue the sufferer. Don't worry about me, Dorothea, I will go and rest now.'

And he would. A bath, an hour flat on his back on the bed, a mouth-puckering tumbler of medicine and he'd last the evening. There were two young ladies to keep an eye on. He told himself that he couldn't trust Sophia not to lure West to the house if there was dancing and, as he had given Lucy the notion that dancing would cure her distress at listening to music, then he had a duty to make sure that really worked when she was in a ballroom with other men. Yes, definitely it was his duty.

'THIS IS A lovely gown, Miss Marsh.' Amy spread out the skirts of the remaining evening dress that Verity had passed on to Lucy.

Amy was still not very skilled with hairdressing, but she was an excellent needlewoman. She had altered the gown to fit and changed the colour of the ribbons from dark brown to an amber that was almost gold, to bring out the tiny dots of gold that were sprinkled across the cream silk fabric. There were two flounces at the hem, puffed sleeves slashed to show a glimpse of gold lining, and a daring, very plain neckline that, when she was laced into the corset that was made to go with the gown, actually gave Lucy a hint of cleavage.

'Do you think this is too…exposed?' She tugged at it. 'You could whip a length of lace around it in a moment.'

'Absolutely not, miss. You'd ruin the elegance of the cut,' Amy said, very much Pringle the lady's maid. 'It's a pity you haven't got a necklace to do it justice, though.'

'I'll put Grandmama's gold locket on some of the narrow amber ribbon.' Lucy rummaged in her small jewellery case. That might prove some distraction from what felt like an expanse of bare flesh. It hadn't felt so bad when she had tried it on in Verity's bedchamber…

She would brave the music, she had decided. Perhaps one of the gentlemen would ask her to dance and, if they left her a wallflower, then she would creep off to one of the antechambers and dance all by herself. It was different from being able to play, but the music would still run through her, lift her. She rather thought that Max had restored happiness to her.

It was a good thing he would not be there this evening, not after such a strenuous day of being active without any rest. She was coming to look for his presence, feel the need to be near him, and that was dangerous, even though he was still infuriatingly authoritarian, cold and conventional.

Amy found her shawl and draped it perfectly from elbow to elbow and Lucy went down to dinner. She was halfway down the final flight of the broad staircase when she stopped, struck by an unpleasant thought: any day now she would find herself back in London, rather better off financially, considerably healed in her mind, but restored to her new life of a music teacher, living in modest respectable lodgings. Her friends would ask her to dinner, to their parties, but she was going to miss this life of ease and elegance.

'You look as though you have lost a guinea and found a groat, Miss Marsh.' Mr Tredgold looked up at her from the foot of the stairs, chubby and beaming in his evening black and white. His victory in the rowing race appeared to have transformed him. 'I hope nothing is amiss. I have to thank you for your support of me—I hear that you placed an early wager, which must have been an act of pure kindness over hope.'

Lucy laughed and came down the rest of the steps to his side. 'I merely remembered something just now that had slipped my mind. And as for the rowing, why, I declare that you are a dark horse, Mr Tredgold, keeping the secret of your prowess like that.'

'I used to be a very good rower when I was a boy,' he confessed, offering her his arm. 'Then I grew sadly stout—the fleshpots of Oxford, you know!—and recently I resolved on a course of exercise on the river at home. I have not my old form yet, and it was a good thing the course was no longer, but I think my style gave me an advantage. Or possibly,' he added with a chuckle, 'the sight of me in the lead so startled the others that they caught crabs and lost their rhythm.'

'It was most impressive,' Lucy assured him as they reached the doors into the drawing room.

'Will you be dancing this evening, Miss Marsh? Might I hope you will partner me for a set?'

'Why, yes, certainly, with pleasure. And I hope I will not reward you for my winnings of a whole crown by treading on your toes.'

They were both laughing as they walked in. The first person Lucy saw was Max looking at her with a coolness that had her chin coming up and which fixed the smile on her lips as though it had been glued.

'Do excuse me a moment, Mr Tredgold.' She swept across the floor. 'Why are you here?'

'As opposed to where? York?'

If he so much as twitches that eyebrow at me, I'll...

'Your bed. You should be resting, you stubborn man.'

'I do not require a nursemaid, Lucy.' There was something in his eyes as his gaze met hers that stirred all the unsettling feelings she had been striving to suppress.

'I do not know *what* you require,' she said tartly.

Max spoke so quietly that she hardly made out the words. 'No, I do not suppose you do. I'm damned if I do either.' Then, 'But Algernon Tredgold is what you fancy?'

'He is a very pleasant young man and he was the cause of my winning a whole crown this afternoon.'

'Hardly a very prepossessing figure of a man.'

'So what if he is not?' she demanded inelegantly. 'Men do not have to cut fine figures any more than ladies have to be beautiful to be worthwhile human beings. It is a pity you have not suffered some losses or setbacks in your gilded life, then you might be less superior and more sympathetic, my lord.'

The lovely gown made a highly satisfying swish as she swept round and stalked back to Mr Tredgold. 'I am so sorry, I just recalled something I had to say to Lord Burnham.'

If Algernon noticed that colour was burning in her cheeks he was too tactful to say anything and at that moment the remainder of the guests came crowding into the room and they were swept up in the conversation.

Lucy received three more requests for a dance before

dinner was announced and was feeling quite dizzy with anticipation, especially when Lady Hopewell let slip that she had instructed the musicians to play at least one waltz.

Lady Moss looked dubious. 'Are you certain that the mothers of all these young ladies would approve? I know it is danced at Almack's these days, but even so…'

'I know just what you mean, my dear. But all the gentlemen are known to us and the party is too small to allow any romping to go unnoticed. If danced with discretion I find it a most elegant dance. I am sure your Clara would shine in it—she is so graceful.'

Lucy noticed that Miss Moss, out of sight of her mother, had just collapsed on the sofa in a fit of giggles at something Lord Overdene had said. Graceful? Well, perhaps. She did not believe she would be either, although she had felt so in Max's arms the other evening. But this was only a private party, not Almack's, and matchmaking mamas would not be observing the young ladies with hawk-like stares, ready to pounce on the slightest misstep in behaviour or deportment. Everyone could relax.

DINNER BROUGHT HER Sir George and Lord Tobias as neighbours and, disconcertingly, Max seated opposite. Sir George, who seemed to have only just noticed her damaged hands, was so tactful in assisting her with everything from her linen napkin to placing the butter just so that she was hard-pressed to thank him civilly. Unless she overstretched her fingers or tried to do anything too fiddly, she was managing now to forget her injuries for hours at a time.

'Thank you. No, I can manage perfectly, Sir George.'

'What happened?' Lord Tobias asked abruptly, ignoring the convention that he should be conversing with his right-hand neighbour during the first course.

'Something heavy fell on them.' Lucy remembered just in time not to say it was a keyboard lid.

'Painful. Can you still write?'

'Yes, although it is uncomfortable.'

'Dreadful not to be able to write. I do not know what I would do if I could not.'

Sir George was cheerfully conversing across the table—it appeared that the casual picnic atmosphere was carrying through to the evening—so Lucy decided she could ignore convention, too.

'You write poetry, I believe?'

Lord Tobias nodded, then had to toss back his hair.

It was very thick, black and glossy, Lucy thought, but it must be a dreadful nuisance. Lord Byron's locks were wavy, she had heard, so they must have been easier to manage. 'I must congratulate you on your punting. I believe it is a lot more difficult than it looks.'

'I learnt on the river when I was at Cambridge. It is a knack more than anything,' he said with surprising modesty.

'Tell me about your poetry,' she asked recklessly. Normally asking young men about their verse was risking mind-numbing boredom, but Lord Tobias shook his head.

'I would if it was better, but I am not satisfied. I wish to write like Byron, but I know I am setting the bar too high. Yet I must attempt it.'

'You have a theme in mind? Or a hero to write about?' She had expected him to talk incessantly—this was like winkling cockles out of their shells.

'You are truly interested?' he asked and she saw he was younger than all his romantic posing had led her to believe. Perhaps it was a mask to shield his uncertainty about his talent.

'If I gave you some to read, would you tell me honestly

what you think?' Yes, he was most certainly younger than the twenty-five or six she had first thought.

'I am no poet, but, yes, I would tell you my honest opinion if you think it would be worth anything.'

'You would understand, I think,' he said seriously, looking at her. 'You would feel it, know if the rhythms are not right. Like music.' His smile took her by surprise and she smiled back. How interesting that two of the people she had almost dismissed on first sight—Mr Tredgold as awkward and uninteresting and Lord Tobias as affected and foolish—had proved her wrong.

'Will you dance this evening?' Lord Tobias asked as the footmen cleared the first course and she told herself she must make conversation with Sir George.

'I will, although I am sadly out of practice.'

'Then you will save at least one for me?'

'I would like that very much,' Lucy said, smiling as she turned to her other partner and found Max regarding her with what looked like frigid disapproval.

For what? Talking to the wrong partner? For smiling?

She turned the smile on him, very sweetly. So sweetly that he seemed at risk of choking on the wine he had just drunk.

SIR GEORGE ALSO claimed a dance and, with so many partners already, Lucy felt an unexpected confidence when they all went through to the ballroom.

The small string band was good and Sir George, who claimed her for the first country dance, was a steady, if rather ponderous, partner. It was not as easy as dancing in hold had been and the effect of the music flowing through her was not as magically all-consuming. Or perhaps that was the effect of dancing with Max, a theory she preferred not to explore too deeply.

Anyway, Lucy told herself as they all clapped and then took their positions for the next dance of the set, she was enjoying this, it felt soothing and invigorating both at the same time and it proved that the magic she had felt when Max had waltzed with her on the terrace had not been a product of the moonlight.

He was not dancing, of course. It was foolish of him to be here at all, when he should be resting. If he threw a fever tomorrow, it would be entirely his own fault. In fact, his arm was probably hurting him, which was why he was looking so severe at dinner.

Algernon Tredgold claimed her for the next set, but he was not as accomplished a dancer as Sir George and trod on her toes three times. Magic was decidedly lacking, but he was cheerfully apologetic and the set passed without too many small mishaps.

There was a short interval while the musicians sorted their music, consulted together and the viola player retuned his instrument. The ladies sat and fanned themselves and the windows were opened on to the garden, bringing in fresh air and the perfume of night-scented stocks.

Lucy saw Max rise and walk over to the little stage, murmur in the ear of the lead violinist who nodded. The musicians settled themselves and the gentlemen began to fan out around the room, seeking their next partner.

'Miss Marsh?' Lord Tobias was at her side.

'My dance, I believe.' She turned to see Max looking, not at her, but at the younger man.

'I had promised Lord Tobias—'

'But not the waltz, I think,' Max said, his eyes still holding Lord Tobias's gaze.

'No, not the waltz. I hope for one of the later dances, Miss Marsh.' Lord Tobias made a small bow and strolled away to Miss Thomas.

'I had not promised you a dance and, anyway, you should be in your bed, not exerting yourself at this hour,' she said crossly. Lord Tobias had not even protested.

She should not have mentioned beds. There was not the slightest flicker of either amusement, let alone anything like desire, on Max's face, but somehow she was convinced that he was thinking of those crowded moments under that bed, of the kiss.

'I assure you, Lucy, I have rested upon my bed, taken a headache powder and generally behaved in the most sensible of manners,' he said, leading her out on to the dance floor.

And now I cannot turn tail and walk off or it will look to everyone as though we are quarrelling.

'Sensible? Of course, my lord, you are always *sensible*.'

The musicians struck a chord, partners took their places and Max gathered her neatly into hold without even a wince.

'I try to be,' he said very seriously as they began to dance. 'I really do—it makes life so much simpler. But recently I find myself wanting to behave in the most irrational manner.'

Oh, there it is, that wonderful feeling, the music flooding through me. So much better than the others, like a cloudy day when the sun comes out.

What had Max just said? She must learn to dance and to think at the same time. 'Irrational? I suppose Lady Sophia's behaviour, however understandable in a woman in love, is enough to make a strict brother, one who has no concept of the emotion, wish to respond irrationally.'

What did he just murmur under his breath? It was hard to tell because they were close to the orchestra now. *Sophia is hardly the problem?* No, it must have been, *Sophia is quite the problem.*

Lucy closed her eyes and found it was not simply the music that was taking over her senses. She was very conscious of Max's hands—light where he held her own, firm where he touched her waist—of the faint scent of starch and soap and the whisper of something citrus and sharp. And the music seemed to fade and the scent became greener and there was the tinkle of water and she opened her eyes.

'We are in the conservatory.'

'It is cooler in here. I was becoming quite dizzy.' He danced on, sweeping her around palms and pots and a statue of a mournful-looking Greek female clutching at her slipping robe in an attempt at modesty.

He was dizzy? She certainly was and Max appeared to have no trouble keeping in step and maintaining his balance.

'*Max.*'

'Yes?' They came to a halt in front of a bench next to the little fountain.

'You are *not* dizzy.'

'Are you calling me a liar?' He seemed amused rather than outraged.

'Yes.'

'I want to kiss you, Lucy—heaven knows why, given that you would probably impale me on your prickles—but I do. Which tells me I am dizzy and probably suffering from the blow to my head.' Max lifted his hand away from her waist as though freeing her to run from him.

CHAPTER FOURTEEN

Lucy stared at Max, up at him, because they were still in the dance position. This close she could see that he had shaved with meticulous closeness, that the slight indentation in his chin *was* a dimple when he smiled—even if it was ruefully—and that those cool grey eyes had intriguing little flecks that were almost black.

'I did not hit my head, I am not dizzy.' *Well, not very.* 'And I would like to kiss you,' she responded. Clearly, she had lost all common sense, but that did not seem very important.

'You understand that I am not attempting to seduce you? That I do not take innocents as lovers? It is just that I feel this quite irrational urge to hold you.' He sounded bemused, which was rather endearing.

Not a word I ever expected to apply to this man...

'Yes, I am quite clear on that. You have made it unflatteringly plain that you cannot imagine why you should wish to kiss me. Let me say in return, I have no idea why I should wish to embrace an arrogant, authoritarian, chilly man like you.'

'I do not feel chilly, Lucy. Not in the slightest.'

She swallowed. Neither did she. 'I doubt that kissing will have a cooling effect, but we could try.'

Max did not reply, only lowered his head slowly, watching her, until their lips touched. She remembered the last time, how his mouth had moved on hers, how his tongue had slid along the seam of her lips, and now she was ready for that, anticipated him, opened to him on a sigh and leaned into his body as his tongue touched hers.

No, he was not at all cold, this man. He was hard as she pressed herself to him, his mouth was hot and she was burning up with the need to be closer to him. She wanted to climb him, wrap herself around him, drown in the delicious sensations his lips were creating.

Everything seemed to be connected, from her mouth to her breasts, to low in her belly, to the wicked little pulse between her legs and from her fingertips in his hair to her toes pressed hard against the unyielding tiled floor.

When he lifted his head a moment or possibly an hour later, she sat down with a bump on the cushioned bench, her knees trembling.

Max stood there, his hands on her shoulders, eyes closed, then he gave himself a little shake and sat down beside her.

'Max...'

'Yes?' He sounded braced for almost anything.

'When I had to hide in the pool that first evening and you lifted me out you seemed so strange, as though you were unwell.' *Or somewhere else entirely.* She had thought about his reaction since, as she had come to know him better. That pallor had not been the result of pulling a muscle in his back lifting her.

She thought he was not going to answer her, then he said, 'You were soaking wet, your clothes were plastered to your body and you were pale. There was weed in your hair. I once saw someone who had drowned in the Thames. A woman. They laid her out on the stinking mud, her gown clinging to her, her hair dark with the water, a strand of weed across her face.'

'Someone you knew?' Of course it was. There was hard-reined emotion under the flat description.

'Her name was Julia. I loved her.'

'Oh. Oh, Max.' Lucy curled her fingers into his hand. 'Were you betrothed?'

'No. It was ridiculous—*I* was ridiculous. She was twenty, I was seventeen and at that age the difference is immense. She was already a woman, I was a romantic boy. She fell for a man, a fortune hunter, and ran away with him, although I pleaded with her not to trust him. She made me promise not to tell anyone and, like a fool, I agreed.'

'Did…did he kill her?'

'He might as well have done. Her father refused to give him money, refused his consent to a marriage, so he discarded her like a worn-out shoe after five months. She was pregnant, the doctor at the morgue said. I had come up to London searching for her when her letters stopped coming. I felt responsible, because I had not told anyone where she had gone, and with whom, until it was too late. I asked the river patrols and they took me to see that night's haul of bodies. They had not even taken her up from the water's edge when I got there.'

His voice was still flat. 'There were bruises on her face.'

'What did you do?'

'I sent for her father, but he wrote back, said she was already dead to them. I had enough money for a simple funeral, so I arranged that in the nearest church, a strange little place by the river. And I saw what damage an ill-considered love affair can do, why it is so important that there is equality of rank and fortune, acceptance by society and family. Otherwise the risk for a woman is too great.

'A week later a letter reached me. Julia had written it

before she…before she went down to the river. She said it was all her fault, that she did not love him enough, that she had thought it was all that was needed to be happy and she was wrong and now she did not know how to go on.

'It had been my fault that she was not stopped and I will not make the same mistake again. I should have known, after all, because one of my uncles made an equally reckless match and they are both unhappy in it.'

'Max, the Reverend West would never abuse Sophia, you must see that in him.'

'It is almost the opposite case. He would come to resent her, her money. His pride is already engaged and he will not take her fortune. And she has no idea what it would be like to live outside her own social circle, to scrimp and save. I want her to be happy, contented, secure.'

Was he right? How could she tell when she hardly knew either of the lovers involved? But for that one tragic incident in his past to have created such certainty, such emotion, proved something to her—Max had felt deep guilt and she had no idea how to help him.

It is not your problem to solve, the voice of common sense said firmly. But yet, for some inexplicable reason, it was…

'Max, I am so sorry.' There were no words, but perhaps touch could soothe, just a little. She lifted her hand to stroke it down his cheek, saw her gloves and, without thinking, stripped them off. She needed to touch him, feel him.

He turned his face into her palm, pressed his lips into it, and with a little sob, she curled her other arm around his neck as he stood, bringing her with him. Something caught, tore, but she hardly heeded it.

The need to comfort had become something else, something entirely new, a sensation close to the ecstasy of making music when everything was right and it flowed from her fingers and possessed her utterly.

She could hear music now, swelling, building—

Someone screamed, a sharp, indignant screech. Max swung round, putting her behind him as he had that other evening in the conservatory, but there was no pool of water to conceal her now.

'Lord Burnham—and *Miss Marsh*. It is true after all! Girls, go out this minute.'

It was Lady Moss, Lucy saw through the fronds of the palm that Max had almost pushed her into. It was not, she realised, very effective cover, judging by the expression on the faces of Lady Moss, her daughter, Miss Thomas—all the young ladies, in fact, plying fans, their cheeks flushed. They had come through from the ballroom to cool themselves, which was why the music had suddenly become louder.

The young ladies ignored the instruction and stood in a little gaggle like nervous, nosy chickens.

'Max, what *are* you doing?' That was Sophia. 'Oh...'

And then Lucy realised that, despite being hot with embarrassment and kisses, there was cool air on her shoulders. What she had felt catch and tear was the little train that fell from the back edge of her neckline. It had ripped away, taking one puffed sleeve and a section of bodice with it, exposing much of her right breast and her stays. She scrabbled to pull it together, her fingers clumsy on the fine fabric, and her gloves fell to the floor.

'Girls, out this moment.' Lady Moss shooed them towards the door with little success. 'Burnham, I had thought better of you and as for you, Miss Marsh, ripping off your clothing in the conservatory! To think I gave you the benefit of the doubt earlier, that I allowed you to associate

with my daughter, with the daughter of my friends who
had entrusted her to my care. Hussy!'

'Miss Marsh is my betrothed and cannot be blamed for
my own lack of self-control.' Max finally managed to get
a word in edgeways.

'No, I am *not*.' There was silence except for the jolly
strains of a lively country dance being played, presumably
to a near-empty ballroom, given that everybody seemed
to be in here, staring at her. 'Lord Burnham is being gallant. We are not betrothed.'

There was another door, the one she and Max had escaped though that first evening. Lucy turned and walked
towards it. She felt Max take her arm and brushed him
away.

Someone said, far too loudly, 'Look at her hands.'

The door banged behind her and she saw it had a latch
which she flicked over. That should stop anyone following
her. She ran upstairs, found her bedchamber and tumbled
in, turning the key in the lock.

Amy was perched on the end of the bed, peering carefully at the heels of a handful of silk stockings.

'Pack, at once. We are leaving.'

'Now, Miss Marsh?'

'Hurry. There's an inn in the village, I can hire a gig to
take us into the nearest town with an inn that the coach
stops at. Then—'

She broke off at a knock on the door. 'Lucy, open this
door.' It was Max.

'Go away.'

Silence. Knowing Max, she doubted that he had done
what she asked. She turned to Amy and whispered, 'Keep
packing, I will help. He can hardly stand out there all
night.'

'What has happened?' Amy asked, but her hands were

already busy rolling the stockings, as her eyes scanned the room, assessing what had to be done.

'A misunderstanding—and a scandal. Are the valises still down here?'

'Yes, miss.'

'What about your things, Amy?'

'I'll just have to go and get them when the coast is clear. Or… Come into the dressing room and look at this.'

Lucy followed her, feeling queasy. Max was still out there, she was certain. And of course he had said they were betrothed. He was a gentleman and so he had done the honourable thing, in public this time, even if it was also something that went directly against what he believed about suitable marriage partners.

But women could have honour, too, and marrying a man simply because of a few kisses in the conservatory and a ripped gown was as logical as trying to train a cat to ride a pedestrian curricle. It did not help that when Max had said *betrothed*, something inside her had fluttered with joy.

'Fool,' she muttered as Amy opened the shutters over the narrow window.

'See, miss?' There's a balcony outside, just like there is outside the bedchamber window. But that one has nothing close to it—this one is paired up with the room next door. I reckon we could climb across.'

Lucy opened the window and leaned out. They were two floors up with only darkness below. Her stomach swooped, but she knew Amy was right—the gap was about two feet and the balustrades were wide and looked in good repair. 'Who is next door?'

'Nobody, miss. And the door for the bedchamber that dressing room belongs to opens out on to the cross-passage at the back. I found it the other day when I needed some blue thread and I thought I'd see if someone's maid was there to borrow from. But it's empty.'

'Right. That's what we will do.'

HALF AN HOUR later Amy hitched up her skirts and climbed out of the window and on to the balustrade. Lucy held up a candle as she took one stride across, then dropped down on to the narrow balcony.

'The window's open, I suppose they don't think anyone can get in at this height,' she whispered. 'Pass the bags across, miss.'

That took only a moment, then it was Lucy's turn. She had put on her most sensible shoes and a plain walking dress, but even so, as she stepped across in the near-dark, she half expected to hear a rip as her heel caught in her skirts and she overbalanced to fall on to the stone terrace below. Then she was down beside Amy, helping get the valises through the window.

The key was in the lock. Amy eased open the door. 'All clear, miss.'

They tiptoed along the passage to the back stairs and Lucy held her breath while Amy ran upstairs and came back ten minutes later with her own valise.

The way down was clear. 'Everyone's in the kitchen clearing up, or up in the ballroom,' Amy murmured as she lifted the latch and they were out into the yard.

They made their way to the stables, then down the track where Max had been riding the afternoon of the archery contest. As Lucy had hoped, it gave out on to a lane and the gate had no lodge with a keeper to stop them.

'That way,' Lucy decided and gave a sigh of relief as they came to a larger lane with a rickety signpost pointing to the village of Staning Waterless. 'It can't be too far,

I heard the church bells quite clearly the other day—the ringers were practising.'

Their luck held. The Hopewell Arms provided them with a gig and a lad to drive them into Blandford Forum and the assurance that they would be in ample time for the early-morning Mail coach to London from The Greyhound in the market square.

YAWNING, THEY CAUGHT it at five o'clock and managed to secure inside seats. It saved Lucy the cost of a night's accommodation and the high price of a post chaise for a journey of at least a hundred miles and, she hoped, gave them sufficient of a start in case Max was still set and determined on putting honour above either sense or his own principles.

It did, however, give her more than ten hours with no privacy to think about what had happened.

Betrothed. Her heart had leapt at the word and she was not so good at self-deception not to understand exactly what that meant. She did not only desire Max's kisses, she wanted him. If their respective stations in life, if their circumstances had been more equal, she would want to marry him.

Which means I am in love with him, I suppose. How had that happened? She hadn't liked the man—she was still not certain that she did. He was too controlled, too authoritative, too... Just *too much*, she supposed.

And yet, he has his good points, she mused as Amy curled up in the opposite corner and fell asleep, buttressed at the side by a serious-looking gentleman who looked like a lawyer.

Max had a strong sense of responsibility and it was clear would do anything to protect his stepsister—whether she wanted it or not. He was honourable. He was intelligent and, she suspected, there was far more of a sense of humour lurking under that glacial expression than he allowed to show. He had kissed her, but only when she had made it clear she wished him to, and he had not taken advantage of her inexperience and simply carried on, swept her away on the tide of her own innocence.

And there was something about him, not simply his good looks, that stirred feelings she had not been aware she possessed. Feelings that must have been buried by the music. Or perhaps Max was part of the music…

'Unlock the door? But—'

'Dorothea, they have been in there since almost midnight last night. It is now midday. Do you propose leaving them to starve? Would that be more proper?' He felt desperate. It had all gone wrong and that was his fault. His fault for wanting to kiss Lucy, his fault for making her unhappy.

His fault for not understanding himself when he saw her all too clearly. She was attracted to him, but was strong enough in her own beliefs to reject even his most pressing attempts to make reparation for his errors, while he felt as though the past and the present, his desires and his fears, were all tugging at him, clamouring for his attention. As Dorothea was now, he realised.

'I am not accepting a lecture from you on propriety, Max Fenton! You bring your paramour to my house when you knew full well it was not that kind of party—'

'I did no such thing. If you believe that I would when my own stepsister is present, then you have formed a very strange idea of my character in the years we have known each other. Now, do you unlock that door or do I kick it down?'

CHAPTER FIFTEEN

Max was angry enough to kick a door down—or shoot a lock off, come to that. He had spent the night on a chair outside Lucy's bedchamber door because he knew she would bolt if she had half the chance and what sleep he had was racked by the old, familiar nightmare of Julia's letter.

He had endured breakfast being glared at by Lady Moss, regarded with disapproval by the older men and with something like awe by the younger ones. The young ladies, herded down to the far end of the table—presumably in case he leapt on them with lustful intent—blushed and giggled.

He had stood up, leaving his food half-eaten, and addressed them. 'I will say this once more. Miss Marsh is not my mistress. I have every hope she will be my wife. If I hear remarks, inside this house or out of it, to the contrary, I will act as appropriate.'

Then he had stalked upstairs to relieve Hobson at the door.

'Not a squeak, my lord. Not so much as the creak of a floorboard.'

Now he had run out of patience. The sooner he extracted Lucy and made her see sense, the sooner he could begin to repair what damage he could. Bitter reality told him that as marriages went it could hardly fail to be a disaster on a personal level, but that was beside the point.

With a tut of disapproval, Lady Hopewell produced a ring of keys and unlocked the door. Max stepped inside and closed it firmly in her face. She promptly opened it and followed him in.

'Lucy?'

The bed was made up. The room empty. He went across to the dressing room. That, too, was empty. Hiding? What would that achieve? The clothes presses were bare, there was no one and nothing under the bed except a prosaic china utensil that brought back inconvenient memories.

'There is nothing of hers here,' Dorothea said. 'But how? There is no other door to the corridor and we are two storeys up.'

Max opened the bedchamber windows on to a tiny balcony, more an architectural feature than a practical place to sit. The corresponding one in the room to the right was a good ten feet away. To the left was the little balcony from the dressing room window and next to that—

He looked down and breathed again. No crumpled body on the flagstones of the terrace.

'Whose room is next door?'

'It is empty. There was a leak in the ceiling from a blocked gutter.'

Dorothea was still talking about falling plaster as Max went out, turned right and right again and found the door, unlocked. The window to the dressing room stood open and there were marks in the lichen on the balustrade of the balcony.

'They left this way,' he said as Dorothea came to stand beside him.

'But why take such a risk?' she demanded. 'If she is your betrothed…'

'She is not my mistress and, as she continues to make clear, she has no wish to be my wife.'

'Yes, but—'

'She is an innocent and I should not have kissed her. The disarray to her gown was due to it catching and tearing, not to unbridled lust,' he added acidly when Lady Hopewell opened her mouth as though to protest.

'If she likes you enough to be kissing you in the conservatory, then why will the foolish girl not marry you?' she retorted. 'You are an earl, for goodness sake. She is clearly gently born, but hardly the sort of young lady I would have imagined you marrying.'

No, and I made that more than clear to her only moments before we were interrupted, Max thought. Lucy must have thought that his pouring out of Julia's story was to emphasise just why he had no intention of marrying her, however much he might enjoy her kisses.

Now she was gone, back to London, he supposed. She would revert to her true name, continue with her pianoforte tuition. He could forget her and put up with a newly acquired reputation for debauched behaviour in respectable ladies' conservatories. Another little scandal would come along soon to eclipse this, he thought with a mental shrug, making his way back to the other bedchamber.

Dorothea tugged the bell pull and when a footman appeared sent him off to see whether Pringle's things had gone from her room. A sensible thing to check, of course. The two of them could have taken refuge in the servant's room until daylight.

The man was back within minutes. 'Everything gone, my lady. Not so much as a hairpin that I could see.'

'Well, you have had a fortunate escape, it seems,' Dorothea remarked when the footman had gone.

'Indeed? From a young lady too principled to take advantage of an offer made out of a sense of obligation? And you would have me just wash my hands of her now? They left in the small hours—where are they now? I shall take out the horse you were considering selling to me. Miss Marsh may not wish to marry me, but I am damned if I'll leave her wandering the lanes of Dorset.'

He strode out, taking consent for granted and ignoring Dorothea's *tut* of disapproval for his language. His old acquaintance was growing puritanical with middle age, he thought darkly.

How did the infuriating female think she was going to get herself and her maid back to London without his money? Walk? The thought of the things that could happen to young women on their own in a journey of over a hundred miles made his blood run cold.

MAX RODE OUT of the same gate he had used the afternoon he was shot, taking it steadily. His arm hurt like the devil after the previous day's activity, followed by a thoroughly uncomfortable night in an upright chair outside Lucy's door, and he did not know how long he would have to be in the saddle now.

The earth at the gate on to the lane was shaded by a big elm and had remained moist, holding the imprints of two sets of small-sized shoes. They pointed towards the direction of the road to the village and he used his heels to send the horse into a trot that took him into Standing Waterless in ten minutes.

A groom was brushing down a neat bay cob in the stable yard and touched a finger to his hat when Max rode in. 'Morning, sir.'

'That's a good animal.' Max noticed a gig to one side, fresh mud splashes on the sides. 'Is he for hire?'

'Aye, sir. But not until this afternoon. He's been out as far as Blandford Forum and back this morning.'

'Ah. So the governess my sister dismissed did find a conveyance.' He leaned down and lowered his voice, man to man on the subject of foolish women. 'I come home and find the household in uproar, the governess dismissed for a mere nothing, the children in tears... I am concerned, as you might imagine.'

'Not to worry, sir. I got them to The Greyhound in plenty of time to catch the Mail.'

Max tipped him and, feeling somewhat relieved, turned his mount. Then something occurred to him. 'Is anything owed for the hire?'

'No, sir, I thank you. The young lady paid just what was asked without a murmur and something for me, too.'

So where the devil did she get the money from? And had she enough for the Mail? He did some calculations as the horse cantered along the wide grass verge. Over a hundred miles, two of them—hopefully inside—a couple of bags, food and tips. She would need at least four pounds, perhaps five.

She must have had more than he realised and, when she threatened to leave before, had demanded what he owed her because otherwise she feared she might not receive it. A wise precaution, but not a very flattering reflection on her opinion of him.

AT THE GREYHOUND the man in charge of the booking office was helpful. Yes, the two young ladies had secured inside seats and he was able to tell Max that the other two inside passengers on their way to London were Mr Promfret, a highly respected local attorney, and Miss Hatch, a most respectable spinster.

Max turned his horse's head back towards Waterless

Manor. There was nothing to be gained by chasing the Mail on horseback, not when it seemed that Lucy had organised her escape most effectively—and with considerable good luck in her timing.

But I know where you live, Miss Marsh–Lambert, he thought as he rode. *If you think this is the end of the matter, you are very much mistaken.*

IT WAS FOUR o'clock in the afternoon before the hackney carriage they had taken from the General Post Office in St Martin's-le-Grand dropped Lucy and Amy at the door, only to find the Duchess of Aylsham's smart town carriage drawn up outside and the lady herself, almost seven months pregnant, descending the front steps with some care.

'There you are! Your landlady said you had gone out of town—and never a word to me, or any of the others. I was beginning to think you had eloped!' Verity smiled as Amy bobbed a curtsy. 'Good afternoon, Pringle.'

'Eloped?' Lucy felt a sudden urge to laugh hysterically. 'Hardly. It was…a commission. In Dorset.'

'*Dorset?* You have only just got back?'

'On the Mail, Your Grace,' Amy said when Lucy merely shrugged.

'Why—? Oh, never mind that now. What am I thinking of, keeping you out here talking when you look exhausted? Come back with me and be looked after for a day or two, and catch up on all the news. The others are all in town, too.'

'I—' Suddenly it was too much effort to resist. She was home and the practical business of travel was done with. Now what was there to keep her from simply sinking down and being miserable? Besides, she and her four friends, Verity, Melissa, Jane and Prue, had always told each other everything and the others' tales of woe caused by men had been equally as shocking as hers—they were hardly likely to be appalled by her story.

'Thank you. I would like that.' She emerged from Verity's embrace to find the footman had already loaded their few bags into the carriage—clearly he knew his mistress too well to doubt that her suggestion would be taken as definite.

Having got her way, Verity was too considerate to demand answers on the short drive to Grosvenor Square. She swept Lucy inside, calling for the housekeeper. 'Mrs Blagden, here is Miss Lambert come to stay. She has been jolted all day on the Mail, so what she needs is a lovely hot bath for a soak and then a quiet rest. The Blue Bedchamber, I think. Are you hungry, Lucy? No? Tea and a little bread and butter then, Mrs Blagden, and please tell Cook, dinner for Miss Lambert in her room.'

She waited until the staff had left before taking Lucy's arm and guiding her up the stairs. 'I will send to the others to come tomorrow morning after breakfast. You don't want to be talking now, I can see. But something is wrong. We'll put it right between us, don't worry.'

LUCY HAD EVERY intention of taking her bath, lying down for an hour and then going down to take dinner with Verity and Will in a civilised manner. Instead, as she explained at breakfast, she fell fast asleep and not even the arrival of the dinner tray woke her.

'You obviously needed the rest,' Verity observed, sifting through the little pile of post and notes the butler brought in. 'Excellent—all the others will be here at ten. Will, you must make yourself scarce, this is a convocation of ladies.'

'Yes, my love,' the Duke said mildly, then winked at Lucy. The Duke of Aylsham had been known as the Perfect Duke, but that was before Verity's influence had done its work on him.

Lucy smiled, recalling Verity's tale of how they had first met when the Duke had plunged down the side of an excavation she was conducting, only to be bitten on the posterior by an ancient skull. After that the poor man had found his life turned upside down by an unconventional lady who was the exact opposite of the wife he had intended to wed.

They lingered over the breakfast table after Will had left muttering about Tatts, boots and Christie's auction house.

'Which sounds expensive,' Lucy observed. She was feeling rather better, but only in the way one feels when a dentist appointment has been made and one's nagging toothache will be dealt with.

'How many pairs of boots can one man require? When I tease him about it he points to my milliners' bills, but surely boots cannot be a matter of fashion like a bonnet? As to Tattersall's, we do need a new pair of carriage horses. But I dread to think what he might find in Christie's—he has conceived a passion for Dutch Old Masters.'

THE DOOR KNOCKER was heard at half past nine, heralding Melissa Taverner's arrival. She was always early for anything she was interested in—and late for things she was not.

'Darling! You look ghastly, what have you been doing? Oh, yes. Tea, please. And I have found a house in Half Moon Street, isn't that bold of me? I have left home now I am in possession of Great Aunt Melly's fortune and intend to be an independent lady author. You see how convenient it will be for harassing Mr Murray, the publisher in Albemarle Street? But never mind me, that can wait until the others come and we have put things to rights for you, Lucy.'

'Thank you,' Lucy said, feeling somewhat as though she had been run over by an over-enthusiastic youth in a pedestrian curricle, the usual result of an encounter with Melissa.

The others arrived shortly afterwards and they retreated to Verity's sitting room where they could kick off their shoes and curl up on the especially comfortable sofas.

'Now,' Verity said. 'Tell us what happened, what is wrong and how we can help.'

Lucy described Lady Sophia's trick to escape to the house party and Max's plan to discover who his sister fancied herself in love with. The others nodded understanding and agreement that, of course, a commission paying such an excellent fee would be irresistible at this precarious early stage of Lucy's business.

'So, what is he like, the Earl of Burnham?' Prue asked. 'I have seen him at a distance, but never met him. Very good-looking, I thought.'

Jane, as Lucy had suspected, did not agree. 'Too perfect, therefore not interesting,' she pronounced. 'And he seems completely without emotion. He would be a nightmare as the subject of a portrait.'

'He is not lacking in emotion,' Lucy said. 'But he is skilled at hiding it.'

'So what happened then?' Melissa demanded.

Lucy took a deep breath and told them everything. Everything except what Max had revealed about his tragic first love. That had been told in confidence. She simply explained that something in his past had convinced him that 'unsuitable' marriages were doomed from the start. The others could be trusted not to betray Sophia's secrets, so she did not hold anything back about the unfortunate Reverend West.

There was silence when she reached the end of her tale.

Then Prue, ever practical, frowned. 'I do hope this will not have any repercussions for your new business, although you said from the start that you thought you would get most custom from the middle-class households, and they are not going to hear any gossip from Lady Hopewell's house guests.'

'You changed your name and nobody there knew you could play the piano, except Lord Burnham,' Jane mused. 'I am sure you would be safe.'

'Yes, I think so,' Lucy agreed. 'And I have some appointments for next month when families are returning to London at the end of the summer—City addresses, not West End ones.'

'That is important, of course,' Verity agreed. 'But surely what is making you so miserable is the fact that you are in love with the man.'

'In love? With Max? I mean, with Lord Burnham? But that is ridiculous, I do not like him, even,' she protested, knowing as she said it that it was untrue.

'Poppycock,' Melissa said. 'I thought from the start that was what we were here to discuss, not pianoforte lessons. I mean, I can understand you wanting to kiss him once, just out of curiosity, and the situation must have been most…provocative. But a second time? A third? I intend to take a lover as part of my plan to be a fully independent woman, but I cannot imagine you risking as much as a lingering glance or a mild flirtation with anyone you were not deeply attached to.'

The others, having heard Melissa's purely theoretical views on free love and female independence many times, did not turn a hair at her declaration, but nodded in unison.

'You are, you know,' Jane said. 'It is perfectly possible to love a man while wishing him at the devil, believe me. That is why you are so miserable and you will be until you reconcile whatever it is that infuriates you about him with the other feelings you have.'

'How?' Lucy demanded.

'He may change or you may find you are mistaken in him. Some things you will disregard as unimportant when the major obstacles are overcome.'

'Such as?' Melissa asked.

'Never you mind,' Jane retorted, blushing.

'This is all beside the point,' Lucy said, trying to be firm and not be distracted. 'Even if I did love him, he is an earl and I am a perfect nobody and a crippled one, to boot.'

'You are not crippled,' Verity said. 'Your hands are getting better. I noticed at breakfast how much easier you were at managing cutlery, how you have stopped lifting a cup as though you expected to drop it at any moment.'

'I still cannot play.'

'But you can do everything else,' Jane pointed out. 'And yours is a perfectly respectable gentry family. Look at me—that is precisely my background, too, and I married an earl. Prue a marquis. Verity's papa is a bishop, to be true, but even so, I cannot imagine he expected her to marry a duke.'

'None of you is estranged from your families.'

'None of us has a father who would slam a keyboard lid down on our hands because they disapproved of us playing on a Sunday.' Melissa, never overly sensitive, could be counted on to mention the one thing everyone in the room was avoiding.

'I do not believe he intended to injure me. I was so shocked at their early return from church when I was engrossed in a new piece of music that I froze, just for a second.'

'And then, instead of being appalled at his own actions, he blames you, says it is a judgement on you for breaking the Sabbath,' Melissa retorted. 'I can understand that no man is actually going to *welcome* Mr Lambert as a father-in-law, but if he loves you, he will set that aside.'

'But Max *doesn't* love me. He offered to marry me because I had been compromised, so he felt honour-bound. He seemed to enjoy kissing me for some reason, although I cannot think why—'

'Men enjoy kissing. Frankly, they are fairly undiscriminating about it,' Jane said sagely.

'There, you see? He would have kissed anyone foolish enough to offer and he proposed out of simple gallantry. And I refused him because I do not love him.'

'No, you didn't,' Prue contradicted. 'You refused him because you have too much pride and honour to accept a proposal made for that reason.'

'Oh, you are exasperating, all of you,' Lucy said. She just wanted to go and sulk somewhere, away from overbearing aristocrats and well-meaning friends who thought they knew her better than she did herself.

'He knows where you live?' Melissa asked.

'Yes. And I am not moving just to avoid him. Besides, I cannot stop advertising. I will not go into hiding. If he has any sense, he will take the very strong hint that I want nothing to do with him and stay away.'

'Hah!' Jane snorted inelegantly. 'I'll wager you a guinea that he is on your doorstep within seven days.'

'Done,' Lucy said. 'I will take your wager. Lord Burnham has too much pride to persist once he has been rejected.'

CHAPTER SIXTEEN

Max arrived back in London three days after Lucy's flight. By an effort of will he had restrained himself from haring off immediately and had successfully chilled the atmosphere of Dorothea's house party by scrupulous civility to everyone, until Lady Moss was driven to apologise for her *misunderstanding* of his actions and motives.

Lucy would have been safe on the Mail, he told himself. She had her maid with her and he was not so inexperienced with women as to expect to turn up on her doorstep hours after she returned home and receive a warm, or even a lukewarm, welcome. She needed a day or so to recover and think things through logically. She was intelligent—she would see the necessity of doing as he said, surely? A woman's honour was so easily lost and there was no way back from a wrong decision, as Julia had found to her cost.

Something nagged at him, an awareness of a contradiction, and he teased it out on the long journey back. Julia had ruined herself in the hope of a marriage for love. Lucy was quite clearly *not* in love, with him or anyone else, it seemed—so why was she risking everything and throwing away a brilliant match, security and reputation? It was deeply puzzling and he had an uneasy suspicion that her motives, too, had something to do with that treacherous emotion.

HIS SECRETARY, PAUL BENTLEY, received him with his usual efficient calm. 'Not being apprised of the date of your return, my lord, I thought it prudent to offer provisional regrets to those invitations where your absence would cause little or no inconvenience. Naturally, I sent apologies to all invitations to dine. There are three invitations for this evening. Lady Fellowes's dinner I have declined. I declined in respect of Lady Twistelton's musicale and, as for Lady Devonham's ball, I said that I thought it unlikely that Your Lordship would be able to attend.'

Lady Twistelton's musicales were to be avoided at all costs and Bentley knew that, just as he knew Emilia Devonham always provided the best of entertainment. 'Thank you, Bentley. Please send a note to Lady Devonham to say that I will be delighted to attend.'

It would be pleasant to be in company that did not regard him as either an unprincipled seducer or a cynical rake.

THAT OPTIMISM LASTED just past the end of the receiving line at Devonham House. A few steps into the already crowded ballroom, he encountered the Duchess of Aylsham, her pregnant form elegantly draped in ice-blue silk, the Marchioness of Cranford and the Countess of Kendall.

Max bowed. Three pairs of eyes narrowed, three mouths pursed and, for a stunned second, Max thought he was about to receive the cut direct from the three of them. At which point he recalled that it was the Duchess who had recommended Lucy to Sophia as a pianoforte teacher.

'Lord Burnham. How…convenient. I was just wishing that I could have a word with you.' Between the Duchess's smile—a shark would have been envious—and the sweetness of her tone, any sensible man would have quailed.

Max had moved from being sensible to downright stubborn at some point in the past few days. He returned her smile. 'Convenient indeed. I would welcome your advice on a problem I have.'

The Countess's inelegant snort was only partly muffled by her fan. The sweet-faced Marchioness, an unlikely match for the privateering Marquis, gave him a look of deep reproach.

The Duchess took his arm. 'I find myself in need of some fresh air. Shall we take a turn on the terrace?'

Bishop's daughter, knowledgeable antiquarian, the unconventional lady who had humanised the Perfect Duke: this was a woman to be wary of if you were a man with something on your conscience.

'I assume this is about a certain mutual acquaintance of ours,' Max said as soon as they were alone outside. This early in the evening the temperature in the ballroom had not reached the point where dancers were driven outside and the crush was not so great that young people could escape chaperons to enjoy a flirtation in the shadows.

'Indeed. You owe the lady in question a not inconsiderable sum for an agreed service.'

'This is about debt collecting?' he asked, incredulous.

'Certainly. I believe you have received a clear answer to your... I suppose I could call it a proposal.'

'You do not think I should persist?'

The Duchess tapped her closed fan to her lips. 'Why should you need to?' she asked. She sounded surprised.

'Because I compromised the lady, of course.' Max felt mystified. Why wasn't the Duchess insisting he marry her friend, or protégée or whatever Lucy was?

'She does not appear to feel compromised and her identity is not known.'

'I am having some difficulty in understanding why she does not wish to marry me,' Max said between gritted teeth.

'Why on earth should she marry a man whose only motivation for offering for her is his pride and his honour?'

'Because I am an earl?'

'I am beginning to understand her point of view very clearly, Lord Burnham. It appears to have escaped your notice that women are also possessed both of pride and of honour.'

'Yet you married after being stranded with the Duke on an island, I believe.' That went well beyond good manners, but this was a lady who had wed a man whose rank was eclipsed only by the royal family.

'Yes, indeed. Was it not fortunate that we were in love with each other?' the Duchess observed sweetly. 'I am certain the lady in question will be delighted to receive the sum owing. It would be best delivered by messenger, don't you think?'

She smiled and this time, as she turned and the light from the ballroom caught her face, he believed it was genuine emotion that warmed the lovely brown eyes. 'Lucy has three friends who married for love. She knows it is possible. Do not expect her to wed for less and at the cost of her conscience.'

Then she was gone with a swish of silk across the flagstones.

Love? What is the matter with everyone? Sophia pining for her confounded Vicar, a duchess lecturing me on the subject, Lucy turning down wealth and status for lack of it?

Were they all suffering from an excess of sensibility? Because they were certainly all lacking in sense. He'd read that novel and the point was clear: sense won over an excess of feeling.

Max went back into the ballroom, scanned the room and identified at least a dozen young ladies of good birth, excellent connections and most respectable fortune. He could work his way around all of those in one evening, he was sure. It was about time he married and found a wife who could deal with Sophia and her emotions, because he was damned if he could.

'Lady Mortain, good evening. Lady Catherine. Might I beg the honour of a dance?'

Yes, this was exactly the kind of girl he should be looking for: pretty, flatteringly pleased at his request, poised and, he was certain, brought up by her mama to be an excellent match for a man of standing. He could not help recognising the calculation behind the expression of sweet attention to his every word. Just as it should be, so why did it send a shiver down his spine?

AFTER TWO NIGHTS with Verity, Lucy returned home the next morning to deal with her correspondence. She matched the encouraging number of enquiries about her services with her diary and did her best not to jump up every time the door knocker was heard. That, given that this was a lodging house with three other ladies in residence on the various floors, plus Mrs Todd, the landlady in the basement, was a frequent occurrence.

She was only alert because she wished to be perfectly poised and cool when Max arrived, as she was quite sure he would, despite her rash wager with Jane. He was stubborn, used to getting his own way and he owed her money.

Or perhaps she would simply tell Amy to accept the payment from him and inform His Lordship that Miss Lambert was not at home. That might be safer after her friends had talked such nonsense about her feelings for Max. Why on earth was she in love with the man? There was nothing lovable about him.

Except for his care for his stepsister, she supposed. And his distress over the girl Julia's tragic mistake. He'd been very brave over being shot, of course, and the way he looked on a horse was certainly productive of a particular…stirring. And, if she was to think of stirrings, there were his kisses and the way she had felt when he danced with her—

And that was most definitely enough of that. His character had some well-hidden good points and she found him physically attractive. That could not amount to love. Her friends were besotted with their own husbands and, being warm and generous women, wished all their acquaintance to be as happy as they were. It would be a mistake to think they possessed some special insight into other people's feelings.

Max had restored her music to her through dance, though. That was a debt she owed him, but love was not founded on debts owed. She wondered when she would dance again. Perhaps if she told the others who had been present at Lady Hopewell's house party they could invite her to their own dances when none of those people would be present.

Her fingers cramped on her pen and she sat back and began her stretching exercises. Her hands were definitely improved, she thought. Less painful, less stiff. She still could not span as widely as she had before and the missing fingertip was still sensitive. Her hands were never going to be perfect again.

And I should stop sitting here brooding. There's the rent due today.

She counted out the money and went downstairs, encountering Amy in the hallway.

'Did you lock the door, Miss Lambert? I was just about to bring up the fresh linen.'

'No, it is open,' Lucy said as the door knocker thumped.

'I'll get that,' Amy said brightly, dumping the sheets

unceremoniously in Lucy's arms. 'Millie downstairs is up to her elbows in washing. It'll be the post at this hour, I expect.'

She flung the front door open with a cheerful, 'Morning, Mr Potts. Oh. Oh, my lord. Er… Miss Marsh—I mean, Miss Lambert isn't At Home, my lord.'

'She appears to have miraculously materialised behind you in the guise of a chambermaid,' Max observed. 'Good morning, Pringle.'

'Good morning to you, my lord. And she might be in, but she isn't receiving.' Amy's ears were red, but she was as stubborn as a little bull terrier, standing squarely in the doorway.

'In that case, could you convey to your mistress that I will be seated out here in my carriage until such time as she is ready to receive me.' He resumed his hat, turned and took his leisurely way down the well-scrubbed steps, across the pavement and into a smart town carriage.

'Look at them horses, miss. Really raises the tone of the street, doesn't it?' Amy was still transfixed in the open doorway.

'*Those* horses and please close the door, Amy. Gawping at the traffic does *not* raise the tone.'

'Yes, miss, sorry, miss. I did right, telling him you weren't receiving, didn't I?'

'You did. Now, what am I going to do? Go out of the back door every time I want to leave the house?'

'He won't stop there for ever, surely, Miss Lambert?' Amy was wide-eyed.

'I would not put it past him to have his butler deliver meals. To resort to hiding is undignified and impractical. I suppose I must get it over with.' A wicked idea occurred to her. 'I know how to make him really uncomfortable.

I'll ask Mrs Todd if I may use her parlour and if she will act as chaperon.'

Her landlady was almost overcome at the thought of an earl in her front parlour, a chamber of the utmost respectability and solid discomfort, but she came to the immediate conclusion that the nobleman in question was a cunning seducer, out to ruin a genteel young working woman. 'He'll get no chance to work his rakish wiles in my house,' she declared stoutly.

Lucy left her ramming extra pins into her already severe coiffure and ran upstairs to tame her own escaping locks into a bun that would have done credit to a workhouse matron.

'Let His Lordship in,' she told Amy as she made her way downstairs to settle on the overstuffed horsehair sofa.

'Lord Burnham,' Amy announced after a few minutes.

'Mrs Todd, may I present Lord Burnham? My lord, Mrs Todd is the householder here.'

Max was looking at his most aloof. 'Ma'am. Miss Lambert, I had hoped to speak to you alone.'

'Not under my roof. This is a respectable house and Miss Lambert is a respectable young lady.'

'Both are clearly apparent, ma'am. However, the conversation I wish to have is of a private nature.' The grey eyes intent on her face were dark with some emotion she could not read. Anger? Desire? *Surely not.*

Even while feeling so inwardly flustered, Lucy was aware of a considerable respect for her landlady. Most people would have quailed in the face of a rigidly controlled, and clearly deeply displeased, aristocrat.

'I should explain, Mrs Todd,' she said meekly. 'Lord Burnham has proposed marriage and I do not wish to accept, but he persists.'

'You don't?' For a second the landlady's facade of gentility dropped, then she recovered herself. 'Then that's that, my lord. No more to be said, although, naturally, I will be honoured to receive you on any future occasion should you call. Pringle will show you out.'

Lucy could only admire Max's dignity. He rose, bowed to Mrs Todd and to her, took his hat from Amy and strode out of the door without further comment.

'Thank you, Mrs Todd. I appreciate your assistance.'

'Well, I can't say I understand you, Miss Lambert, for he's a fine-looking gentleman, never mind the title. But I expect you are right: no good comes of marrying far above, or far below, I always say.'

She was halfway up to the hall when she realised that Amy was talking to Max and stopped, her head just below the level of the floor.

'...as well as the money you owe Miss Lambert. There's the hire of the gig and the Mail coach fare and the tips. I wrote that down. Here it is. And then there's the guinea she wagered with Lady Kendall that you'd be too proud to turn up on her doorstep.'

'Have you considered a career as a clerk, Pringle?'

'No, my lord. They don't employ women in jobs like that, more's the pity.' There was a rustle of paper. 'Thank you, my lord. I'll find you some change.'

'Keep it for yourself, Pringle. You have earned it.'

When the front door closed she climbed the rest of the way. 'Amy, you are wonderful—you got the money?'

'To be fair, miss, he'd got it all ready. And he must have estimated the fare and so forth coming back. And it's almost ten pounds too much, even allowing for Lady Kendall's guinea.' She clutched the banknotes tight as they tried to roll back up again. 'Wasn't Mrs Todd clever? He'll not come back and risk being greeted by her again.'

'Very clever.' Lucy bit her lip as she looked at the closed

front door. 'But Lord Burnham's not a man to give in to threats and he's used to getting what he wants. I wonder what he will do now?'

LUCY WAS RIGHT: he did have too much pride to beg. Max ordered his driver to take him to the bottom of St James's Street. He got out, walked through Cleveland Row past the front of the Palace and out into Green Park.

He wanted to ride hard, gallop off the anger and the frustration, but London parks in the late morning were no places for furious riding. Instead, he would walk off the edge of his temper through the Park, then walk along Piccadilly to Old Bond Street and Gentleman Jackson's Salon. There would be someone willing to strip off and fight, or Jackson himself might condescend to give him a bout. It wouldn't do his healing arm any good, but to hell with that.

Confound the woman. He slashed at an innocent clump of dog daisies with his cane. There was no denying Lucy's intelligence—setting her landlady on him was a stroke of genius. He should give up now. She was clearly not being coy. He had paid his debt to her—his monetary debt, that is—so logic insisted that he walk away, stop thinking about her and get on with his life.

And keep well away from that coven of friends she possesses, he added as he reached the south-east corner of the reservoir. Aristocratic ladies advocating marrying for love? That was dangerous, almost heretical, thinking.

HE ENCOUNTERED TREVOR ATKINSON, an old friend, on the doorstep.

'Max, my dear fellow! What have I done to offend you? That expression could kill a nest full of wasps at ten paces.'

'Not a thing, Trevor.' Max managed an apologetic smile.

'Just thinking through a problem—a difficult employee. Fancy a round or two?'

'If you promise not to take my head off—and no black eyes, I'm off courting this afternoon, I'll have you know.' Atkinson held the door for him.

'What, heading for parson's mousetrap? Who is the lucky lady?'

His friend lowered his voice. 'Eugenia White. No, don't raise that devilish eyebrow, I know her father's a liability and her brother's a hell-born babe. But it's love, you know. I must have her, even if it means towing her family out of the River Tick.'

'I seem to be hearing a lot about marriages for love recently,' Max said as they went through to the changing room and began to strip off down to their shirt sleeves.

'It's the devil, believe me, old man. I tried to be sensible.' Atkinson began to unwind his elaborate neckcloth. 'But I was just too miserable. My valet threatened to leave me because I threw my boots at him, my sister said she'd not have my escort anywhere and I quarrelled with Lawson.'

'What, Sidney Lawson?' Max looked up from the bench where he was tugging off his boots. 'That's impossible, surely?'

'Almost,' Trevor said gloomily. 'Anyway, I realised after that I had to do something and the only thing that works is surrender. I love her, I think she loves me and, if she accepts me today, I'll be the happiest man alive.'

'Let me see if I can knock some sense into you,' Max said, rolling up his sleeves. 'I'll do my best not to spoil your beauty while I'm at it.'

CHAPTER SEVENTEEN

'I promise, none of the guests who encountered you and Lord Burnham at Lady Hopewell's will be there. I was talking to Mrs Plaistow only this morning when we met in Berkeley Square where she was deciding on the ice-cream order from Gunter's. It will be a delightful small dance—not even big enough to be called a ball. Her two nieces are coming out next Season and she wants to give them a little polish beforehand. Nice girls, both of them, but rather shy.' Jane poured Lucy a fresh cup of tea. 'I asked her if I might bring a friend and she was delighted. Do say you'll come.'

'Well, I suppose I could,' Lucy said cautiously. 'It would be very pleasant and I have no students this afternoon, which means that I can prepare. So, thank you, I will.'

'I think it is quite safe, you know. I mean—Burnham has stopped calling, hasn't he?'

'It is almost a week, yes. I think Mrs Todd would be enough to rout the Regent, frankly. Max—Lord Burnham, I mean, has paid me, I sent him a receipt and that is that.'

'You do not look very happy about it.'

'Of course I am,' Lucy protested. If she said it often enough, she might come to believe it.

'Yes, I suppose it is for the best now. You might love him—' Jane waved one hand holding a biscuit when Lucy began to protest '—no, don't argue with me, I know best. You might love him, but the beast clearly does not love you or he would find some way to be with you.'

'Absolutely. Not that I am in love with him,' she lied. She might tell herself she didn't, but she knew she was only deceiving herself. 'I mean, even if he did love me, which is impossible, he is far too sensible to persist. I will put him behind me. I already have,' she added hastily.

'Of course you have,' Jane said briskly. 'It will be painful, I know, but better that than finding yourself married to such a proud, unyielding man. Now, tell me, how is your business prospering? Do you have many wealthy cits clamouring to employ you to teach their daughters?'

Lucy pushed away the inexplicable feeling of disappointment at the change of subject and conjured up a smile. 'Yes. I had expected a slow start, but it only took Mrs Grisholm, a banker's wife, to tell all her friends for me to receive a positive flood of enquiries and I now have ten regular pupils and several more appointments to call and discuss terms.'

'That is good news,' Jane said warmly. 'Oh, I almost forgot. You know that new rose-coloured gown I had from Madame Mirabelle? I haven't even worn it and I was showing it to Ivo in his study and he stood up and knocked his inkwell to the floor and it soaked the ruffle around the hem. My maid cut it off, but now it is far too short for me, but it would be the perfect length for you.'

'She could sew on a new ruffle, surely?'

Jane wrinkled her nose. 'She could, but we will never get a match—Madame said it was the last of a batch of French lace. And I think it actually looks better plain because it draws more attention to the lace at the bodice and on the sleeves. And that is ornate enough for you to need nothing more than your pearl ear drops. I think it was *meant*.'

'But you've had no wear from it. And Madame Mirabelle is not cheap. I couldn't—'

'Yes, you could. And I have had full value from it, believe me. Darling Ivo was so remorseful about the accident. He had to help me out of it before the ink stained my petticoats and so forth and then he felt he had to make it up to me…'

So Lucy went home with a new evening gown, the prospect of being able to dance again and a warm glow at the kindness of her friends. She only wished she could do something to help them in return.

Jane collected her in her carriage and Lucy was glad of the interior gloom to hide her blushes when Lord Kendall—*Darling Ivo*—greeted her. He and Jane were so much in love, she thought, firmly refusing to consider what memories the gown she was wearing might evoke in him. Jane came from exactly the same background as she did, the respectable squirearchy and country gentry, and here she was, happily married to an earl.

Who loves her, she reminded herself.

She also realised, as the carriage drew to a halt, that Jane's idea of what constituted a 'small dance' had changed a great deal since they were unmarried girls. There was a strip of red carpet from kerbside to the front steps, the footmen wore powdered wigs and Mrs Plaistow's modest ballroom hummed with conversation, laughter and the sounds of a good-sized string ensemble tuning up.

An anxious scan of the room revealed no familiar faces. Because of the presence of a number of very young ladies there were to be no waltzes, Jane told her and, as there also appeared to be a number of rather young male guests as well, the punch was much milder than the norm.

'Catering to the infantry,' said Ivo, grimacing at his first sip. 'And there are no card rooms.'

'Do your duty and charm the young ladies,' Jane told him.

'I shall begin by asking Lucy to dance,' Ivo said and promptly led her out for the first set.

He was a good dancer and Lucy enjoyed herself, felt the thrill of moving with the music and the newly discovered pleasure of moving in harmony with a partner. It seemed to amplify the impact. Ivo was not Max, of course.

Even as she thought it she and Ivo reached the head of the line and turned and she saw Max. She was standing still, otherwise she thought she would have tripped.

Lucy blinked. Yes, he was there, not watching the dancers but in conversation with a red-headed man. Then he turned and she saw him full face and almost missed Ivo reaching for her to promenade down the double row of dancers.

'Ivo, that was Max.' She had no doubt that her married friends took their husbands into their confidence. 'His arm was in a sling again and his face... Did he have a black eye?'

'I saw. He's been fighting by the look of it. The bruising has turned yellow, so it wasn't in the last day or so.' Ivo appeared to find that amusing.

'But what can have happened? Footpads, do you think?'

'Doubt it. Probably a bout at one of the boxing salons.'

'Surely not when his arm cannot have been healed.'

Ivo managed to turn her under arm and shrug at the same time.

'Men are so peculiar,' Lucy said, anxious and baffled. When they came off the floor she found Jane and pulled her to one side. 'You told me that no one from the house party would be here.'

'No, I didn't. I said that none of the guests who were there with you and Burnham would be present. I didn't say he wouldn't.'

'You… You… Words fail me.'

'Good, because Lady Playfair is giving us a very peculiar look.'

'And the wretched man is hurt—his arm is in a sling, his face is bruised.'

'It cannot be serious if he is here, can it?'

'He's a man. They do any number of ill-advised, ridiculous things,' Lucy retorted and stalked off.

She found Max still in conversation with his red-headed acquaintance. He saw her and murmured something to his friend who bowed to her and walked away.

Max was sporting a fading black eye and a healing split on his cheekbone and his arm was supported in a black silk sling.

'Have you been fighting?' Lucy demanded.

'And good evening to you, Miss Lambert. I have been boxing, since you ask.'

'With stiches in your arm? Presumably you burst them.'

He grimaced. 'It was worth it.'

'And I suppose I should see the other fellow and marvel at your superior skill in making even more of a mess of him.'

'Actually, no. It was Trevor Atkinson to whom I was talking when you arrived to lecture me. I promised not to mark his face because he was going courting that afternoon.'

'Idiots, the pair of you.'

'But we felt much better for it,' Max assured her.

'How could you? You would have had to have your

wound re-stitched and your eye must have been closed, never mind all the bruises I can't see.'

'Spiritually, I can assure you, we were greatly uplifted. Trevor worked off his pre-proposal nerves and I recovered my temper.'

'So what are you doing here?' she demanded.

'Not following you about, I can assure you, Miss Lambert. I am enjoying the company of my friends, assuring Trevor I will support him at the altar and regretting the absence of card tables. Naturally, I would ask you to dance, but as you can see, I am not equipped with sufficient functioning limbs.'

'And I would refuse in any case,' she said, then caught herself. 'No. That was rude of me, I beg your pardon. You are a very good dancer and I would, of course, accept.'

'But without pleasure?'

'With pleasure in the dance and irritation at your company,' Lucy confessed.

'But why? I am no longer pressing you to marry me. Why else should you be annoyed with me?'

'Because… I find you unsettling,' she admitted without thinking.

Max smiled enigmatically. 'How very flattering.'

'Oh! You are impossible.'

She turned to walk away and found herself face to face with his stepsister.

'Lady Sophia. Good evening. Um…what a delightful gown.' She sounded gauche, she knew, but she was so shocked by the other woman's looks that she found herself burbling. 'I am here with my friends Lord and Lady Kendall. Perhaps you know them?'

'No, I have not had the pleasure.' Sophia was as beautifully dressed and turned out as ever, but there were dark shadows under her eyes that powder could not conceal and she had lost weight in the short time since Lucy had last seen her. Her voice sounded artificially light and her smile was forced.

'Oh. Well, I must get back. How lovely to see you again.'

'THAT WAS LUCY MARSH,' Sophia said when she reached Max.

'Yes. I spoke to her.'

I unsettle her...

'She looked nice, I thought. A lovely gown.' Her voice was flat.

'Sophia, are you feeling unwell?' He had hardly seen her for the past few days and this evening, when they were ready to go out to the carriage, she had the hood of her cloak pulled up. Now he realised that he had not noticed her because she had been unusually quiet. She looked as though she had not slept for nights.

'I am perfectly well, thank you, Max.' That was definitely a brave smile.

'You look tired.' It was a test question—normally any suggestion that she was not looking her best, or that she might wish to leave an entertainment early, would be met with cries of protest.

'Perhaps, a little. But I would not wish to drag you away. After all, you asked specifically if I would like to come this evening. I had not realised we had been invited.'

They had not until the last minute. Mrs Plaistow had sent a note with the invitation, apologising because she had not thought he would be entertained by such a small affair, but her dear friend Lady Kendall had wondered if Lady Sophia would be there.

Lady Kendall was one of the coven, of course, and that made him wary, but curious. She was matchmaking, it seemed, because she had certainly not been acting at Lucy's request. Most peculiar...

But now he was worried about Sophia. 'Come, we will go home. My arm is aching,' he added, although it wasn't. Not, at least, as much as his head.

MAX SPENT A thoroughly unsettled week. It was inexplicable and peculiar. He wasn't sleeping well—and he always slept well except when the nightmares struck. His concentration was all to pieces and he was restless. He waved away the invitations that Bentley gave him every day because nothing appealed and when he came back from his morning ride and was changing, Hobson startled him by announcing that, 'If Your Lordship is on a reducing regime, then perhaps it would be best if I were to cancel the preliminary fitting for your new evening suit.'

'I am doing no such thing,' Max protested as he shrugged on his waistcoat. 'I have no need to, I would hope.'

'So I would have said, my lord. Your Lordship has a fine figure: enough to give any valet great satisfaction in the finished effect, if I may be so bold. But, if you will excuse me—' Hobson hooked one finger in the waistband of Max's breeches that he had just fastened and tugged gently. 'An inch too loose, my lord.' He cleared his throat. 'I would not wish to presume, but perhaps it might be as well to consult Your Lordship's physician.'

He wasn't ill, surely? He was certainly not, unlike that mountebank Byron, on some ghastly diet involving soda water and dry biscuits. But Max realised he didn't seem to be hungry. In fact, he had found himself missing luncheon and waving away desserts.

Perhaps he should consult Dr Finnegan. He would mention it that afternoon when the man came to remove the stitches he had replaced with much tutting and disapproval after Max's bout with Atkinson. Perhaps he had caught whatever was ailing Sophia.

He went down to luncheon, for which he had no appetite, just to see how she was. The answer was decidedly wan. She picked at her food, but answered his attempts at conversation brightly enough and with a smile.

Max knew his stepsister. She was putting on a brave face. Not sulking—no one could miss Sophia sulking. No, this was different—she was miserable, but pretending not to be.

'What is wrong, Sophia?' He pushed away his plate and looked at hers, almost identical, with hardly anything eaten.

'Nothing that you can do anything about, Max.' She set her knife and fork down on her plate, her concentration apparently fixed on aligning them exactly.

'Are you unwell?'

'No. Just not... Just not sleeping, that is all.'

'Or eating. Or smiling unless you think someone is looking at you.'

She kept looking down at her plate.

'Sophia, what is wrong?'

'My heart is broken,' she said with a calm that made him catch his breath at the pain in it. Sophia raised her gaze to look at him. 'There is nothing to be done, I see that now. Anthony will not accept my money and he will not marry me because he cannot support me in the way he believes he should on his income as a clergyman. I expect I will become used to it in time and it will hurt less, but for now I find it impossible to sleep and I do not have much appetite. I am sorry if I am a blight on your spirits—I have noticed that you seem very unlike your usual self lately.'

'There is nothing wrong and you are not blighting my

spirits.' *Except that I should have realised earlier how unhappy you were.* 'Is there anything—?'

'No.' Her smile was more genuine this time. 'Eat your luncheon, Max.' She got up and went out.

What *could* he do? Not go back in time and make West's father marry his mother, that was certain. He could hardly get the man elevated to a high position in a few months. Even if he had that kind of influence on church quarters, West had admitted himself he had no great vocation for the life, just the ability to make a reasonable country parson. If he would not take Sophia's money, or his father's, then he certainly would not accept Max's.

What was needed was buried treasure or a legacy from some distant relative, but he had no belief in fairy stories or any confidence that something would just happen to heal Sophia's broken heart. She was in love, he had to accept that. For her it was real and for the first time in his adult life Max felt powerless in the face of something that he did not understand and he had no ability to make right.

'DOCTOR FINNEGAN IS HERE, my lord.'

Startled, Max looked at the clock. Two-thirty. He had been sitting here chasing a mangled piece of cold beef around his plate and brooding on Sophia's lover for almost an hour.

'Send him to my bedchamber. I will be with him directly.'

He submitted to having the stiches removed and to another lecture on the inadvisability of extreme physical exertion with half-healed wounds.

'There is no infection?'

'No, none.' Finnegan began packing away his instruments. 'A very clean healing process. Are you experiencing any discomfort?'

Max recounted his lack of appetite and loss of weight, restlessness, difficulty sleeping.

After prolonged prodding and probing and a series of highly intrusive questions, the doctor sat back. 'It is, I believe, all in your mind, my lord. You are worrying about something, I should imagine. I would not like to suggest that you have anything on your conscience. That just leaves us with the possibility that you are in love.' He chuckled. 'I jest, of course, my lord.'

'Of course,' Max agreed and managed a hollow laugh. It had been a difficult few weeks, disrupted and aggravating. That was all that was wrong and he was not going to let some sawbones' foolish quip get under his skin. He had, somehow, to make things right for Sophia.

CHAPTER EIGHTEEN

Strangely, being exceedingly busy with teaching, meeting with prospective students and keeping her accounts did not prevent Lucy's brain from filling with inappropriate daydreams about Max Fenton. He would arrive on her doorstep, braving Mrs Todd and drop to one knee before declaring his undying love for her, a love that overcame every scruple about their inequality of status. He would send her letters revealing the torment in his heart because she refused him. Slim volumes of tender verse would arrive by every post…

'Oh, for goodness sake, stop this nonsense,' she said aloud and realised she had been sitting with her pen in mid-air while a large blot of ink fell on to her account book.

If her friends were right and she had fallen in love with Max, then there was nothing she could do about it. Thank goodness the thought had not occurred to her when he was asking her to marry him or she might have weakened to such an extent that she agreed.

People fell hopelessly in love all the time—look at poor Lady Sophia and Mr West—and they just had to learn to live with it. Not that she was absolutely convinced that she did love Max, she thought, confused.

If she did, wouldn't she think him perfect in every way? Wouldn't she forget his more aggravating habits and his cool perfection? This was doubtless some kind of foolish infatuation, probably an after-effect of her injury, the upset of leaving home, the disruption of her new life.

But she might be able to do something about Sophia. If Mr West did not want to be a clergyman, then perhaps he was suited to some other occupation that would pay him more. Normally, she knew, young men found such positions due to the influence of their fathers' friends, but Anthony West would never have dreamt of asking his father for help, whoever he was. But perhaps she could consult an influential man herself and see what his advice would be. And they did not come with much more influence than the Duke of Aylsham.

Lucy was on the point of handing a coin to the hackney carriage driver when the door of the familiar house in Grosvenor Square opened behind her. Goodness, but the staff were efficient.

'Thank you.' She smiled up at the driver and turned, feeling the smile freeze on her lips. Not a highly trained footman, on the alert. *'You.'*

'Me,' Max agreed. His smile looked as convincing as hers felt.

'What are you doing here?'

'Calling on the Duke. Have you any objection?' Max appeared to have recovered himself because he came slowly down the steps, drawing on his gloves.

She could hardly demand to know why he was here. Perhaps they were friends. Perhaps they had business together.

'The Duchess is not at home, by the way,' Max said helpfully. 'Apparently she is visiting an elderly relative in Hampstead.'

'Yes, I know, she goes every fortnight.' Lucy found that she was walking away from the house, her hand tucked firmly into the crook of Max's elbow. How had that happened?

'So you were visiting the Duke yourself? He was not expecting you, I think.'

'No, he was not, but I hardly need an appointment to call upon a friend.'

Max turned into Charles Street.

'Where are we going? And why?'

'Berkeley Square. I feel the need to buy you an ice at Gunter's. You seem a little flushed and it may cool you down.'

'I am flushed because I am being kidnapped in broad daylight!'

'But not at all. If you do not wish for an ice, tell me where you would like to go?'

'Back to see the Duke, of course.'

'He was on his way out, hot on my heels, I imagine. He was good enough to spare me ten minutes, but he had an appointment at the Home Office.'

'Botheration. I particularly wanted his advice.'

'Can I help?'

'Hardly,' Lucy retorted. 'You are the problem.' Then she realised what she had said. 'I mean, not you, only—'

'I had believed that when I stopped asking you to marry me I had ceased to be a thorn in your side,' Max said, and she glanced up at him sharply. It was difficult to tell, what with the brim of her bonnet and the fact that he was looking straight ahead, but there had been something in his voice that caused a little stab, just under her heart.

'I think I would like that ice cream after all,' she said. 'They do a wonderful one with black cherries, Verity tells me. You would enjoy it.'

THE FASHIONABLE CONFECTIONER'S shop was as busy at that hour as it ever was, but Max found a table in a far corner.

When the waiter came with his menu on a board he ordered the cherry ice cream for them both with *langue du chat* biscuits and coffee. 'Although I recall your predilection for more exotic ices.'

She waved that away. 'What is wrong?' Lucy asked as soon as the man had gone back to the counter. 'You called to see Will without him expecting you, it is urgent enough for him to have to squeeze you in to a spare ten minutes—and it would have only been ten, because Will, being perfect, is never late for anything. And you look—' She studied him, trying to read what was different behind that mask of composure. 'Unhappy.'

He would not tell her, of course. Lucy braced herself for the snub.

'It is Sophia. I am concerned about her. It seems she truly does care deeply for her highly unsuitable clergyman. What they need, if they are ever to overcome his very correct scruples and marry, is for him to find some better paid occupation, one where his birth may not be a hindrance. I have no influence in the Church, let alone in government circles, and I thought the Duke might be able to advise me.'

'But that is wonderful—it is precisely why I was calling on Will. He is just the person. Sophia must have told you what she confided to me and I am so happy that she felt able to do so.'

'What, exactly, did my stepsister tell you?' That darkness was back behind his eyes again, and Lucy felt she had blundered.

'It wasn't a confidence as such,' Lucy hastened to tell him. 'Just that Anthony never wanted to be a clergyman, but, without any other options or sponsors than Lady Hopewell, that was his only choice of respectable occupation. He cannot take chances with his career, you see, not with his mother to support. But Sophia told me that his education was very good—it was the one thing they would accept from his father—so I thought that Will might know of an opening for someone intelligent and honest. He is very hard-working and conscientious, you know. Even though he does not feel a calling to the church, he is doing his very best for his parishioners. And you know that he is honourable.'

'Yes, I do. And I knew about his education and character from Dorothea Hopewell, who knows about the circumstances of his birth. She could not break confidences, of course, but it is clear the entire blame lay with his father. Aylsham seems to have some ideas of how to advance West and has promised to get back to me when he has made enquiries.'

The waiter came with their ices and coffee. Lucy picked up her spoon, tasted and gave a little moan of pleasure. 'This is so good.' She licked her lips, reluctant to lose the slightest taste, and watched as Max sampled his.

He closed his eyes and she indulged herself with the sight of his thick black lashes, then looked away quickly when he opened his eyes.

'Did you know that the Reverend Sydney Smith said that a friend of his thought that heaven would be like eating *pâté de foie gras* to the sound of trumpets? I think he was wrong. I believe it may be eating black cherry ice cream and watching you lick it from your bottom lip with the very tip of your tongue.' He apparently ignored her gasp. 'I have to tell you, it is one of the most erotic sights I have seen.'

'*Max.*' Lucy swallowed. 'We are in the middle of Gunter's, for goodness sake.'

'Nobody can hear us. Your ice is beginning to melt.' He sounded quite cheerful, all of a sudden.

'I am not surprised! I hardly dare take another spoonful.'

'Please, eat. I promise not to make another shocking remark.'

They ate in silence. Lucy had no idea what Max was thinking, other than, apparently, quite shocking things, but she made herself focus on the tart sweet taste on her tongue and tried to shepherd her stampeding thoughts into some sort of order.

Finally, as she crunched the last of the little biscuits, she realised what it was. Max desired her. Why, when the world was full of far more desirable women, goodness knew, but he had enjoyed kissing her and wanted to do so again. That was all it was. And perhaps her stubborn refusal to marry him added piquancy to his feelings.

Max industriously scraped every last trace of ice from his bowl, for all the world like a schoolboy with a treat.

'Walk with me,' he said, putting down his spoon at last.

'Why?'

'Because I wish to test a theory. Because we have not been on good terms and I would like to change that. Because the sun is shining.'

He poured coffee and sat sipping his while Lucy stared fixedly at the top button of his waistcoat and tried to think.

Yes, she was in love with the man, she could not deny it now, not after the way her heart had skipped a beat when she had seen him on those steps, not after the way her pulse still fluttered. But what did he want of her? Kisses, it seemed, but something more? He wouldn't try to seduce her, would he? He was too honourable, she told herself.

'Where shall we walk?'

'It is not far to Green Park. We could stroll down to the reservoir, find a seat in the shade and watch small children feed the ducks.'

That seemed safe enough and excited toddlers, swarms

of nursemaids and quacking ducks were hardly the sort of company a wicked seducer would choose.

'Very well, I would like that.' It would be a mixed pleasure and pain, she thought sadly as Max paid the waiter. He said something to the man, who looked startled, but he came back after a moment with a small parcel tied with a loop of string as a handle.

Gentlemen did not normally stroll along the streets of Mayfair carrying brown paper parcels, but Max seemed oblivious to the stares as they made their way southwards to the park.

They found a bench at the western end of the reservoir, a safe distance from shrieks, splashing and quacking. Max dusted the seat off for her, sat down and began to untie the string to reveal a mass of bread crusts and what looked like stale cake. 'I thought you might like to feed the ducks.'

'You are the Earl of Burnham and you walk through the street carrying a package of scraps and want to feed the ducks?'

'I haven't since I was about six years old,' he said. A flock of sharp-eyed sparrows had already gathered around their feet, followed by the inevitable pigeons. Ducks, alert to any likelihood of food, were already swimming towards them like a flotilla of ships of the line going into battle.

'I imagine there are any number of things you haven't done since you were six,' Lucy said. She threw a piece of cake to a particularly scruffy sparrow. 'Why have you changed your mind about helping Sophia? You were so convinced about the perils of unequal marriages.'

'She has changed,' Max said slowly, apparently intent on lobbing bread to a duck whose parentage appeared to include a variety of farmyard fowl. 'I expected tears, sulks, tantrums and slammed doors. My stepsister is not self-centred, precisely, but she is heedless, lacking in introspection, endlessly optimistic that everything will work out just as she wants it.

'Now Sophia is quiet, sad but controlled. It is as though something inside her has died, or has been so crushed it has changed out of all recognition. When I finally got her to talk she acknowledges that it is hopeless, that West's sense of honour will not allow him to make this match. She says her heart is broken.'

He took some more bread from the brown paper and seemed intent on seeing how far he could send the sparrows with a wide scatter of crumbs. Lucy waited: there was more to be said, she was certain.

'I believe her,' Max said abruptly. 'I thought that sort of thing was nonsense. But you know what affected me most? She said she would get used to it in time and it would hurt less. And she apologised for blighting my spirits. This is Sophia—if I held up a notice to say my left foot had dropped off and I was bleeding on the carpet, then she would be all attention, all concern, but otherwise she might not notice. Yet now, when she is truly miserable, she notices that my spirits are low.'

Lucy shifted on the bench so that she could see Max better. Were his spirits low? Other than worrying about his stepsister, what had he to depress his mood? He had escaped an unsuitable marriage, after all.

'Hearts cannot break, or we die,' she said, conversationally. 'But *something* breaks when a person or a thing that is truly essential to us is with us no more. And it changes us profoundly. Your heart broke when Julia died. Mine broke when my fa—when I injured my hands and could no longer play. I can see now that before I was so wrapped up in my music that I was careless of my friends, hardly noticed the world around me. Finding that world was all I had now and knowing I had not been as good a friend as I should have been if I had been paying attention, that hurt. It made me cross and prickly.'

'I noticed,' Max said with a little huff of laughter. 'Go on.'

'You were still a youth when Julia died. I imagine you were full of daydreams and idealism, not ready to be an adult yet. But you found yourself dealing with tragedy and loss and having to take responsibility for her funeral because her parents would not. I imagine you grew up very fast.'

'Too fast,' Max said, his gaze resting, unfocused, on the melee of squabbling waterfowl.

For a moment Lucy thought he was going to say more, then he reached out and took her left hand in his. 'What happened to your hands?'

He needed to change the subject and she could understand that. 'I told you—an accident with the keyboard cover falling unexpectedly.'

'It was not an accident, was it?' He was as implacable as a prosecuting attorney. 'A falling cover might break a finger, cause bruises or cuts, but not so much damage, not unless it was slammed down with force. Who did it, Lucy? Your father?'

She had not spoken of it since she had fled to London and had stammered out the whole story to her friends, almost incoherent through anger and misery and pain. But she trusted Max.

I love him, she acknowledged, finally facing the truth. *What change is this heartbreak going to make in me, I wonder?*

'Yes, my father. My parents, you see, are country gentry. Respectability is their watchword. They are also deeply observant of every dictate of the church, far beyond what most parishioners are, even the most devout of them. There is a little coterie of them, all, it seems to me, striving to outdo each other in holiness.'

'And they have not joined one of the more rigorous Protestant sects?' Max asked.

'Dissenters are not *respectable*,' Lucy said. 'The Church of England is. They were beside themselves with joy when I became friends with Verity Wingate whose father is a retired bishop. They never questioned what I was doing there at the Bishop's Palace and what I *was* doing was playing. Verity was pursuing her antiquarian interests, Melissa was writing, Jane painting and Prue studying the Classics. At home I was only allowed to play hymns and uplifting music.

'Sundays, of course, was for attending church twice. That day I had some new sheet music that Verity had ordered for me. I pretended to have a hacking cough—I made my throat sore with it—and, of course, nothing could be allowed to disrupt the service, so I was allowed to stay at home. The Vicar broke his leg falling down the pulpit steps and the service broke up. I was so lost in the music that I didn't hear my parents come in and Papa slammed down the keyboard lid. I wasn't fast enough, I was taken so by surprise…'

Max said something under her breath that Lucy was glad she could not make out. 'I suppose it was all your fault?'

'Of course. I brought it on myself by lying to avoid church; I was playing scandalous music; I was disobedient. The list goes on. Fortunately I had a small inheritance that they could not control so, when I was well enough, I said I was leaving home and coming to London. When they tried to stop me I threatened to tell everyone in the parish what had happened. Goodness knows what *respectable* tale they've come up with to explain my disappearance.'

'I know what I would like to do about their so-called respectability,' Max said grimly. He looked down at her hand, still in his. 'You know, I think you are using your hands more freely. Are they getting better?'

Lucy looked down and spread her free hand. 'I think you are right, this one is a little improved.'

Max opened his own hand, gently parting the fingers and taking hers with them. 'And this, too, I think. Which doctor are you seeing?'

'None now. The doctor at home said they would never get better, but gave me some exercises to help the stiffness.'

'I know a doctor who has been helping a friend of mine who was wounded at Waterloo. He lost a finger and his thumb on one hand. I can give you his name if they don't continue to improve.'

'They will never be perfect,' she said sadly, looking down. 'There is the missing fingertip and those fingers will never be quite straight.'

'Lucy.' She looked up and found Max was watching her intently. 'Do you insist that everything and everyone is perfect?'

CHAPTER NINETEEN

'Do I insist on perfection?' Lucy repeated, puzzled. 'No, of course not. Only in my music. No one is perfect.'

'I wondered, that is all,' Max said. 'Was your music perfect before? Were you the very best pianist in the world?'

'Of course not. I was good, I believe, but never perfect. I could always improve and, if nothing had happened to my hands, I would have become better. But not faultless, I know that.'

'So what is stopping you playing now? The pain? The fear of failing?' Max was back to being the prosecutor again. 'Does this hurt?' He spread his fingers a little wider, hers still enmeshed with them.

'Hurt? No. But they are stiff. I could never be perfect…' Her voice trailed away as she realised where he had led her. 'But I never was perfect, was I?'

'And at some time in the past you had to begin, to learn. It would be like going back many stages and I should imagine you would have to modify your technique, but couldn't you accept that?'

'I don't know whether the magic would be there,' she admitted, shaken. Why had she never thought of learning to play again? Because she had been so unconsciously arrogant about how good she had been before?

'It is there when we dance. I suspect it may be there

when we kiss,' Max said, his voice low and warm. He shifted on the bench, his broad shoulders shielding her from the group of chattering nursemaids farther along the bank of the reservoir. 'Shall we see?'

She should say, *No*. Or at least, *Why?* But Lucy knew neither word was going to cross her lips. She loved Max, he wanted to kiss her and it would be the last time.

So she lifted her face to him and sighed into his mouth as their lips met. She felt warm and safe, protected by his body, even though they were right out in the open where anyone might see. Oh, and the magic was there, coursing through her veins, hot and dangerous and fizzing with need and energy. It reached all those forbidden places, it made her breasts ache for his hands, it filled her limbs with the need to twine around his and her hands with the desire to rip off his clothes, her clothes.

Something—not amorous hands—tugged at her hem and Lucy jumped, opened her eyes and met Max's gaze. He looked like a man who had taken a blow to the head.

'Max—ouch!' She looked down. Ducks crowded around their feet and a goose was attacking her skirts where the remains of the brown paper parcel was squashed.

Max took one corner and shook it hard, sending bread and cake crumbs flying. The birds chased after them in a noisy, wing-flapping mass, leaving them looking out at the reservoir and, at least on Lucy's part, attempting to gather both wits and breath.

She brushed down her skirts. 'I should be going home. I have a lesson to prepare for this afternoon.' Yes, her legs would support her when she stood. A firm hand with her bonnet, which was decidedly askew, and she would be able to hail a hackney carriage without causing passersby to stare.

Max rose, too, of course. All he had to do was put his

hat back on to look perfectly respectable, although he was still holding the sheet of wrapping paper in front of him. Lucy held out her hand. 'If you give me that, I will fold it up and put it in my reticule.'

'In a moment.' He took a deep breath and began to fold the paper, making rather a long business of it. 'I will walk you home,' he said when he eventually handed her the neat square.

'I will hail a hackney carriage. I really should get back.' *I really should not spend any more time with you. Ever.* She began to walk the short distance to the nearest gate out on to Piccadilly.

Max caught up with her. 'Thank you.'

'For a goodbye kiss?'

'Is that what it was? I meant for your help and advice about Sophia.'

'Yes, it was goodbye. I do hope Will finds some way to help the Reverend West. I expect we may see each other again in the street or at social events. I do not think it would be a good idea to acknowledge that we know each other, do you?'

They walked through the gate just as a hackney carriage drew up and a portly gentleman got out. Lucy waved at the driver who touched his whip to his hat brim. 'Little Windmill Street, if you please. Goodbye, my lord.'

She did not look out of the window as they drove off and she managed to get inside her own door and take off her bonnet before she gave way to misery and dissolved in tears.

AYLSHAM, THE PERFECT DUKE, lived up to his name. Four days later he called on Max with a proposal for Anthony West's new career.

'Is he competent at languages?' he asked after he had

accepted a cup of coffee and settled himself in a chair in Max's study.

'I have no idea. He has a university education, but beyond that I cannot say. Why do you ask?'

'You are aware, naturally, that Brazil is a Portuguese possession? And, of course, Portugal is our oldest ally. There are enormous opportunities for trade—exports from Britain and imports that this country would benefit from. Trade does exist now, but it is not as well developed as it might be. A delegation will sail next month to take the new British consul and a number of, shall we say, trade experts, to assess the possibilities and to cement good relations. An organised and competent secretary is required. The opportunity to impress a number of influential people is considerable.'

'I imagine that various government departments can provide a number of suitably qualified men.'

Will smiled. 'But not anyone for whom I am the patron. I suggest that you make the proposition to Mr West immediately. It cannot be guaranteed, of course, and if his language skills are so poor that he cannot learn functional Portuguese in the length of the ocean voyage, we will have to think again. But the sooner I speak to him, the better.'

THE LETTER WAS sent and Anthony West was on Max's doorstep two days later, leaving his curate in charge. No, he did not speak Portuguese, but he did speak Spanish, French and Italian and he was confident he could master it. The prospect of the Duke's patronage seemed to dazzle him, but he had no hesitation in saying that he wanted to try for the position.

'My birth will not affect this?' he asked abruptly.

'With the favour of a duke and your betrothal to the

daughter of an earl? No, I think that may conveniently slip people's minds.'

West's mouth opened, but no words came out.

'If you still want to marry the chit, that is,' Max had drawled. 'It is up to you, of course, but I suggest that some arrangement is made that you draw on an equivalent sum from her fortune to match your salary and the balance is held in trust for the children.'

MAX SAID NOTHING to Sophia until West returned the next day, dizzy with his good news. Max called her down to the drawing room, closed the door on them and ignored the long silence that followed her shrieks of delight. He thought he could trust the Vicar-turned-diplomat not to anticipate the wedding night.

Sophia's happiness was the one bright light in Max's life. He could see clearly now that he was in love with Lucy and equally clearly that she did not love him. The more he brooded on her words in the park, the more he came to recognise what had happened to him after Julia's death and the desperate words in her letter. He had grown up with a jolt, that was true, but like any very young man he had fixed some very black-and-white theories in his head and had not let them go.

Theories about his duty, theories about marriage and utterly unfounded ideas about love and its dangers were like those strange creatures turned to rock that scientists were beginning to say were not from Noah's flood, but the relics of some immeasurably distant past.

They had acted like a bulwark against loneliness and hurt and had long since served their turn. Now they only stifled him. But worse, they had stopped him recognising what he felt about Lucy, about seeing, right from the start, that something in her attracted him and that it was more than simple physical attraction.

Now what was he to do, when the person who seemed to give him the best advice was the last one that he could ask?

LUCY STOOD AND eyed the piano in the Duchess of Aylsham's music room. It had taken her a week to work up the courage to come and ask Verity if she could use it and her friend had simply waved a hand towards the instrument, said, 'Whenever you want, Lucy dear', and had left her alone.

Now her skimpy reserves of courage seemed to have run out and the one person who had given her enough to have even got here was impossible to ask for support.

She sat down, adjusted the stool, opened the lid. Max had faith in her or he would not have suggested she try to play, so she would. She peeled off her gloves and folded them carefully, then did her finger-stretching exercises. She adjusted the stool once more.

Then Lucy closed her eyes, thought of Max and laid her hands on the keys.

She was uncomfortable and clumsy. The wrong notes, the lack of subtlety, the impossibility of playing with one finger slightly shorter than it had been—the result was awful. Dreadful. A travesty.

Without opening her eyes, she reached out and closed the lid over the keys again before her tears fell on the ivory.

But Max had reminded her that once she had not been able to play at all. She'd had to learn. Lucy opened her eyes, lifted the lid again and studied her hands. What if she thought of them as belonging to a pupil? How would she advise that person? She just had to forget that she was the one who was leaning to play all over again.

Adjust the position of her hands to accommodate the

shorter finger, of course. Work with the finger-span that the pupil had. Do not expect too much from digits that were unpractised and stiff. Be patient.

She tried again. It felt awkward still, there was no magic yet, but if she took it slowly…

She did not have to be perfect, he was right. 'Thank you, Max,' Lucy breathed. She could not have him, but now she would always have this.

TEN DAYS LATER she sat and massaged her aching fingers and marvelled at how much progress she had made. She had rented the pianoforte owned by Mrs Todd, who kept it more for appearances than anything, and she hired labourers to move it upstairs and a tuner to repair the neglect of years.

The new hand position had become automatic, the span of her fingering had increased and slowly, slowly, the result was becoming less about technique and more about pure music.

It gave her pleasure and satisfaction, joy, even, but the old all-consuming magic was not happening. Perhaps that was because she was so much more aware of the world around her, of other pleasures.

There was the satisfaction of working with her pupils, the constant interest of the city around her, the company of her friends whose own lives had widened to more than they had ever been. Yes, perhaps it was that and not the endless ache, the hollowness in her chest, the absence of Max and the pain of loving him.

It might be that the magic would never return, she thought sometimes when she lay awake in the small hours of the morning and the satisfaction of her playing was hours away and the distractions of London were silent and still.

But now she ran her hand lightly over the black and white keys and smiled. There was a lesson in the afternoon with Master James Cricklewood, aged eight, one of her few male pupils. Master James was wildly enthusiastic, very naughty and a pleasure to be with. She had found a wonderfully thumping march that he would enjoy and she was looking—

The door knocker thudded. Really, she had to stop that ridiculous habit of stopping, listening, every time a knocker sounded. It wouldn't be Max, it would *never* be Max.

But there were feet climbing the stairs. Several pairs of feet. Some of her friends, perhaps, unless they were going upstairs. No, they had stopped on her landing. Lucy went across, opened the door and stepped back abruptly.

'*Mother?*'

'There, I knew it would be a lovely surprise for her,' her mother said to Mrs Todd. The landlady nodded and went back downstairs, leaving Mr and Mrs Lambert on the threshold, their fixed smiles fading along with the sound of the landlady's feet.

Lucy's lunge at the door handle was too late and they were inside the room, the door closed behind them.

'What are you doing here?' she demanded.

'How could we not come when we heard what you had been doing, you wicked girl?' her mother said. She placed her bonnet on the table and sat down on one of the upright chairs, her husband behind her, one hand on her shoulder, for all the world like a portrait of rectitude.

'Your flouting of the Sabbath, your lies, your frivolous music—those were bad enough, but to learn that you have disgraced the family name by becoming a…' She flushed, her throat and cheeks flaming.

'Trollop,' Lucy's father stated. 'A nobleman's plaything. A harlot.'

'I am no such thing,' Lucy said hotly. 'I am a respectable pianoforte teacher. Where have you got those lies from?'

'Did you think you could come back to Dorset, to virtually our doorstep, and flaunt your paramour without word reaching us? How can we hold our heads up in the parish after this?'

'Who has been lying about me?' Somehow word of her presence at Lady Hopewell's house had got back, but how?

'The third parlourmaid is Jenny Hawkins and the Hawkinses—'

'The Hawkinses have that smallholding with all the chickens on the edge of the village,' Lucy said wearily. She should have thought of that—a big house drew in servants from miles around.

'And she came home on her monthly day off and told her sister Annie who works at the inn and after that it was all over the village.' Her mother shook her head, the picture of righteous sorrow. 'You arrive alone in a closed carriage with a man, you cause an uproar, then you flee the house. How could you, Lucy?'

'As all you have heard is unfounded gossip, you are very quick to judge, Mama. I was employed by the gentleman in question to help him with a family problem which, thanks to that intervention, has been solved. Because of necessary discretion some people got the wrong idea and I felt it prudent to leave. I am not that man's mistress. I am nobody's mistress and, if your sole reason for visiting me was to lecture me on the subject, then I suggest you leave. Now.'

'No, it is not the sole reason, as you should know. You have been compromised, now you will marry that man.'

'I will do no such thing.' Lucy fought the instinct to retreat into her bedchamber and push a chair under the door handle. 'You cannot make me.'

'We can make him,' her father said grimly.

'As you do not know who he is—'

'The Earl of Burnham.'

Behind her parents the door opened and Max walked in. 'Did someone say my name?'

Lucy sat down on the pianoforte stool.

'I was about to knock.' He looked around the room from her doubtless white face to the two middle-aged people in their Sunday best and his face took on the expression of icy control that Lucy hated.

'You are Burnham?' her father demanded.

'I am the Earl of Burnham, yes. You would appear to have the advantage of me.'

'I am Frederick Lambert and this is my wife. We are Lucy's parents. Now, what do you have to say to *that*, my lord?'

'Good morning.' When her father merely glowered at him, Max raised one eyebrow. 'What would you have me say?'

'You compromised my daughter!'

'I can assure you, madam, I have done no such thing.' Max looked across at Lucy. 'Unless, of course, Miss Lambert says I did.'

'*No.* I have not and I *will* say no such thing. Ignore them. They have heard gossip and rumour and lies and have seen an opportunity.'

'Wicked girl! We have seen our duty and that is to ensure this man makes good the damage he has done and marries you.'

'Mother, I do not wish to marry Lord Burnham. He most certainly does not wish to marry me. There is no reason why he should.'

'He should know his duty!'

'Which is to follow Miss Lambert's wishes. Not yours. Not society's. Your daughter does not wish to marry me and she has made that abundantly clear.'

Her father ignored Max, or pretended to, and spoke directly to her. 'I have no doubt,' he said, 'that you would not have strayed so far from your upbringing as to have wantonly given yourself to this man without the assurance of marriage. If he does not marry you, then we will have recourse to a suit for breach of promise.'

'Blackmail does not appear to be a very promising beginning to a happy marriage,' Max said with deceptive mildness. 'We are all aware, I think, of the effect of such a suit, successful or unsuccessful, on a lady's reputation.'

'What reputation?' lamented her mother. 'We will have to leave the parish, move far away where we are not known. I cannot bear the humiliation.'

'Your humiliation?' Lucy sprang to her feet and began to pace. 'Never mind mine! You listen to lies about me and do not defend me, you try to force me into marriage to save your own face—and because you would love to gloat about *My daughter the Countess*.'

'How dare you speak to your mother like that.'

Her father took a step towards her and Max moved, like a fencer going in to attack, and stood between them.

'You, sir, are the person responsible for the damage to Miss Lambert's hands, I believe.' The sound of an invisible rapier being drawn was almost audible.

'It was an accident. She should not have been playing on a Sunday. I merely closed the lid.'

Max seized the older man by the arm, jerked him towards the piano, pushed him down on to the stool and held his hand flat over the keys and took hold of the keyboard lid. 'I will *merely close it*, shall I, and we will see what effect that has.'

Lucy froze as her father, no weakling, struggled against the implacable grip. Max's hand tightened on the lid... Then he shut it, just as though he was doing so after playing. It rested lightly on her struggling father's knuckles. 'What a very strong man you must be, Mr Lambert.' He released her father and stepped away, still keeping between her and her parents. 'We can only be grateful that you did not slam the lid down in a fit of temper.'

She would not hide behind him. Lucy side-stepped and looked at her shaken mother and father. 'I think you should go now.'

Have you ever loved me? she wondered. Or, if they had, when had it stopped, when had she become simply a projection of their own vision of themselves—virtuous, godly, upstanding figures who were very large fish indeed in their tiny country pond? 'You can go back ho—go back to Dorset and tell everyone that you have cast me off. They will be impressed that you have done the right thing.'

'I will not leave you with that man.' Her mother was on her feet, trembling but defiant.

'I can assure you, ma'am, I will be right behind you,' Max said. 'We are all unwelcome intruders here.'

He did not look at Lucy as he opened the door and followed her parents out on to the landing. She stood listening as footsteps descended the stairs, two hurried pairs, one more measured, heavy, almost.

Then the front door closed and she ran to the window and looked down. Her parents had hailed a hackney carriage and she saw only the top of Max's tall hat as he stood watching them drive off. Then he turned and walked away towards Mayfair. He did not look back, he did not look up. He turned left across the road, into a side street and was gone.

CHAPTER TWENTY

It was not until Lucy had fled the house and gone for a long walk around St James's Park that she felt calm enough to think about what had just happened. As she was growing up she had sometimes wondered whether those tales about fairies changing babies over, just to cause chaos in the human world, did not have some grain of truth. Perhaps somewhere there was a staid, obedient young woman who had grown up in a house full of cheerfulness and music.

She should feel sorry for her mother and father, she knew. They never seemed happy. Why had they married? Perhaps, thirty years ago, another set of parents had arranged a *suitable* marriage and the two of them had been forced together and whatever joy they had in their lives had curdled so that only appearance and respectability were left to them.

Anger and resentment would curdle her spirits, too, she suspected, if she slammed the door on them and left those feelings to fester. Perhaps, in a day or so, she could find it in herself to write to them, tell them about her life, send them news. But not yet. She was too sore to do it now.

And there was Max to think about, to feel sore over. Worn out with her angry striding, and with a blister on her heel, Lucy sat down wearily on the nearest bench and contemplated a pair of pelicans perched on a log at the edge of the lake.

They seemed wildly exotic in the middle of London, but Prue had told her that the original ones were a gift from the Russian ambassador to Charles II. She tried to imagine the man transporting the creatures all the way from Russia— in the diplomatic bag?—terrified they would expire before he could deliver them and having his fingers snapped at. As she thought it, a pigeon strayed too close and one lunged at it. The pigeon escaped, much to Lucy's relief.

Max had been furious with her father, she recalled with a shiver. His expression as he had held the older man's hand flat on the keyboard had shown emotions Lucy had never seen in him. He had moved, so protectively, to stand between her and her parents and he had refused to bow to threats and do something he thought she did not want.

But why had he been there at all? He could not have known her parents would descend on her like that. It could not have been to give her news of Mr West and Sophia, because Sophia had written to her to tell her that she was to be married the day before Anthony sailed and that she had every intention of sailing with him. Although, she had added, she had not told Max this. Lucy would receive an invitation, of course, but as the wedding was to be in the port of Falmouth, Sophia said she quite understood if it was too far for her to travel. Lucy wondered whether Anthony West was also aware that his bride intended joining him and decided it was none of her business to interfere.

Limping slightly from the blister, she began to walk slowly back home, giving the pelicans a wide berth. It made her think of that kiss beside the Green Park reservoir and the squabbling ducks around their feet. Probably she would not even have noticed a pelican attacking her skirts if Max had carried on kissing her like that.

SHE LET HERSELF in with her latch key and climbed the stairs to her floor. It was gloomy now and the curtain on the landing window was still closed. As she reached out to draw it back her foot disturbed something and she bent to pick it up: a little bouquet of rosebuds in all shades of pink, tightly bound with a trailing ribbon.

It had been right under the window next to her door, as though kicked there by a careless foot or tossed away. Someone carrying it upstairs could not have dropped it there. Yet it was quite fresh, only a trifle dusty, and one bud had a bent stem.

She unlocked her door and carried it inside, puzzling over it.

'Oh, what lovely flowers, miss.' Amy got up from her seat at the table where she had been darning stockings.

'Yes, and quite a mystery. I found them on the floor under the landing window just now, as though someone had dropped them.'

'Did you have any callers while I was out, miss?' Amy asked as she went into the bedchamber. She came back with a large flat package. 'I got ever such a nice material to make a new underskirt for that blue gown.'

'My parents,' Lucy said, opening the parcel.

'Oh, gawd, miss.'

'It was not amusing,' Lucy admitted. She saw no reason to tell her maid that Max had also called. 'Yes, this is very nice, you have such a good eye for these things, Amy.'

The maid began to repack the fabric. 'I…er… I suppose someone might have called with the flowers and heard… um…raised voices and went away again.'

'Yes, perhaps. Where are you going?'

'Just to check there isn't anything else, Miss Lambert.'

Amy reappeared a moment later. 'There was this card, right in the corner, and it's got your name on it.'

Lucy. Nothing else. No message, no signature. She did not recognise the handwriting.

'It's a man, don't you think?' Amy was craning to see.

'Rather hard to tell from four letters,' Lucy said, turning it over. She lifted it to her nose and sniffed. Dust—and just the very faintest hint of…spice?

One thing was certain, her parents would certainly not be bringing her flowers. But Max had been her only other caller, unless someone else had come and, as Amy said, heard the raised voices and went away without knocking. But why throw down the flowers?

But if it had been Max who brought them, if he had been on the point of knocking and had then walked in because of what he heard—then, yes, he might well have either dropped them, unheeded, or tossed them away because he would not wish to appear in the middle of an argument like a suitor at her door.

Which was the only reason she could think of why a man would turn up with an exquisite little bouquet, complete with trailing pink ribbons.

Lucy sat down with an inelegant thump.

'Miss?'

'I have such a painful blister on my heel. I walked a long way in these shoes and they are still too new and stiff for that.'

'I will get a dressing for it,' Amy said. 'And I'll put these in water.'

If Max was bringing her flowers, what did that mean? Was it possible that he had feelings for her after all? That he wanted to make a fresh start? Or was he simply another man who thought that if a woman allowed kisses she might permit far more?

No. This was Max and she loved him and she would not believe that of him. But how to ask him? It would be ghastly if the flowers were not from him. He might think she was angling for him to marry her after all.

'Save the ribbon!' Lucy called to Amy. She had an idea.

'Oh, yes, miss. It's a lovely colour, isn't it?' She came back in with the roses in the white china vase from Lucy's dressing table in one hand, the ribbon around her neck and some soft cloth in her hand. 'If I cut a pad of this and you slip it inside your stocking and put on some older shoes, that should make you more comfortable.'

'Amy, can you make a rosette with that ribbon? Something I could pin to my gown like a corsage?'

Amy looked up from snipping the cloth. 'Oh, yes, that's easy to do.' She handed Lucy the little pad for her heel. 'I'll just get my sewing box.'

AN HOUR LATER Lucy came out on to the street wearing a soft brown walking dress with a cream spencer decorated by an elaborate knot of pink ribbon over her heart, hailed a passing hackney carriage and gave him an address in Cavendish Square. She felt hollow inside with nerves, but she told herself that this was too important to allow terror to get in her way. This was the rest of her life, the difference between true happiness and making the best of things.

She had it all worked out. She would tell Max that she had called to thank him for defending her in front of her parents and to apologise for the embarrassment it must have caused him. She would say nothing about her own feelings, nothing about rosebuds. Then she would see what happened when he saw the rosette of pink ribbon.

After all, what have I got to lose but my pride if I make a fool of myself? she thought, gazing out of the window.

Then, as the carriage rounded the first corner, she saw a familiar figure on the pavement ahead.

The driver pulled up with an oath as she flung the

door open. 'Wait till I've stopped, won't you, you stupid woman!'

'Sorry.' She half fell out into the road, scrabbled in her reticule and tossed him a coin. 'Max!'

Like most of the passers-by he had stopped and turned at the cabby's shout. He strode towards her and almost towed her on to the pavement out of the way of a coal wagon. 'Are you trying to get yourself killed?'

Lucy grabbed hold of his lapels to steady herself. He was clearly furious and she felt her dream of a calm meeting where their true feelings might become clear vanishing like a faint mist in the morning sun. Then she realised that he was far too angry for mere irritation at her carelessness. This was the anger of someone who cared.

'I was coming to see you,' she said. She kept hold of his lapels and he still held her wrist. Surely he must feel her pulse hammering under his fingers?

Max lifted his free hand and touched the ribbon. 'That is…pretty.'

'It is from a bunch of rosebuds someone brought me this morning. They dropped it outside my door.'

She was half aware of other pedestrians, of people staring at them as they passed. Max seemed totally oblivious to the fact they were not alone.

'Have you any idea who it was?'

'I think so. I hope I am right.'

His expression was no longer controlled, there was no icy calm now. A nerve twitched at the corner of his eye and she could see the tension in his jaw. 'Why do you hope that?'

'Because I would like it very much if that person brought me roses. Or if they came to see me bringing nothing at all.'

The world had gone still and quiet around her. There

was only Max staring down at her, her reflection in his eyes looking back, the way his lips parted as though he was about to speak. Or—

'For Gawd's sake, guv'nor, kiss the wench or move out the way!'

Max's gaze did not even flicker as a burly porter shouldered his way past them. 'Ah,' he murmured. 'The voice of common sense.' And he lowered his mouth to hers.

The now familiar magic was there, but something new, something better. Max was not kissing her because it was a pleasurable thing to do, he was kissing her because he had to, because he was compelled, just as she was compelled to ignore the fact they were in the midst of a crowd, on a public street. This was Max and she loved him and she was filled with hope that he loved her, too.

It was the near silence as much as anything that broke the spell. Lucy opened her eyes, blinked up at Max as he lifted his head. Around them there was a collective sigh.

'We have an audience,' he murmured and smiled.

'Go on then, miss. Say *yes*,' a female voice urged and was seconded by a chorus.

Lucy looked, blinked. They were surrounded. There were two women hefting a load of laundry between them, an errand boy with his mouth open, a porter with a parcel on his shoulder, Miss Wilkins, who lived in the apartment above her, a trio of giggling maidservants with laden baskets from the nearby market and the looming figure of the parish constable.

'Move along there, now, you're causing an obstruction and I'm not sure as that ain't indecent behaviour.'

''Ere, Albert Prewitt, they can't do that, not until she's said *yes*,' one of the washerwomen protested.

'I haven't asked her yet, ma'am,' Max said, making the woman blush and simper.

'Well, go on then! Better than that serial story they're reading out loud every week down at the Fox and Geese, this is.'

'The middle of the street was not quite where I had planned to do this, but will you do me the honour of becoming my wife, Miss Lambert?'

Lucy swallowed. It was what she wanted and she was terrified. He was an earl. Her parents were a nightmare. They had already caused a small scandal. It was impossible.

'Yes,' she said firmly. 'Yes, Lord Burnham, I will marry you.'

There was a ripple of applause and a whistle from the messenger boy.

Max grinned and looked around. 'Hey! Cabbie!'

He bundled her into the hackney carriage and they sank back against the lumpy upholstery, side by side and silent.

'Did I just do that?' Max asked after a moment. 'Kiss you and then propose in the street?'

'Yes.'

'That's a relief. I thought I was dreaming.' His hand found hers, but they still did not look at each other.

'So did I,' Lucy confessed. She gripped his hand tightly. 'But I think it is true.' The nasty insidious worm of doubt squirmed, intent on crushing her happiness. 'I know why I said yes, but Max, why did you ask me?'

He turned then, twisting on the seat so that he could look at her. 'Because I love you.'

'Oh. Thank goodness, because I love you so much and I think I knew it even as I was on the Mail coming back to London. But I couldn't tell you, not when you kept proposing out of honour.'

They sat and smiled at each other with no need to speak. Lucy remembered the number of times she had watched her friends and their husbands exchange long, lingering looks tinged with a smile and an edge of something that sent shivers to her toe-tips and made her feel like an intruder. But now she and Max were the insiders, this was *their* lingering look and the smile and the shivers were for her.

'Make love to me, Max.'

'Oh, yes.' It sounded like a vow. 'But not here. I have been on the point of making love to you under a bed, on a terrace and on a bench in Green Park and I have no intention of actually doing so in a hackney carriage. I told the driver to take us home.'

'Home.' Home with Max. She held his hand tighter and the nasty worm of uncertainty gave a final, desperate wriggle. 'Max, my parents—'

'I told myself that they are more to be pitied than anything. What a very joyless life they seem to lead. I told myself to wonder what had made them like that, on the grounds that to understand all is to forgive all, but I'm afraid that, unless I ever do understand, then I am never going to forgive them for making you unhappy, for taking your music from you.' He let go of her hand only to put his arm around her and pull her close. 'Perhaps grandchildren will soften them.'

'Children? Max, we haven't discussed children.'

'We have never discussed anything except my stepsister and your music.' The carriage lurched to a stop. 'We're here. Home.'

'One of them,' she said faintly as he handed her out. 'How many houses do you own?'

'To live in as opposed to those with tenants? Just the four. This one, Knight's Acre, my country seat in Shropshire; the hunting lodge in Northamptonshire and a villa on the south coast that I bought last year. Is that enough?'

Max teasing her was new and unsettling. Almost as unsettling as the reality that she had agreed to marry an earl.

The front door swung open. 'Good afternoon, my lord.' The butler was surprisingly young to Lucy's eyes.

'Miss Lambert, this is Pomfret. Pomfret, Miss Lambert has just agreed to marry me. I do not expect that information to move beyond these walls at present.'

'Certainly, my lord, and congratulations. Ma'am, I am honoured.'

'Thank you, Pomfret.'

'Miss Lambert and I have a great deal to discuss. See that we are not disturbed.'

'My lord. Dinner, my lord? Lady Sophia is dining at Lady Henderson's with the Reverend West.'

'Lady Henderson is her other godmother,' Max said to Lucy. He glanced at the long-case clock. 'At eight, Pomfret.'

'Max,' Lucy whispered as he guided her towards the stairs. 'We are going *upstairs*.'

'My study is upstairs,' Max said. 'Where better place to discuss the details of our marriage.'

She did not know whether to be relieved or sorry. She had thought Max was bringing her home to make love to her. And then she had realised, the moment she saw the butler, that if he took her upstairs the entire household would know what was happening. So, if the study was up there, too, this was much less embarrassing and she was still with Max.

There is nothing to be disappointed about. She scolded herself for wanting so much when, already, her dream had come true. He loved her. They would marry. She could wait.

Max opened a door at the head of the stairs and she went in to his study. Then he locked the door and went across to open a door in the far corner. 'This is rather more comfortable.'

It was his bedchamber. Max turned the key in what must be the door on to the landing, then another she supposed was his dressing room.

'And now, Lucy my love, we are alone with only the truth between us.'

CHAPTER TWENTY-ONE

Now she was nervous. 'Max, why *did* you come to my rooms this morning?'

'To propose,' he said as he shrugged out of his coat, sat down and began to take off his shoes. 'It took me a while to realise just why I was feeling so very out of sorts, you see. I ended up needing to fight someone or pack up and drive to the other end of the country—and at the same time I hated the idea of leaving London. I couldn't concentrate, I lost my appetite, nothing gave me any pleasure. It took me far too long to realise that I was missing you and it was not until I looked at Sophia that I understood that I was in love with you.'

'But you went away again. You threw away the roses.'

Max untied his neckcloth and tossed it aside. 'What would you have thought if I had offered to marry you this morning?'

'That my parents had forced it on you,' she admitted. 'I would not have believed anything else you told me.'

'So I went away, almost convinced that you truly did not want me and that it was hopeless.'

'Almost?' Lucy put her bonnet on the dresser and began to unbutton her pelisse with fingers that had not fumbled so badly since before she had left home. She peeled off her gloves and did not look at her hands.

'Almost.' Max smiled, his eyes that she had always thought so hard speaking to her gently of love. 'I brooded and paced and snapped at Hobson and kicked the furniture and then told myself I was being a coward, that I should go back and tell you, from my heart, what I felt. Not ask you to marry me yet, but ask you if you could love me.' He stood and took her in his arms.

They kissed as he undressed her down to her shift, then broke apart for her to pull his shirt over his head. Max fought his way out of his breeches, she kicked off her shoes and snagged her stockings wrenching them off. Then they stood, just looking at each other.

She ought to feel shy. Max was naked—not that she dared drop her gaze below the middle of his chest—and she was, almost. Lucy realised that she was not embarrassed, but she was uncertain.

'I'm not pretty,' she said abruptly. 'I'm skinny and I've not got much bosom and my hands—'

'Aren't you pretty? I hadn't noticed.' Max stepped close, ran his thumbs over her cheekbones, teased one finger down her nose, traced the line of her lips. 'Perhaps a little pampering and being happy will put more flesh on your bones, but I am very fond of them, just as they are.' His hands gently cupped the small swells of her breasts. 'And these—' He dipped his head and ran the tip of his tongue over first one nipple, then the other through the fine lawn. 'These are delicious.

'And as for your hands, these are the fading battle scars of a courageous fight. Nobody is perfect, Lucy. No one needs to be. I am certainly not and yet you say you love me.'

She tugged at the shift, pulled it over her head and then, shy at last, stepped close and curled one arm around his neck. 'I think you are *almost* perfect. You can be colder than an ice house in winter when you are annoyed and you are far too handsome.'

Max snorted.

Lucy ran her finger down the faint depression in his chin. 'But I even love your dimple.'

'I do *not* have a dimple.'

They landed on the bed, more by luck than judgement, she thought, and then stopped thinking, only feeling.

A man's body was a fascinating collection of different sensations and she found she was rubbing herself against Max as though she was a cat. There was the friction of hairy legs entwined with hers, the surprising softness of his hair at his nape, the smoothness of his upper arms with the hard muscle beneath that shifted under her roving fingers. His hands strayed lightly over her body as she explored his, caressing, not demanding, sending shivers and tingles through her.

His chest was even more fascinating. A dusting of hair that narrowed down, nipples that hardened and puckered to her touch and more of those impressive muscles. He was such a different shape, so powerful.

Then she leaned forward and touched her tongue-tip to his right nipple, and Max growled, rolled over, and she found herself between a very soft mattress and a very hard man. Her legs seemed to know what to do, curling around his hips, opening her to the urgent pressure. He moved his hips, rubbing against her until she began to pant and squirm. Vaguely, she realised that the soft pleading gasps were her own, begging for more, needing it all.

There was more pressure, fullness, an alarming moment when this seemed impossible, painful, not right and then they both shifted, stilled and they were one and it was…

'Perfect,' she whispered against Max's cheek.

Slowly, he began to move and the magic began, better

than dancing, better than music. This was both of them, in harmony, giving and taking pleasure, making something that was only for them, building and building to a crescendo she could not imagine.

'Come with me,' Max said, and Lucy let go and soared.

'Lucy?'

'Mmm?' She was not certain where she was, but it was a very pleasant place to be when her body was as limp as a half-filled feather pillow and little lightning flashes of delicious sensation kept darting through her body. She let her eyes open and found she was lying with her head on Max's chest, his heart beating reassuringly under her ear. His arm was around her and his breath whispered in her hair and she knew she was home.

'Speak to me.' He sounded almost as stunned as she felt.

'I love you.' She felt rather than heard his sigh. 'And that was magical and mysterious and the most perfect thing that has ever happened to me.'

'You leave me no words because you have taken them from my lips.' She felt him shift and press a kiss to the top of her head. 'You know, when you first described how playing had made you feel, I thought about making love. That was the closest I had ever been to that feeling. And now I have felt it, too.'

The warm body she was resting on was so still that Lucy wondered if he had fallen asleep. Then Max said, 'We had better get married soon.'

'Very soon, if we are going to do this often.' Lucy found the strength to sit up. 'You look like a very superior cat who has stolen the cream and has eaten so much of it he cannot move.'

Max levered himself up against the pillows and smiled that slow, secret smile.

Perhaps after all I am not so very exhausted...

'Where?' he asked. 'St George's would be the obvious choice. The chapel at Knight's Acre is another. Your parish church here in London. Or your parish church at home in Dorset?'

'That is not my home any longer. Home is where you are.' She thought about it. 'Knight's Acre, I think, if that is what you would like.'

'It is. And my mother will be happy. She has severe arthritis and finds travel difficult. Will a month give you long enough for whatever preparations brides have to make?'

'It will be with my friends helping. I imagine that if a duchess, a marchioness, a countess and one very determined spinster cannot extract a trousseau for the bride of the Earl of Burnham from London's best modistes, then there is something very wrong with the city's shopkeepers.'

'Open accounts with whomever you need to and have them send the bills to me,' he said. He looked more alert now, more the everyday Max, not the new, sensual, heavy-lidded lover. 'No, don't poker up. I know by the time your friends have finished with you the total will be beyond your means.'

Lucy nodded. He was right and she was not going to stand on her pride and look less than a suitable bride for an earl. He had enough to contend with marrying someone from an obscure county parish with thoroughly awkward parents.

'And we will invite your parents,' Max said, as though reading her mind. 'It will be interesting to see if they accept. If they do, it may be the beginning of a reconciliation.'

'Soft words turn away wrath,' Lucy said. 'You see—I did attend church most of the time and listen, too. You are right, I would hate our children to be estranged from two of their grandparents, and they say that anger corrodes the soul.'

A clock struck, seven thin, silver notes.

'Shall I ring for hot water? I expect you would like a bath.' Max got off the bed and picked up a heavy silk robe from a chair. 'Put this on and take your clothes.' He opened the door on to the corridor and looked out. 'Quite clear. Second door on the left is a guest room. I'll send a maid and everything you'll need.' He turned. 'What is it?'

'I was simply admiring you. I haven't seen you all over at the same time before,' she admitted, considering fanning herself. Not that Max's self-esteem appeared to suffer from neglect—he stood there perfectly assured, without a stitch on. It was she who was blushing.

But when she reached him at the door and looked up into his face, Lucy realised this was not the composed, controlled man she thought she had come to know. There was warmth in his gaze and questions in his eyes, and an air of openness and vulnerability that she could never have imagined Max Fenton revealing.

'I love you,' she said and kissed him. 'I loved you before and now I love you even more.'

He took her in his arms and she felt the last of the ice shatter.

LUCY WAS LOLLING in the bath, trying to ignore the rapidly cooling water because she was so happy lying there remembering and looking forward and generally being happy.

There was a tap on the door and Amy peeped in. 'Oh, miss! His Lordship sent a note to say how you was staying for dinner and he'd see you home after and I wasn't to worry. But I thought, I can't have my lady eating dinner with an earl in her walking dress, now, can I?' She came

right in, revealing a sheet-wrapped bundle in her arms. 'So
I've brought an evening gown and the right slippers.' She
gazed around her. 'Lovely room, miss. I s'pose you'll live
here when you're married and a countess.'

'How did you guess I am going to be married?'

Amy just rolled her eyes.

'Yes, I suppose I will live here. Could you pass me
the towel? Thank you.' She looked at the maid. 'What's
wrong, Amy?'

'Nothing, miss. I expect you'll give me a decent character when I leave, won't you? Only I like being a lady's
maid.'

'Of course I would—if you were leaving. But why?'
Lucy climbed out of the bath and snuggled into a vast
length of very soft linen.

'Well, you'll be a countess, won't you? You'll need one
of those starched-up dressers, not a girl from a village who
can't do your hair properly.'

'You will learn how to do my hair—I'm sure you can
get lessons—and then you'll learn how to be starched-up,
too, I expect. I hope you'll stay, Amy—I'm going to need
all the help I can get to learn how to do this.'

LUCY FOUND MAX in what Pomfret described as, 'The Small
Dining Room, Miss Lambert.'

It was still large enough to hold a table that, with all
the leaves out, could seat eight, but the two places were
set together, one at the head and the other next to it on the
right, and there were no servants. Lucy felt her shoulders
drop a little. She had imagined sitting at one end of a long
board with Max at the other and making polite conversation while a small regiment of footmen lurked around the
room. Even her friends' dining rooms were like that unless
they all gathered together for an informal supper.

'Come in. Do you mind if we serve ourselves?' Max caught her hand. 'It is all on the sideboard—or shall I serve you?'

He is talking too much. He is nervous. Max, nervous?

She felt better still and returned the pressure of his fingers. 'Show me what there is. It smells delicious.'

But Max was frowning, looking down into her face. 'What is wrong?' He traced a fingertip under her eyes. 'You have been crying.'

'Amy thought I would dismiss her and employ a starched-up dresser because I will be a countess. And I promised her I wanted her to stay with me and she burst into tears and so did I. We have been having a happy weep.' She leant against his shoulder, just for the pleasure of feeling him, solid and strong.

'I suppose, when I am married to one, I may come to understand women better,' Max said solemnly. But there was a smile in his voice. 'Tell me about happy weeping when you have tried the pea soup.'

They talked about weeping and happiness, about how good the soup was and whether Lucy would like to redecorate the whole London house from top to toe. They talked about Max's mother and whether Max was absolutely certain she would be happy to move to the Dower House. Lucy complimented him on his carving of the roast guinea fowl and he wanted to know which type of pianoforte she wanted to be installed in each house.

It seemed to Lucy that they spoke of everything and nothing and it was all a miracle. Then Max put down the delicate silver spoon with which he had been eating the lemon posset.

'I may be hell to live with, you know. I am used to having my own way since I was eighteen and left home.' He frowned at her. 'You'll want to leave me after a week, I'm sure of it.'

'If you are difficult, then I will tell you,' Lucy said firmly. 'I'll be just as bad, you know. I have been getting my own way by subterfuge for years, sneaking off to play at the Bishop's Palace. And then when I was thwarted I left.' She picked up her spoon, eyed the posset and put it down again. Rich food, happiness and lovemaking were quite enough for one evening without adding sweets.

'Will we have arguments?' Max asked.

'Terrible ones, I expect,' she said and laughed. 'Then we can make it up afterwards.'

'Perhaps we could pretend we have just had the most terrible, blazing row,' he suggested as he pushed her untouched dessert to one side, leaned across and kissed her.

Max tasted of lemons and sugar and wine and himself, an intoxicating mixture. He stood up, drawing her with him, then, to her surprise, kicked her chair out at an angle to the table and sat her down again as he went to his knees before her.

'The door…'

'Is locked. And, yes, I know you do not wish to appear to the staff later all rumpled.' His hands were sliding her skirts up to her knees. 'I have no intention of rumpling you. None whatsoever.' Irresistible pressure spread her thighs apart as the skirt rode higher and Max leaned in.

'Max? Max!'

It was indecent, improper, outrageous and… Lucy ran out of words. She should stop him. This couldn't be right. She would push him away. Yes, that was what she would do. In a moment when his clever tongue paused, then she would… She would…

Lucy's hands closed on Max's bent head and clung until she had to lift them away to stifle her own cries.

At last he sat back on his heels and grinned at her. 'See? Not rumpled at all.'

'Oh, you *wicked* man.' She swooped forward and kissed him. Lemon and wine and Max and… Oh, goodness, that must be her that she was tasting on his lips. *Wicked, wicked man.*

'I do love you so,' she said and burst into tears.

MORE HAPPY TEARS, Max diagnosed, as he got to his feet, scooped Lucy into his arms and went to sit on the sofa. He was glad she had told him about that, because otherwise he'd have been shaken. *More* shaken.

He couldn't claim to be inexperienced. He'd had his share of mistresses, he thought he was reasonably well practised in the arts of love and what his partners felt had always been important. But he had never loved anyone before, never felt this shattering responsibility, as though he held something very fragile, very precious, cupped in his hands. Making love to Lucy had been a revelation and the responsibility had almost brought him to his knees.

Had brought him there, he thought, and enjoyed a brief flicker of masculine smugness. Lucy's reaction from shock and outrage to melting, squirming, delirious female had been delicious. Exploring lovemaking together was going to be a wonder.

But that did not explain the way he felt about her. She was not a beauty, she had no figure to speak of, she was lacking in sophisticated conversation and society graces— and none of that mattered because she was simply Lucy and he loved her. Honest, prickly, brave, talented. Lucy. Somehow he knew that the nightmares that had haunted him had fled.

He found a handkerchief by dint of some determined

wriggling and managed to apply it to her face before his shoulder was completely soaked.

She snuffled inelegantly, which made him smile, and blew her nose with even less elegance and eventually emerged damply and smiled. 'Sorry.'

'Was it that awful?' Max asked, managing to keep a straight face.

'It was *dreadful*. Can I do the same thing to you?'

CHAPTER TWENTY-TWO

One month later—Knight's Acre, Shropshire

The chapel was all dark polished panelling and dully gleaming marble. Light streamed in through the high windows, painting the floor and the guests with rich reds and blues, striking gold off the candlesticks on the altar and saturating the masses of flowers with even richer colours.

Max studied the altar frontal in forensic detail. Counting the embroidered flowers was doing little for his nerves.

Beside him his best man, Trevor Atkinson, nudged him in the ribs. 'You all right, old fellow? You've gone awfully white. It'll be fine, just you wait and see.'

Trevor had married his Eugenia three weeks before and was radiating the smugness of a newly married man who did not have to experience this ordeal again.

It was all very well for Trevor to talk. Even if Eugenia hadn't loved him, her father and brother, unable to believe their good fortune, would have marched her up the aisle and into his arms. They were learning now that Trevor was not the amiable soft touch they had thought he was.

But Lucy had every reason for not marrying him. She was independent. She had her music again now. He knew he could be arrogant and icy and difficult to live with. She wasn't used to vast houses and numerous servants and—

The organist, who had been producing soft, twiddling music, opened up all the stops, or whatever it was they did, and the organ trumpeted, bringing the congregation to its feet.

Max swung round. *There you are. My love.*

Lucy was a very slender column of cream and white lace on her father's arm: repentance on his part, forgiveness on hers, Max thought. A fragile miracle that might last beyond this day.

Then, halfway towards him, she threw back her veil and smiled, slid her fingers from her father's arm and walked alone to Max, both hands held out.

It seemed as though trumpets had joined the organ as she reached his side.

'HAVE I TOLD you I love you, Lady Burnham?'

'Not for the past ten minutes.' Lucy side-stepped into an alcove away from the mass of chattering, laughing guests and leaned against Max for a moment. 'And I love you, too. I thought I would hate this—all these people—but it is going so well, don't you think? Not that I can recall half the names, but it doesn't seem to matter. Oh, look, your mother is talking to mine. Do you think that's safe?'

'They've been in conversation for at least ten minutes, so I think so. Although it is mainly my mother telling yours that *of course* she doesn't mind being the Dowager Countess now, given that my wife is *such* a charming girl. Which means that your mother has to tell her what I paragon I am and as a result they are in perfect harmony.'

'And the Bishop was congratulating my father on my upbringing, which has utterly dumbfounded him. Oh, look, there's Melissa waving at me from the door to the little sitting room. I'll just go and sit with her for ten minutes and get my breath back.'

It took five minutes to work her way across to the room and when she did finally reach it Melissa promptly closed the door behind her and turned the key in the lock. All four of her friends were in the room and no one else. They sat in their wedding day gowns and beamed at her.

'We thought you needed a rest,' Jane said. 'We've got tea and we promised Will to make Verity put her feet up for half an hour.'

Verity, eight months pregnant now, rolled her eyes, but her feet were obediently propped on a stool.

'Oh, bliss.' Lucy flopped into the nearest chair, and Melissa handed her a cup. 'I didn't realise how much I need this.'

'It is a lovely wedding,' Prue said. 'I cried all through the service and even Ross had to blow his nose and clear his throat and pretend he wasn't welling up.'

As her husband, Ross, the Marquis of Cranford, was a tough, scarred ex-privateer, this was, indeed, something.

'And when you threw back your veil and I saw Max's face— Oh, here I go again.' Jane produced a crumpled handkerchief.

'Put your feet up, too.' Melissa pushed a footstool across. 'You need to be well rested for your wedding night.'

'Oh, yes,' Lucy agreed.

'Your face! You smug thing, you've already been to bed with him.' Melissa was never the reticent one.

'Of course.' *Just once, although I'm not telling them any more. And now I can't wait...*

'Where are you going on your honeymoon?' Verity asked. 'Last time you said it was still a secret.'

'Max realised that he had to tell me so I had the right clothes. We're going to the new villa he has recently bought on the coast and he is going to teach me to ride and to swim.'

'Very energetic,' Melissa said with a grin.

'Don't smirk,' Verity chided. 'You, Melissa, are the last of us unmarried, so our efforts must be focused on finding you the right man and then we will all have gorgeous husbands.'

'Not me.' Melissa poured herself another cup of tea and lifted it in a toast. 'Here's to freedom. I am coming to London. Papa is letting me have the little house he has just inherited and I will write and find myself interesting and handsome lovers and be an outrageous bluestocking spinster.'

'MELISSA SAYS SHE is going to be an outrageous bluestocking spinster and live in London.' Lucy curled up against the bedhead and waited for Max who, clad in his dressing gown and little else, was rummaging in a cupboard. 'What are you doing?'

'I knew there was one in here somewhere.' He produced a blanket. 'Come on, it is a lovely night.'

'For what?' Lucy slid off the bed and found her slippers. She was disappointed—she had waited a long time, it seemed, for them to be alone—but she was also intrigued.

'Star watching.' He turned back. 'Perhaps two blankets.'

They crept down the winding stairs from his dressing room like a pair of eloping lovers and then ran across the lawn down to the edge of the little lake. Max spread out one of the blankets and they sat side by side, hands linked.

There was no breeze, the air was heavy with the day's heat and somewhere, distantly, a fox barked. A fish jumped out on the lake with a splash and above them the stars were sharp and bright in the sky.

'I am happy,' Max said. 'It isn't something one thinks about, is it? You know when you are *un*happy or afraid or bored or having fun, but being aware of simple, plain happiness is rare. There is nothing to worry about. We are safely married, tomorrow we will slip away and go south and it will be someone else's problem to worry about our guests. When we arrive at the villa there will be nothing to do but make love and enjoy ourselves and get to know each other even better.'

He lay down, pulling her with him so they lay side by side. 'Look up. There is the music of the spheres, the celestial harmonies playing for us. And down here, on earth, we can make our own music, even though I cannot play a note.'

Lucy lay and watched the stars as Max shrugged off his robe and then parted hers, baring her skin to the soft night air. He began to kiss his way down her body, his own silvered by the moonlight, making her sigh and then cry out as he found her nipples, caressed her breasts until she was shifting, writhing, the scent of crushed grass rising around them.

'Now, Max. *Now*.'

His body was warm over hers, his weight both a prison and a liberation as she rose to meet his thrust, took him in, arched to match his rhythm, stared up blindly at the cold arch of the skies above them as the magic and the music took them both.

'I love you.'

Who said that? She did not know, only that it was true and a miracle and, like Max, she was utterly, purely happy.

She came to herself to find Max wrapping her in his robe, then both of them in the second blanket.

'I am going to make love to you for as long as my strength lasts and, one day, when I am too old and decrepit to do more than remember, I will still be making love to you in my mind and my soul,' Max said.

And Lucy laid her head on his chest and heard his heart beat under her cheek, and knew it was true.

* * * * *

Rumours

Author Note

To be asked to write about a place I know well and love is a rare privilege and I did not have to think twice when it was suggested that I set a novel among the real inhabitants of Wimpole Hall, a magnificent National Trust property in Cambridgeshire, England.

Everything I read about the Yorke family, who lived at Wimpole at the beginning of the nineteenth century, convinced me they must have been delightful people and I knew my hero and heroine would relish their company, too. I hope you enjoy exploring Wimpole Hall and its lovely park alongside Isobel and Giles as they fall in love. It is a love that seems doomed, but then, as now, Wimpole Hall has a certain magic and things may not be as black as they seem!

DEDICATION

For the staff at Wimpole
who were a mine of information and
who were so patient with my endless questions.

CHAPTER ONE

February 2nd, 1801—the Old North Road,
Cambridgeshire

The chaise rattled and lurched. It was an almost welcome distraction from the stream of bright and cheerful chatter Isobel's maid had kept up ever since they left London. 'It isn't *exile* really, now is it, my lady? Your mama said you were going to rusticate in the country for your health.'

'Dorothy, I know you mean to raise my spirits, but *exile* is precisely the word for it.' Lady Isobel Jervis regarded the plump young woman with scarce-concealed exasperation. 'To call it *rustication* is to draw a polite veil over the truth. Gentlemen rusticate when they have to escape from London to avoid their creditors.

'I have been banished, in disgrace, and that is exile. If this was a sensation novel the fact that it is completely undeserved and unjust would cast a romantic glow over the situation. But this is not a novel.' She stared out through the drizzle at the gently undulating farmland rolling past the post-chaise window. In reality the injustice only increased her anger and misery.

She had taken refuge in the country once before, but that had been justified, essential and entirely her own doing. This, on the other hand, was none of those things.

'That was the sign to Cambridge we've just passed,' Dorothy observed brightly. She had been this infuriatingly jolly ever since the scandal broke. Isobel was convinced that she had not listened to a word she had said to her.

'In that case we cannot be far from Wimpole Hall.' Isobel removed her hands from under the fur-lined rug and took the carriage clock from its travelling case on the hook. 'It is almost two o'clock. We left Berkeley Street at just before eight, spent an hour over luncheon and changing horses, so we have made good time.'

'And the rain has eased,' Dorothy said, bent on finding yet another reason for joy.

'Indeed. We will arrive in daylight and in the dry.' The chaise slowed, then swung in through imposing gateposts. From her seat on the left-hand side Isobel glimpsed the bulk of a large brick inn and a swinging sign. 'The Hardwicke Arms—we are in the right place, at least.'

As they passed between the gateposts Isobel began to take more interest in the prospect from the window: it would be her home for the next two months.

The tree-dotted parkland rose gently on the left-hand side. She glimpsed a small stone building on the top of one low knoll, then, as the carriage swung round, the house came into view.

'Lawks,' Dorothy observed inelegantly.

'It *is* the largest house in the shire,' Isobel pointed out. 'I thought it might be a small palace from what Mama said, but it looks curiously welcoming, don't you think? Quite like home at Bythorn Hall.' It was no simple mansion, to be sure, but the red brick looked warm, despite the chill of the sodden February air.

The chaise drew up close to the double sweep of steps that led to the front door. *Too soon.* Isobel fought the sudden wave of panic. The Earl and Countess of Hardwicke had offered her shelter for the sake of their old friendship with her parents—Philip Yorke, the third earl, had met her father, the Earl of Bythorn, at Oxford—so they were hardly strangers, she told herself, even if she had not met them for several years.

'Be on your best behaviour, Dorothy,' she warned. 'The earl has been appointed the first Lord Lieutenant of Ireland, so he will soon be the king's representative.'

'Foreign, that's what Ireland is,' the maid said with a sniff. 'Don't hold with it.'

'It is part of the new United Kingdom,' Isobel said repressively. 'You enjoyed the celebrations at the beginning of the year, do not pretend that you did not! I must say I would like to see Dublin when the earl and countess move there in April, but they will have far more important things to worry about then than a house guest.'

In fact it was very kind of Lord Hardwicke and Elizabeth, his witty blue-stocking countess, to give sanctuary to their old friend's disgraced daughter at such a critical juncture in their lives. It might suit the Jervises to put it about that Isobel was helping the countess with her preparations, but she was sure she would be more of a distraction than a help.

She had wanted to flee to her friend Jane Needham's cheerful country manor in the depths of the Herefordshire countryside. It was remote, it was safe and it held warmth and love. But Mama had been adamant: if scandal forced her daughter to retreat from London, then she would do so, very ostentatiously, under the wing of a leading aristocratic family.

The doors opened, footmen came down the steps, and Dorothy began to gather up their scattered shawls and reticules as Isobel tied her bonnet ribbons and strove for poise.

It was too late to back away now: the carriage door was

opened, a footman offered his arm. Isobel put back her shoulders, told herself that the shivers running down her spine were due entirely to the February chill and walked up the steps with a smile on her lips.

'My dear Isobel! The cold has put roses in your cheeks—let me kiss you.' The entrance hall seemed full of people, but Lady Hardwicke's warm voice was an instant tonic, lifting spirits and nerve. 'What a perfectly ghastly day, yet you have made such good time!'

Caught before she could curtsy, Isobel returned the embrace wholeheartedly. 'Thank you, ma'am. It was an uneventful journey, but it is a great relief to be here, I must confess.'

'Now please do not *ma'am* me. Call me Cousin Elizabeth, for we are related, you know, although rather vaguely on your mother's side, it is true. Come and greet my lord. You are old friends, I think.'

'My lord.' This time she did manage her curtsy to the slender man with the big dark eyes and earnest, intelligent face. Philip Yorke was in his mid-forties, she recalled, but his eager expression made him look younger.

'Welcome to Wimpole, my dear Isobel.' He caught her hands and smiled at her. 'What a charming young woman you have grown into, to be sure. Is it really four years since I last saw you?'

'Yes, sir. After Lucas…after Lord Needham's funeral.' As soon as she said it Isobel could have bitten her tongue. Her host's face clouded with embarrassment at having reminded her of the death of her fiancé and she hurried into speech. 'It is delightful to meet you again in happy circumstances—may I congratulate you upon your appointment to the lieutenancy?'

He smiled in acknowledgement of her tact. 'Thank you, my dear. A great honour that I can only hope to be worthy of.' Behind him one of the two men standing beside the butler shifted slightly. 'You must allow me to introduce our other guests.' The earl turned to motion them forwards. 'Mr Soane, who is doing such fine work on the house for us, and Mr Harker, who is also an architect and who is assisting in some of Mr Soane's schemes for improvements in the grounds. Gentlemen, Lady Isobel Jervis, the daughter of my old friend the Earl of Bythorn.'

'My lady.' They bowed as one. Isobel was fairly certain that she had shut her mouth again by the time they had straightened up. Mr Soane was in his late forties, dark, long-faced and long-chinned, his looks distinctive rather than handsome. But Mr Harker was, without doubt, the most beautiful man she had ever set eyes upon.

Not that she had any time for handsome bucks these days, but even a woman who had vowed to spurn the male sex for ever would have had her resolution shaken by the appearance of this man. He was, quite simply, perfection, unless one would accept only blond hair as signifying true male beauty. His frame was tall, muscular and elegantly proportioned. His rich golden-brown hair was thick with a slight wave, a trifle overlong. His features were chiselled and classical and his eyes were green—somewhere, Isobel thought with a wild plunge into the poetic, between shadowed sea and a forest glade.

It was preposterous for any man to look like that, she decided while the three of them exchanged murmured greetings. It was superfluous to be quite so handsome in every feature. There must be *something* wrong with him. Perhaps he was unintelligent—but then, the earl would not employ him and Mr Soane, who had a considerable reputation to maintain and who had worked for the earl at Hammels Park before he succeeded to the title, would not associate with him. Perhaps he was socially inept, or effeminate or had a high squeaky voice or bad teeth or a wet handshake...

'Lady Isobel,' he said, in a voice that made her think of honey and with a smile that revealed perfect teeth. He took her hand in a brief, firm handshake.

Perfection there as well. Isobel swallowed hard, shocked by the sudden pulse of attraction she felt when she looked at him. A purely physical reflex, of course—she was a woman and not made of stone. He would be a bore, that was it. He would talk for hours at meals about breeding spaniels or the importance of drainage or the lesser-known features of the night sky or toadstools.

But the perfect smile had not reached his eyes and the flexible, deep voice had held no warmth. Was he shy, perhaps?

The two architects drew back as the countess gave instructions to the butler and the earl asked for details of her journey. Isobel realised she could study Mr Harker's profile in a long mirror hanging on the wall as they chatted. What on earth must it be like to be so good looking? It was not a problem that she had, for while she knew herself to be tolerably attractive—*elegant* and *charming* were the usual words employed to describe her—she was no great beauty. She studied him critically, wondering where his faults and weaknesses were hidden.

Then she saw that the remarkable green eyes were fixed and followed the direction of his gaze, straight to her own reflection in the glazing of a picture. She had been staring at Mr Harker in the most forward manner and he had been observing her do it.

Slowly she made the slight turn that allowed her to face him. Their gazes locked again as she felt a wave of complex emotion sweep through her. Physical attraction, certainly, but curiosity and a strange sense of recognition also.

His eyes, so hypnotically deep and green, held an awareness, a question and, mysteriously, a darkness that tugged
at her heart. Loneliness? Sadness? The thought flickered
through her mind in a fraction of a second before they both
blinked and she dismissed the fancy and was back with the
social faux pas of having been caught blatantly staring at
a man. A man who had been staring at her.

The polished boards did not, of course, open up and
swallow her. Isobel fought the blush that was rising to her
cheeks with every ounce of willpower at her disposal and
attempted a faint smile. They were both adult enough to
pass this off with tolerable composure. She expected to see
in return either masculine smugness coupled with flirtation or a rueful acknowledgement that they had both been
caught out staring. What she did *not* expect was to see
those complex and haunting emotions she had observed a
moment earlier turn to unmistakable froideur.

The expression on Mr Harker's face was not simply
haughty, it was cold and dismissive. There was the faintest
trace of a sneer about that well-shaped mouth. She was no
doubt intended to feel like a silly little chit making cow's
eyes at a handsome man.

Well, she was no such thing. Isobel lifted her chin and
returned his look with one of frigid disdain. *Insufferable
arrogance!* She had hardly been in the house five minutes, they had exchanged a handful of words and already
he had taken a dislike to her. She did not know him from
Adam—who was he to look at her in that way? Did he
think that good looks gave him godlike superiority and
that she was beneath him? He no doubt produced an eyeglass and studied women who interested him without the
slightest hesitation.

'Shall we go up?'

'Of course, ma'am… Cousin Elizabeth,' Isobel said with

the warmest smile she could conjure up. 'Gentlemen.' She nodded to the earl and Mr Soane who were in conversation, ignored Mr Harker, and followed her hostess through into the inner hall and up the wide staircase.

That snub on top of everything else felt painfully unjust. What was wrong with her that men should treat her so? Isobel stumbled on the first step and took herself to task. *She* had done nothing to deserve it—they were simply unable to accept that a lady might not consider them utterly perfect in every way.

There was a faint odour of paint and fresh plaster in the air and she glanced around her as they climbed. 'Mr Soane has done a great deal of work for us, including changes to this staircase,' the countess remarked as they reached the first-floor landing. She did not appear to notice that her guest was distracted, or perhaps she thought her merely tired from the journey. 'There was a window on the half landing on to an inner court and that is now filled in and occupied with my husband's plunge bath, so Mr Soane created that wonderful skylight.' She gestured upwards past pillared balconies to a view of grey scudding clouds. They passed through double doors into a lobby and left again into a room with a handsome Venetian window giving a panoramic view across the park.

'This is your sitting room. The view is very fine when the sun shines—right down the great southern avenue.' Lady Hardwicke turned, regarding the room with a smile that was almost rueful. 'This was one end of a long gallery running from back to front until Mr Soane put the Yellow Drawing Room into what was a courtyard and then, of course, the upstairs had to be remodelled. We seem to have lived with the builders for years.'

She sighed and looked around her. 'We had just got Hammels Park as we wanted it and then Philly's uncle died and he inherited the title and we had to start all over again here ten years ago.'

'But it is delightful.' Lured by sounds from next door, Isobel looked in and found that her pretty bedchamber had an identical prospect southwards.

Dorothy bobbed a curtsy as they entered and scurried through a door on the far side to carry on unpacking. Isobel saw her evening slippers already set by the fire to warm and her nightgown laid out at the foot of the bed.

'Catherine, Anne and Philip will have been sorry not to be here to greet you.' The countess moved about the room, shifting the little vase of evergreens on the mantelpiece so it reflected better in the overmantel mirror and checking the titles of the books laid out beside the bed. 'We did not expect you to make such good time in this weather so they went out after luncheon to call on their old governess in Royston.'

'Cousin Elizabeth.' On an impulse Isobel shut the connecting door to the dressing room and went to catch the older woman's hand so she could look into her face. 'I know you wrote that you believed my account of the affair—but was that simply out of your friendship for Mama? You must tell me honestly and not try to be kind. Mama insisted that you would never expose your daughters to a young woman who had participated in a veritable orgy, but I cannot help but wonder if you perhaps think that there was no smoke without some flicker of fire?

'Do you believe that I am completely innocent of this scandal? I feel so awkward, thinking you might have reservations about my contact with the girls.' She faltered to a halt, fearful that she had been gabbling. Guilt for sins past and hidden, no doubt. But this scandal was here and now and the countess, however kind, had a reputation for strict moral principles. It was said she did not even allow a beer house in the estate village.

'Of course I believe you would never do anything immoral, Isobel.' Her conscience gave an inward wince as the countess drew her to the chairs set either side of the fire. 'But your mother was so discreet I have no idea exactly what transpired. Perhaps it is as well if I know the details, the better to be prepared for any gossip.'

Isobel stared into the fire. 'When Lucas died I was twenty. I stayed in the country for almost a year with my old school friend Jane, who married Lucas's half-brother. You will recall that he drowned in the same accident. Jane was pregnant, and their home was so remote: it helped both of us to be together.

'I wanted to remain there, but Mama felt strongly that I should rejoin society last year because I had missed two Seasons. I hated it—I was older than the other girls, none of the men interested me in the slightest and I suppose I allowed it to show. I got a reputation for being cold and aloof and for snubbing gentlemen, but frankly, I did not care. I did not want to marry any of them, you see.

'Mama thought I should try again this year and, to ease me in, as she put it, I went to the Harringtons' house party at Long Ditton in January. I knew I was not popular. What I did not realise was that what might have been acceptable in a beauty with a vast fortune was merely regarded as insulting and irritating in a tolerable-looking, adequately dowered, second daughter of an earl.'

'Oh, dear,' Lady Hardwicke murmured.

'Quite,' Isobel said bitterly. 'It seems that instead of being discouraged by my snubs and lack of interest, some of the gentlemen took them as an insult and a challenge and resolved to teach me a lesson. I was sitting up reading in my nightgown late one night when the door opened and three of them pushed in. They had all been drinking, they had brought wine with them and they were bent, so they said, on "warming me up" and showing me what I had been missing.'

A log collapsed in a shower of sparks, just as one had in the moment before the door had burst open that night. 'I should have screamed, of course. Afterwards the fact that I did not seemed to convince everyone that I had invited the men there. Foolishly I tried to reason with them, send them away quietly before anyone discovered them. They all demanded a kiss, but I could see it might go further.

'I pushed Lord Halton and he collapsed backwards into a screen which smashed with the most terrific noise. When half-a-dozen people erupted into my room Halton was swigging wine from the bottle where he had fallen, Mr Wrenne was sprawled in my chair egging on Lord Andrew White—and he had me against the bedpost and was kissing me, despite my struggles.

'One of the first through the door was Lady Penelope Albright, White's fiancée. No one believed me when I said I had done nothing to encourage the gentlemen, let alone invite them to my room. Lady Penelope had hysterics, broke off the engagement on the spot and has gone into such a decline that her parents say she will miss the entire Season. Lady Harrington packed me off home at dawn the next day.'

'Oh, my dear! I could box Maria Harrington's ears, the silly peahen. Had she no idea what the mood of the party was? I suppose not, she always had more hair than wit.' Lady Hardwicke got to her feet and paced angrily to the window. 'And what now? Do your parents think this will have died down by mid-April when we go to Ireland and you return home?'

'They hope so. And I cannot run away for ever. I suppose I must face them all some day.' Isobel put a bright, determined smile on her face. The thought of going into society again was daunting. But she could not live as a recluse in Herefordshire, she had come to accept that. She had parents and a brother and sister who loved her and who had been patient with her seemingly inexplicable desire to stay away for far too long.

She might wish to be removed from the Marriage Mart, but not under these humiliating circumstances. And London, which she enjoyed for the theatres and galleries, the libraries, the shops, would become a social minefield of embarrassment and rejections.

'That is very brave,' the countess said. 'I could call out all those wretched young bucks myself—such a pity your brother is too young to knock their heads together.'

'I would certainly not want Frederick duelling at sixteen! It is not as though I feel any pressing desire to wed. If I had found a man who was the equal of Lucas and this had caused a rift with him, then I would have something to grieve over, but as it is…' *As it is I am not faced with the awful dilemma of how much of my past life to reveal to a potential husband.*

CHAPTER TWO

Isobel stared into the fire and finally said the things she had been bottling up inside. She had tried to explain at home, but it seemed her mother would never understand how she felt. 'I suppose I should be fired up with righteous indignation over the injustice of it all. I was so hurt and angry, but now I feel no spirit for the fight any more. What does it matter if society spurns me? I have not felt any burning desire to be part of it for four years.'

She bit her lip. 'The men believe I am putting on airs and think myself above them, or some such foolishness. But the truth is, even if I did wish to marry, they all fail to match up to my memories of Lucas. I still remember his kindness and his intelligence and his laugh. People say that memory fades, but I can see his face and hear his voice.'

'But you are no longer mourning him, only regretting,' the countess suggested. 'You have accepted he is gone.'

'Oh, yes. I know it, and I have accepted it. There was this great hole full of loss and pain and now it is simply an empty ache.' And the constant nagging doubt—had she done the right thing in those months after Lucas's death? The decisions had seemed so simple and yet so very, very hard.

'I do not want to go through that again. Or to settle for something less than I felt for him.' Isobel turned, reached out to the older woman. 'Do you understand? Mama does not, she says I am fanciful and not facing up to reality. She says it is my duty to marry.'

'Yes, I understand.' Lady Hardwicke gave her hand a squeeze. 'But I should not give up on men *quite* yet,' she added with a shake of her head. 'Do you mind if I tell Anne in confidence what happened at the house party? She is almost eighteen now and will be making her come-out in Dublin. She might pick up something from gossip in friends' letters and I would have her know the truth of matters. It will serve as a warning to her.'

'To fawn on young gentlemen in case they turn on her?' Isobel enquired.

'To lock her bedroom door at night and to scream the moment she feels any alarm,' the countess said with a smile.

'No, I do not mind.' Isobel returned the smile. The older woman was right to reprove her for that note of bitterness. If she became a sour old maid as a result of this, then those rakes would have made her exactly what they jeered at her for being.

'I will have tea sent up and hot water. Relax and rest until dinner time, then you will feel strong enough to face at least some of my brood. Charles and Caroline must have nursery tea and wait until the morning to meet you, but I will allow Lizzie and Catherine to have dinner with us, and Anne and Philip will be there, of course.'

'And the architects?' Isobel asked with studied nonchalance.

'Yes, they will join us. Mr Soane will travel back to London tomorrow. It is never easy to persuade him to stay away from his wife and his precious collection of art and antiquities in Lincoln's Inn Fields, but Mr Harker is staying. I confess, I wish he were not *quite* so good looking, for the girls are all eyes and attitudes whenever they see him, but to do him credit, he gives them not the slightest encouragement, which is just as well, considering who he is.'

She swept out, adding, 'Do not hesitate to ring if you need anything, my dear, I am so pleased to have you here.'

Isobel sank back into the chair, puzzled. *Who Mr Harker is? He* was an architect, but so was Mr Soane. Architects of good breeding—or even the sons of bricklayers like Mr Soane, if they were cultivated and successful—were perfectly acceptable socially, even at the dining table of an earl. Mr Harker's accent had been impeccable, his manners—if one left aside his hostile gaze—without reproach, his dress immaculate. He was a gentleman, obviously, and as eligible as a houseguest as Mr Soane. But who *was* he? Isobel shrugged. 'Why should I care?' she asked the crackling fire. 'He is insufferable whoever he is.'

THE CLOCK IN the inner hall struck seven as Isobel reached the foot of the stairs. Where was everyone? There were no footmen to be seen and the doors ahead and to the right were closed, giving her no clues.

'If you say so…' A low masculine rumble. At least two of the party were down already, she realised with relief. It was always so awkward, standing around in a house one did not know.

Isobel followed the voices into the front hall and realised they came from the rooms to the left of the entrance. The cues lying on the billiard table in the first hinted that perhaps some of the gentlemen had only recently left. The conversation was clearer now, coming from the room beyond. The door stood ajar.

'…pleasant young lady, she will be companionship for Lady Anne, no doubt.' That was Mr Soane. Isobel stopped in her tracks. Was he talking about her?

'She is a good six years older than Lady Anne,' Mr Harker replied with disastrous clarity. 'One wonders what she is doing unwed, although I imagine I can hazard a guess. She has too bold an eye—no doubt it attracts the wrong sort of attention, not honourable proposals.'

'You...' Isobel bit back the words and applied her eye to the crack between door and hinges.

'You think she might prove to be an embarrassment?' the older man asked. He sounded concerned. 'I have seen the lengths you have to go to to prevent young ladies from becoming…um, attached.'

'I have no intention of allowing her to so much as flirt with me. She was staring in the most brazen manner in the hall—presumably she thinks it sophisticated. That, or she is on the shelf and signalling that she is open to advances.'

Harker was strolling around the room, looking at the pictures that hung on the panelling. For a moment the exquisite profile came into view, then he vanished with a flick of dark blue coat tails.

You arrogant, vain swine! Isobel's fingers uncurled, itching to slap that beautiful face.

'I do hope not.' A slice of Soane's long, dark countenance appeared in the slit, furrowed by a frown. 'Lady Hardwicke would be most upset if there was any untoward flirtation. You know her reputation for high standards.'

'And it would rebound on you by association, Soane, as I am your protégé. I have no intention of risking it, have no fear. It is hardly as if she offers irresistible temptation in any case.' Both men laughed, covering Isobel's gasp of outrage.

'A pity gentlemen cannot have chaperons in the same way as the ladies,' Soane remarked. 'Being a plain man myself, I never had any trouble of that kind. Find yourself a wife, preferably a rich one, and settle down as I have, that is my advice, but I have no doubt you enjoy your freedom and your dashing widows too much, eh, Harker?'

'Far too much, sir. Besides, finding the right wife, in my circumstances, will take more application than I am prepared to expend upon it just now.'

As if anyone would have you! The words almost left Isobel's mouth as the sound of their voices faded away. Her vision was strangely blurred and it took a moment to realise it was because her eyes had filled with tears of anger and hurt. It was so unjust to be stigmatised as a flirt, or worse, simply for staring at a man. And then to be labelled as *on the shelf* and too ordinary to offer any temptation to a connoisseur, such as Mr Harker obviously considered himself to be, was the crowning insult.

It took a few moments to compose herself. Isobel turned back the way she had come, unwilling to risk walking into them again. Was that cowardice or simply the wisdom to keep well away from Mr Harker while her palm still itched to slap him?

There was a footman in the hall when she emerged. 'May I help you, my lady? The family is in the saloon, just through here, ma'am.'

Ushered back through the inner hall, Isobel found herself in a pleasant room with a large bay window. It was curtained now against the February darkness, but she assumed it would look out onto the gardens and park stretching off to the north.

The earl was poring over what looked like architectural drawings with Mr Soane and a fresh-faced youth was teasing a giggling girl of perhaps twelve years—Lord Royston and Lady Lizzie, she guessed.

The countess sat on a wide sofa with Lady Anne and her fifteen-year-old sister, Catherine, who were making a show of working on their embroidery.

Mr Soane must have come through a connecting door, but there was no sign of the viper-tongued Mr Harker. Where was he? Isobel scanned the room, conscious of butterflies in her stomach. The evidence of nerves gave her another grudge against Mr Perfection.

The children saw her first. 'Ma'am.' Philip bowed. 'Welcome to Wimpole Hall.'

'Are you our Cousin Isobel?' Lizzie was wide-eyed with excitement at being allowed to a grown-up party. Isobel felt her stiff shoulders relax. *He* was not here and the children were charming.

GILES HARKER STRAIGHTENED up from his contemplation of the collection of Roman *intaglio* seals in a small display table set against the wall. Lady Isobel had entered without seeing him and he frowned at her straight back and intricate pleats of brown hair as she spoke to Philip and Lizzie. She was a confounded nuisance, especially in a household presided over by a lady of known high standards. Lady Hardwicke's disapproval would blight his chances of commissions from any of her wide social circle. She might be a blue-stocking and a playwright, but she was the daughter of the Earl of Balcarres and a lady of principle.

The Yorke daughters were charming, modest and well behaved, if inclined to giggle if spoken to. But this distant cousin was another matter altogether. At his first sight of her a tingle of recognition had gone down his spine. She was dangerous, although quite why, Giles would have been hard pressed to define. There was something in those wide grey eyes, her best feature. Some mystery that drew his unwilling interest.

Her frank and unabashed scrutiny had been an unwelcome surprise in an unmarried lady. He was used to the giggles and batted eyelashes of the young women making their come-outs and made a point of avoiding them. His birth was impossibly ineligible, of course, even if his education, style and income gave him the entrée to most of society. But he was unmarriageable and dangerous and that, he was well aware, was dinned into the young ladies he came into contact with.

Yet those very warnings were enough to make some of them think it irresistibly romantic that the illegitimate son of the Scarlet Widow was so handsome and so unobtainable.

For certain married ladies Giles Harker was not at all unobtainable—provided his notoriously capricious choice fell on them. Something the son of the most scandalous woman in society learned early on was that one's value increased with one's exclusivity and he was as coolly discriminating in his sins as his mother was warmly generous in hers. Even in her fifties—not that she would ever admit to such an age despite the incontrovertible evidence of an adult son—her heart was broken with delicious drama at least twice a year. His remained quite intact. Love, he knew from observation, was at best a fallacy, at worst, a danger.

Lord Hardwicke and Soane straightened up from their litter of plans, young Lord Royston blushed and the countess smiled. 'Come in, my dear. Philip, bring that chair over to the sofa for Cousin Isobel.'

Giles watched as she walked farther into the room with an assurance that confirmed him in his estimate of her age. 'Thank you, Lord Royston,' she said as he brought her chair. 'And you are Lady Lizzie?'

'Yes, ma'am.'

'I think I must be Cousin Isobel to you and Philip, for your mama assures me we are all related. Will you take me and introduce me to your sisters?'

Giles let the lid of the display table drop for the last

fraction of an inch. Lady Isobel turned at the small, sharp sound. There was a friendly smile on her lips and it stayed, congealed into ice, as her gaze passed over him without the slightest sign of recognition.

A most-accomplished cut direct. It seemed an extreme reaction. He had sent her that chilling look in the hall out of sheer self-defence, as he did with any over-bold young woman who seemed interested. Mostly they took the hint and retreated blushing. This one seemed to have taken deep offence instead. She turned back and went to take her seat, sinking on to it with trained elegance.

For the first time in a long time Giles felt a stirring of interest in an utterly ineligible woman and it made him uneasy. That meeting of eyes in the hallway had been astonishing. He had intended to warn off yet another wide-eyed virgin and instead had found his snub returned with interest and hostility. Why she was so forward, and why he was so intrigued, was a mystery.

The earl began to pour drinks for the ladies without troubling to ring for a footman. Giles strolled over. 'Allow me to assist, sir.' He took the two glasses of lemonade for the youngest girls, noting how tactfully their father had used wine glasses to make them feel grown up. He came back and fetched the ratafia for Lady Anne and Lady Isobel, leaving the earl to serve his wife.

'Lady Isobel.' He proffered the glass, keeping hold of it so that she had to respond to him.

'Thank you.' She glanced up fleetingly, but did not turn her body towards him. 'Would you be so good as to put it on that side table, Mr Harker?' He might, from her tone, have been a clumsy footman.

Giles put the glass down, then spun a chair round and sat by her side, quite deliberately rather too close, to see if he could provoke her into some reaction. He was going to get to the bottom of this curiosity about her, then he could safely ignore her. As good breeding demanded, Lady Isobel shifted slightly on the tightly stuffed blue satin until he was presented with her profile.

Now she was rested from her journey she was much improved, he thought, hiding a connoisseur's assessment behind a bland social smile. Her straight nose was no longer pink at the tip from cold; her hair, freed from its bonnet, proved to be a glossy brown with a rebellious wave that was already threatening her hairpins, and her figure in the fashionable gown was well proportioned, if somewhat on the slender side for his taste.

On the other hand her chin was decided, her dark brows strongly marked and there was a tension about her face that suggested that she was braced for something unpleasant. Her mouth looked as though it could set into a firm line of disapproval; it was full and pink, but by no stretch of the imagination did the words *rosebud* or *bow* come to mind. And she was quite definitely in at least her fifth Season.

Lady Isobel took up the glass, sipped and finally turned to him with a lift of her lashes to reveal her intelligent dark grey eyes. 'Well?' she murmured with a sweetness that did not deceive him for a second. 'Have you studied me sufficiently to place me in your catalogue of females, Mr Harker? One well-bred spinster with brunette plumage, perhaps? Or do I not quite fit into a category, so you must bring yourself to converse with me while you decide?'

'What makes you think I have such a catalogue, Lady Isobel?' Giles accepted a glass of claret from the earl with a word of thanks and turned back to her. Interesting that she described herself as a spinster. She was perhaps twenty-four, he guessed, five years younger than he was. The shelf might be in sight, but she was not at her last prayers yet and it was an unusual young woman who would admit any danger that she might be.

'You are studying me with scientific thoroughness, sir. I half expect you to produce a net and a pin to affix me amongst your moth collection.'

Moth, he noted. *Not butterfly. Modesty? Or is she seeing if I can be provoked into meaningless compliments?*

'You have a forensic stare yourself, ma'am.'

Her lips firmed, just as he suspected they might. *Schoolmarm disapproval*, he thought. Or embarrassment, although he was beginning to doubt she could be embarrassed. Lady Isobel seemed more like a young matron than an unmarried girl. She showed no other sign of emotion and yet he could feel the tension radiating from her. It was strangely unsettling, although he should be grateful that his unwise curiosity had not led her to relax in his company.

'You refer to our meeting of eyes in the hall? You must be tolerant of my interest, sir—one rarely sees Greek statuary walking about. I note that you do not relish being assessed in the same way as you study others, although you must be used to it by now. I am certain that you do not harbour false modesty amongst your faults.'

The composure with which she attacked began to nettle him. After that exchange she should be blushing, fiddling with her fan perhaps, retreating from their conversation to sip her drink, but she seemed quite calm and prepared to continue the duel. It confirmed his belief that she had been sounding him out with an intention to flirt—or more.

'I have a mirror and I would be a fool to become swollen-headed over something that is due to no effort or merit of my own. Certainly I am used to stares,' he replied. 'And do not welcome them.'

'So modest and so persecuted. My heart bleeds for you, Mr Harker,' Lady Isobel said with a sweet smile and every appearance of sympathy. Her eyes were chill with dislike. 'And no doubt you find it necessary to lock your bedchamber door at night with tiresome regularity.'

'That, too,' he replied between gritted teeth, then caught himself. Somehow he had been lured into an utterly shocking exchange. A well-bred unmarried lady should have fainted dead away before making such an observation. And he should have bitten his tongue before responding to it, whatever the provocation. Certainly in public.

'How trying it must be, Mr Harker, to be so troubled by importunate members of my sex. We should wait meekly to be noticed, should we not? And be grateful for any attention we receive. We must not inconvenience, or ignore, the lords of creation who, in their turn, may ogle as much as they please while they make their lordly choices.'

Lady Isobel's voice was low and pleasant—no one else in the room would have noticed anything amiss in their conversation. But Giles realised what the emotion was that had puzzled him: she was furiously angry. With him. Simply because he had reacted coldly to her unladylike stare? Damn it, she had been assessing him like a housewife looking at a side of beef in the butchers. Or did she know who he was and think him presumptuous to even address her?

'That is certainly what is expected of ladies, yes,' he said, his own temper rising. He'd be damned if he was going to flirt and cajole her into a sweet mood, even if Lady Hardwicke noticed their spat. 'Certainly unmarried ones—whatever their age.'

Her chin came up at that. 'A hit, sir. Congratulations. But then a connoisseur such as yourself would notice only ladies who offer *irresistible temptation*. Not those who are *on the shelf and open to advances*.'

She turned her shoulder on him and immediately joined in the laughter over some jest of Philip's before he had time to react to the emphasis she had put on some of her phrases. It took a second, then he realised that she was quoting him and his conversation with Soane a few minutes earlier.

Hell and damnation. Lady Isobel must have been outside the door. Now he felt a veritable coxcomb. He could have sworn he had seen the glitter of unshed tears in her eyes. Now what did he do? His conscience stirred uneasily. Giles trampled on the impulse to apologise. It could only make things worse by acknowledging the offending words and explaining them would simply mire him further and hurt her more. Best to say nothing. Lady Isobel would avoid him now and that was better for both of them.

CHAPTER THREE

'Dinner is served, my lady.' There was a general stir as the butler made his announcement from the doorway and the party rose. Giles made a hasty calculation about seating plans and realised that ignoring Lady Isobel might be harder than he had thought.

'We are a most unbalanced table, I am afraid,' the countess observed. 'Mr Soane—shall we?' He went to take her arm and the earl offered his to Lady Isobel. Giles partnered Lady Anne, Philip, grinning, offered his arm to fifteen-year-old Catherine and Lizzie was left to bring up the rear. When they were all seated Giles found himself between Lady Isobel and Lizzie, facing the remaining Yorke siblings and Mr Soane. Conversation was inevitable if they were not to draw attention to themselves.

Lizzie, under her mother's eagle eye, was on her best behaviour all through the first remove, almost unable to speak to him with the effort of remembering all the things that she must and must not do. Giles concluded it would be kinder not to confuse her with conversation, which left him with no choice but to turn and proffer a ragout to Lady Isobel.

'Thank you.' After a moment she said, 'Do you work with Mr Soane often?' Her tone suggested an utter lack of interest. The question, it was obvious, was the merest dinner-table conversation that good breeding required her to make. After his disastrous overheard comments she would like to tip the dish over his head, that was quite clear, but she was going to go through the motions of civility if it killed her.

'Yes.' Damn it, now he was sounding sulky. Or guilty. Giles pulled himself together. 'I worked in his drawing office when I first began to study architecture after leaving university. It was a quite incredible experience—the office is in his house, you may know—like finding oneself in the midst of Aladdin's cave and never knowing whether one is going to bump into an Old Master painting, trip over an Egyptian sarcophagus or wander into a Gothic monk's parlour!

'I am now building my own practice, but I collaborate with Soane if I can be of assistance. He is a busy man and I owe him a great deal.'

Lady Isobel made a sound that might be interpreted, by the wildly optimistic, as encouragement to expand on that statement.

'He employed me when I had no experience and, for all he knew, might prove to be useless.'

'And you are not useless?' She sounded sceptical.

'No.' *Hell, sulky again.* 'I am not.' Deciding what to do with his future during that last year at Oxford had not been easy. It would have been very simple to hang on his mother's purse strings—even her notorious extravagances had not compromised the wealth she had inherited from her father, nor her widow's portion.

Somehow the Dowager Marchioness of Faversham kept the *bon ton*'s acceptance despite breaking every rule in the book, including producing an illegitimate child by her head gardener's irresistibly handsome soldier son, ten months after the death of her indulgent and elderly husband. She was so scandalous, so charming, that Giles believed she was regarded almost as an exotic, not quite human creature, one that could be indulged and permitted its antics.

'I work for my living, Lady Isobel, and do it well. And I do not relish indolence,' he added to his curt rejoinder. He would have little trouble maintaining a very full, and equally scandalous, social life at the Widow's side, but he was not prepared to follow in her footsteps as a social butterfly. Society would have to accept him as himself, and on his own terms, or go hang if they found him too confusing to pigeonhole.

'You had an education that fitted you for this work, then?' Lady Isobel asked, her tone still inquisitorial, as though she was interviewing him for a post as a secretary. Her hands were white, her fingers long and slender. She ran one fingertip along the back of the knife lying by her plate and Giles felt a jolt of heat cut through his rising annoyance with her, and with himself for allowing her to bait him.

Stop it, there is nothing special about her. Just far more sensuality than any respectable virgin ought to exude. 'Yes. Harrow. Oxford. And a good drawing master.'

Lady Isobel sent him a flickering look that encompassed, and was probably valuing, his evening attire—from his coat, to his linen, to the stick-pin in his cravat and the antique ruby cabochon ring on his finger. Her own gown and jewellery spoke of good taste and the resources to buy the best.

'What decided you on architecture?' she asked. 'Is it a family tradition?'

No, she quite certainly did not know who he was or she would never have asked that. 'Not so far as I am aware. My father was a soldier,' Giles explained. 'I did not realise at first where my talents, if I had any, might lie. Then it

occurred to me that many of the drawings in my sketch-
books were buildings, interiors or landscapes. I found I
was interested in design, in how spaces are used.' His en-
thusiasm was showing, he realised and concluded, before
he could betray anything more of his inner self, 'I wrote
to Mr Soane and he took me on as an assistant.' He lowered his voice with a glance down the table. 'He is generous to young men in the profession—I think his own sons
disappoint him with their lack of interest.'

And now, of course, many of his commissions came
from men he met socially, who appreciated his work, liked
the fact that he was 'one of them' and yet was sufficiently
different for it not to be an embarrassment to pay his account. Giles was very well aware that his bills were met
with considerably more speed than if he had been, in their
eyes, a mere tradesman. And in return, he stayed well clear
of their wives and daughters, whatever the provocation.

'So, have you built your own house, Mr Harker?'

'I have. Were you thinking of viewing it, Lady Isobel?'

'Now you are being deliberately provocative, Mr
Harker.' Her dark brows drew together and the tight social smile vanished. 'I am thinking no such thing, as you
know perfectly well. This is called *making polite conversation*, in case you are unfamiliar with the activity. You
are supposed to inform me where your house is and tell
me of some interesting or amusing feature, not make suggestive remarks.'

'Are you always this outspoken, Lady Isobel?' He
found, unexpectedly, that his ill temper had vanished, although not all his guilt. He was enjoying her prickles—it
was a novelty to be fenced with over dinner.

'I am practising,' she said as she sat back to allow the
servants to clear for the second remove. 'My rather be-
lated New Year resolution is to say what I mean. Scream

it, if necessary,' she added in a murmur. 'I believe I should say what I think to people to their faces, not behind their backs.'

Ouch. There was nothing for it. 'I am sorry that you may have overheard some ill-judged remarks I made to Mr Soane earlier, Lady Isobel. That is a matter for regret.'

'I am sure it is,' she said with a smile that banished any trace of ease that he was beginning to feel in her presence. If she could cut with a smile, he hated to think what she might do with a frown.

'However, I do not feel that any good will be served by rehearsing the reason you hold such...*ill-judged* opinions.' Giles took a firm grip on his knife and resisted the urge to retaliate. He had been in the wrong—not to feel what he did, but to risk saying it where he might be overheard. Now he must give his head for a washing. He braced himself for her next barb. 'You were telling me about your house.'

Excellent tactics, he thought grimly. *Get me off balance while you work out how to knife me again.* 'My house is situated on a small estate in Norfolk. My paternal grandfather lives there and manages it for me in my absence.' It was also close enough for him to keep an eye on his mother on those occasions she descended on the Dower House of Westley Hall for one of her outrageous parties, causing acute annoyance and embarrassment to the current marquess and his wife and scandalised interest in the village. When she was in one of her wild moods he was the only person who could manage her.

'Your father—'

'He died before I was born.' It had taken some persuasion to extract his grandfather from the head gardener's cottage at Westley and persuade him that he would not be a laughing stock if he took up residence in his grandson's new country house. 'My grandfather lives with me. His health is not as robust as it once was.' Stubborn old Joe had resisted every inch of the way, despite being racked with rheumatism and pains in his back from years of manual labour. But now he had turned himself into a country squire of the old-fashioned kind, despite grumbling about rattling around in a house with ten bedchambers. Thinking about the old man relaxed him a little.

'How pleasant for you,' Lady Isobel said, accepting a slice of salmon tart. 'I wish I had known my grandfathers. And does your mama reside with you?'

'She lives independently. Very independently.' Things were relatively stable at the moment: his mother had a lover who was a year older than Giles. Friends thought he should be embarrassed by this liaison, but Giles was merely grateful that Jack had the knack of keeping her happy even if he had not a hope of restraining her wilder starts. To give the man his due, he did try.

'She is a trifle eccentric, perhaps?'

'Yes, I think you could say that,' Giles agreed. How quickly Lady Isobel picked up the undertones in what he said— No wonder she was able to slip under his guard with such ease when she chose.

'My goodness, you look almost human when you grin, Mr Harker.' She produced a sweet smile and turned to join in the discussion about the Irish language the earl was having with his eldest daughter.

You little cat! Giles almost said it out loud.

He had succeeded—far more brutally than he had intended—in ensuring he was not going to be fending off a hand on his thigh under the dinner table, or finding an unwelcome guest in his bedchamber, but at the expense of making an enemy of a close friend of the family. Now he had to maintain an appearance of civility so the Yorkes did not notice anything amiss. He could do without this—

the tasks he had accepted to help Soane were going to be as nothing compared with the challenge of keeping his hands from Lady Isobel's slender throat if she continued to be quite so provocative.

She was idly sliding her fingers up and down the stem of her wine glass as she talked. The provocation was not simply to his temper, he feared.

Giles took a reviving sip of wine and listened to young Lizzie lecturing John Soane on the embellishments she considered would make the castle folly on the distant hill even more romantic than it already was.

That was one possibility, of course: wall up Lady Isobel in the tower and leave her for some knight in shining armour to rescue. Which was a very amusing thought, if it were not for the fact that he had a sneaking suspicion that through sheer perversity she would never wait around for some man to come to her aid. She would fashion the furniture into a ladder, climb out of the window and then come after him with a battleaxe.

She laughed and he turned to look at her, the wine glass halfway to his lips. That laugh seemed to belong to another woman altogether: a carefree, charming, innocent creature. As if feeling his regard, she turned and caught his eye and for a long moment their glances interlocked. Giles saw her lips part, her eyes darken as though something of significance had been exchanged.

A stab of arousal made him shift in his chair and the moment was lost. Lady Isobel turned away, her expression more puzzled than annoyed, as though she did not understand what had just happened.

Giles drank his wine. He knew exactly what had occurred; two virtual strangers had discovered that they were physically attracted to each other, even if one of them might not realise it and both of them would go to any lengths to deny it.

THERE WERE PEOPLE in her bedroom. Voices, too low to make out, a tug on the covers as someone bumped into the foot of the bed. Isobel opened her eyes to dim daylight and a view of lace-trimmed pillow. With every muscle tensed, she rolled over and sat up, ready to scream, her heart contracting with alarm.

There was no sign of the party of rowdy bucks who had haunted her dreams. Instead, three pairs of wide eyes observed her from the foot of the bed, one pair so low that they seemed on a level with the covers. *Children*. Isobel let out a long breath and found a smile, restraining the impulse to scoot down the bed and gather up the barely visible smallest child and inhale the warm powdered scent of sleepy infant. 'Good morning. Would one of you be kind enough to draw the curtains?'

'Good morning, Cousin Isobel,' Lizzie said. 'I knew it would be all right to wake you up. Mama said you should sleep in and eat your breakfast in your room, but I thought you would like to have it with us in the nursery.'

The contrast between her own dreams of drunken, frightening bucks invading her bedroom, of the presence of Giles Harker somewhere in the mists of the nightmare, and the wide, innocent gaze of the children made her feel as though she was still not properly awake.

'That would be delightful. Thank you for the invitation.' Isobel rubbed the sleep out of her eyes and regarded the other two children as they came round the side of the bed. 'You must be Caroline and Charles. I am very pleased to meet you.'

Charles, who was four, if she remembered correctly, regarded her solemnly over the top of his fist. His thumb

was firmly in his mouth. He shuffled shyly round the bed
to observe her more closely. Isobel put out one hand and
touched the rosy cheek and he chuckled. She fisted her
hands in the bed sheets. He was so sweet and she wanted…

Caroline beamed and dragged the wrapper off the end
of the bed. 'You'll need to put this on because the pas-
sageways are draughty. But there is a fire in the nursery.'

The children waited while she slid out of bed, put on
the robe, ran a brush through her hair and retied it into
a tail with the ribbon before donning her slippers. 'I'm
ready now.'

'We can go this way, then we will not disturb Mama.'
Lady Caroline led her out of the door on the far side of
the bedchamber, through the small dressing room and out
of another door on to what seemed to be the back stairs.
'We just go through there and up the stairs to the attic—'

There was the sound of whistling and the soft slap of
backless leather slippers on carpet. Across the landing a
shadow slid over the head of the short flight of stairs that
must lead to the suites at the back of the house. Someone
was coming. A male someone. Trapped in the doorway,
with a chattering seven-year-old in front of her, a small
boy hanging on to her skirts and Lizzie bringing up the
rear, Isobel just had time to clutch the neck of her wrapper together as Mr Harker appeared.

He stopped dead at the sight of them, his long brocade robe swinging around his bare ankles. His face was
shadowed with his unshaven morning beard, his hair was
tousled and an indecent amount of chest was showing in
the vee of the loosely tied garment. He must be naked beneath it. 'Good morning, Lady Isobel, Lady Lizzie, Lady
Caroline, Master Charles. I hope you do not represent a
bathing party.'

Cousin Elizabeth had said something about a plunge

bath in this area, so that was presumably where he was
going. He might have had the decency to have turned
on his heel the moment he saw them, Isobel thought, resentment mingling with sensations she tried hard not to
acknowledge. Now she was in the position of having to
exchange words with a scarcely clad man while she was in
her nightwear. The fact that her wrapper was both practical and all-enveloping was neither here nor there.

'We are going to the nursery for breakfast,' she said, her
gaze, after one glimpse of hair-roughened chest, fixed a
foot over his head. 'Lead the way, please, Caroline.'

'Good morning, Mr Harker,' the children chorused. Isobel scooped up little Charles as a shield and they trooped
across the landing, past the architect and through into the
sanctuary of the door to the attic stairs. She was furiously
aware that she was peony-pink and acting like a flustered
governess. All her anger-fuelled defiance of him over dinner was lost in embarrassment.

They climbed the stairs and Caroline took them around
the corner and on to a landing with a skylight overhead
and a void, edged with rails and panelled boards, in the
centre. As she tried to orientate herself Isobel realised it
must be above the inner hallway her room opened on to,
with the snob-boards to prevent the servants looking down
on their employers.

'Papa had Mr Soane make him a plunge bath in the old
courtyard that used to be behind the main stairs.' Lizzie
waved a hand in the general direction. 'I think it would
be great fun to learn to swim in it, but Mama says it is for
Papa to relax in, not for us to splash about.'

*Now I have the mental picture of Mr Harker floating
naked in the warm water... Thank you so much, Lizzie.*

'Here we are. This is where Caroline and I sleep, and
here is Charles's room and here is the nursery. Nora, we

have brought Lady Isobel, I told you she would like to have breakfast with us.'

A skinny maid bobbed a curtsy. 'Oh, Lady Lizzie! I do hope it is all right, my lady, I said you'd be wanting to rest, but off they went...'

'That is quite all right. I would love to have breakfast here.' The children and their staff appeared to occupy this entire range of south-facing rooms with wonderful views over the long avenue and the park towards Royston. A pair of footmen carried in trays. Charles twisted in her arms and she made herself put him down.

'I told them to bring lots of food because we had a special guest. Those are my designs for the tower—Mr Soane says I show a flair for the dramatic,' Lizzie pronounced, pointing at a series of paintings pinned on the wall. 'I expect I get that from Mama. She writes plays, you know and sometimes when we have a house party they are acted in the Gallery. Papa says she is a veritable blue-stocking. We will go for a walk this morning and I will show you the tower.' Lizzie finally ran out of breath, or perhaps it was the smell of bacon that distracted her.

'That would be very pleasant, provided your mama does not need me.' Isobel sat down at the table. 'It would be wonderful to get out in the fresh air and it looks as though the morning will be sunny, which is such a relief after yesterday's drizzle.' And there was the added advantage that if she was out of the house she would be at a safe distance from Mr Harker's disturbing presence.

While she ate she contemplated just how maddening he was. He was arrogant, self-opinionated, far too aware of his own good looks, shockingly outspoken and did not do his robe up properly. He was, in fact, just like the drunken bucks at the house party, only sober, which was no excuse, for that meant he should know better. He also made her feel strangely unsettled in a way she had almost forgotten she could feel. There was no doubting that his relaxed, elegant body would strip to perfection, that his skin would feel—

Isobel bit savagely into a slice of toast and blackcurrant conserve. What was the use of men except to make women's lives miserable? She contemplated Master Charles, chubby-cheeked, slightly sticky already, full of blue-eyed innocence. Little boys were lovely. She felt a pang at the thought of what she was missing.

Kind fathers and husbands like her own papa, or Lord Hardwicke, were obviously good men. Lucas had been almost perfect. But how on earth was one to tell what a candidate for one's hand would turn out to be like? Most males, by the time they turned eighteen, appeared to be rakehells, seducers, drinkers, gamblers...

Perhaps she could become an Anglican nun. They did have them, she was sure, and it sounded safe and peaceful. A mental image of Mr Harker, laughing himself sick at the sight of her in a wimple, intruded. She would look ridiculous and she would be quite unsuited to the life. Besides, she would not be free to travel, to visit Jane and the children. An eccentric spinster then. She had enough money.

Only she did not *want* to be a spinster. She would rather like to fall in love again with a good man and marry. Her daydream stuttered to a halt: he would doubtless want children. But where did she find one she could trust with her heart and all that was most precious to her? And even if she did find this paragon, was he going to want her when he knew the truth about her?

CHAPTER FOUR

'More coffee, Cousin Isobel?'

'Thank you, Lizzie.' Her mind was going round in circles. Isobel forced herself into the present. 'At what time shall we go for our walk?'

'Shall I meet you in the garden at ten o'clock?' the girl suggested. 'I must explain to Miss Henderson, my governess, that I am going on an educational nature expedition with you.'

'You are?'

'There are the lakes—we will see all kinds of wild birds,' Lizzie said with irrefutable logic. Isobel found herself experiencing a pang of sympathy for the unfortunate Miss Henderson.

A VISIT TO Lady Hardwicke's unusual semi-circular sitting room, almost next to her own, reassured Isobel that her hostess did not require her assistance, and that Lizzie was permitted to escape from French conversation for one morning.

Isobel snuggled her pelisse warmly around herself as she stepped out into the garden that lay between the north front and the parkland. It wanted at least fifteen minutes until ten o'clock and there was no sign of Lizzie yet. The bleak, wintry formal beds held little attraction, but the shrubbery that lay to one side behind the service wing looked mysterious and worthy of exploration.

A glimpse of a small domed roof intrigued her enough to brave the dense foliage, still dripping on to the narrow paths after yesterday's drizzle. The building, when she reached it down the twisting paths, was small, low and angular with an odd dome and no windows that she could see. It looked vaguely classical, but what its function might be, she had no idea. The gloomy shrubbery seemed an odd place for a summer house. Perhaps it was an ice house.

Isobel circled the building. Under her boots the leaf mould yielded damply, muffling her footsteps as she picked her way with caution, wary of slipping.

The sight of a pair of long legs protruding from the thick clump of laurel bush that masked the base of the structure brought her up short. The legs were visible from midthigh, clad in brown buckskin breeches. The polished boots, smeared with mud, were toes down—their owner must be lying on his stomach. As she stared there was a grunt from the depths of the bush—someone was in pain.

A keeper attacked by poachers? A gardener who had fainted? Isobel bent and pushed aside the branches with her hands. Even as she crouched down she realised that gamekeepers and gardeners did not wear boots of such quality. She slipped, landed with an ungainly thump, threw out a hand and found she was gripping one hard-muscled, leather-clad thigh.

'Oh! Are you all right?' The man was warm at least— perhaps he had not lain there very long. There did not seem to be any room to move away now she was crouched under the thick evergreen foliage.

The prone figure rolled over and she went with him in a tangle of thin branches to find herself flat on her back, her body pinned under the solid length of a man who was quite obviously neither fainting nor wounded, but very much in possession of his senses. All of them.

'My dear Lady Isobel, have you come to assist me with the plumbing?' Harker drawled as he looked down at her through the green-shadowed gloom. After a fraught moment he raised his weight off her and on to his elbows.

'Plumbing?' Isobel stared at him. 'What on earth are you talking about? Let me go this—ouch!'

'You are lying on a hammer,' he explained. 'If you will just move your shoulder a trifle… There. Is that more comfortable?'

'No, it is not. Will you let me up this instant, Mr Harker!'

'The ground is quite dry under these evergreens and you are lying on sacking.' There was the hint of a smile tugging at one corner of those sculpted lips. 'You are being very demanding—I really do not feel you can expect anything better if you will insist on an alfresco rendezvous with me in early February.'

Isobel tried to sit up and succeeded merely in pressing her bosom against his chest. Harker's eyes darkened and the twitch of his lips became an appreciative smile. She fell back, opened her mouth to scream and then remembered Lizzie—the last thing she wanted was to frighten the child by bringing her to this scene.

Furious at her own powerlessness, she put up her hands and pushed against his shoulders. He did not shift. Isobel felt her breath become shorter. *Oh, the humiliation*—she was positively panting now and he doubtless thought it was with excitement. Even more mortifying was the realisation that he would be right—her instincts were responding and she *was* finding this exciting. This was her punishment for daydreaming about his body. The reality was just as deliciously hard and lean and—

'Get off!' She felt aroused, flustered and indignant, but

she did not feel afraid, she realised as the green eyes studied her. 'I have not the slightest intention nor desire of making a rendezvous with you, Mr Harker, inside or outside.'

'Then whose thigh did you think you were fondling?' he asked with every appearance of interest.

'*Fondling?* How dare you! I lost my balance.' The feel of those taut muscles under the leather was imprinted on her memory. 'I thought a gardener had fainted, or hit his head, or a gamekeeper had been attacked by poachers or something.' His body was warm and hard and seriously disturbing to a lady's equilibrium, pressed against her just there…and the wretch knew it. He shifted slightly and smiled as she swallowed. Oh, yes, he was finding this *very* interesting. No doubt she should be flattered.

'And there I was, thinking that the sight of me in my dressing gown was enough to lure young ladies into a damp shrubbery,' Harker said. 'I was, of course, about to decline what I assumed was your most flattering offer.'

'Decline?' She stared at him. That he could imagine for one moment that she had actually followed him there in order to…to…canoodle… Indignation became fury. 'Why—?'

'Why? Because well-bred virgins are far more trouble than they are worth.'

'Oh!' The insufferable arrogance of the man!

'This is probably madness, but as we are here, it seems a pity to waste the moment.' She realised too late that her hands were still on his shoulders and tried to pull herself away, but there was nowhere to go. He bent his head and took her mouth, all with one smooth, well-practised movement.

The last man to kiss her had been both drunk and clumsy. Harker was neither. His mouth was hot and demanding and sent messages straight to her belly, straight to her breasts, as though wires connected every nerve and he was playing with them. Panic at her own response threatened for a fleeting moment and then she got one hand free, twisting as she did so. The smack of her palm against the side of his face was intensely satisfying.

'You...you *bastard*,' she spat, the moment he lifted his head. The word seemed to rock him off balance. The green eyes darkened, widened and he pushed himself up and away from her. The wave of anger brought her to her feet, shoving against him for balance as she crashed out of the shrubs onto the path. 'Is this revenge because I took you to task for your insulting words to Mr Soane last night? You arrogant, lustful, smug *bastard*!' It was a word she never used, a word she loathed, but now she threw it at him like a weapon.

'Cousin Isobel? Are you in the shrubbery?' Lizzie's voice sounded as though she was coming towards them.

'Stay there,' Isobel said fiercely, jabbing a finger at him. 'Just you stay there.' Harker straightened up, one hand rubbing his reddening cheek, his mouth twisted into a rueful smile. The mouth whose heat still seemed to burn her own.

Isobel turned on her heel and almost ran along the twisting path to meet the child. The tug of the ribbons at her throat stopped her in time to rescue her bonnet. She brushed leaf mould from her skirts, took a deep breath and stepped out onto the lawn.

'Here I am. I went exploring.' Somehow her voice sounded normal, if a little over-bright.

'Oh, I expect you found the Water Castle. *Castello d'Aqua*, Mr Soane calls it. He had it built to supply the boiler when the plunge bath was put in, but it hasn't been working very well.' Lizzie chattered on as she led the way across the garden and out of the gate into the park. 'Papa said the pressure was too low and the steward should call a plumber, but Mr Harker said he'd see if he could free up the valve, or something. I expect having a bath this morning reminded him.'

That must have been what he was doing in the bushes, not lying in wait for passing females to insult. Apparently he could manage to do that with no prior warning whatsoever.

They let themselves out of the iron garden gates and Lizzie led the way across the park that lay between the house and the hill surmounted by the folly tower. A small group of deer lifted their heads and watched them warily.

'What a delightful park.' Isobel kept her side of the conversation going while she forced her somewhat-shaky legs to keep up with Lizzie's exuberant pace.

Harker had leapt to the most indecent conclusion about her motives—her desires, even. He had not let her get more than a word out, he had taken advantage of her in the most appalling way.

She had stood up to him last night—was this then to be her punishment? To be taken for a lightskirt? Or was this insult simply retaliation for her refusal to meekly treat him as wonderful? That made him no better than those wretched bucks who had invaded her bedroom and she realised that that was disappointing. Somehow, infuriating though he was, she had expected more of him.

She had responded to him, she thought, incurably honest, as she trudged in Lizzie's exuberant wake through a gate and across a narrow brick bridge crossing a deep stock ditch. Had he realised? Of course he had—he was experienced, skilful and had slept with more women than she had owned pairs of silk stockings. So now she could add humiliation to the sensations that would course through her when she next saw Mr Harker and he, no doubt, would

use it to torment her mercilessly for as long as the game
amused him.

She toyed with the idea of telling Cousin Elizabeth,
then realised that she did not come out of the incident well
herself, not unless she was prepared to colour the encounter so she appeared a shrinking violet and he a ravisher.

'See—is it not splendid?' Lizzie gestured to the tower
and ragged length of curtain wall that crowned the far hill.
'But I think Papa should have Mr Soane build an entire
castle. Or Mr Harker could do it. He is younger so perhaps
he is more romantic. It would not be an extravagance, for
all the gamekeepers and under-keepers could live in it,
which would be a saving in cottages.'

'Do you not think the keepers might find it uncomfortable?' Isobel enquired as they took the winding sheep path
down towards the sheet of water. She resisted the temptation to remark that, in her opinion, Mr Harker was as romantic as a ravaging Viking horde.

'That had not occurred to me. You are very practical,
Cousin Isobel.' Practicality did not seem to appeal much
to Lizzie. She frowned, but her brow cleared as the lake
opened out in a shallow valley before them. A long narrow ribbon of water ran away to their right. Ahead and to
the left was a smaller, wider lake.

'When Mr Repton was here to do the landscaping he
said we should have a ship's mast on the bank of the lower
lake.'

'A rowing boat or a skiff, you mean?'

'No, a proper big ship's mast so the tops of the sails
would be seen from the house and it would look as though
there was an ocean here.' Lizzie skipped down the somewhat muddy path. 'Papa said it was an extravagant folly.
But I think it would be magnificent! I liked Mr Repton,

but Papa says he has expensive ideas, so Mr Sloan and Mr Harker have come instead. You see, there is a bridge here.'

As they got closer Isobel could see that the valley had been dammed and that the smaller lake was perhaps fifteen feet above the lower one, with a bridge spanning the point where the overflow ran from one to the other.

Lizzie gestured expansively. 'Mr Repton said we need a new bridge in the Chinese style.' She ran ahead and leaned over the rail to look into the depths below.

Isobel dragged her mind away from trying to decide whether she ought to tell Cousin Elizabeth about Mr Harker's kiss, however badly it made her appear. 'That does look a trifle rickety. Do be careful. Lizzie!'

As she spoke the rail gave a crack, splintered and gave way. Lizzie clung for a moment, then, with a piercing shriek, tumbled into the water and vanished under the surface.

'Lizzie!' Isobel cast off her bonnet and pelisse as she ran. 'Help! Help!' But even as she shouted she knew they had seen no one at all in the broad sweep of park, let alone anyone close enough to help.

Could the child swim? But even if she could, the water was cold and muddy and goodness knew how deep. There were bubbles rising, but no sign of Lizzie. Isobel ran to the edge, waded in and forced her legs, hampered by her sodden skirts, through the icy water. She couldn't swim, but perhaps if she held on to the bridge supports she could reach out a hand to Lizzie and pull her up.

Without warning the bottom vanished beneath her feet. Isobel plunged down, opened her mouth to shriek and swallowed water. Splinters pierced her palm and she lost her hold on the wooden supports. The light was blotted out as the lake closed over her head.

GILES CURSED UNDER his breath and held the grey gelding to an easy canter up the sweeping slope. Had he completely misread her? Had Lady Isobel simply chanced to come upon him in the shrubbery and lost her balance as she maintained? He had thought it a trick to provoke him into kissing her and that her protests had been merely a matter of form. But now his smarting cheek told him her protests had been real enough. So had her anger last night. He had let his desires override his instincts and he had completely mishandled the situation.

Bastard. He had learned to accept and ignore that word, to treat it with amusement. But for some reason it had stung more from her lips than the flat of her hand on his cheek had done

He should seek her out and apologise. *Hell.* If he did, then she would either slap his face again or she would be all too forgiving and…and might kiss him again with that delicious mixture of innocent sensuality and fire.

No. Too dangerous. Concentrate on work and forget one provoking and unaccountably intriguing woman who, it was becoming painfully clear, he did not understand. She was no schoolroom miss—she would soon forget it, or at least pretend to.

He reined in as the grey reached the earthworks that marked the base of the old windmill. From here there was a fine view north over the lakes to the Gothic folly and, stretching south along the edge of the woodland, an avenue of trees leading to his destination, the Hill House.

The avenue stretched wide and smooth, perfect for a gallop. Giles gathered up the reins, then stopped at the sound of a faint shriek. A bird of prey? A vixen? He stood in his stirrups and scanned the parkland. There was nothing to be seen.

'Help!' It was faint, but it was clear and repeated, coming from the direction of the lakes. A woman's voice. Giles dragged the gelding's head round and spurred down the slope, heedless of wet grass, mud and thorn bushes. The deep stock ditch opened up before them and the grey gathered his hocks under him and leapt, then they were thundering down towards the lake.

As Giles reined in on the flat before the dam he could see no signs of life—only a bonnet and pelisse lying discarded at the water's edge.

There were footprints in the mud, small woman's prints, and a disturbance, bubbles, below the centre of the bridge where the rail was broken. Giles flung himself out of the saddle, wrenched off his coat and boots and strode into the lake. The muddy water churned and two figures broke the surface for a few moments, the larger flailing desperately towards the bridge supports, the smaller limp in her grasp before they sank again. Lady Isobel and Lizzie.

It took a dozen strokes to reach them. Giles put his head down and dived under, groped through the muddy water and touched a hand, so cold that for a moment he thought it was a fish. He kicked and broke the surface hauling the dead weight of both woman and child after him.

'Take her,' Isobel gasped as they broke the surface and she thrust the child's body into his reaching arms. When he tried to take hold of her too, she resisted. 'No, there's weed tangled round her. I couldn't… You'll need both hands to pull her free.'

Treading water, Giles wrenched and tugged and the slight body was suddenly floating in his arms. 'Hang on!' he ordered Isobel as though he could keep her afloat by sheer force of will. He towed Lizzie back to the shore, dumped her without ceremony and turned back to Isobel. She had vanished.

CHAPTER FIVE

Numb, shaking with cold and fear for Isobel, Giles launched himself back into the water in a shallow dive. She was beyond struggling now as he caught one slender wrist and pulled her, gasping and choking, back to the surface again.

As soon as they reached the shallows she managed to raise herself on hands and knees and shake off his hold. 'Go and see if she's breathing. Help her—I can manage.'

Giles stumbled to the shore and dragged Lizzie farther up onto the grass, turned her over his knee and slapped her hard between the shoulder blades. 'Come on, breathe!' She coughed, retched up quantities of muddy water, then began to cry.

'Lizzie, it is all right, Mr Harker rescued us,' a hoarse voice croaked beside him. 'Come here now, don't cry.' Somehow Isobel had crawled up the bank to gather the child in her arms, petting and soothing. 'There, there. We'll get you home safe to your mama, don't worry.'

Giles found his coat and wrapped it round them. Lady Isobel's hair hung in filthy sodden curtains around her face, her walking dress clung like a wet blanket to her limbs and she was shuddering with cold, but her voice was steady as she looked up at him. 'Please, go for help,

Mr Harker.' She dragged the coat off her own shoulders and around the child.

He stared at her for a moment, a bedraggled, exhausted Madonna, somehow the image of desperate motherhood and feminine courage. 'Felix will take all of us at a walk, it will be faster.' He dragged on his boots and unsaddled the gelding to make room for the three of them. 'Let me get you up first, then I'll hand Lizzie to you. Can you manage?'

Lady Isobel let him drag her to her feet, then boost her onto the horse. She ignored the display of bare flesh as her skirts rode up her legs and held out her hands to steady Lizzie as the child was put in front of her. Giles vaulted up behind.

Felix, well trained and willing, plodded up the slope with his burden while Giles tried to hold Isobel and Lizzie steady as their shivering increased. Through his own wet shirt he could feel how cold Lady Isobel was growing, but she did not complain. He could hear her murmuring reassurance to Lizzie, the words blurred as she tried to control her chattering teeth.

'Thank God you can swim,' he said as the house came in sight. He steered Felix towards the service wing where there would be plenty of strong hands to help.

'I c-can't.'

'Then why the hell did you go in?' Giles demanded, his voice roughened with shock.

'I th-thought I might be able to reach her if I held on to the bridge supports. She did not c-come up, you see. By the time I had got to the house and brought help she would have drowned. But the bottom shelved and I was out of my depth—as I went down I found her.' She broke off, coughed, and he did his best to support her until the racking spasms ceased. 'I untangled enough of the weed to push us up to the surface, but then I could not keep us there.'

Every other female of his acquaintance would have stood on the lakeside and screamed helplessly while the child drowned. 'Isobel, that was very brave.'

She did not react to the way he addressed her—she was probably beyond noticing such things. 'There didn't seem to be any other option—she was my responsibility.' The retort held a ghost of her tart rejoinders of the night before and Giles smiled with numb lips even as a pang of shame reminded him how easily he had judged this woman.

She seemed to slump and Giles tightened his arms around them. 'Steady now.' Isobel let her head fall back on his shoulder and she leaned against him as though seeking for the slight heat he could give her. He wanted to rip off their clothes, hold her against his bare flesh to force his remaining warmth into her. 'Almost there now, my brave girl.'

As they rode into the yard the boot boy gawped, a scullery maid dropped an armload of kindling, but one of the footmen ran forwards shouting, 'Here! Everyone—quick— and bring blankets! Hurry!'

Hands reached for Lizzie and Isobel and he let them be taken before he threw a leg over Felix's withers, dropped to the ground and ran to find the countess.

ISOBEL RATHER THOUGHT she had fainted. One minute she was held against Mr Harker's comfortingly broad chest, and he was calling her his brave girl, the next hands were lifting her down and then she found herself in the countess's sitting room with Cousin Elizabeth ordering hot baths and towels and more coals for the fire and no recollection of how she had got there.

'I'm sorry,' she managed to say when the hubbub subsided enough to make herself heard. Her voice sounded raspy and her throat was sore. 'The rail on the bridge broke and Lizzie tumbled in. Mr Harker…'

Mr Harker had saved her and the child. She looked at Lizzie, white-faced, her vulnerable, naked body and thin little arms making her look much younger than her years. She wanted to hold her, convince herself the child was safe, but that was not her right. Lizzie had her mother to hold and comfort her. Her mother was with her, every day, saw every change in her growing child, felt every emotion…

'Mr Harker said you went in after Lizzie even though you cannot swim,' Cousin Elizabeth said. She looked up from the tub where she was on her knees helping the nursery nurse rub her daughter's pale limbs amidst clouds of steam. Isobel blinked back the tears that had blurred her vision and with them the pang of jealousy towards the older woman with her happy brood of children all around her. 'She owes her life to you both.' The shock was evident on the countess's strained face, even though she managed to keep her voice steady.

'Let me help you into the bath.' Lady Anne, who had been peeling off Isobel's sodden, disgusting clothes, pulled her to her feet and urged her towards the other tub set before the fire. 'Papa insisted on sending his valet to look after Mr Harker. Tompkins went past just now muttering about the "State of Sir's Breeches" in capital letters. One gathers that Mr Harker's unmentionables may never be the same again.'

As Anne must have intended, the women all laughed and Isobel felt herself relax a little as she slid into the hot water. To her relief Lizzie began to talk, her terrifying brush with death already turning into an exciting adventure. 'And Mr Harker galloped up like a knight in shining armour and dived into the lake…'

He must have done—and acted without hesitation—or neither of them would be here now. He might be a rake, and an arrogant one at that, but he had been brave and effective. And kind in just the right way: brisk and bracing enough to keep them both focused.

Isobel bit her lip as Anne helped her out of the tub and into the embrace of a vast warm towel. She was going to have to thank Mr Harker, however hard that would be. 'Sit by the fire and let me rub your hair dry,' Anne said as she and the maid enveloped Isobel in a thick robe.

Finally Lizzie was bundled off to bed. Her mother stopped by Isobel's chair and stooped to kiss her cheek. 'Thank you, my dear, from the bottom of my heart. Will you go to bed now?'

'No. No, I want to move around, I think.' She was filled with panic at the thought of falling asleep and dreaming of that black, choking water, the weed like the tentacles of a sea monster, her fear for the child. As Lizzie had slid through her hands she had thought she had lost her. She shuddered. To lose a child was too cruel and yet they were so vulnerable. *No, stop thinking like that.*

'If you are sure.' The countess regarded her with concern. 'You are so pale, Isobel. But very well, if you insist. Perhaps you could do something for me—I know my husband will have said all that is proper, but will you ask Tompkins to tell Mr Harker that I will thank him myself tomorrow? For now I must stay with Lizzie.'

'Yes, of course. As soon as I am dressed,' Isobel promised. Anne pressed a cup of tea into her hands and stood behind her to comb out her hair.

'Mr Harker is very handsome, don't you think?' the younger girl remarked as soon as they were alone.

'Oh, extraordinarily so,' Isobel agreed. To deny it would be positively suspicious. 'Although I find such perfection not particularly attractive—quite the opposite, in fact. Do you not find his appearance almost chilly? I cannot help but wonder what lies behind the mask.' What was he hiding behind that handsome face? Puzzling over his motives kept drawing her eyes, her thoughts, to him. He had courage and decision, he was beautiful, like a predatory animal, but he was also rude, immoral…

'How exciting to have your come-out in Dublin,' she said, veering off the dangerous subject of rakish architects. 'And with your papa representing his Majesty, you will be invited to all the very best functions.'

The diversion worked. Anne chatted happily about her plans and hopes while Isobel let the strength and courage seep slowly back into her as the warmth gradually banished the shivers.

Mr Harker's rooms would be on the north side of the house, judging by his appearance en route to the plunge bath. There were three suites on the northern side and the westernmost one of those belonged to the earl. So by deduction Harker must be in either the centre or the eastern one. Isobel hesitated at her sitting-room door and was caught by Dorothy as her maid bustled past with an armful of dry towels.

'Lady Isobel! How did you get yourself dressed again? You should be in your own bed and wrapped up warm. Come along, now, I'll tuck you up and fetch some nice hot milk.'

'I would prefer to warm myself by exploring the house a little and for you to see what can be done with my walking dress. I fear it must be ruined, but I suppose it might be salvageable.'

There was a moment when Isobel thought Dorothy was

going to argue, then she bobbed a curtsy and retreated to the dressing room with pursed lips, emanating disapproval.

Isobel's footsteps were muffled as she crossed the landing. Somehow that made the nerves knotting her stomach worse, as though she was creeping about on some clandestine mission. But she had to thank Mr Harker for saving her life and she had to do that face-to-face or she would be uncomfortable around him for her entire stay at Wimpole. It did not mean that she forgave him for that kiss, or for his assumptions about her.

It occurred to Isobel as she lifted her hand to knock on the door of the central suite that this visit might reinforce those assumptions, but she was not turning back now.

She rapped briskly. A voice within, somewhat smothered, called 'Come!' Isobel rapped again. The door opened with a impatient jerk and Mr Harker stood on the threshold, a towel in his hand, his damp-darkened hair standing on end. He was in his shirt sleeves, without his neckcloth. Like this he seemed inches bigger in both height and breadth.

'Isobel?'

'Do not call me—' She took a breath, inhaled the scent of sandalwood and soap and moderated her tone. She was here to make peace, she reminded herself, not to lash out to prove to herself just how indifferent she was to him. 'I have a message from the countess and something I wish to say on my own account. Lady Hardwicke wants very much to thank you herself, but she feels she must be with Lizzie today and she hopes you will understand if she does not speak with you until tomorrow. I think you may imagine her emotions and will therefore forgive her sending a message.'

He tossed the towel away towards the corner of the room without taking his eyes from her face. 'I do not need

thanking and certainly do not expect her to leave the child
in order to do so. How is Lady Lizzie?'

'Much better than one might expect, after that experience. She will be perfectly all right, I believe.' She could
turn tail and go now. Isobel took a deep breath instead.
'And I, too, must thank you, Mr Harker, on my own account. I owe you my life.'

'I was in the right place to hear you, that is all. Anyone would have done the same.' He frowned at her. 'You
should not be here.'

For him to be preaching the proprieties was intolerable!
'Please, do not be afraid I have come with any improper
purpose, Mr Harker. Surely even your elevated sense of
self-esteem would not delude you into thinking that after
this morning's experiences I have either the desire or the
energy to attempt to seduce you.'

The acid in her tone made him blink and the sweep of
those thick dark lashes did nothing to moderate her irritation with him. 'Rest assured,' she added rather desperately, 'I have no intention of crossing the threshold. Your...
virtue is perfectly safe.'

He studied her in silence for a moment. Isobel pressed
her lips together to control the other things she would very
much like to say on the subject of men who made assumptions about ladies with no evidence and then discussed
them with their friends and then ravished them in wet
shrubberies and made them feel...made them...

'What a relief,' he said finally. 'I was about to scream
for help.' She glared at him. 'However, I believe I have an
apology to make.'

'Oh? So you are sorry for that outrage in the shrubbery,
are you?' It was very hard to hang on to a sense of gratitude when the wretch stood there, the gleam in his eyes
giving the lie to any hint of penitence in his voice.

'I am sorry for coming to an incorrect conclusion about your intentions. I cannot be sorry for the kiss, for I enjoyed it too much.'

'If that is intended to flatter, Mr Harker, it failed. I imagine you enjoy virtually any kisses you can snatch.' She should turn on her heel and walk away, but it was impossible to leave him before she had made her indifference to him clear beyond any possible doubt. It was very strange—the last time she had felt this stubborn and light-headed had been after an incautious second glass of champagne on an empty stomach.

'I do not find you in the slightest bit attractive and, even if I did, my upbringing and my personal standards would prevent me acting in any way that might hint at such foolishness,' she stated, crossing her fingers tightly in the folds of her skirt. 'If your delusions about your personal charms have suffered a correction, I can only be glad of it for the sake of other females you may encounter.' It must be the effect of expressing her irritation so freely, but she was feeling positively feverish. Isobel shivered.

Instead of taking offence at her lecture, or even laughing at her, Harker took a step closer, his face serious. 'Why are you not in your bed, Isobel?'

'Because I do not need to mollycoddle myself. And grateful as I am to you for rescuing me, I did not give you the use of my name.'

'If you desire to thank me for getting wet on your behalf, I wish you will let me use it. My name is Giles and I make you free of that,' he said as he lifted one hand and laid the back of it against her cheek. 'You are barely warm enough, Isobel. I am sorry for this morning, and last night. I have become…defensive about single ladies. I was wrong to include you with the flirts and, worse, upon no more evidence than a very frank stare and a willingness to stand up to me.'

Somehow his hand was still against her cheek, warm and strangely comforting, for all the quiver of awareness it sent through her. If her limbs felt so leaden that she could not move, or brush away his hand, then at least she could speak up for herself. 'Surely you are not so vain as to believe that good looks make you somehow superior and irresistible to women? That every lady who studies your profile or the width of your shoulders desires you?' Oh, why had she mentioned his shoulders? Now he knew she had been looking.

He did not take her up on that revealing slip. 'Unfortunately there are many who confuse the outer form, over which I have no control, and for which I can claim no credit, for the inner character. And, it seems, there are many ladies who would welcome a certain amount of… adventure in their lives.' He shrugged. 'Men are just as foolish over a pretty face, uncaring whether it hides a vacuous mind or fine intelligence. You must have observed it. But the pretty young ladies are chaperoned,' he added with a rueful smile.

'And no one protects the handsome men?' Isobel enquired. She had managed to lift her hand to his, but it stayed there instead of obeying her and pushing his fingers away. She felt very strange now, not quite in her own body. There was a singing in her ears. She forced herself to focus. 'You are telling me that you are the victim here?'

'We men have to look after ourselves. I am vulnerable, certainly. If I acquire a reputation for flirting, or worse, with the unmarried daughters of the houses where I work, I will not secure good commissions at profitable country estates.' His mouth twisted wryly. 'Repelling single young ladies has become second nature and a certain cynicism about the motives of those who show an interest is, under the circumstances, inevitable.'

'What circumstances?'

Giles had caught her left hand in his, his fingers long and strong as they enveloped it. 'You do not know? Never mind.' Isobel thought about persisting, then restrained herself—probably this was something that would reveal her as painfully naive. Giles drew her closer and slid his hand round to tip up her chin. 'You are exhausted and probably in a state of shock. Why will you not rest?'

'I do not want to dream,' Isobel confessed. 'I have night…' The man must be a mesmerist, drawing confessions out of her as she stood there, handfast with him. She should go at once, stop talking to him about such personal matters. If only her body would obey her, because she wanted to go. She really wanted…

'You suffer from nightmares?'

'When I have a lot on my mind.' Her voice sounded as though it was coming from a long way away. She stared at Giles Harker, who was moving. Or perhaps the room behind him was. It began to dawn on her that she was going to faint.

'You are in no fit state—' Harker caught her as her knees gave way and gathered her against his chest. He ought to put her down because this was improper. She should tell him… But he was warm and strong and felt safe. Her muddled brain questioned that—Giles Harker was not safe, was he?

There was the sound of footsteps on the great staircase below them, muted voices carrying upwards. Giles stepped back into his room, pulling her with him, and closed the door. 'Damn it, I do not want us found by a brace of footmen with you draped around my neck and me half dressed.' His voice was very distant now.

'Put me down, then,' Isobel managed as she was lifted and carried into another room, deposited on something. A bed?

'Stay there.'

'I do not think I could do anything else…' It was an effort to speak, so she lay still until he came back and spread something warm and soft over her.

'Go to sleep, Isobel. If any nightmares come, I will chase them away.'

He will, promised the voice in her head. It was telling her to just let go, so she did, and slid into a darkness as profound as the blackness of the lake water.

CHAPTER SIX

Giles locked the door from his dressing room on to the landing and studied the sleeping woman stretched out on the chaise. Isobel must be utterly drained to have fainted like that. He supposed he should have done something, anything, rather than carry her into his room, but it was a trifle late to worry about that now and they were probably safe enough. The family would be too concerned about Lizzie to wonder where their guest had got to and his borrowed valet believed him to be resting and would not disturb him.

He sat down in a chair, put his elbows on his knees and raked his fingers through his damp hair. Nothing had changed, so why the devil was he ignoring the self-imposed rules that had served him so well all his adult life? Isobel was a single young lady of good family and one, it would appear, that he had misjudged. The wild sensuality he had sensed in her must have either been his own imagination or she was unaware of it in her innocence.

He shot a glance through the door into the dressing room, but she seemed deeply asleep. He was discovering that he liked her, despite her sharp tongue and unflattering view of him. He admired her courage and her spirit, enjoyed the sensation of her in his arms. But all of that meant nothing. She should be, literally, untouchable and they both knew it.

Why, then, did she make him feel so restless? He wanted something, something more than the physical release that his body was nagging about. There was a quality, a mood, about Isobel that he simply could not put his finger on. Giles closed his eyes, sat back, while he chased the elusive emotions.

'MR HARKER. GILES! Wake up, you are having a nightmare.'

Giles clawed his way up out of a welter of naked limbs, buttocks, breasts, reaching hands and avid mouths. 'Where the hell am I?'

'In your bedchamber at Wimpole Hall.' He blinked his eyes into focus and found Isobel Jervis kneeling in front of him, her hands on the arms of the chair. His body reacted with a wave of desire that had him dropping his hands down to shield the evidence of it from her as she asked, 'What on earth were you dreaming about? It sounded very...strange.'

'I have no idea,' he lied. 'How long have we been asleep?' Long enough for her to have lost the pallor of shock and chill. Her body, bracketed by his thighs, was warm. *Hell.* 'You should not be here.' And certainly not kneeling between his legs, as though in wanton invitation to him to pull her forwards and do the outrageous things his imagination was conjuring up.

'I am well aware of that, Mr Harker! It is four o'clock. I heard the clocks strike about five minutes ago when I woke. Are you all right? You were arguing about something in your sleep.'

'I am fine,' Giles assured her. Already his head was clearing. It was the familiar frustrating dream about trying to break up a party at the Dower House, the one that had got completely out of hand. It was after that fiasco that he began to lay down the law to his mother—and to his surprise, she had listened and wept and things had become marginally better. But that night, when he had to cope with a fire in the library, a goat in the salon—part of a drunken attempt at a satanic mass—and the resignation of every one of his mother's long-suffering staff, had burned itself into his memory.

'I was supposed to be making sure you did not dream,' he apologised. 'And you had to rescue me instead.'

'I had no nightmares,' she assured him. 'But it was a good thing that your voice woke me.' Her hair had dried completely and the loose arrangement was beginning to come down in natural waves that made him want to stroke it as he might a cat's soft coat. Isobel shook it back from her shoulders and a faint scent of rosemary touched his nostrils, sweet and astringent at one and the same time, like the woman before him.

'You must go before anyone starts looking for you.' He kept his hands lightly clasped, away from temptation.

Isobel nodded and sat back on her heels and the simple gown shifted and flowed over breast and thighs. Giles closed his eyes for a moment and bit back a groan.

'I will go out of your dressing room and across the inner landing to my sitting room. Provided no one sees me leaving your chamber, there are any number of ways I could have reached my own door.'

'You have an aptitude for this kind of intrigue,' Giles said in jest. Isobel got to her feet in one jerky movement and turned towards the door in a swirl of skirts. He saw the blush on her cheek and sprang up to catch her arm. 'I am sorry, I did not mean that as it sounded. You think clearly through a problem, that is all.'

'Yes, of course.' She kept her head averted, but the tension in her body, the colour in her cheek, betrayed acute mortification. 'I have a very clear head for problems.' The unconcern with which she had knelt before him had gone—now she was uncomfortably aware of him as a man.

'Isobel.'

She turned, her eyes dark and her mouth tight. He no longer thought it made her look like a disapproving governess. This close, he could read shame behind the censorious expression.

'I am sorry.' How she came to be in his arms, he was not certain. Had she moved? Had he drawn her close—or was it both? But with her there, warm and slender, those wide, hurt grey eyes fixed questioningly on his face, it seemed the most natural thing in the world to kiss her.

Isobel must have sensed his intent, although once his arms had encircled her she did not move for a long moment. Then, 'No!' She jerked back against his hold, as fiercely as if he had been manhandling her with brutal intent. 'Let me *go*.'

Giles opened his hands, stepped back. 'Of course.' There had been real fear in her eyes, just for a moment. Surely she did not think he would try to force her? Perhaps she had recovered enough to realise just how compromising it was to be in a man's bedchamber.

Or was this all a tease, a way of punishing him for his kiss that morning? But then she would have to be a consummate actress. Puzzled, uneasy, he knew this was not the time to explore the mystery that was Isobel Jervis. In fact, now was the time to stop this completely before his curiosity about her got the better of him.

He opened the door and looked out. 'It is safe to leave.'

'Thank you,' Isobel murmured and brushed past him without meeting his eyes.

That was, of course, the best possible outcome. All he

had to do now was to maintain a civil distance. He could only hope he was imagining the expression in her eyes and that he could ignore the nagging instinct that he should be protecting her from whatever it was that caused it.

'YOU'RE NOT HAVING anything to do with that man, are you, my lady?' Dorothy set the breakfast tray across Isobel's lap with unnecessary firmness. 'You go vanishing goodness knows where yesterday when you should have been resting and I worry you were with him. He's too good looking for any woman to be around—it shouldn't be allowed. You can't trust any of them—men—he knows you're grateful for him saving you and the next thing you know he'll be—'

'I told you, I had a nap in one of the other rooms, Dorothy.' Isobel made rather a business of wriggling up against the pillows and setting the tray straight on her knees. 'Will you please stop nagging about it?'

'What your sainted mama would say if she knew, I do not know.'

'And how could you?' Isobel said between gritted teeth. 'There is nothing to know.'

'He's no good, that one. He's not a gentleman, despite all those fine clothes and that voice,' Dorothy pronounced as she bustled about, tidying the dressing table. 'They don't say much in front of me in the servants' hall, me being from outside, but I can tell that there's something fishy about him.'

'Dorothy, if Lady Hardwicke trusts Mr Harker sufficiently to entertain him in her own home, with her daughters here, I really do not feel it is your place to question her judgement.'

'No, my lady.'

'And one more sniff of disapproval out of you and you can go straight back to London.'

Silenced, the maid flounced out, then stopped to bob a curtsy in the doorway.

'May I come in?' Cousin Elizabeth looked round the door and smiled when she saw Isobel was eating. 'It seems everyone is much recovered this morning, although I have forbidden Lizzie to leave her room today.'

'How is she?' Isobel's sleep had been disturbed by vivid dreams of loss, of empty arms and empty heart. She felt her arms move instinctively as though to cradle a child and fussed with the covers instead.

'She is fine, although a trifle overexcited. What would you like to do, my dear? Stay in bed? I can bring you some books and journals.'

The sun was pouring through the window with a clarity that promised little warmth, but exhilarating views. 'I thought I might take another walk, Cousin Elizabeth. If you do not require me to assist you with anything, that is. Perhaps Anne or Philip might join me?'

'Of course, you may go and enjoy this lovely weather, just as long as you do not overtire yourself.' She looked out of the window and nodded, as though she could understand Isobel's desire to be outside. 'Philip would join you, but his father has sent him to his studies—his tutor's report on his Latin was very unsatisfactory, poor boy. And Anne has fittings with the dressmaker all morning—I declare she has not a single thing fit to wear for her come-out.'

'Never mind. I do not mind exploring by myself,' Isobel said. 'It is such a sunny day and who knows how long the weather will hold at this time of year.'

'Do you want me to send one of the footmen to go with you?'

'Goodness, no, thank you. I will probably dawdle about looking at the view and drive the poor man to distraction.'

The countess smiled. 'As you wish. The park is quite

safe—other than the lake! Mr Harker and my husband will be in a meeting this morning.' She delivered this apparent non sequitur with a vague smile. 'And now I fear I must go and have a long interview with the housekeeper about the state of the servants' bed linen. Do not tire yourself, Isobel.'

ISOBEL CAME DOWN the front steps an hour later, then stopped to pull on her gloves and decide which way to go.

Over to her left she could glimpse the church with the stables in front of it. Time enough for viewing the family monuments on Sunday. A middle-aged groom with a face like well-tanned leather came out from the yard and touched his finger to his hat brim.

'Roberts, my lady,' he introduced himself. 'May I be of any assistance?'

'I was trying to decide which way to walk, Roberts.' Isobel surveyed the long avenue stretching south. It would make a marvellous gallop, but would not be very scenic for a walk. The park to the north, towards the lake, she did not feel she could face, not quite yet. To the east the ground was relatively flat and wooded, but to the west of the house it rose in a promising manner. 'That way, I think. Is there a good view from up there?'

'Excellent, my lady. There's very fine prospects indeed. I'd go round the house that way if I was you.' He pointed. 'Don't be afeared of the cattle, they're shy beasts.'

Isobel nodded her thanks and made for the avenue of trees that ran uphill due west from the house. At the first rise she paused and looked back over the house and the formal gardens.

Why, she wondered, had Cousin Elizabeth made a point of mentioning where Giles Harker would be that morning?

Surely she did not suspect that anything had transpired between them beyond his gallant rescue?

And what *had* happened? Gi… Mr Harker seemed to accept that she was not some airheaded flirt. She was, she supposed, prepared to believe that he suffered from an irritating persecution by women intent on some sort of relationship with a man of uncannily good looks. But that kiss in the shrubbery, the look in his eyes as they stood at the door of his room, those moments made her uneasily aware that she could not trust him and nor could she trust herself. He was a virile, attractive male and her body seemed to want to pay no attention whatsoever to her common sense.

There was something else, too, she pondered as she turned and strode on up the hill, her sturdy boots giving her confidence over the tussocky grass. There was another man behind both the social facade and the mocking rake, she was sure. He had a secret perhaps, a source of discomfort, if not pain.

Isobel shook her head and looked around as she reached the top of the avenue and the fringe of woodland. The less she thought about Giles Harker the better and she had no right to probe another's privacy. She knew what it was to hold a secret tight and to fear its discovery.

To her right was an avenue along the crest, leading to the lake and, beyond it, she could see the tower of the folly. To her left the view opened out beyond the park, south into Hertfordshire across the Cambridge road. A stone wall showed through a small copse. She began to walk towards it, then saw that it was the building she had noticed from the chaise when she had first arrived. As she came closer to the grove of trees it revealed itself as a miniature house with a projecting central section and a window on either side.

It was set perfectly to command the view, she realised,

but as she got closer she saw it was crumbling into decay, although not quite into ruin. Slates had slipped, windows were broken, nettles and brambles threatened the small service buildings tucked in beside it.

Isobel walked round to the front and studied the structure. There was a pillared portico held up by wooden props, a broken-down fence and sagging shutters at the windows. The ground around it was trampled and muddy and mired with droppings and the prints of cloven hooves.

And through the mud there were the clear prints of a horse's hooves leading to where a rope dangled from a shutter hinge: a makeshift hitching post.

Giles Harker's horse? Why would he come to such a sad little building? Perhaps he was as intrigued by it as she was, for it had a lingering romance about it, a glamour, as though it was a beautiful, elegant woman fallen on hard times, perhaps because of age and indiscretion, but still retaining glimpses of the charms of her youth.

But he was not here now, so it was quite safe to explore. Isobel lifted her skirts and found her way from tussock to tussock through the mud until she reached the steps. Perhaps it was locked. But, no, the door creaked open on to a lobby. The marks of booted feet showed in the dust on the floor. Large masculine footprints. Giles.

With the delicious sensation of illicit exploration and a frisson of apprehension that she was about to discover Bluebeard's chamber, Isobel opened the door to her right and found the somewhat sordid wreckage of a small kitchen. The middle door opened on to a loggia with a view of the wood behind the building and the door to the left revealed a staircase. The footprints led upwards and she followed, her steps echoing on the stone treads. The door at the top was closed, but when she turned the handle it opened with a creak eerie enough to satisfy the most romantic of imaginings.

Half amused at her own fears, Isobel peeped round the door to find a large chamber lit patchily by whatever sunshine found its way through the cracked and half-open shutters.

It was empty except for a wooden chair and a table with a pile of papers and an ink stand. No mysterious chests, no murdered brides. Really, from the point of view of Gothic horrors it was a sad disappointment. Isobel cast the papers a curious glance, told herself off for wanting to pry and opened the door on the far wall.

'Oh!' The room was tiny and painted with frescoes that still adhered to the cobwebbed walls. A day-bed, its silken draperies in tatters, stood against the wall. 'A love nest.' She had never seen such a thing, but this intimate little chamber must surely be one. Isobel went in, let the door close behind her with a click and began to investigate the frescoes. 'Oh, my goodness.' Yes, the purpose of this room was most certainly clear from these faded images. She should leave at once, they were making her feel positively warm and flustered, but they were so pretty, so intriguing despite their indecent subject matter…

The unmistakable creak of the door in the next room jerked Isobel out of a bemused contemplation of two satyrs and a nymph engaged in quite outrageous behaviour in a woodland glade. She had heard nothing—no sound of hooves approaching the building, no footsteps on the stairs. The wind perhaps…but there had been no wind as she walked up the hill. The consciousness that she was not alone lifted the hairs on the nape of her neck.

CHAPTER SEVEN

'I know you are in there, Isobel.' Giles Harker's sardonically amused voice made her gasp with relief, even as she despised herself for her nerves and him for his impudence.

'How did you know?' she demanded as she flung the door wide.

He was standing hatless in the middle of the room in buckskins and breeches, his whip and gloves in one hand, looking for all the world like an artist's model for the picture of the perfect English country gentleman. He extended one hand and pointed at the trail of small footprints that led across the room to the doorway where she stood.

Isobel experienced a momentary flicker of relief that she had resisted the temptation to investigate what was on the table. 'Good morning, Mr Harker. I came up here for the view, but I will not disturb you.'

'I thought we were on first-name terms, Isobel. And I am happy to be disturbed.' Was there the slightest emphasis on *disturbed*? She eyed him warily. 'It is an interesting building, even in this sorry state. Whether I can save it, or even if I should, I do not yet know.'

So this was what he was about, the rescue of this poor wreck. 'It is charming. It is sad to see it like this.'

'It was built as a prospect house and somehow was never used very much for forty years. Soane had sug-

gestions for it some time ago, Humphrey Repton countered with even more ambitious ones. His lordship points
out that it cost fifteen-hundred pounds to build, so hopes
that I, with no previous experience of the place, will tell
him what can be done that will not cost a further fifteen-
hundred pounds.' He smiled suddenly and she caught her
breath. 'Now what is it that puts that quizzical expression
on your face?'

'It is the first time I have heard you sound like an architect.'

'You thought me a mere dilettante?' The handsome face
froze into pretended offence and Isobel felt the wariness
that held her poised for flight ebb away as she laughed at
his play-acting. Surely he was safe to be with? After all,
he had let her sleep untouched when she was at her most
vulnerable yesterday and the moment when they had stood
so close and she had thought he was about to kiss her had
been as much her own fault as his. But it had troubled her
sleep more than a little, that moment of intimacy, the sensual expertise she knew lay behind the facade of control.

'I knew Mr Soane would not associate with you, nor
the earl employ you, if that was so. But you are the perfect
pattern of the society gentleman for all that. You should
not object if that is all you are taken for.'

'Appearances are deceptive indeed. You should look
out for the glint of copper beneath the plating when you
think you are buying solid silver,' he said with an edge
to his voice that belied the curve of his lips. He turned to
the table before she could think of what to reply. 'You are
that impossibility, it seems—a woman without curiosity.'

'Your papers? Of course I was curious, but curiosity
does not have to be gratified if it would be wrong to do so.'

'Even if these are simply sketches and elevations?'

'For all I knew they might be the outpouring of your

feelings in verse or love letters from your betrothed or even your personal accounts.'

'I fear I am no poet and there is no letter from a patient betrothed, nor even—do not think I cannot read that wicked twinkle in your eyes, Isobel—billets-doux from females of quite another kind.'

'I have no idea what you are talking about,' she said repressively. 'Tell me about this house. Or is it not a house?'

'A prospect house is a decoration for a view point, not for living in. As was fashionable when it was built, this room was designed as a banqueting chamber. It *is* rather splendid.' He swept a hand around the space which was perhaps twenty feet square. 'Repton's plans would make this open for picnics. He proposed moving the pillars up from the front portico to frame the opening and turning the ground floor into an estate worker's cottage.'

'Oh, no.' Isobel looked around her at the wide fireplace and the walls that had once been painted to resemble green marble. 'I love this as it is. Could it not be repaired?'

'I share your liking. But I fear the initial building was so poorly done that repair or alteration may be a positive money pit for the earl.'

'And there I was imagining it renovated and turned into a little house. I love looking at houses,' she confessed. 'I think I must be a natural nest-builder.' She could imagine herself, an almost-contented spinster, in a little house like this. But she would be alone with a cat, not with the sound of a child's feet running towards her—

'You found the painted room.' He strolled past her and into the little chamber she had been examining. Isobel shook off the momentary stab of sadness and followed. She would not be a prude, she would simply ignore the subject matter of the tiny, intricate scenes that covered the mildewed walls. 'The frescos are in the Etruscan style,' he explained. 'I think this room was intended for trysts, don't you?'

'Or as the ladies' retiring room,' Isobel suggested.

'So prosaic! I hoped you would share my vision. Or perhaps you have examined the designs and are shocked.'

It rankled that he should think her unsophisticated enough to be shocked. 'Your vision is of a history of illicit liaisons taking place here?' Isobel queried, avoiding answering his question.

'Do you not think it romantic?' Giles leaned his shoulder against the mantel shelf and regarded her with one perfect eyebrow lifted.

'Thwarted young lovers might be romantic, possibly, but I imagine you are suggesting adulterous affairs.' She could easily imagine Giles Harker indulging in such a liaison. She could not believe that he was celibate, nor that he repulsed advances from fast widows or wives with complacent husbands, however much he might protest the need to keep young ladies at a safe distance.

'Not necessarily. How about happily married couples coming here to be alone, away from the servants and the children, to eat a candlelit supper and rediscover the flirtations of their courtship?'

'That is a charming thought indeed. You are a romantic after all, Mr Harker. Or a believer in marital bliss, perhaps.' She kept her distance, over by the window where the February air crept through the cracks to cool her cheeks.

'Giles. And why *after all*? An architect needs some romance in his soul, surely?'

'Yesterday your views on the relationships between men and women seemed more practical than romantic.' Isobel picked at a tendril of ivy that had insinuated itself between the window frame and the wall.

'Merely self-preservation.' Giles came to look out of the

window beside her, pushing the shutter back on its one remaining hinge. 'How is it that you have avoided the snare of matrimony, Isobel?'

Surprised and wary, she turned to look at him. 'You regard matrimony as a snare for women as well as for men? The general view is that it must be our sole aim and ambition.'

'If it is duty and not, at the very least, affection that motivates the match, then I imagine it is a snare. Or a kindly prison, perhaps.'

A kindly prison. He understood, or could imagine, what it might mean for a woman. The surprise loosened her tongue. 'I was betrothed, for love, four years ago. He died.'

'And now you wear the willow for him?' There was no sympathy in the deep voice and his attention seemed to be fixed on a zigzagging crack in the wall. Oddly, that made it easier to confide.

'I mourned Lucas for two years. I find it is possible to keep the memory of love, but I cannot stay in love with someone who is no longer there.'

'So you would wed?' He reached out and prodded at the crack. A lump of plaster fell out, exposing rough stone beneath.

'If I found someone who could live up to Lucas, and he loved me, then yes, perhaps.' *He would have to love me very much indeed.* 'But I do not expect to be that fortunate twice in my life.'

'I imagine that all your relatives say bracingly that of course you will find someone else if only you apply yourself.'

'Exactly. You are beset with relatives also, by the sound of it.'

'Just my mother and my grandfather.'

Which of those produced the rueful expression? she

wondered. His mother, probably. He had described her as eccentric.

'If this paragon does not materialise, what will you do then?' Giles asked.

'He does not have to be a paragon. I am not such a ninny as to expect to find one of those. They do not exist. I simply insist that I like him and he is neither a rakehell nor a prig and he does not mind that I have...a past.'

'Paragons of manhood being fantastic beasts like wyverns and unicorns?' That careless reference to her past seemed to have slipped his notice.

Isobel chuckled. 'Exactly. I have decided that if no eligible gentleman makes me an offer I shall be an eccentric spinster or an Anglican nun. I incline towards the former option, for I enjoy my little luxuries.'

Giles laughed, a crow of laughter. 'I should think so! You? A nun?'

'I was speaking in jest.' How attractive he was when he laughed, his handsome head thrown back, emphasising the strong line of his throat, the way his eyes crinkled in amusement. Isobel found herself smiling. Slowly she was beginning to see beyond the perfect looks and the outrageous tongue and catch glimpses of what might be the real man hiding behind them.

There was that suspicion about secrets again. What would he be hiding? Or was it simply that his faultless face made him more difficult to read than a plainer man might be? 'I thought about a convent the other day when I was reflecting on just how unsatisfactory the male sex can be.'

'We are?' He was still amused, but, somehow he was not laughing at her, but sharing her whimsy.

'You must know perfectly well how infuriating men are from a female point of view,' Isobel said with severity, picking up the trailing skirts of her riding habit to keep them out of the thick dust as she went to examine one of the better-preserved panels more closely. Surely they could not all be so suggestive? It seemed they could. Was it possible that one could do that in a bath without drowning?

'You have all the power and most of the fun in life,' she said, dragging her attention back from the erotic scene. After a moment, when he did not deny it, she added, 'Why is the thought of my being a nun so amusing?'

Giles's mouth twitched, but he did not answer her, so she said the first thing that came into her head, flustered a little by the glint in his eyes. 'I am amazed that the countess allows this room to be unlocked. What if the girls came in here?'

'The whole building has been locked up for years. Lady Hardwicke told the children that they were not to disturb me here and I have no doubt that her word is law.'

'I think it must be, although she is a very gentle dictator. So—will you recommend that the place is restored?'

'I do not think so.' Giles shook his head. 'It was badly built in the first place and then neglected for too long. But I am working up the costing for the earl so he has a fair comparison to set against Repton's ambitious schemes.'

'But that would be such a pity—and you like the place, do you not?'

'It is not my money. My job is to give the earl a professional opinion. I am not an amateur, Isobel. I am a professional, called in like the doctor or the lawyer to deliver the hard truths.'

'But surely you are different? You are, after all, a gentleman—'

Giles turned on his heel and faced her, his expression mocking. 'Do you recall what you called me when I kissed you?'

'A…*bastard*,' she faltered, ashamed. She should never

had said it. It was a word she had never used in cold blood. A word she loathed.

'And that is exactly, and precisely, what I am. Not a gentleman at all.'

'But you are,' Isobel protested. He was born out of wed-lock? 'You speak like a gentleman, you dress like one, your manner in society, your education—'

'I was brought up as one, certainly,' Giles agreed. He did not appear at all embarrassed about discussing his parentage. Isobel had never heard illegitimacy mentioned in anything but hushed whispers as a deep shame. How could he be so open about it? 'But my father was a common soldier, my grandfather a head gardener.'

'Then how on earth…? Oh.' Light dawned. His *eccentric* mother. 'Your mother?' His mother had kept him. What courage that must have taken. What love. Isobel bit her lip.

'My mother is the Dowager Marchioness of Faversham.' Isobel felt her jaw drop and closed her mouth. An aristocratic lady openly keeping a love child? It was unheard of. 'She scorns convention and gossip and the opinion of the world. She has gone her own way and she took her son with her.' He strolled back into the large chamber and began to gather up the papers on the table.

'Until you left university,' Isobel stated, suddenly sure. A wealthy dowager would have the money and the power, perhaps, to insist on keeping her baby. Not everyone had that choice, she told herself. Sometimes there was none. 'She did not want you to study a profession, did she?' She made herself focus on the man in front of her and his situation. 'That was when you went your own way.'

'Perceptive of you. She expected me to enliven society, just as she does.' He shrugged. 'I am accepted widely—I know most of the men of my age from school and university, after all. I am not received at Court, of course, and not in the homes of the starchier matrons with marriageable girls on their hands.'

Isobel felt the colour mount in her cheeks. No wonder he was wary of female attention. If his mother was notorious, then he, with his looks, would be irresistible to the foolish girls who wanted adventure or a dangerous flirtation. Giles Harker was the most tempting kind of forbidden fruit.

'Of course,' she said steadily, determined not to be missish. 'You are not at all eligible. I can quite see that might make for some…awkwardness at times. It will be difficult for you to find a suitable bride, I imagine.'

'Again, you see very clearly. I cannot marry within society. If I wed the daughter of a Cit or some country squire, then she will not be accepted in the circles in which I am tolerated now. There is a careful balance to be struck in homes such as this—and I spend a lot of my time in aristocratic households. We all pretend I am a gentleman. A wife who is not from the same world will not fit in, will spoil the illusion.'

'It will be easier as your practice grows and your wealth with it.' Isobel bit her lip as she pondered the problem. 'You could wed the daughter of another successful professional man, one who has the education and upbringing to fit in as you do.'

Giles stopped in the act of rapping a handful of papers on the desk to align them. Isobel's reaction to his parentage was undeniably startling—it was almost as though she understood and sympathised. 'Do you plot all your friends' lives so carefully for them? Set them all to partners?'

'Of course not. It is just that you are a rather different case. Unusual.' She put her head on one side and contemplated him as though trying to decide where to place an exotic plant in a flower border or a new ornament on a shelf. 'I would never dream of actually matchmaking.'

'Why not? It seems to be a popular female preoccupation.'

Now, why that tight-lipped look again, this time accompanied by colour on her cheekbones? 'Marriage is enough of a lottery as it is, without one's acquaintances interfering in it for amusement or mischief,' she said with a tartness that seemed entirely genuine.

'You are the victim of that?' Giles stuffed his papers into the saddlebag he had brought up with him.

'Oh, yes, of course. I am single and dangerously close to dwindling into a spinster. It is the duty of every right-thinking lady of my acquaintance to find me a husband.'

There was something more than irritation over being the target of well-meaning matchmaking, although he could not put his finger on what it was. Anger, certainly, but beneath that he sensed a deep unhappiness that Isobel was too proud to show.

'Ah, well,' Giles said peaceably, 'we are both safe here, it seems. The Yorke girls are well behaved and well chaperoned and there are no eligible gentlemen for the countess to foist upon you.'

'Thank goodness,' Isobel said with real feeling. 'But I am disturbing you when you have work to do. I will go on with my walk now I have admired the view from up here.'

'I do not mind being disturbed.' He thought he had kept the double meaning out of his voice—he was finding her unaccountably disturbing on a number of levels—but she bit her lower lip as though she was controlling a sharp retort. Or just possibly a smile, although she turned abruptly before he could be quite certain. 'Where are you going to go now?'

'I do not know.' Isobel stood looking out of the window.

'The avenue running north from here is pleasant. It skirts the wood.'

'And leads to the lake.'

'That frightens you?'

'No. No, of course not.' The denial was a little too emphatic.

'Then you did not dream?' Giles buckled the saddlebag, threw it over his shoulder, picked up his hat and gloves and watched her.

'No…yes. Possibly. I do not recall.'

'I will come with you,' he said. 'I have been sitting too long.'

'But your horse—'

'I will lead him. Come and see the best view of the Gothic folly.'

Isobel followed him down the stairs and out into the sunshine, allowed him to take her hand as they negotiated the mud and then retrieved it as she fell in beside him. They walked beneath the bare branches of the avenue, Felix plodding along behind them, the reins knotted on his neck, the thin February sunlight filtering through the twigs.

CHAPTER EIGHT

Afterwards Giles found it difficult to recall just what they talked about on that walk. His memories seemed to consist only of the woman he was with. Isobel seemed to be interested in everything: the deer grazing in the park, the lichen on the tree trunks, the view of the roofs of the Hall, complex and interlocking, the reason why he had named his horse as he had and what an architect must learn. He made her laugh, he could recall that. She stretched his knowledge of botany with her questions and completed his verse when he quoted Shakespeare. But under it all there was still a distance, a wariness. She was no fool, she knew she was playing with fire being with him, but it seemed, just now, as if she was suspending judgement.

She held her bonnet against the breeze. 'A lazy wind—it does not trouble itself to go around,' she said. 'Oh.' The lakes spread out below them in the valley, chill and grey.

'And there is the folly.' Giles pointed to the tower on the opposite hill to bring her eyes up and away from the source of her apprehension. 'Shall we go and look at it?'

If you fell off a horse, then the best thing was to get right back on, and the narrow bridge where the broken timbers showed pale, even at this distance, was her fall. 'Of course, if you are too tired...'

Isobel's chin went up. 'Why not?'

They followed the path down into the stock ditch and through the gate in the fence at the bottom. Felix's hoof-prints from the previous day were clear in the turf. It had been a good jump, Giles thought as they climbed out at the other side.

Isobel was silent as they walked down the hillside towards the lake. Then, as the muddy patch where they had clawed their way out came in sight, she said, 'I thought she had drowned. I thought I was not going to be able to save her. What if you had not heard us?' The words tumbled out as though she could not control them and he saw her bite her lip to stem them. Her remembered fear seemed all for Lizzie, not for herself, and he recalled how she had cradled the child on the bank. For the first time it occurred to him that a single woman might mourn her lack of children as well as the absence of a husband.

'Don't,' Giles said. 'What-ifs are pointless. You did save her, you found her and hung on until I got there. Now run.'

She gasped as he caught her hand and sprinted down the last few yards of the slope, along the dam, on to the wooden bridge, its planks banging with the impact of their feet. Moorhens scattered, piping in alarm. A pair of ducks flew up and pigeons erupted from the trees above their heads in a flapping panic. Giles kept going, past the break in the rail and on to the grass on the other side.

He caught Isobel and steadied her as she stopped, gasping for breath. 'You see? It is quite safe.' Felix ambled in their wake.

'You—you—' Her bonnet was hanging down her back and she tugged at the strings and pulled it off. She was panting, torn between exasperation and laughter. 'You idiot. Look at my hair!'

'I am.' The shining curls had slipped from their pins and tumbled down her back, glossy brown and glorious. Her

greatest beauty, or perhaps as equally lovely as her eyes.
Isobel stood there in the pale February sunlight, her face
flushed with exertion and indignation, her hair dishevelled
as though she had just risen from her bed, her breasts rising and falling with her heaving breath.

Kiss her, his body urged. *Throw her over the saddle and
gallop back to the Hill House and make love to her in the
room made for passion.* 'You are unused to country walks,
I can tell,' he teased instead, snatching at safety, decency,
some sort of control. 'I will race you to the folly.' And he
took to his heels, going just fast enough, he calculated, for
her to think she might catch him, despite the slope.

There was no sound of running feet behind him. So
much the better—he could gain the summit and give himself time to subdue the surge of lust that had swept through
him. Just because Isobel was intelligent and poised and
stood up to him he could not, *must not*, lose sight of the
fact that she was a virgin and not the young matron she
often seemed to be.

The thud of hooves behind him made him turn so
abruptly that his heel caught in a tussock and he twisted
off balance and fell flat on his back. Isobel, perched side-
saddle on Felix's back, laughed down at him for a second
as the gelding cantered past, taking the slope easily with
the lighter weight in the saddle.

God, but she can ride, Giles thought, admiring the sight
as she reached the top of the hill and reined in.

'Are you hurt?' Her look of triumph turned to concern
when he stayed where he was, sprawled on the damp grass.

'No, simply stunned by the sight of an Amazon at full
gallop.' He got to his feet and walked up to join her. 'How
did you get up there?' She had her left foot in the stirrup
and her right leg hooked over the pommel. Her hands were
light on the reins and she showed no fear of the big horse.

Her walking dress revealed a few inches of stockinged leg above the sturdy little boot and he kept his gaze firmly fixed on her face framed by the loose hair.

'There's a tree stump down by the fence. Felix obviously thought someone should be riding him, even if his master was capering about like a mad March hare.'

'Traitor,' Giles said to his horse, who butted him affectionately in the stomach. 'Would you care to explore the folly, Isobel?'

She sent an interested, curious glance at the building, then shook her head. 'We had better go back or we will be late for luncheon, will we not? Perhaps I can look at it tomorrow.'

Pleasure warred with temptation. They could be together safely, surely? He had self-control and familiarity would soon enough quench the stabs of desire that kept assailing him. It was too long since he had parted with his last mistress, that was all that ailed him. The challenge to make Isobel smile, make her trust him, was too great.

'I am not too busy to walk with you. Or we could ride if you prefer?'

'Oh, yes. If only it does not rain. I had better get down.' She lifted her leg from the pommel and simply slid, trusting him to catch her. Obviously his dangerous thoughts were not visible on his face. Her waist was slender between his hands. He felt the slide of woollen cloth over silk and cotton, the light boning of her stays, and set her down with care.

It took him a minute to find his voice again, or even think of something to say. 'What have you done with your bonnet, you hoyden?' Giles asked halfway down the hill as they walked back towards the lake. Isobel pointed to where the sensible brown-velvet hat hung on a branch beside the

path. 'And what are you going to say to Lady Hardwicke
about your hair if she sees you?'

'Why, the truth, of course.' Isobel sent him a frowning
look. 'Why should I not? Nothing happened. We ran, my
bonnet blew off, my hair came down. It is not as though
we are in Hyde Park. Or do you think she will blame you
in some way?'

'No, of course not. She trusts you, of course—she would
suspect no impropriety.' Now why did that make her prim
up her lips and blush?

'Exactly,' Isobel said, her voice flat. But when they
reached the garden gate and Giles turned to walk Felix
back to the stables, she caught his sleeve. 'Thank you for
chasing my nerves away at the bridge.'

'That is what friends do,' he said. That was it, of course:
friendship. It was novel to be friends with an unmarried
woman but that was surely what this ease he felt with Isobel meant.

She smiled at him, a little uncertain. He thought he
glimpsed those shadows and ghosts in her eyes still, then
she opened the garden gate and walked away between the
low box hedges.

A FRIEND. ISOBEL was warmed by the thought as she walked
downstairs for breakfast the next morning. It had never
occurred to her that she might be friends with a man, and
certainly Mama would have the vapours if she realised
that her daughter was thinking of an architect born on the
wrong side of the blanket in those terms.

But it was good to see behind the supercilious mask
Giles Harker wore to guard himself. After a few minutes as
they walked and talked she had quite forgotten how handsome he was and saw only an intelligent man who was kind
enough to sense her fears and help her overcome them. A

man who could laugh at himself and trust a stranger with his secrets. She wished she could share hers—he of all men would understand, surely.

He was dangerous, of course, and infuriating and she was not certain she could trust him. Or perhaps it was herself she could not trust.

Giles was at the table when she came in, sitting with the earl and countess, Anne and Philip. The men stood as she entered and she wished everyone a good morning as the footman held her chair for her.

'Good morning.' Giles's long look had a smile lurking in it that said, far more clearly than his conventional greeting, that he was happy to see her.

The morning was fine, although without yesterday's sunshine. They could ride. Isobel did not pretend to herself that she did not understand why the prospect of something she did almost every day at home should give her such keen pleasure. Perhaps she felt drawn to him because Giles was of her world but not quite in it, someone set a little apart, just as she was by her disgrace. She wanted to like him and to trust him. Could she trust her own judgement?

'Might I ride today, Cousin Elizabeth?'

'This morning? Of course. You may take my mare, she will be glad of the exercise. I have been so involved with the endless correspondence that this change in our life seems to be producing that I have sadly neglected her. And it is not as though my daughters enjoy riding, is it, my loves?'

A heartfelt chorus of 'No, Mama!' made the countess laugh. 'One of the grooms will accompany you, Isobel.'

Isobel caught Giles's eye. 'I...that is, Mr Harker is riding out this morning, ma'am, I believe. I thought perhaps...'

She feared the countess would still require a groom

as escort, but she nodded approval. 'I will have Firefly brought round at ten, if that suits Mr Harker?'

'Thank you, ma'am, it suits me very well. Shall I meet you on the steps at that hour, Lady Isobel?'

'Thank you,' she said demurely and was rewarded by a flickering glance of amusement. Was she usually so astringent that this meekness seemed unnatural? She must take care not to think of this as an assignation, for it was nothing of the kind. *Friendship*, she reminded herself. That was what was safe and that, she had to believe, was what Giles appeared to be offering her.

'Mama, I have been thinking,' Lady Anne said. 'With Cousin Isobel and Mr Harker here we might have enough actors to put on a play. We could ask the vicar's nephews to help if we are short of men. Do say *yes*, it is so long since we did one.'

'My dear, it is not fair to expect poor Mr Harker to add to his work by learning a part. He and Papa are quite busy enough.'

'You have a theatre here, Cousin Elizabeth?' Isobel asked, intrigued.

'No, but we have improvised by hanging curtains between the pillars in the Gallery.'

'That was where we had the premiere performance of Mama's play *The Court of Oberon*,' Lizzie interrupted eagerly. 'And then it was printed and has been acted upon the London stage! Is that not grand?'

'It is wonderful,' Isobel agreed. Many families indulged in amateur dramatic performances, especially during house parties. She caught Giles's eye and smiled: he looked appalled at the possibility of treading the boards.

'Perhaps on another visit, Lizzie,' the countess said. 'I am writing another play, so perhaps we can act that one when it is finished.'

'The post, my lord.'

'And what a stack of it!' The earl broke off a discussion with his son to view the laden salver his butler was proffering. 'And I suppose you will say that all the business matters have already been dispatched to my office? Ah well, distribute it, if you please, Benson, and perhaps my pile will appear less forbidding.'

'Feel free to read your correspondence,' Lady Hardwicke said to her guests as her own and her daughters' letters were laid by her plate.

After a few minutes Isobel glanced up from her mother's recital of a very dull reception she had attended to see Giles working his way through half-a-dozen letters. He slit the seal on the last one and it seemed to her, as she watched him read, that his entire body tensed. But his face and voice were quite expressionless when he said, 'Will you excuse me, Lady Hardwicke, ladies? There is something that requires my attention.'

Isobel returned to her own correspondence as he left the room. It was to be hoped that whatever it was did not mean he would have to miss their ride. She told herself it was not that important, that she could take a groom with her, that it was ridiculous to feel so concerned about it, but she found she could not deceive herself: she wanted to be alone with Giles again.

The earl departed to the steward's office, Philip to his tutor and Cousin Elizabeth and Anne for a consultation with the dressmaker. Isobel followed behind them a little dreamily. Where would they ride this morning? Up to the folly and beyond, perhaps. Or—

'Lady Isobel.' Giles stepped out from the Yellow Drawing Room. 'Will you come to the library?'

It was not a request; more, from his tone and his unsmiling face, an order. 'I—' A footman walked across the

hallway and Isobel closed her lips on a sharp retort. Whatever the matter was, privacy was desirable. 'Very well,'
she said coolly and followed him through the intervening
chambers into the room that was one of the wonders of
Wimpole Hall.

But the towering bookcases built decades ago to house
Lord Harley's fabled collection were no distraction from
the sick feeling in the pit of her stomach. Isobel could not
imagine what had so affected Giles, but the anger was radiating from him like heat from smouldering coals.

'What is this autocratic summons for?' she demanded,
attacking first as he turned to face her.

'I should have trusted my first impressions,' Giles said.
He propped one shoulder against the high library ladder
and studied her with the same expression in his eyes as
they had held when he had caught her staring at him in
the hall. 'But you really are a very good little actress, are
you not? Perhaps you should take part in one of her ladyship's dramas after all.'

'No. I am not a good actress,' Isobel snapped.

'But you are the slut who broke up Lady Penelope Albright's betrothal. You do not deny that?' he asked with
dangerous calm.

When she did not answer Giles glanced down at the letter he held in his right hand. 'Penelope is in a complete nervous collapse because you were found rutting with Andrew
White. But I assume you do not care about her feelings?'

Isobel felt the blood ebbing from her cheeks. That foul
slander...and Giles believed it. 'Yes, I care for her distress,'
she said, holding her voice steady with an effort that hurt
her throat. 'And I am very sorry that she chose such a man
to ally herself with. But you must forgive me if I care even
more that Lord Andrew mauled and assaulted me, ruined

my reputation and that very few people, even those who I thought were my friends, believe me.'

'Oh, very nicely done! But you see, I have this from my very good friend James Albright, Penelope's brother—and he does not lie.'

'But he was not there, was he? He knows only what Penelope saw when she came into my room that night: four people engaged in a drunken romp. Only one of them, myself, was not willing and the other three—the men—were set on giving a stuck-up spinster a good lesson, a retaliation for snubbing their patronising flirtation.

'That is the truth and if you have not the perception to know it when you hear it, then I am sorry, but there is nothing I can do.' Isobel turned on her heel. One more minute and she was going to cry and she was *damned* if she would give Giles Harker the satisfaction of knowing he had reduced her to that. A fine friend he had turned out to be!

'Who would believe such a tale?' he scoffed as he caught her by the arm and spun her back to face him. 'No one there did and they were on the spot.'

'You think it improbable they would be deceived?' Yes, after all there *was* something she could do, something to shake that smug male complacency.

'Of course,' Giles began as Isobel threw herself on his chest, the suddenness of it knocking him off balance back against a bookcase full of leather-bound volumes. 'What the devil—'

As he tried to push her away she used the momentum of his own movement to swing around in his grip until she was pressed by his weight against the books, then she threw her arms around his neck, pulled his head down and kissed him hard, full on the mouth.

For a moment Giles resisted, then he opened his lips over hers and returned the kiss with a ruthless expertise

that was shocking and, despite—or perhaps because of—
her anger, deeply arousing. Isobel had been kissed passion-
ately by her betrothed, but that was four years ago and she
had loved him. The assault of Giles's tongue, his teeth, the
fierce plundering exploration, fuelled both anger and the
long-buried desire that had been stirring with every encounter they had shared. When he lifted his head—more,
she thought dizzily, to breathe than for any other reason—
Isobel slapped him hard across the cheek.

'Now, if someone comes in and I scream, what will they
think?' she panted. His face was so close to hers that she
could feel his breath, hot on her mouth. 'What will they
have seen? Giles Harker, a rake on the edge of society,
assaulting an innocent young lady who is struggling in
his arms. Who will they believe? What if I tear my bodice and run out, calling for help? You would be damned,
just as I was.

'I do not have to justify myself to you. But I was sitting
in my room, reading by the fireside in my nightgown, and
three men burst in. I thought I could reason with them. I
did not want a scandal, so I did not scream—and that was
my mistake. And for that I am condemned by self-righ-
teous hypocrites like you, Giles Harker. So now will you
please let me go?'

For a long moment he stared down at her, then those
gorgeous, sinful lips twisted. 'Yes, I believe you, Isobel.
I should never have doubted you.'

Kiss me again, a treacherous inner voice said. *Listen
to your body. You want him.* 'You called me a slut. You
just kissed me as though I was one.' She did not dare let
go of her bitterness.

'I believe you now.' He looked at her, all the anger and
heat gone from his face. 'I am sorry I doubted you. Sorry

I called you… No, we won't repeat that word. But I am not certain I can be sorry for that kiss.'

'Unfortunately, neither can I,' Isobel admitted and felt the blood rise in her cheeks. 'You kiss very…nicely.' And as a result her body had sung into life in a way it had not done for a long time. 'No doubt you have had a great deal of practice. But kindly do not think that is why I…why I did what I did just now. I could think of no other way to prove my point.'

'Nicely?' Giles seemed a trifle put out by the description. 'We will not pursue that, I think. I should not make light of what has happened to you. I was wrong and you have been grievously slandered. What is your family doing about it?'

Isobel shrugged and moved away from him to spin one of the great globes that stood either side of the desk. It was easier to think away from all that intense masculinity. The man addled her brain. She had let herself be almost seduced into friendship and then he believed the worst of her on hearsay evidence. And instead of recoiling from her angry kiss he had returned it. He was not to be trusted. Not one inch.

'They denied it everywhere they could, of course. But my brother is a schoolboy, my father a martyr to gout. Neither of them is going to be taking up a rapier in my defence! Besides, my hostess threw me out the next morning, so the lie is widely believed. There is nothing to be done except take refuge where I am trusted—here with old friends of my parents.'

CHAPTER NINE

Giles paced down the length of the library to the other globe, the celestial one showing the heavens, and spun it viciously. 'Something should be done.' Hell's teeth, he had called an innocent woman a foul name, he had accused her on hearsay evidence. He was having trouble getting past his own self-loathing for that, and for wanting to kiss her again. Kiss her…and more. That made him a rutting beast like Andrew White and he was not. Please God, he was not that.

'Why is your old friend not calling out the man who betrayed his sister? Andrew White seems to be getting away scot-free,' Isobel demanded. It was a reasonable question.

'James is almost blind. He can see well enough to get around, but that is all. His sight was failing when we were at Harrow and it has deteriorated since.'

'Poor man. I had no idea. I was aware that he did not come into society, of course,' Isobel said, instantly compassionate. She was sweet when she was soft—pitying for James, tender with the child. He wanted that softness, but all she would give him was the fire.

'He is a scholar, a great mind. When we were children at school he held the bullies at bay because they were frightened of his rapier intelligence and his sharp tongue. He protected me with his wits when I was new, terrified and a victim because of my parentage. As I grew in size and confidence I defended him with my fists. Fortunately he can afford to keep secretaries and assistants so his studies are not affected by his sight. He is working on a new translation of the Greek myths.'

'A true friendship,' Isobel murmured, her head bent over the spinning globe, her long index finger tracing a route across continents. Was she imagining an escape from all this? 'Will you help me? Tell Lord James you believe me? If he can convince his parents and Penelope, then it might do some good.' She sounded doubtful that he would support her, even now.

'Of course.' *Of course. But that is not enough. You are mine. I saved your life so you are mine.* The anger boiling inside him became focused. He would tell James, of course, and Penelope, whom he had known since she was six, but there must be justice for Isobel. White and the other two had got off from this almost unscathed.

Out of the corner of his eye he saw Isobel put back her shoulders and straighten her back as if bracing herself to carry this burden of disgrace. Alone, she believed. But she was not alone any more. The fierce sense of possessiveness was unsettling, but he had never saved someone's life before—perhaps that accounted for the way he felt about Isobel now.

'You are very brave,' he said and her chin came up with a defiance that tugged at his heart.

'I refuse to go into hiding because I am the victim of an injustice, so what else can I do but carry on? Besides, if I was truly courageous I would be in London now, brazening it out, would I not?' Isobel threw at him.

'I think you are too much of a lady to be brazen about anything. And what well-bred virgin would not shy away from such behaviour?' Now, what had he said to make her blush so? 'It takes a wicked widow like my mother to carry off that kind of thing.'

She gave herself a little shake. 'There is nothing to be done about the situation beyond you telling your friend the truth. Look, the sun is shining—I think I will ride after all.'

'Then I hope the weather holds for you. I find I must go to London this morning.' There *was* more he could do and it seemed that Isobel had no one else to do it for her. Besides, Giles thought, the fierce possessiveness burning hot inside him, this would be both his right and a pleasure. The experience of defending a lady was not new, but it was an ironic twist that this time he would be on the side of innocence instead of mitigating his mother's latest outrages.

'It is not a problem with your business that takes you there, I see,' she said, watching him with narrowed eyes. 'That was the smile of a man who positively relishes what is in front of him.'

'Oh, yes,' Giles agreed. 'I am looking forward to it, although it is an unexpected development.' It was easy to resist the temptation to tell her what he was intending to do. This could all be covered by his willingness to stand up for his friends the Albrights. Isobel's name need not come into it.

'How mysterious! Or perhaps you are simply missing your mistress.'

'No.' He made himself smile at the jibe. 'It is a secret, but I will tell you when I get back.' He would have to do that, for she needed to know that the insult and the calumny had been answered. Giles lifted a hand to touch her cheek, pale and sweetly curved, but she flinched away as though she feared even that caress.

He wanted to protect her, needed to possess her. It seemed his wants might be satisfied, but never his needs. Nor should they be, of course, he thought with a stab of regret.

Behind them the library doors opened and he let his hand fall away as Isobel pretended a renewed interest in the globe.

'Ah! There you are, Harker.'

'My lord?'

'Excuse me, Isobel my dear—a matter of urgent business.'

'But of course. I hope your journey to London is uneventful, Mr Harker.' Isobel smiled politely and turned from him. 'I will see if they can spare me a groom—the morning is too fine to waste the opportunity of a ride.'

In the silence that followed the swish of her skirts through the door the earl strode across the room and half sat on the edge of the big desk.

'London? I need you here, Harker. My steward tells me that my banker is due the day after tomorrow to discuss how the financial affairs of the estate will be handled in my absence in Ireland. I need to confirm the figures Soane left with me for the further building work and to make a final decision on the Hill House and the other matters you were looking into for me. I must have the funds and authorities in place to allow matters to proceed without my agents having to endlessly send to Dublin for my agreement on every detail.'

'I will be back by then, my lord.' He could be in London by that night, have a day to do what he had to do and a day at most to travel back. 'I assure you of it.'

'You are certain? You will forgive me if I press you, but it would be extremely inconvenient if this were delayed and Delapoole had to return to town.'

'My word upon it, my lord.'

'Excellent. I will let you get on then. Safe journey, Harker.'

GILES WALKED UP the steps into Brookes's, one hand unobtrusively under Lord James Albright's elbow. It was all the guidance his friend needed, other than a murmured word now and again to help him orientate himself in the blurred world he refused to allow to defeat him.

'Good evening, my lord, Mr Harker.' The porter came forwards for their hats and canes.

'Evening, Hitchin. Lord Andrew White in?'

'Yes, my lord. He is in the library with Mr Wrenne and Lord Halton, I believe.'

'Excellent,' James remarked as they made their way down the corridor. 'Three birds with one stone. I've never felt so helpless before—I wish I could get my hands on that swine White myself.'

'I'll hold him for you,' Giles offered with a grin as he opened the library door. The room was empty except for the three men lounging in deep leather armchairs by the fireside. They looked round as the friends entered and Giles saw the mixture of wariness and defiance on White's face when he realised who his companion was.

He guided James's hand to rest on the back of a chair, then walked across. The three got to their feet to face him. 'Harker. Do they let you in here? I thought this was a club for gentlemen.'

'Quite patently it is not,' Giles countered. 'They appear to have admitted the three of you and you are lying scum who think nothing of assaulting a lady and blackening her reputation. Or perhaps you crawled in here through the sewers like rats?'

'Wrenne, be so kind as to pull the bell, will you?' White drawled, but Giles could see the wariness in his eyes. The beginning of fear. 'Get a porter to throw out this bastard.'

'And what about me?' James asked. 'Do you expect the porters to expel two club members on no grounds whatsoever?'

'This is damned awkward, Albright.' White's bluff tone

was at odds with the look of dislike he shot at James. 'Your sister took exception to a situation that was completely misinterpreted, made a scene, accused me of lord knows what, broke off the engagement— If I had been permitted to come and explain at the time, this could all have been put behind us.'

'You could hardly blame Penelope for her reaction,' Albright said with dangerous calm. 'You were found in another woman's bedchamber.'

'All a bit of fun that got out of hand. If Penelope had been a bit more sophisticated about it, we would still be betrothed.'

'And what a pity that would be,' James remarked. 'This is bad enough, but at least she discovered that you were a philandering cheat before she was irretrievably tied to you.'

'The devil!' White strode across the room until he stood immediately in front of James. Giles shifted his position so he could watch the other two—he did not want a brawl in the club, but if James lost hold of the threads of his temper, that is what they might well have. 'No one calls me a cheat! If you weren't as blind as a bat I would call you out for that, Albright.'

'And I would refuse your challenge, White. My grievance predates yours. You will apologise both to my sister and to the lady who you so grievously offended that night, or give me satisfaction.'

'I will do no such thing,' White blustered. 'And meet *you*? You couldn't hit a barn door with a blunderbuss.'

'I fear you are correct,' James said with such politeness that Giles felt his mouth twitch in amusement. 'However, as in all cases where a duellist cannot fight because of infirmity, my second will take my place.'

'And who is that?' White swung round as Giles cleared

his throat. 'You? I'll not meet a bastard on the field of honour.'

'No?' Giles drawled. 'Then it will be all around town within the day that you and your friends are cowards who will not fight, even when the odds are three to one. My friend did not make it clear, perhaps, that the challenge includes all of you. The choice of weapons is, of course, yours, as is the order in which you meet me. We stay at Grillon's tonight and I expect word from you as to place, time and weapons by nine tomorrow morning. I have no time to waste on you—the matter will be concluded by dawn the day after tomorrow.'

He took James's arm and guided him out of the door, closing it on an explosion of wrath. 'That went well, I think.' The picture of Isobel struggling in that lout's grip while he pawed at her was still painfully vivid in his imagination, but at least the gut-clenching anger had been replaced with the satisfying anticipation of revenge for her. He hoped they would choose rapiers; he would enjoy playing with them, making it last.

'Exceedingly well. I might not be able to see much, but I could tell that rat's face changed colour. Where shall we dine tonight?'

'WE ARE BEING FOLLOWED.' Giles took a firmer grip on James's arm. In the darkness with only occasional pools of light, or the wind-tossed flames of the torches carried by passing link-boys, his friend was completely blind.

'Who? How many?'

'Five, I think.' Giles turned a corner, aiming for King Street and the bright lights around the entrance to Almack's. They had been eating in a steak house in one of the back streets that criss-crossed the St James's area. Now they were only yards from some of the most exclusive clubs, gracious houses and the royal palace, but surrounded by brothels, drinking dens and gambling hells. It was not an area to fight in—not with a blind man at his side.

'As to who it is, I suspect our three friends and a pair of bully boys they've picked up.' He lengthened his stride. 'We rattled them, it seems. We're almost to King Street, James. If anything happens you'll be able to make out the lights if you just keep going down the slope and you'll be on the doorstep of Almack's.'

'And leave you? Be damned to that,' James said hotly.

'Go for help—hell, too late, here they come.'

There was a rush of feet behind them. Giles swung round, pulled the slim blade from the cane he carried and pushed James behind him as he let his sword arm fall to his side. The two big men, porters by the look of them, skidded to a halt on the cobbles, their shadowed faces blank and brutal.

Beyond three figures lurked, too wary to approach. Giles stepped back as though in alarm, flailed wildly with the cane and the big men laughed and rushed him. The rapier took the nearest through the shoulder, then was wrenched from Giles's hand as the man fell against his companion. As the second man fended off the slumped body Giles jabbed him in the solar plexus with the cane, kneed him in the groin as he folded up, then fetched him a sharp blow behind the ear as he went down.

'Stay behind,' he said sharply to James as his friend moved up to his side. The three men who had held back rushed them, so fast that he was only just aware as they reached him that they were masked. His fist hit cloth, but there was a satisfying crunch and a screech of pain as the man—White, he suspected—fell back. Then one of the others had him in a bear hug from behind and the other began to hit him.

Through the blows and the anger he kept control, some-how, and began to fend off the man in front of him with lashing feet and head butts when he got close enough. Dimly he was aware of the sound of breaking glass and James's voice, then he wrenched free and could use his fists.

James shouted again, there was a thud and swearing, a fast-moving shadow and pain in his face, sharp and over-whelming. Giles's fist connected with the chin of the man in front of him and he saw him fall. As he went down the alleyway was suddenly full of figures and the flare of light.

James was there at his side, gripping his arm, and a stranger who seemed strangely blurred, stood close, a torch in his hand. 'Gawd! They've made a right bloody mess of you, guv'nor.'

'Made more of a mess of them,' Giles said, his voice coming from a long way away. Then there was silence.

GILES HAD BELIEVED HER. Isobel hugged that to herself through the rest of the day and into the next, allowing his faith to warm her like a mouthful of brandy. He believed her and he would convince Penelope's family of her in-nocence. Somehow that was less important than Giles's acceptance, although it should not have been.

She could not deceive herself: Giles Harker aroused feelings in her that no unmarried lady should be feeling— anger and exasperation amongst them. But there was more, something between friendship and desire that every in-stinct of self-preservation told her was dangerous.

Perhaps it *was* simply desire. Isobel sat and sorted tan-gled embroidery silks for the countess without taking con-scious note of the vivid colours sifting between her fingers.

He aroused physical feelings in her and that, of course, was wrong and sinful.

If she was the unawakened innocent that he believed her, then perhaps she would not have recognised this ache, this unsettled feeling, for what it was. Or she would have been shocked at herself and put it out of her mind, convinced that she was simply attracted by a handsome face and fine figure.

But she was not innocent and not a virgin. She had made love with her betrothed twice and, although Lucas had been almost as shy and inexperienced as she, it had been intense and pleasurable and had left her body wanting more. In her grief, and through the heartrending decisions to be made after his death, those feelings had vanished. Unaroused and unimpressed by the men she met when she returned to society, Isobel had assumed that passion had died for her.

But it seemed that desire had only been sleeping and all it had taken was a kiss from the right man to awaken it. Giles Harker had not been the first man to kiss her since Lucas Needham's death, but he was the only man who made her feel like this.

What did that mean? Isobel held up two hanks of orange silk and tried to focus on whether they were exactly the same shade. She knew how she felt: happy and apprehensive, warm and slightly shaky. Very restless. Her lips retained the feel of his, her tongue the taste of him.

Isobel shifted uncomfortably in the deep armchair. He was a rake, he had behaved disgracefully as well as heroically, and he made her want to cross verbal swords with him at every opportunity. She knew, none better, the dangers of giving in to physical passion—she should find an excuse and leave Wimpole before she was tempted any further.

Coward, an insidious little voice murmured in her head. *Why not enjoy being with him, even snatch a few kisses? You are far too sensible to—*

'Cousin Isobel, you are wool-gathering!' It was Anne, laughing at her. Isobel looked down at her lap and found greens carefully paired with blues, the orange arguing with a rich purple and pinks looped up with grass-green.

'So I am! Listen—is that a carriage arriving?' They were in the South Drawing Room and the sound of wheels and of the front doors opening came clear in the still of the house.

'Who on earth can that be?' Anne glanced at the clock. 'Past three. Too late for a call and we are expecting no one for dinner.'

'And Mr Harker is not due back until tomorrow.' Isobel dumped the silks unceremoniously into their basket and went to peep out of the window. 'Very unladylike of me, I know! Now who is that? I do not recognise him.'

'Neither do I.' Anne came to look over her shoulder. 'The groom is helping him down, even though he is quite a young man. I do believe he is blind—see his stick? But we do not know anyone who is blind, I am sure.'

'It must be Lord James Albright. Mr Harker mentioned that he had a blind friend of that name. But…' Her voice trailed off. If James Albright had heard from Giles of her innocence and had called to tell her so, surely he could not have arrived so speedily and uninvited by the Yorkes? Unless he had met Giles in town and had set out that morning without pausing to write.

'What on earth is going on?' Anne tugged her hand. 'Come on, we will find out better from the hallway—see, four footmen have gone out *and* Mama!'

'They are helping someone who is sick or injured,' Isobel said. Her feet did not want to move. Her stomach was possessed by a lump of ice. It was Giles, she was certain, and something was horribly wrong.

CHAPTER TEN

Isobel clutched the draped brocade at the window while Peter, the brawniest of the footmen, backed out of the carriage, supporting a tall figure. *At least he is alive.* Only then could she admit to herself the depth of her sudden irrational fear. With the thought her paralysis ended. It was Giles and he was injured. His head was swathed in bandages, his legs dragged as the men held him. *'Giles.'* She brushed past Anne, uncaring about the other girl's startled expression, and ran through the anteroom into the hall.

'Giles!'

'I can walk upstairs perfectly well,' he was saying to the footmen on either side of him. 'I do not need carrying up in a chair, I assure you.' His voice was slurred. As she ran forwards she saw his face was bruised. He did not seem to hear her, or see her.

'Giles.'

'Leave him.' Cousin Elizabeth caught her arm while she was still yards away. 'He is hurt, but the last thing he needs is women fussing over him. Peter and Michael will get him upstairs. The doctor has been sent for. I will go and have Mrs Harrison gather up salves and bandages and plenty of hot water.'

'But—'

'It is nothing mortal, I assure you, ma'am,' an unfamiliar voice said behind her. 'He is in a great deal of discomfort, but there are no deep wounds. Sore ribs, broken nose, bruising, cuts—so my doctor tells me. He should not have travelled today, but he said he had given the earl his word he would be here tomorrow and he's a stubborn devil.'

'You are Lord James Albright?' Giles had vanished unsteadily around the turn of the stair. The man who stood to one side, leaning on a light cane, wore thick spectacles on a pleasant face that showed both bruises and a graze along the jaw. When he held out his hand to her she saw his knuckles were raw. 'You have been in a fight? Is that what happened to Giles... Mr Harker?'

'The same fight,' he said with a grin. 'I might be nearly as blind as a bat, but when you put a big enough target in front of me, I can hit it.' As she took his hand he closed his fingers around hers, as if to detain her. 'I think you must be Lady Isobel?'

'Yes.'

'Then I have an apology to make to you on behalf of my sister.'

'There is no need. I understand why she thought as she did. But why have you and Giles been fighting?'

'Is there somewhere we can sit and talk?'

'Of course, forgive me. Lady Anne, do you think a room could be prepared for Lord James, and some refreshments sent to the South Drawing Room?'

'Yes, of course. I'll arrange that and then go and help Mama.' Anne hurried away.

'Through here, Lord James.' Uncertain how much assistance he would need, Isobel laid her hand on his arm and guided him to where she and Anne had been sitting. 'Are you in need of any medical attention yourself?' The bruises seemed alarming as he settled into the armchair with the last of the fading light on his face.

'It is nothing some arnica will not help,' he said with a smile, then fell silent as the tea tray was brought in, candles lit and the fire made up.

Isobel served him tea, then forced herself to wait patiently while he drank.

'You are wondering why I am here and what Harker and I have been doing,' James Albright said after a minute. 'He came to London yesterday to tell me the truth of what occurred when my sister's engagement was broken. At the time Penelope was adamant that she did not want any action taken against White, that in drink and high spirits he must have been entrapped by—forgive me—a designing female. She just wanted to put it all behind her.

'But once I heard the truth, that he had not only been unfaithful to my sister but had plotted to assault another woman in the process, then I knew I must challenge the three men involved. My family honour was involved twice over—once in the insult to Penelope and secondly in the role we unwittingly played in your disgrace.'

'But, forgive me, you are—'

'Almost blind. Quite. But, as my second, Harker could legitimately take up the challenge on my behalf. He would have called them out in any case, but that would raise questions about his, er…relationship with you. This way we both achieved satisfaction and the matter appeared to be entirely related to the insult to my sister.'

'His relationship with me?' What had Giles said to this man? *What* relationship?

'You are friends, are you not?'

'Oh. Yes, of course.' Isobel's pulse settled back down again.

'We challenged them and they apparently decided it would be easier if we suffered an unpleasant accident and fell foul of some footpads. Foolish and dishonourable, and even more foolish in practice. They thought that two large bully boys would make mincemeat out of one blind man and an architect with a pretty face. Unfortunately for them they were not at school with us. I learned to defend myself in a number of thoroughly ungentlemanly ways and Giles, when he is angry, fights like a bruiser raised in Seven Dials.'

'And you beat them—five of them?'

'Almost. It turned nasty by the end, but then the noise brought out a crowd from the nearby ale houses and, er, another place of entertainment and they soon worked out who the aggressors were and the odds against us. White, Wrenne and Halton have been taken up by the watch for assault and affray and their two thugs proved to be wanted by the magistrates already.'

'But Giles—how badly is he hurt?'

'Sore ribs where he was kicked. He was kicked in the head, too, I suspect, so he is probably concussed. The broken nose. Bruises and grazes all over. But that will all heal.'

A chill ran down her spine. What was Albright not saying? 'And what will *not* heal?' Isobel demanded bluntly.

'Oh, it will all knit up again. It is just that his face… there was a broken bottle.'

It seemed it was possible to become colder, to feel even more dread. 'His eyes?' she managed to articulate.

'His sight is all right, I promise. As to the rest—I couldn't see well enough to judge.'

'No, of course not. Thank you for explaining it all to me so clearly.'

'Harker said you were not a young lady to have the vapours and that you would want the truth whole.'

'Indeed, yes. Please, allow me to pour you some more tea. Or would you prefer to go to your room now?' Giles expected her to be strong and sensible and so, of course, she would be.

THE EVENING SEEMED INTERMINABLE. The doctor came and went after speaking to the countess, the earl and Lord James. Dinner was served and eaten amidst conversation on general matters. The explanation that Mr Harker and Lord James had been set upon by footpads was accepted by the younger members of the family and everyone, once concern for Mr Harker's injuries had been expressed, seemed quite at ease. The earl was delighted with his intellectual guest and bore him off to the library after dinner to discuss the rarer books.

Isobel thought she would scream if she had to sit still any longer with a polite smile on her lips, attempting to pretend she had nothing more on her mind than helping Lady Anne with her tangled tatting. She wanted to go to Giles so badly that she curled her fingers into the arm of the chair as though to anchor herself.

Finally Cousin Elizabeth rose and shooed her elder daughters off to their beds. 'And you too, Isobel, my dear. You look quite pale.'

'Cousin Elizabeth.' She caught the older woman's hand as the girls disappeared, still chattering, upstairs. 'How is he? Please, tell me the truth.'

'Resting. He is in some pain—the doctor had to spend considerable time on the very small stitches on his face, which was exhausting for Mr Harker of course. He will be able to get up in a day or so.'

'I must see him.'

'Oh, no!' Lady Hardwicke's reaction was so sharp that

Isobel's worst fears flooded back. 'He needs to rest. And, in any case, it would be most improper.'

'And those are the only reasons?'

'Yes, of course.' But the countess's gaze wavered, shifted for a second. 'Off to bed with you now.' As they reached the landing she hesitated. 'Isobel... You have not become unwisely fond of Mr Harker, have you? He is not... that is...'

'I know about his parentage. I hope we are friends, ma'am,' Isobel said with dignity. 'And he helped Lord James clear my name, so I am grateful and anxious about him.'

'Of course.' Reassured, Cousin Elizabeth patted her hand. 'I should have known you would be far too sensible to do anything foolish. Goodnight, my dear.'

Anything foolish. She is worried that I have become attached to him in some way. And I have. I desire him, I worry about him. I want to be with him.

At her back was the door to his room. In front, her own with Dorothy waiting to put her to bed. Isobel walked across the landing and laid her right palm against the door panels of Giles's room for a moment, then turned on her heel and walked back to her own chamber.

'What an evening of excitements, Dorothy,' she remarked as she entered, stifling a yawn. 'I declare I am quite worn out.'

HALF AN HOUR later Isobel crept out of her room, her feet bare, her warmest wrapper tight around her over her nightgown. At Giles's door she did not knock, but turned the handle and slipped into the room on chilly, silent feet.

There was a green-shaded reading lamp set by the bed, but otherwise the room was in darkness, save for the red glow of the banked fire that was enough to show the long

line of Giles's body under the covers. His left arm lay outside, the hand lax, and the sight of the powerful fingers,
open and still, brought a catch to her breathing. It was
unexpectedly moving to see him like this, so vulnerable.

On the pillow his head was still, with a bandage around
the forehead, down over one cheek and around his neck.
It was lighter than the heavy turban he had been swathed
in when he arrived—Isobel tried to take comfort from
that as she crept closer. The doctor had paid no attention
to anything but getting his dressings right, it seemed—
Giles's normally immaculate golden-brown hair stuck out
incongruously between the linen strips.

She felt the need to smooth it, touch it and feel the rough
silk, convince herself that he was alive and would soon be
well, although he lay so immobile. Even as she thought it
Giles moved, caught himself with a sharp breath. His ribs,
or perhaps it was just the accumulation of bruised muscles.

'Lie still,' Isobel murmured and took the last few steps
to the bedside. His unbandaged cheek was rough with
stubble and unhealthily hot when she laid her palm against
it. They had placed him in the centre of the wide bed and
she had to lean over to touch him.

'Isobel?' His eyes opened, dark and wide in the lamp-
light, the pupils huge. 'Go 'way.'

'Did the doctor drug you?' It would account for the wide
pupils, the slur in his speech. 'Are you thirsty?'

'Stubborn woman,' he managed. 'Yes, drug. Tasted
foul…thirsty.'

There was a jug on the nightstand. Isobel poured what
seemed to be barley water and held it to Giles's bruised
lips. He winced as it touched, but drank deeply.

'Better. Thank you. Now go 'way.' His eyelids drooped
shut.

'Are you warm enough?' There was no answer. She

should go now and let him sleep. There was nothing she could do and yet she could not leave him. He had fought for her honour and for his friend who could not demand satisfaction for his sister. If she had only screamed when those men broke into her room, then none of this would have happened.

'Idiot man,' she murmured. 'You try to convince me that you are a rake and then you almost get yourself killed for honour.'

Giles shifted restlessly. He should not be left like this. There was a chair by the fireside, she could sit there and watch him through the night; she owed him that.

She eyed the bed. It was wide enough for her to lie beside him without disturbing him. Isobel eased on to the mattress, pulled the edge of the coverlet up and over herself. When Giles did not stir she edged closer, turned on her side so she could watch his shadowed face and let herself savour the warmth of his body.

It was very wrong to feel like this when he was injured, she knew that. It was not only wanton, it was unbefitting of a gentlewoman. She should be concerned only with nursing a sick man, not with wanting to touch every inch of him, kiss away every bruise and graze, caress him until he forgot how much he hurt.

She must not do it. But she could lie there, so close that their breath mingled, and send him strength through her presence and her thoughts. Tomorrow she must face the consequences of his defence of her, of the debt she now owed him and her own jumbled emotions, but not tonight.

'Oh, my Gawd!'

Giles woke with a jerk from a muddled, exhausting dream into pain that caught the breath in his throat and

the sound of the valet's agitated voice. He must look bad
to shake that well-trained individual.

He kept his eyes closed while he took stock. Ribs, back,
a twisted shoulder, aching jaw, white-hot needles down the
side of his face and a foul headache. Nothing lethal, then,
only bruises, cuts and the effects of the good doctor's enthusiastic stitchery and drugs on top of a thoroughly dirty
fist fight. But he had little inclination to move, let alone
open his eyes. All that would hurt even more and, damn
it, he had earned the right to ignore the world for a few
minutes longer.

'My lady!'

That brought him awake with a vengeance as the bedding next to him was agitated and a figure sat upright.

'Oh, hush, Tompkins! Do you want to rouse the entire
household?'

'No, my lady. That's the last thing I'd be wanting,'
Tompkins said with real feeling. 'But you can't be in here,
Lady Isobel! What would her ladyship say?'

'I was watching over Mr Harker last night and I fell
asleep,' Isobel said with composure, sitting in the midst
of the rumpled bedding in her nightgown and robe. Giles
closed his eyes again. This had to be a nightmare. 'She
would say I was very remiss to lie down when I became
sleepy and we don't want to upset her, do we?'

'No, my lady,' said the valet weakly.

'So you will not mention this, will you, Tompkins?'

'No, my lady.'

Neither the valet nor the woman in bed with him—*in
his bed*—were paying him the slightest attention. Giles
gritted his teeth and pushed himself up on his elbows as
the valet went to draw back the curtains. 'What the devil
are you doing here, Isobel?'

'I wanted to make sure you were all right.' Her voice
trailed away as she stared at him in the morning light and

the colour ebbed out of her cheeks, leaving her white. 'Of all the insane things to do, to tackle five men like that!' She sounded furious.

'Insane? I did not have a great deal of options. I could have run away and left James, I suppose.' Damn it, he had fought for her and she was calling him an idiot?

'That is not what I meant.' Isobel slid from the bed and he turned his head away and tried to push himself upright, humiliated to find himself too weak to sit up and argue with her.

'Sir, you shouldn't try to sit up,' Tompkins said. By the sound of it he was trying to envelop Isobel in Giles's robe.

'Pillows,' Giles snapped, mustering his strength and hauling himself up. 'And a mirror.'

'Now I don't think that would be wise, sir.'

'Your opinion is not relevant, Tompkins. A mirror. At once.'

'Sir.' The valet piled pillows behind him, handed him a mirror and hovered by the bedside, his face miserable.

'Unfasten this bandage.'

'Giles—'

'Sir—' Giles lifted his hand to try to find the fastening and the man shook his head and leaned over. 'The doctor will have my guts for garters, sir.'

The process was unpleasant enough to make him feel queasy. When the dressing was finally unwrapped Giles lifted the glass and stared at the result. His nose had been broken, his mouth was bruised, but down the right side of his face where he had expected to find a single cut on his cheek, perhaps reaching to his cheekbone, were two savage parallel slashes from just above his eyebrow, down his cheek to his jaw.

'The swelling and the stitches made it look worse than it is, sir, I'm sure.' Tompkins rushed into speech. 'The doctor's very good, sir, lots of tiny stitches he took. Lucky it missed your eye, sir. A miracle, the doctor said that was.'

A miracle. A miracle that had changed his face for ever in seconds. Giles stared back at familiar eyes, a familiar mouth, eyebrows that still slanted slightly upwards. As for the rest… He had always taken his looks for granted. His glass had told him he was handsome. Some women called him beautiful. It was nothing to be proud of: his looks came from his parents and good fortune and had proved enough of a nuisance in the past. He would get used to the changes.

He had forgotten Isobel until she stammered, 'No… Giles…' She fled for the door, wrenched it open and, with the barest glance around to check outside, ran from the room.

So this new face sent a courageous young woman fleeing from the room in revulsion, a young woman who was not a lover, but who had called him her friend. That hurt, he discovered, more than the injuries themselves. 'Put back the bandage, Tompkins,' he said harshly. 'Then bring me hot water, coffee, food.'

'But, sir, you should be resting. Her ladyship told Cook to prepare some gruel.'

'Tompkins, I have a job to do and I cannot do it on gruel. His lordship requires my attendance today. Either you bring me proper food or I will go down to the kitchen myself and speak to Cook. And send for the doctor. I cannot go about looking like an Egyptian mummy.'

The valet left, shaking his head. Giles lay back against the pillows and told himself that it did not matter. He would heal in time and scars and a crooked nose were not the end of the world. But he could not forget the look on Isobel's face when she had stared at him, appalled. That felt as though something had broken inside him.

CHAPTER ELEVEN

By breakfast Isobel was no nearer overcoming the guilt. Giles's beautiful face was scarred for life and it was her fault. He had done it for her. The shock of how injured he was, her own helplessness, had made her angry—with herself as well as, irrationally, with him.

She should not have shouted at him, she thought penitently as she looked across the table to where James Albright sat, coping efficiently with bacon and eggs after a few moments' discreet exploration of the table around him with his fingertips. Giles had fought for him, too.

Cousin Elizabeth pressed Lord James to stay on, but he shook his head. 'You are very kind, but I will leave after luncheon if that is convenient. I must go and tell my family the truth of this matter.' He smiled in Isobel's direction before turning back to his hostess. 'I am sorry to trouble you for so long, but my groom tells me that one of the horses has cast a shoe and they must send to the village blacksmith. I thank you for your hospitality under such trying circumstances,' he added.

'Helping an injured man, and one who is a friend of the family now, is no hardship, Lord James. And I know Mr Harker insisted that you bring him, although what on earth he was thinking about, I cannot imagine. Surely he did not think that he would be in any state to work with

my husband and his advisers today—' She broke off and
stared at the door. 'Mr Harker!'

'Good morning. I apologise for my appearance.' Giles
walked into the room with a deliberation that Isobel realised must be the only alternative to limping. She found
she was on her feet and sat down again. He did not spare
her a glance.

Giles had discarded the swathes of bandage, although
there was a professional-looking dressing across his injured cheek. The swelling around his nose was less, although the bruising was colourful. He sat down next to
his friend and touched his hand briefly.

'Mr Harker, you should go back to bed immediately!
What can you be thinking of?'

'Lady Hardwicke, I assure you I am quite capable of
working with the earl and his advisers.' He accepted a cup
of tea from Anne and reached for the cold meats.

The countess shook her head at him, but did not argue
further, apparently recognising an impossible cause
when she saw one. 'Benson, please tell his lordship that
Mr Harker will be joining him and Mr Delapoole after
breakfast.'

Isobel ate in silence, almost unaware of what food
passed her lips. Giles not so much ignored her as managed to appear not to notice her presence. When he rose
to leave she got to her feet with a murmured excuse to her
hostess and followed him out, padding quietly behind him
until he reached the Long Gallery.

'Giles! Please wait.'

He stopped and turned. 'Lady Isobel?' The beautiful
voice was still slightly slurred.

'Don't. Don't be like that.' She caught up with him and
laid her hand on his arm to detain him. 'Why are you angry
with me? Because I have not thanked you for what you

did for me? Or because I slept in your room? I am sorry if it was awkward with Tompkins. If you had to give him money, I will—'

'What were you doing in my room? In my bed?'

'I was not in it, I was on it.' She knew she was blushing and that her guilty conscience was the cause. She desired him. She had lusted after him. 'I was worried about you. I came to your room to make certain you were all right. You were thirsty so I gave you something to drink. You were drugged and I thought someone should watch over you. The bed was wide. I only expected to doze, not sleep so soundly that anyone would find me in the morning.'

'A pity you did not turn up the lamp and see at once just how repulsive I look now: then you could have fled there and then and not waited until Tompkins and daylight revealed the worst.' His bloodshot eyes fixed her with chilly disdain as she gaped at him. 'You have had time to pluck up the courage to look at me. Pretty, isn't it?'

'You thought I was repulsed? Giles, for goodness' sake! No, it isn't *pretty*, it is a mess. But it will get better when the bruises come out and the swelling subsides. Your nose will be crooked, but surely you are not so vain that will concern you?'

'And the scars?' he asked harshly.

'Will they be very bad? The stitches will make it look and feel worse at first. My brother had them in his arm last year and they looked frightful. But now all there is to show is a thin white line.'

'Isobel, I am not a sixteen-year-old boy needing reassurance.' Giles turned away, but she kept her grip on his sleeve.

'No, you are a—what?—twenty-nine-year-old man in need of just that! Physical imperfections are no great matter, especially not when they have been earned in such a way. You will look so much more dashing and rakish that your problems with amorous ladies will become even worse.'

'Then why did you look at me as you did this morning? Why did you flee from my room?' he demanded.

'Because it was my fault, of course! You had been hurt, you must have been in such pain, and it was all because of me. I know you felt you had to defend your friend's sister, but if I had not told you my story you would never have known. I was angry with myself, so I shouted at you.'

'Of all the idiotic—'

'I am not being idiotic,' she snapped, goaded. 'You could have been killed, or lost an eye.'

'Isobel, I could not let them do that to you and not try to defend you. How could I not fight?' Giles turned fully and caught her hands in his. The chill had gone from his expression, now there was heat and an intensity that made her forget her anger. But with it, her vehemence ebbed away.

'You hardly know me. We have been friends for such a short time,' Isobel stammered.

'Friends? Is that really what you think we are?' She could see the pulse beat in his temple, hard, just as her heart was beating. 'I saved your life—that makes you mine. I want to be so much more than friends with you, Isobel, did you not realise?'

'You do? But—'

'But it is quite impossible, of course,' he said with a harsh edge beneath the reasonable tone. 'You might be mine, but I can never have you. You do not have to say it. I am who I am—you are what you are. You must forgive me for speaking at all,' he added with a smile that did not reach his eyes. 'I have embarrassed you now.'

'No. No, you have not.' What did he really mean? What did he want, feel? She did not know, dared not ask. This was not some smooth attempt at seduction, this was bitter and heartfelt—the words seemed dragged from him against his will.

'I want you as more than a friend. I had hoped that I had hidden it. I knew I should not feel it. But I cannot help it,' she added despairingly.

'I should never have kissed you.'

'Two kisses are not what makes me feel like this.' She put her hand to her breast, instinctively laying it across the heart that ached for him.

'You fought very hard against what you feel?' he asked. His hands had come up to her shoulders. He was holding her so close that her skirts brushed his boots and she had to tip her head back a little to look into his face. The taut lines had relaxed into a wary watchfulness.

'Not as hard as I should have,' Isobel admitted. 'But I was afraid you would think me like the women you have to avoid, the ones who pursue you.'

'I doubt any of them would stand here, this close, with me looking like this,' Giles said with a return to the bitterness.

'I have seen better shaves,' Isobel admitted, seeing what humour might do. No good was going to come of this, she knew that. How could it? He was, as he said, who he was. But that was for tomorrow. Today she knew only that she was desired by this man. 'And I could wish your mouth was not so bruised.'

'Just my mouth?' He raised an eyebrow and winced.

'I would like to kiss you,' Isobel admitted, beyond shame at saying it. 'But I do not want to hurt you.'

'Kiss it better,' he suggested, pulling her closer and bending his head so his words whispered against her lips.

She slid her hands up to the nape of his neck to steady herself and trembled at the unexpected, vulnerable softness of the skin beneath her fingertips. With infinite care she met his lips with her own: the slightest pressure, the gentlest brush. He sighed and she opened to him and let him control the kiss.

This was so much more than that passionate exchange in the library, that foolish tumble in the shrubbery. So much more intimate, so much more trusting. Giles made a sound deep in his throat, a rumble of masculine satisfaction, and she met the thrust of his tongue with her own, learning the taste of him, the scent of his skin, the rhythm of his pulse. Their lips hardly moved as the silent mutual exploration went on, but Giles's hands travelled down her back until he held her by the waist, drew her tighter against his body.

He was lean and long and fit and Isobel pressed against him out of need and yearning and felt the heat and the hardness of his need for her. She wanted to get closer, to wrap herself around him, but she stopped herself in time, recalling his ribs.

'What is it?' Giles lifted his head.

'Your ribs. Lord James said you had been kicked.'

'If you can be thinking about my ribs while I am kissing you, it does not say much for my lovemaking.' Giles bent and brushed his uninjured cheek against hers, his mouth nuzzling at the warm angle of her neck and shoulder.

'You want to make love to me?' How brazen she was to ask such a thing. How wonderfully liberating it felt to do so.

'I would give a year of my life for one night in your arms.' His voice was muffled against her skin as she lifted her hand to touch his hair.

Isobel gasped. It was all her fantasies about Giles, all her wicked longings, offered to her to take. All she needed was the courage to reach out.

Almost as soon as he said it, she felt him hear his own

words. The enchanted bubble that surrounded them shattered like thin glass. Giles's body tensed under her hands, then he released her and stepped back.

'I am sorry. I should never have spoken, never touched you.' His face was tight with a kind of pain that his physical injuries had not caused. 'I did not mean— Isobel, forgive me. I would not hurt you for the world.' He turned on his heel and walked away without looking back, up the gallery and into the book room that led to the library.

She stared after him, still shaking a little from the intensity of that kiss, unable to speak, unable to call him back.

He had only wanted a brief amorous encounter and his sense of honour had stopped him before they both were carried away. Isobel sank down on the nearest chair, stared unseeing at a landscape on the opposite wall and tried to tell herself she had just had a narrow escape.

THE EARL BROKE up the meeting shortly before noon. Giles suspected that such a short morning's work was on his behalf, but he could not feel sorry for it. Between the lingering effects of the doctor's potions, the pains in his body and his anger with himself over Isobel, it had been an effort to think straight at all, although the other men did not appear to notice anything amiss.

Of all the damnably stupid things to have done. But somehow he had not been able to forget that moment of waking to find her beside him in the big bed. All his good resolutions, all his self-deception that he could treat her as a friend, had fled to leave only a raw, aching need for her.

He could have controlled it, he told himself savagely, as he turned left out of the steward's room and, on impulse, took the steps up from the basement. He emerged into the grey light of a blustery, cold day that threatened rain before nightfall. Giles jammed his hands into his breeches'

pockets. He *would* have controlled it if she had not chosen
that moment to come to him, her face full of hurt at the
way he had coolly ignored her.

That vulnerability, that honesty, the way she confronted
him so directly had somehow wrenched equal frankness
from him. And because she was older than most of the
unmarried girls he encountered, because he had been so
open with her, he had let himself believe that they could
have an affaire.

And of course she was too innocent to understand where
their kisses were leading—even if she was not, it would
have been wrong. By his own action he had cleared her
name of all disgrace—now she could go back into society,
find a husband, marry.

She was a lady and that meant marriage—but not to
him, he told himself savagely. Not to him and she knew
it, had remembered it when he had blurted out his desire
for her. He had thought he had come to terms with his
birth and with the limits it placed upon him: it seemed
he was wrong.

'Idiot,' he muttered, kicking gravel. Of course a woman
like her would not offer herself to a man she did not love.
She had thought him her friend, nothing more, and he had
betrayed her trust. 'Damnation.' What had he done?

'Harker, I could follow you across Cambridgeshire just
from the muttered oaths.' He looked up to find James, his
cane in his hand, standing in front of him. 'What is the
matter? Are you in pain?'

'Not as much as I deserve to be. What are you doing
out here?' Giles took in his friend's thick greatcoat and
muffler. 'It is no weather for a walk.'

'I went over to the stables to see how they were pro-
gressing in the search for a blacksmith. What's the matter
with you? If you want to talk about it, that is.'

He could trust James, more than he could trust his own sense, just at the moment. 'Strictly between ourselves I've made a mull of things with Lady Isobel. More than a mull. Are you warm enough to walk? I don't want to risk being overheard.'

'Of course.' James fell in beside him as he walked past the stables and the church down the drive to the east. 'Have you told her you love her?'

'*What?* Of course not! I'm not in love with her. I do not fall in love with well-bred virgins. In fact, I do not fall in love with anyone.' James snorted. 'I want her, that's the trouble, and she caught me with my guard down and I damn nearly propositioned her.'

'Clumsy,' James remarked. 'And unlike you. But of course she, being female and having more intuition than the average male, presumably took your intentions to be honourable.'

'I don't know what she took them to be,' Giles retorted, goaded. 'She knows who I am, so how could she believe them to be anything but dishonourable? And what makes you think she wants me? Your fine understanding of female sensibility?'

'Not being able to see means I use my ears, my dear Harker. And I listen to the silences between the words as well. You two are, as near as damn it, in love with each other. What are you going to do about it?'

'Nothing. Because you are wrong, and even if you were correct, even if I was fool enough to allow myself to fall in love, I would do nothing. I am not even going to apologise for what happened between us in the Long Gallery and perhaps that will bring her to her senses. And stop snorting, it is like having a conversation with a horse. I'll leave as soon as I can.'

'So you make love to her and then snub her. An excel-

lent plan if you wish to break her heart, although I doubt
Lady Isobel deserves that.'

'Then what do you suggest?' Giles demanded.

'Marry her.'

CHAPTER TWELVE

'Marry her? Are you insane?' Giles slammed to a halt. 'Isobel is the daughter of an earl.'

'And so? She's a second daughter, she's perilously close to being on the shelf and she's had a brush with scandal. From what my sister tells me she was only doing the Season reluctantly in any case. Perhaps her father would be delighted for her to marry an up-and-coming architect with society connections, a nice little estate and a healthy amount in the bank.'

'You *are* insane,' Giles said with conviction.

'All right.' Albright shrugged. 'Go right ahead and break her heart because you won't risk a snub from the Earl of Bythorn.'

'Snub? I'd be lucky if he didn't come after me with a brace of Mantons and a blunt carving knife. I would in his shoes.'

'Coward,' James said.

'I am trying to do the honourable thing,' Giles said between gritted teeth. 'And that includes not knocking your teeth down your throat. You're the only man who can get away with calling me a coward and you know it.'

'If you want to do the honourable thing, then you want to marry her,' Albright persisted. 'Let's go back inside, it is raw out here and it must almost be time for luncheon.'

'Of course I do not.' Giles took the other man's arm and steered him down a path towards the back of the house. 'I am not in love. I have never been in love, I do not intend on falling in love. I intend,' he continued with more force when that declaration received no response, 'to make a sensible marriage to a well-dowered young woman from a good merchant family. Eventually.'

'That's three of you who'll be unhappy then,' James retorted as they went in through the garden door. 'Give me your arm as far as my room, there's a good fellow.'

LORD JAMES WAS particularly pleasant to her over luncheon, Isobel thought. Perhaps he was trying to make up for the misunderstanding over the house-party incident. Sheer stubborn pride made her smile and follow all his conversational leads. She wished she could confide in him, for he seemed both intelligent and empathetic and he knew Giles so well. That was impossible, of course—he would have no more time for her foolish emotions than Giles had and, besides, she could not discuss Giles with anyone.

She had bathed her red eyes and dusted her nose with a little discreet rice powder. Giles would never guess she had been weeping, she decided, studying her own reflection in the overmantel glass.

'You think this new census is a good idea?' he was saying now in response to Lord James's speculation on how accurate the results of the government's latest scheme might be. He sounded not one wit discomforted by what had occurred that morning. Isobel tried to be glad of it.

'What do you think, Mr Harker?' she challenged him, frustrated by his impenetrable expression. He was treating her as though she was unwell, fragile, which was humiliating. It seemed to her that when he spoke to her his voice was muted. His face, when their eyes met, was politely bland. But she knew him too well now to believe he was indifferent to what had passed between them that morning. There were strong emotions working behind the green, shuttered eyes.

'I think that it will all depend on the competence of the parish priest entrusted to fill in the return in each place,' he said now. 'Better if each person was questioned individually. Or every householder, at least.'

'You think that would expose more of the truth?' Isobel asked. 'That people would reveal their circumstances honestly?'

'Perhaps not,' Giles said slowly. 'And perhaps it is a mistake ever to ask for too much honesty.' Isobel had no difficulty reading the meaning hidden in his words. He had been honest about his desires, had led her to the point of seduction and now he was regretting it.

'Sometimes people do not know the truth because they are too close to it,' Lord James observed, making her jump. She had forgotten that she and Giles were not alone. 'The observer often sees more of the picture, don't you think?'

'So gossips and old maids like to say in order to justify their meddling,' Giles said harshly.

Startled, Isobel glanced between the two men. Albright's mouth twisted into a wry smile, but he did not appear to feel snubbed by what had sounded like a very personal remark. Giles, on the other hand, looked furious with his friend. Something had passed between them that morning, it was obvious.

The earl looked up from his plate of cold beef, unconscious of the undercurrents flowing around his luncheon table. 'The census? Very good idea in my view. I'd be glad if they did it in Ireland, then I might have a better idea of what to expect of conditions and problems there. I may suggest it when we see how this works out.'

The talk veered off into discussion of Irish politics, social conditions and, inevitably, sporting possibilities. Isobel placed her knife and fork neatly on her plate, folded her hands on her lap and watched Giles.

He guarded his feelings well at the best of times, except for his betraying eyes. But now, with his face so damaged and his eyes bruised, she was not at all sure she could read him at all. Except to know he was unhappy. *Good*, she thought, and went back to chasing a corner of pickled plum tart around her plate with no appetite at all.

IN THE GENERAL stir at the end of the meal Isobel found herself beside James Albright. 'I hope you have a safe journey home, Lord James.'

'Rest assured I will make your innocence known to Penelope and all my family,' he said. 'And we will ensure the facts are spread far and wide. Unless, of course...' he lowered his voice '...you would prefer to stay ruined?'

'Whatever can you mean, sir?'

'It might widen your choice of marriage partner, perhaps,' he suggested with a slight smile.

'Are you suggesting what I think you are?' Isobel demanded. *Marriage?* 'There is no question of a match between myself and...and anyone.'

'No? Of course *anyone* would say that, too, and, if...er, *anyone's* defences were not down, he would never have got himself into a position where he betrayed his feelings to me quite so blatantly, as I am sure you realise.'

'As we are speaking very frankly, Lord James,' Isobel hissed, furious, 'the feelings betrayed to me were not those which lead to a respectable marriage—quite the opposite, in fact!'

'Oh, dear. Hard to believe that anyone could make such a mull of it, let alone my friend. He is usually more adroit,'

Lord James observed. Isobel glanced round and found they were alone in the room. His sharp hearing must have told him that also, for he raised his voice above the murmur he had been employing. 'If I am mistaken in your sentiments, Lady Isobel, then pray forgive me. But if I am not, then you are going to have to fight for what you want. Not only fight your parents and society, but fight Harker as well.'

'I have no intention of throwing myself at a man who only wants me for one thing,' she said. 'And I do not want him at all, so the situation does not arise.'

'You know him better than that. Try to forgive him for his clumsiness this morning. If his feelings were not engaged he would have been…smoother.'

'How did you—?' She took a deep breath. 'My feelings are not engaged.'

'I found him in some agitation of mind. He told me he had erred and distressed you—I could fill in the rest. He let himself dream and hope and then woke up to the problems which are all for you, not for him. Giles Harker has a gallantry that will not allow him to harm you, so, if you want him, then you must take matters into your own hands.'

'Lord James—are you insinuating that I should seduce him?' Isobel felt quite dizzy. She could not be having this conversation with a man who was a virtual stranger to her.

The unfocused eyes turned in her direction. 'Just a suggestion, Lady Isobel. It all depends what you want, of course. Forgive me for putting you to the blush, but Giles Harker is an old and dear friend and I will happily scandalise an earl's daughter or two if it leads to his happiness. I wish you good day, ma'am.'

WITH LORD JAMES'S departure the men went back to their meeting and Lady Hardwicke swept up Catherine, Anne, Lizzie and Isobel, ordered them into bonnets, muffs and warm pelisses and set out for the vicarage to call on Mrs Bastable, the vicar's wife.

'I have sadly neglected my parish duties these past few days and it is Sunday tomorrow,' she remarked as she led her party down the steps. 'What with Lizzie's drama and all our preparations for the move and the pleasure of having Isobel with us and now Mr Harker's accident, the Clothing Fund has been sadly neglected.'

'Was it an accident, Mama?' Lizzie demanded. 'Mr Harker, I mean. You said it was footpads who broke his nose and cut his face like that.'

'It was accidental in that he fell amongst criminals who tried to hurt him,' her mother said repressively.

'And Lord James was the Good Samaritan who rescued him?'

'I rather think he was rescuing himself quite effectively,' Isobel said, then closed her lips tight when Anne shot her a quizzical glance.

'And the bad men?'

'Have been taken up and will stand their trial, as all such wicked persons should,' her mother pronounced.

'The wages of sin is death,' Caroline quoted with gruesome relish.

'Really, Caro!'

'It is from the Bible, it was mentioned in last Sunday's sermon,' Caroline protested. 'Mr Harker is very brave, isn't he, Cousin Isobel?'

'Very, I am certain.'

'And he was very handsome. Miss Henderson said he's as handsome as sin. But will he still be so handsome when they take the bandages off?'

Lady Hardwicke's expression did not bode well for the governess, but she answered in a matter-of-fact tone, 'He will have scars and his nose will not be straight. But those things do not make a man handsome: his morals and character and intelligence are what matter.'

She pursued the improving lecture as they made their way across the churchyard and through the wicket gate into the vicarage garden. Isobel brought up the rear, her mind still whirling from that extraordinary conversation with James Albright.

Had he really meant that Giles was in love with her? Worse, he seemed to believe she shared those emotions.

THE VICAR'S WIFE was grateful for help with the results of a recent clothing collection and, after serving tea, set her visitors to work that was familiar to Isobel from her own mother's charitable endeavours.

Isobel helped sort clothing into a pile that would be reusable by the parish poor after mending and laundering. The remaining heaps would be organised by the type of fabric so that when they had been washed the parish sewing circle could make up patchwork covers, rag-rugs or even suits for small boys from a man's worn-out coat.

It was worthy work and the kind of thing that she would be organising if she married a wealthy landowner, as she should. Lord James had spoken of marriage. An architect's wife would not have these responsibilities, although Giles had said he had a small country estate, so perhaps there were tenants. What would the duties of an architect's wife be? Not organising the parish charities, or giving great dinner parties or balls, that was certain. Nor the supervision of the staff of a house the size of Wimpole Hall, either. Not any of the things she had been raised to do, in fact.

This was madness. She would not marry save for love— on both sides—and Giles Harker wanted one thing, and one thing only.

'Cousin Isobel, you are daydreaming again,' Anne

teased. Isobel saw she was waiting for her to take the corners of a sheet that needed folding. 'What on earth were you thinking of? It certainly made you smile.'

'Of freedom,' Isobel said and took the sheet. They tugged, snapping it taut between them, then came together to fold it, their movements as orderly as a formal minuet.

'Goodness, are you one of those blue-stockings?' Anne put the sheet in the basket and shook out a much-worn petticoat. 'I do not think this is any use for anything, except perhaps handkerchiefs.'

'Me, a blue-stocking? Oh, no. And I was not thinking of freedom from men so much as from expectations.' Anne looked blank. 'Oh, do not take any notice of me, I am wool-gathering.'

'I think everyone is behaving most strangely,' Anne said and tossed the petticoat onto the rag pile. 'There is the fight Mr Harker was involved in—and Lord James. I do not believe for a moment that it was simply bad luck with footpads, do you? Then you are daydreaming all the time and Mama is lecturing and there are peculiar conversations that seem to be about one thing, but I don't think are, not really. Like you and Mr Harker talking about the census and honesty.'

'Well, you know why I am here,' Isobel said. 'I have a lot on my mind, so I suppose that makes me seem absent-minded. And men are always getting into fights. It was probably over a game of cards or something. And I expect Cousin Elizabeth has a great deal to worry about with your father's new post, so that makes her a little short. And as for peculiar conversations, I cannot imagine what you mean.'

Anne looked unconvinced, but went back to sorting shirts while the countess tried to persuade the vicar's wife that she could take over judging the tenants' gardens for a prize, as Lady Hardwicke did every year.

Isobel picked up some scissors and began to unpick the seams of a bodice, letting Mrs Bastable's protestations that she knew nothing about vegetable marrows and even less about roses wash over her head.

Was she falling in love with Giles? Had Lord James, with whatever refined intuition his blindness had developed in him, sensed it when she could only deny it? Had Lord James really been serious when he had told her to take the initiative? Now Giles was no longer in shock, half-drugged and in so much pain, he would not take the first step—whatever his feelings, his defences were up.

I don't want to fall in love with him! That can't *be what I feel.* She had not felt like this over Lucas, so torn, so frightened and yet so excited. But then, Lucas had been completely eligible, there had been no obstacles, no secrets. No reasons to fight against it. Or was she simply in lust with the man and finding excuses for her desires?

'Cousin Elizabeth, I would like to speak to Mr Harker alone after dinner, if you will permit. He will not let me thank him properly for what he did—perhaps if I can corner him somewhere I can say what I need to.'

The countess put down her hairbrush and regarded Isobel with a frown. 'That will be all, Merrill.' Her dresser bobbed a curtsy and went out, leaving the two women alone in the countess's bedchamber.

'He has certainly put you in his debt and a lady should thank a gentleman for such an action, I agree,' Lady Hardwicke said, a crease between her brows. 'But a tête-à-tête is a trifle irregular.'

'I have been alone with him before,' Isobel pointed out. But the countess was obviously uneasy. Perhaps she suspected, just as Lord James did, that there was something more between Isobel and Giles. 'A walk or a ride in the open are one thing, but in the house… Oh, dear. Perhaps one of the downstairs reception rooms would not be so bad—if you can persuade him to stand there long enough to be thanked! But for a man determined on escape there is a way out of all of them into another room. Unless you speak to him in the antechapel—there is no way out of that except into the gallery of the chapel and no one could object to a short conversation in such a setting.'

'Thank you, Cousin Elizabeth. Now all I have to do is lure him in there.'

Isobel left the countess shaking her head, but she did not forbid the meeting.

CHAPTER THIRTEEN

Giles schooled his face into an expressionless mask when Isobel, assisting the countess at the after-dinner tea tray, brought him a cup. He wanted to look at her, simply luxuriate in watching her, not have to guard every word in case he made things even worse.

He braced himself for murmured reproaches, or even hostility. 'Have you formed an opinion on the crack in the antechapel wall?' she asked without preamble. 'It sounds quite worrying, but perhaps the earl is refining too much upon it.'

'What crack?' It was the last thing he expected to hear from her lips. Giles put the cup down on a side table and the tea slopped into the saucer.

'Oh, he was saying something about it before dinner. I understood that he had asked you to look at it.' Isobel sat down beside him in a distracting flurry of pale pink gauze and a waft of some delicate scent. Now he did not want to look at all: he wanted to hold her, touch her. Did she not realise what she was doing to him? Was she trying to pretend nothing had happened in the Long Gallery?

'I was not aware of it,' he said, forcing his brain to deal with structural problems.

'Perhaps he did mention it and the blow to your head has made you forget it,' she suggested.

That was a disturbing thought. His memory was excellent, but then, he had believed his self-control to be so also and that episode with Isobel had proved him very wrong on that score.

'Or perhaps he meant to ask you, then decided it was not right while you feel so unwell,' she said with an air of bright helpfulness that made him feel like an invalid being patronised.

'I will go and look at it now.' Giles got to his feet and went into the hall. He took a branch of candles from the side table and opened the door into the chamber that led to the family gallery overlooking the chapel.

Once the room had been the State Bedchamber, but the great bed had long been dismantled and was somewhere up in the attics. Giles touched flame to the candles in the room and began to prowl round, trying to find cracks in the plaster, not think about Isobel's soft mouth, which seemed to be all he could focus on.

There in the left-hand corner was, indeed, a jagged crack. It would bear closer investigation in daylight, he decided, poking it with one finger and watching the plaster flake.

'Is it serious?'

'Isobel, you should not be in here.' In response she closed the door behind her, turned the key in the lock and slipped it into her bodice. 'What the devil are you doing?' Behind him was the double door into the gallery pew. Short of jumping fifteen feet to the chapel's marble floor, he was trapped, as she no doubt knew full well.

'I need to talk to you.' She was very pale in the candle-light and the composure she had shown over the tea cups had quite vanished. Giles saw with a pang that her hands were trembling a little. She followed his gaze and clasped them together tightly. 'About this morning.'

'I am sorry— I allowed my desires to run away with me. I had no right to kiss you, to hold you like that. It will not happen again.'

'That is a pity,' she said steadily. 'I would very much like you to do it again. I think I am in love with you, Giles. I am very sorry if it embarrasses you, but I cannot lie to you, I find. Not even to salve my pride.'

He stared at her, every bone in his body aching to go to her, to hold her, every instinct shouting at him to tell her… What? That he loved her? Damn James for even suggesting it. Of course he was not in love—he simply could not afford the luxury of hopeless emotion. But he did not want to hurt Isobel. 'I am very sorry, too,' he said, staying where he was. 'I never wanted to wound you.'

'I might be wrong, of course. I might not be. I thought perhaps…you…' Saying it brought the colour up under the delicate skin of her cheeks, soft pink to match her gown. He thought he had never seen her look lovelier or more courageous.

'No,' he said and kept his voice steady and regretful. He did not know what he felt, but surely it was only desire and friendship and liking. The emotion was stronger than any he had ever felt for a woman, but that was simply because he had never saved the life of one before, never fought for her honour, never met a woman like Isobel.

Isobel valued honesty above her own pride, but he could protect her from herself. 'No, I do not love you, Isobel. And that is a mercy, is it not? We could not possibly marry.'

'If you had not cleared my name and restored my reputation, and we did love each other, then perhaps we might have done.'

Hell, she's been talking to James, the interfering romantic idiot that he is.

'But not if I do not love you,' he pointed out. It felt like turning a knife in his chest, the pain of denying her, the knowledge that he was hurting her. 'And I do not think you love me, either. You feel desire, as I do, and it is easier for a woman to accept if you dress it up as love.'

'Do not patronise me! If I desire you I am not such a hypocrite as to pretend it is something else,' she flashed back at him. Her eyes were very bright, although if it was because they were full of tears, she did not shed them and he dared go no closer to see, in case she should read in his face how much he cared and took that for love. 'But you want me.'

'Oh, yes, and you know that too well for me to attempt to deny it. I want you so much it keeps me awake at night. So much that I ache and I cannot concentrate. But, Isobel, I might be many things, but I do not seduce virgins.'

'No,' she said, and smiled wryly. 'I am sure that you do not.'

'You will forget me soon enough,' he offered, flinching inwardly at the banality of the words.

'You think so? I thought we could talk this through with honesty, but it seems I misjudged you. Goodnight, Giles.'

She removed the key from her bodice, unlocked the door and walked away, leaving him, for once in his life, unable to think of a word to say.

GILES DID NOT come back to the saloon afterwards. Isobel smiled and nodded to Cousin Elizabeth to reassure her that her mission to thank him had been successful, stayed to drink one cup of tea and then made her excuses and went up to bed.

He said he did not love her, but then he would say that whatever he felt, it was the honourable course of action in his position. And he said he wanted her—although he was quite correct and she hardly needed him to tell her that. If they made love, it would be hard for him to hide his true feelings, she was certain. She could try to seduce him, and if he made love to her then he would be trapped between a rock and a hard place—to marry her would be, in his eyes, dishonourable, but then not to marry her after sleeping with her would be equally bad.

And to put Giles in that position would be very wrong of her whether he loved her or not. Isobel wrestled with her conscience while Dorothy brushed out her hair and helped her into her nightgown. 'I cannot do it.'

'What, my lady?'

'Never mind. Something I had been wondering about.'

'You look sad, my lady. Aren't you pleased that Lord James knows the truth? It will be all over town in a twinkling, then you can go back and do the Season, just like all the other young ladies.'

'I do not want to, Dorothy.' It was the first time she had said it out loud, but it sounded so right. She had tried hard to please her parents, but the thought of entering the Marriage Mart again with this aching in her heart was agony. How could she even contemplate marriage to another man? She had thought she would never get over Lucas's death. Now that she had and had found Giles, it was impossible to believe she would recover from it. It must be love, she thought drearily. But love should make you happy, not confused and angry and scared.

'Now, my lady, that is foolishness indeed!' Dorothy bustled about tidying up until Isobel thought she would scream. 'All young ladies want to get married and have children.' An ivory hairpin snapped between Isobel's fingers. 'You had a nasty time at that horrid house party and then you almost drowned and then there's the shock of poor Mr Harker coming back with his face all ruined. No wonder you are feeling out of sorts, my lady. You'll find a nice titled gentleman with a big estate and live happily ever after with lots of babies.'

'I don't want lots of babies. I just want my—' Isobel caught herself in time. 'His face is not ruined,' she snapped. 'The bruises and swelling will go down, the scar will knit and fade in time.'

'Yes, but he was so handsome. Perfect, like a Greek god.' The maid sighed gustily. 'Terrible blow to his pride, that will be.'

'He has more sense than to let such a thing affect him,' Isobel said, hoping it was true. Then a thought struck her. Surely Giles did not think she was saying she thought she loved him because she felt guilty that he had been wounded defending her good name? No, that was clutching at straws and she would go mad if she kept trying to guess at his motives. All she had was the bone-deep conviction that he did care for her and no idea how she could ever get him to admit it.

'I will go to bed and read awhile. Thank you, Dorothy, I will not need you again tonight.'

The maid took herself off, still talking about the joys of the London Season. Isobel stuffed another pillow behind her back and tried to read. *It might as well be in Chinese for all the sense it is making*, she thought, staring at the page and wondering why she had selected such a very gloomy novel in the first place.

THE SOUND WOKE her from a light sleep that could only have lasted an hour at the most, for the candles were still burning. What was it? A log collapsing into fragments in the fire? No, there it was again, a scratch at the door panels. Isobel scrambled out of bed and went to open the door, half expecting Lizzie, intent on a midnight feast.

Giles stood on the threshold in the brown-and-gold brocade robe open over pantaloons and shirt, his feet in leather slippers. In the dim light his eyes sparked green from the flame of the candle he held.

'What on earth is wrong? Does Lady Hardwicke need me?'

'No. May I come in?' The clock on the landing struck one.

'Quickly. Before someone sees you.' Isobel pulled him inside and closed the door before the thought struck her that he was even more compromising on this side of the threshold. 'Giles, you should not be here.' How could he be so reckless? He spoke about her reputation and then he came to her room in the small hours. Isobel let her temper rise: it was safer than any of the other emotions Giles's presence aroused.

'I am aware of that.' He put down the candle and went to stand in front of the fire. 'I could not sleep because of you.'

'A cold bath is the usual remedy for what ails you, is it not?' she demanded.

He gave a short, humourless bark of laughter. 'Guilt, I find, trumps lust for creating insomnia.'

'What are you feeling guilty about and why, if I may be frank, should I care?' Isobel pulled on a warm robe and curled up in the armchair, her chilly feet tucked under her. There stood Giles, close enough to touch, and there was her bed, rumpled and warm, and if that was not temptation, she had no idea what was.

He stooped to throw a log on the fire and stirred it into flame with the poker. The firelight flickered across his bruised, grim face and made him look like something from a medieval painting of hell, a tormented sinner. 'You might care. I lied to you. I care for you very much, Isobel.'

It seemed she had been waiting to hear those words from him for days, but now all that filled her was a blank, hurt misery. Isobel blinked back the welling tears. 'I had not thought you so cruel as to mock me.' The heavy silk of the chair wing was rough against her cheek as she turned her head away from him.

'Isobel—no! I am not mocking you.' The poker landed in the hearth with a clatter as Giles took one long stride across to the chair to kneel in front of her.

'Then you are cynically attempting to make love to me.' She still would not look at him. If he had come to her room with a heartfelt declaration of love then he would not have looked so grim.

'That would make me no better than those three, tricking my way into your room.' His hands, strong and cold, closed over hers and she shivered and looked down at the battered knuckles. 'Isobel, my Isobel, look at me.'

With a sigh she lifted her eyes to meet his. 'Whatever your feelings, Giles, they do not seem to make you very happy.'

'That is true,' he agreed. 'And it is true that I care for you, and like you and want you, all those things. And it shakes me to my core that you might love me.'

'Then why deny it? Why hurt me, play with my feelings like this?'

He released her hands, rocked back on his heels and stood up to pace back to the fire. 'Because what I feel for you is not love and I dare not let either of us believe that it is. Because even if it was, I can see no way to find any happiness in this, however we twist and turn. I do not want to play with your feelings, I would never hurt you if I could help it. But we can do nothing about it. I believed it for the best if you thought I did not care—you might forget about me. Then I realised how much that wounded you and I could not bear not to tell you that I do care, that I want you, that in some way I do not understand, you are mine.'

The hard knot of misery inside her was untwisting, painfully, as hope warred with apprehension. *I am his, he wants me, he likes me, but he does not believe he loves me?* 'And what you feel for me is not love?' she asked.

'I do not think I know how to fall in love,' Giles said flatly. 'I have been with more women than I care to admit to you, Isobel. And I have never felt more than desire and a passing concern for them, pleasure in their company.'

How carefully he guards his heart, she realised with a flash of insight. *He knows he is ineligible for any of the women he meets socially, so he does not allow himself the pain of dreaming.*

'You think it is hopeless, then? My love for you, your... feelings for me?' *Yes*, she thought as she said it. *Yes, I do love him.*

'Of course it is hopeless. Even if I was a perfectly respectable second son, say, earning my own living as an architect, your father would consider it a poor match. As it is, he would never permit you to ally yourself to me. And you deserve a man who loves you. We can be strong about this, Isobel. Avoid each other, learn to live our separate lives.'

'Will you not even *try* to find some way we can be together?' Isobel scrambled out of the chair and went to stand in front of him. The heat of the fire lapped at her legs, but every other part of her was cold and shivery. 'If we talk about it, perhaps we can see some way through.'

'No. It would be wrong to wed you.'

'I am of age, I can decide who to marry. Love grows. I would take a risk on yours.'

'Your father would cut you off,' Giles said. 'Disown you.'

'Do you want my money, then?' she jibed at him, wanting to hurt him as he was so unwillingly hurting her.

'No—but I do not want to deprive you of it.'

'As your wife I would hardly starve,' she pointed out. 'And I am not at all extravagant. We would not be invited to all the most exclusive events, so that would be a saving in clothes—'

'Do not jest,' Giles said, shaking his head at her. But she could see the reluctant curve of his mouth. Misery and pessimism did not come easily to him. 'A scandal would affect my business and then how could I support you?'

'You are imagining the worst.' Isobel shook his arm in exasperation. 'What if marriage to the daughter of an earl was good for your business? I would keep the other women at bay, I would entertain, I know all the people who might commission you. You say you do not think you will ever fall in love—well then, why not take the nearest thing to it?'

'Stop it, Isobel.' Giles put both hands on her shoulders and looked down into her face. 'You are talking yourself into an emotion you do not feel. I will go back to London. In a week or two you will go home and take part in the Season and you will find an eligible, titled husband and live the life you were born to live.'

'No. I will not,' she stated with conviction. 'I was waiting for a man to fall in love with. One who loved me. One I could confess my secret to and who might accept me despite it. I do love you, I know that now—this could not hurt so badly if it was simply desire. But I cannot believe that after Lucas, and now you, that I will find a third man to love, and one who feels the same. So I am resolved to give up on the Season. I will become a spinster, a country mouse who will dwindle quietly away as a good daughter and sister. One day, no doubt I will be an aunt and much in demand.'

'You are talking rubbish.' Giles's voice was rough. 'What secret?'

'That I am not a virgin.' There was the other thing as well, the thing that tore at her heart, but she could not tell him that, however much she loved and trusted him. 'Lucas and I were lovers in the weeks before he died, you see. Men seem to place such importance on that, in a bride. I could hope that someone who loved me would understand, but not a man who was making a marriage for other reasons. I could lie, I suppose, and hope he would not notice. I could pretend to be ignorant and innocent—but that is hardly the way to begin a marriage, by deceiving one's husband.'

She shrugged, his hands still heavy on her shoulders. The truth, but not the whole truth. But Giles, of all men, would not understand why she had done what she had done, why she had made the dangerous, desperate choice that she had.

He stood there silent and she wondered if she had shocked him. Was he like all the rest, the respectable ones who would condemn her for the sin of loving? 'I have disappointed you,' she stated, unable to wait for the condemnation on his tongue, the rejection on his face.

'Then you misjudge me,' Giles said. 'You were in love with him. He was a fortunate man. I can feel jealousy, I will admit that. But how can I condemn you? But you are right about one thing—it would have to be a deliberate act of deception to pretend to your husband that you are completely unawakened. Even holding you in my arms, kissing you, I felt the sensuality, the awareness of your own body's needs and of mine.'

'Giles?'

'Mmm?' He drew her in close and held her warm and safe against his bruised body and she felt his breathing as she slid her arms under his robe and around his waist. Suddenly it was all very simple.

'Make love to me.'

CHAPTER FOURTEEN

Giles's heartbeat kicked and his hands tightened. 'Isobel, think of the risk. You making love with the man you were going to marry is one thing. But I'll not chance getting you with child.'

'There are ways of making love that hold no risk,' she said. It was easier to be bold with her burning face hidden against his shirt front. 'We… Lucas and I, made love like that the first time.'

'You trust my self-control?' His voice rumbled in his chest against her ear and she felt the pressure as he rested his uninjured cheek against her hair. He had not rejected her out of hand. Her pulse quickened, the heaviness of desire settled low inside her. If he touched her intimately he would feel the evidence of her desire for him. And she wanted him to touch her, shamelessly.

'Yes.' The second time with Lucas, neither of them had had any self-control. But it had not mattered, they told themselves, lying tangled in a happy daze afterwards. They would be married within weeks. 'Am I asking too much of you?'

'There is nothing you could ask me that is too much, except to forget you. This is only going to make things worse for us, you know that?'

'I know. But it will not be worse until tomorrow.'

Giles gave a muffled snort of laughter. 'Feminine logic,' then gasped as she pulled a handful of shirt from his breeches and put her hands on his bare skin. 'Isobel, if we are found out—'

'Lock the door. Lock the door and make love to me, Giles.' Isobel stepped back out of his arms. 'Please. Make me yours, as much as we can.'

As he went to the door she blew out all but two of the candles.

'Isobel?' Giles turned back, the key in his hand.

'I am shy—a little,' she confessed and knew her blush added veracity to the half-truth. She did not want to risk what he might read from her body.

'There is no need,' he said, smiling at her as he let his robe drop then pulled his shirt over his head. 'It is all right,' he added as she ran forwards with a cry of distress at the sight of his ribs, marked black and blue with bruises. 'Bruised, not broken. Let me see you, Isobel.'

Her robe slithered to the floor. Under it all she wore was her nightgown, warm and sensible flannel for February. 'Ah. My little nun,' Giles teased and pulled it over her head before she could protest. 'Oh, no, not a nun. My Venus.'

'I am not that,' Isobel protested, her hands instinctively shielding her body, even as she warmed with shocked pleasure at Giles's expression as he looked at her in the shifting shadowlight.

'Slim and rounded and pale.' His hands traced down over her shoulders, down her arms, over her hips. His touch was warm now. 'When I first saw you I thought you were too thin and your nose was red from the cold. You seemed quite plain to me. I must have been blind.'

'And I thought you were a cold statue, too perfect to be real.' She let her hands stray to his chest and played with the dusting of dark hair. 'So cold.' His breath hitched as her fingernail scratched lightly at one nipple.

'No. Not cold,' Giles said thickly. 'Hot for you.' He kissed her, held her tight against him so her breasts were crushed against the flat planes of his chest and her thighs felt the heat of his through the black silk of his evening breeches. The thin fabric did nothing to disguise the hard thrust of his erection against her belly. This was no shy and tentative young lover, this was a mature, experienced man. Isobel moaned into his mouth, pressed herself against him.

She wanted him, needed him inside her so she could possess and be possessed, know that she was his. But they must not, she knew it. Whatever she did, she must not put Giles into a position where he felt honour-bound to marry her, come what may. Somehow—if only he would come to realise that he loved her—they would find a way, but not like that.

Giles slowed the kiss, gaining control after the first shock of their lips meeting. He edged her against the bed until she tumbled backwards and he followed her, rolling her into the centre of the mattress and coming to lie beside her.

'Your breeches.' Isobel felt for the fastenings, but his hand stilled hers, pressing it down over the straining weight of his erection.

'Better leave them on.' He was having trouble controlling his breathing, she realised.

'No.' She shook her head and burrowed her fingers beneath his. 'I know what to do. Let me touch you, Giles.'

'You are— Oh, God.' He sank back as her determined hands pulled down his breeches and tossed them away.

'Oh.' He was…magnificent. The fight had battered and bruised his upper body, but below the waist the skin was unblemished, winter-pale. The dark hair that arrowed down from his waist added emphasis to a masculinity that did not need any enhancement. Isobel realised he was holding his breath and did what instinct was clamouring at her to do. She bent and kissed him there, her hands curved over the slim hips.

Satin over teak beneath her lips, the scent of aroused male musk in her nostrils, lithe muscles in tension beneath her hands, his sharply indrawn breath—every sense was filled with him as she trailed her lips upwards.

'Isobel.' He sounded in pain, but she knew enough to realise this was not agony. 'Not yet. Let me…'

She did not fight him as he pulled her up to lie beside him. She would let him lead because it was on him that the burden of control fell. But she would help, she would be rational and—

Giles took her right nipple between his lips and tugged and all rational thought vanished. Isobel pulled his head against her breast with a sob and the knowledge that he could do what he wished with her, she had absolutely no will to stop him.

His mouth, wicked and knowing, tormented each tight, aching nipple in turn, until she was writhing against his flank, gasping his name and some incoherent plea she did not even understand herself. Her body, the flesh she had thought immune to desire for so long, ached and clamoured and, as his fingers stroked down, laced into the damp curls, slipped between the swollen lips, she simply opened to him, quivering with need as he slipped into the tight heat that clenched around his fingers.

'I love you,' she managed and was silenced by his mouth, his tongue. Against her hip she could feel his straining body and reached for him, finding the rhythm as her fingers curled around him and his thumb worked wicked, knowing magic at her core. 'I love you,' she gasped, the words lost in his kiss as her body arched, pressing up into the heel of his hand, shuddering as the bliss that was almost pain took her.

'Isobel,' she heard through the firestorm and Giles thrust into her circling fingers, shuddered and was still.

How long they held each other afterwards, she did not know. She must have drowsed, for she woke to find him gently washing away the evidence of his passion, then he pulled the covers over them, snuggled her against his side and she felt the long body relax as he slid into sleep.

There was only one candle alight now, Isobel noticed hazily. And Giles had said nothing. Her body had not betrayed her as she feared. He had not realised she had borne a child and her secret was still safe from the man she loved.

'WHAT TIME IS IT?'

'I can't tell with you wrapped round me like this,' Giles said, disentangling the clinging limbs that chained him so deliciously to the bed. He managed to raise himself on one elbow and lift the carriage clock that stood on the night table. It was almost completely dark and he had to bring it to his face to squint at the hands in the faint glow from the fire. 'Half past four. I must go soon.'

'Already?'

Isobel sounded peevish, he noted, amused, as she burrowed back against his side. The chuckle turned to a gasp as she slid one hand down and stroked. 'Ten minutes. Fifteen,' he amended as the caress tightened into a demanding grip.

'Only fifteen?' Isobel wriggled up to kiss his stubbled jawline. 'You are all bristles.'

'You would be amazed at what I can do in fifteen minutes with these bristles,' Giles said and burrowed down the bed, ignoring the twinges from his ribs.

'Oh, do mind your nose and the stitches,' Isobel said. Then, '*Oh*!' in quite another tone as he pressed her thighs apart and began to make love to her with mouth and tongue and, very gently, his teeth.

She was not shocked, he realised as he luxuriated in the scent and taste of warm, sleepy, aroused woman. Her fiancé must have made love to her like this as well. He half expected a twinge of jealousy, but surprised himself by feeling none, only pity for the other man. He would have married her if only he had lived, poor devil.

Then everything but the present moment and the pleasure of pleasuring Isobel was driven from his mind as she took his head in her hands and moaned, opening for him with complete trust, total abandon.

'TEN MINUTES,' GILES said with what even he recognised as smug masculine satisfaction when they lay panting in each other's arms, half inclined to laughter, completely relaxed.

'Fast is almost as good as slow,' Isobel murmured, kissing her way up from the tender skin just below his armpit to his collarbone. 'Giles, do you regret that your mother kept you instead of finding you a home where you would grow up with a family you thought were your own?'

'What on earth makes you ask that?' He sat up and struck a light for the candle beside them. Isobel rolled on to her back, her hair a tangled, wanton mass of shifting silk on the pillows. Giles bent and kissed her between her breasts.

'I don't know. Do you regret it? It cannot have been easy, being known as the Scarlet Widow's illegitimate son. It sounds as though you were bullied at school and there are some in society who shun you.'

'I would probably have been bullied anyway,' he said with a shrug. 'I was far too pretty—a real little blond

cherub until I started to grow and my hair darkened. And
if Geraldine had tried to give me away my grandfather
would have had something to say about it, so I would have
ended up with him and been an illegitimate gardener's boy
instead of having the education and the opportunities I
have had. No, I do not regret it. I know who I am, where I
came from. I am myself and there is no pretence, no lies.'

'You call your mother by her first name?'

'The last thing she wants is an almost-thirty-year-old
man calling her "Mama." It makes people do the arithmetic
and I doubt she'll admit to forty, let alone fifty.'

'I suppose her position protected her at the time, made
it easier for her to keep you.'

'No.' At first he had assumed that, but with matu-
rity had come understanding. 'It was anything but easy.
I picked up some of the story from her, some from my
grandfather, but she kept me when it would have been an
obvious thing for her to have pretended she was with child
by her late husband. All she had to do was to apparently
suffer a miscarriage late on, then retire from sight to recover, give birth and hand me to Grandfather.

'But she brazened it out and never pretended I was anything but my true father's son. I remember that whenever she is at her most outrageous. She is a very difficult
woman.'

'She must have loved him very much,' Isobel ventured.
She was pale and seemed distressed. Perhaps this was
bringing back memories of her fiancé's death.

'She had been in a loveless, if indulgent, marriage to a
man old enough to be her father for four years. She must
have needed youth, heat, strength.' Had it been love? Or, as
he suspected, had Geraldine simply needed to feel the emotion as she did with every lover since? It was such an easy
excuse, love. But how did you learn to feel it genuinely?

'My father was young, handsome, off to fight in his scarlet uniform. Perhaps he was a little scared under all the bravado. By all accounts it was not some wanton seduction by an experienced older woman or some village stud taking advantage of a vulnerable widow.'

'How brave she was.'

'It cut her off from her own family, from her in-laws and, for a long time, from society. But she fought her way back because I think she realised that my future depended upon it.' Giles got out of bed and began to dress. 'Not that she was ever the conventional maternal figure. And the shocking behaviour is probably a search for the love and affection she experienced for such a short time. Not that she would ever talk about it.' What had she felt when she heard of his father's death in battle? He had never wondered about that before. Now with someone to care about himself, the thought of his mother's pain was uncomfortably real.

Isobel still looked pensive. 'Giles, what are we going to do?'

'I am going to my own bed and you are going back to sleep. And check the pillow for hairs when you wake.' He rummaged under the bed for a missing slipper, determinedly practical.

'Our hair is close enough in colour for Dorothy not to notice. You have had a lot of practice at this sort of thing,' she said slowly. 'Only I presume it is suspicious husbands you need to deceive, not protective ladies' maids.'

'Complacent, neglectful husbands—a few in my time,' he confessed. 'I do not make a habit of it. Are you jealous?'

'Of course.' Isobel sat up straight and shook her hair back. It seemed her brooding mood had changed. The sight of her naked body filled him with the desire to rip his clothes off and get back into bed again.

'Yes, of course I am jealous even though I have no right to be,' she said with a half smile. 'My brain is all over the place—I am not thinking straight. When I asked what we are going to do, I did not mean now. I meant afterwards. In the morning.'

'And for the rest of our lives?' Giles pulled on his robe and made himself meet her eyes, too shadowed to read. 'I do not know, Isobel. I honestly do not know anything, except that this has no future.'

He turned the key in the lock and eased the door ajar. 'The servants are beginning to stir, I can hear them moving about on the landing above.' He looked back at her, upright, shivering a little in the morning air, her lips red and swollen from his kisses, her eyes dark. What he wanted was to drag her from the bed, bundle her in to her clothes and flee with her, take her home to Norfolk and be damned to the consequences. Was that love? If it was, it was selfish, for nothing would more surely destroy her.

'Go back to sleep,' Giles said instead and went out into the darkness.

WHAT SHE WANTED to do was to get up, get dressed, throw her things into a portmanteau and follow him, beg him to take her away, to his home and his grandfather and let the world say what it would. Because this was love, however much she might fight it. Love was too precious, too rare, to deny.

But it was impossible to act like that, as though she had only her own happiness to think of. Her parents would be appalled and distressed. Cousin Elizabeth and the earl would be mortified that such a scandal had occurred while she was under their roof. Giles's business, his whole future, would suffer from the scandal.

He cared for her and that was a miracle. He had shown

her love, all through the night, as much by his care and re-
straint as by the skill of his lovemaking. Perhaps he would
come to realise that he loved her, but some deep feminine
instinct told her that he would be wary of admitting it,
even if his upbringing, his past, the constraints upon him,
allowed him to recognise it.

She had given him everything she could, except that one
deep, precious secret. Annabelle. Lucas's child was being
raised as a legitimate Needham, believed by all the world
to be the twin of little Nathaniel, the child of her friend
Jane and Jane's husband Ralph Needham, Lucas's half-
brother. The two men were drowned together when their
carriage overturned into a storm-swollen Welsh mountain
beck late one winter's night.

No one knew except Jane, her small, devoted household
in their remote manor and the family doctor. Annabelle
was growing up secure and happy with all the prospects
of a gentleman's daughter before her and Isobel dared not
risk that future in any way. She saw her child once or twice
a year and lived, for the rest, on Jane's letters and Annabelle's messages to *Aunt Isobel*. Her parents would never
know their own grandchild. She had not heard her daughter's first words nor seen her first steps.

If she married again Isobel knew her conscience would
tear her apart. How could she take her marriage vows while
hiding such a thing from her husband? But how could she
risk telling a man when he proposed? If he spurned her
and then could not be trusted with the secret it would be
a disaster.

Giles had said he was glad he had stayed with his
mother, that he knew who he was. No pretence, no lies,
he had said and he obviously admired and loved the Dowager for the decision she had taken. He would not understand why Isobel gave her child away; he would think she

did not have the courage of his own mother to keep Annabelle and defy the world.

There was a very large lump in her throat and her face was wet, Isobel realised. She dared not let Dorothy find her like this. She slid out of bed, her legs still treacherously weak at the knees from Giles's lovemaking, and splashed her cheeks in the cold water on the washstand. Then she smoothed the right-hand side of the bed, tucked it in and got back in, tossing and turning enough to account for the creases.

A CLOCK STRUCK six and Isobel knew she had been lying, half asleep, half waking and worrying, since Giles had left her. In an hour and a half Dorothy would bring her chocolate and hot water. She must try to sleep properly despite the warm tingling of her body and the agitation of her mind. Whatever the day brought, she would need her wits about her.

CHAPTER FIFTEEN

There was no sign of Giles at breakfast, nor was he with the earl, Isobel discovered after some carefully casual questions. Lizzie finally gave her a clue.

'I think it is such a pity,' she was protesting to Anne as they entered the breakfast room. 'Good morning, Cousin Isobel. Have you heard the awful news? Mr Harker is conspiring with Papa to demolish the Hill House.'

'Really, Lizzie! You are dramatising ridiculously,' Anne chided as she sat down. 'Papa has decided it is not worth reconstructing, that is all. Much better that it is safely demolished.'

'But Mr Repton said—'

'Mr Repton is not always right and it is Papa's decision. Anyway, we would not be here to use it for ages, even if it was rebuilt.'

'Well, I am very disappointed in Mr Harker,' Lizzie announced darkly. 'He had better not try to knock down my castle.'

'I believe he is going to see what can be saved of the stonework to go to strengthening the Gothic folly,' her sister soothed. 'I expect that is what he is doing today. I heard him say something to Papa about good dressed stone not going to waste.' Lizzie subsided, somewhat mollified.

'Is Cousin Elizabeth coming down to breakfast or have

I missed her?' Isobel asked. 'I was going to ask her if I might ride this morning.' If Giles was not at the Hill House, then she would ride over the entire estate to find him, if necessary.

'Oh, Mama left early to drive into Cambridge to take Caroline to the dentist,' Anne said. 'I know it is Sunday, but she woke with the most terrible toothache. Mama says we can all go to evensong instead of matins. But I know she will not mind you taking her mare. Benson, please send round to the stables and have them saddle up Firefly for Lady Isobel.' As the butler bowed and crooked a finger for a footman to take the message, Anne added, 'I do not think this sunshine will last—my woman predicts a storm coming and she is a great weather prophet.'

THE SKY WAS certainly dark to the west as the groom tossed Isobel up into the saddle of the countess's pretty little chestnut mare. 'Shall I come with you, my lady? She's a lively one.'

'No, thank you. I can manage her.' She held the mare under firm control as they crossed in front of the house and then gave her her head up the hill towards the derelict prospect house.

Giles's big grey was tied up outside and whickered a greeting as Isobel reined Firefly in. A movement caught her eye and she glanced up to find Giles sitting at the window over the portico. One foot up on the sill, his back against the frame, he turned his head from the distant view he had been contemplating and looked down.

'Isobel. You should not be here.' But he smiled as he said it and a tremor of remembered pleasure ran through her.

She brought the mare up next to the grey and slid down to the steps, managing to avoid the mud. 'But we need to talk,' she said, tilting her face to look at him as she tied the reins to the same makeshift hitching post.

'Come up, then.' Giles disappeared from sight and met her at the top of the staircase.

'This feels so right. So safe,' she said and walked into his arms without hesitation. 'I do love you so, I know that now.'

Giles's reply was muffled in her hair, but she heard the words and the happiness was so intense it made her shiver. 'Last night was very special for me, Isobel.' Then he put her away from him and the look on his face turned the frisson into one of apprehension. 'But I have been up here for hours thinking—without any conclusion other than this is wrong and we must part.'

'No! No,' she repeated more calmly as she walked past him into the chamber. 'We are meant to be, meant for each other. I refuse to give up.'

'There is no way. We cannot change who I am and that is that.' The bruises on his face were yellowing now, the swelling subsiding. Isobel stood biting her lip and looking at his profile as Giles stared out of the window, his mouth fixed in a hard line.

'Your nose is not so very crooked,' she said after a moment. 'It is not as bad as when it was so swollen. Now it just looks interesting. Perhaps this—us—is not so bad either if we give it time and think.'

'The only thing that would make our marriage acceptable is your ruin, and you know it as well as I do. And there is no alternative for you other than marriage.'

'Then what is to become of us?' she said, her voice cracking on the edge of despair.

'We will learn to live without each other,' Giles said harshly. 'Just as you learned to live without Lucas when he died.'

'I would not call it living,' Isobel whispered. At first, despite the bitter grief, it had been bearable. That year when she had been with Jane, their pregnancies advancing together, the month after the births when she could hold Annabelle, truly be a mother to her—that had been a time of happiness mixed with the mourning. It was only after she had returned home, doubly bereaved of both fiancé and child, that Isobel had plunged into deep sadness.

'I do not think I realised how depressed I was,' she said, looking back over the past four years. 'Even when I felt better I did not want to mix socially, look for another man to love, because I did not believe there was one. I could not see what the future held for me. Now—'

'Now you must start afresh,' Giles said and turned from the window to look at her. 'You have the courage and the strength, you know you have. And you are better off without me, even ignoring my birth. I have been— I am—a rake, Isobel. I have never courted a respectable young woman.'

'So will you forget me easily?' He had made love with her, slept with her, been thinking about her for hours— and he still did not know if he loved her, she thought, her confidence shaken.

'No.' He shook his head. 'You have marked my heart as surely as these scars will mark my face. I will never forget you, never cease to want you. You are, in some way I do not understand, mine.'

'But you will find a wife and marry and have children.' She could see it now. He would find an intelligent, socially adept daughter of some wealthy city merchant and she would love him and he would be kind to her and together they would raise a family and Isobel would see them sometimes and smile even though her heart was cracked in two...

'Yes. And you will find a husband. We will find contentment in that, Isobel.'

How the sob escaped her, she did not know; she thought she could control her grief. 'It sounds so dreary,' she said and bit her lip.

'You will make a wonderful mother,' Giles said. 'You will have your children.'

'Oh, no. Do not say that. Do not.' And then the tears did finally escape, pouring down her face as she thought of Annabelle and the children she would never have with Giles.

'Sweetheart.' Giles pulled her into his arms, kissing away the tears. 'Please don't cry. Please. I am sorry I cannot be what you want me to be.'

She turned her head, blindly seeking his mouth, tasted her own tears, salt on his lips. 'Love me again, Giles. Now and every night while we are both here.' He went so still she caught herself with a pang of guilt. 'I'm sorry, that is selfish, isn't it?' She searched his face, looking for the truth she had learned to read in his eyes. 'It isn't fair to expect you not to make love fully.'

'I would want to be with you even if all I could do was kiss your fingertips,' Giles said, his voice husky. 'You gave me so much pleasure last night, Isobel. But I have no right to let you risk everything by coming to your chamber again.'

'If that is all we have, just the time we are both here, then surely we can take that, make memories from it to last for ever? We will not be found out, not if we are careful as we were last night.' It was Sunday, so perhaps it made what she was asking even more sinful. But how could loving a man like this be a sin?

'Memories?' He held her away from him, studying her face, and then he smiled. It was a little lopsided, but per-

haps that was simply because of the stitches in his cheek.
'Yes. We will make one of those memories here and now
and use that little chamber one last time for the purpose
for which it was intended.'

There was a rug thrown over the chair at the desk he
had been using to write his notes. Giles spread it over the
frame and ropes that were all that remained of the daybed
in the painted chamber and while he closed the battered
shutters Isobel shed her riding habit, pulled off her boots
and was standing, shivering slightly in her chemise and
stockings, when he turned.

'Goose bumps,' she apologised, rubbing her hands over
her chilled upper arms.

'I'll warm them away. Don't take any more off, it is too
cold.' He wrapped his greatcoat around her, then eased her
on to the bed before stripping to the skin.

Isobel lay cocooned in the Giles-smelling warmth of
the big coat and feasted her eyes on him. He would be embarrassed if she told him how beautiful his body was, she
guessed, and besides, many other women had told him that,
she was sure. Instead she wriggled her arms free to hold
them out to him. 'Giles, come into the warm.'

'I am warm.' He wrapped her up snugly again, then
parted the bottom of the coat so he could take her feet in
his hands, stroking and caressing them through her stockings, teasing and warming and arousing as he worked his
way up. Then he flipped the coat back over her lower legs
and proceeded to kiss and lick and nibble her knees until
Isobel was torn between laughter and desperation.

'Giles!'

'Impatience will be punished.' He covered her knees,
then shifting up the bed, left precisely the part she wanted
him to touch shrouded. He pushed up her chemise to lick

his way over the slight swell of her belly, into her navel, up between her breasts without once touching the curve of them, the hard nipples that ached for his touch.

Only when he reached her chin and she was whimpering with desire and delicious frustration did he lie on the bed beside her, lower his mouth to hers and kiss her with languorous slowness while his hands caressed her, edging her to the brink, then pulling back, building the pleasure until Isobel thought every nerve must be visible as they quivered under the skin, then leaving her again teetering on the edge of the abyss.

'Oh, you wretch,' she sobbed, her fingers tight on the hard muscle of his shoulders as she arched, seeking his touch. 'You torturer.'

'Touch me,' Giles said, bringing her hand to clasp around him. 'Take me with you.' Then he held nothing back, his body at her mercy, his hands demanding, demanding, until Isobel lost all sense of what was her and what was Giles and surrendered to the mindless oblivion of pleasure.

She came to herself to find him slumped across her, relaxed into sleep. 'Giles?'

'Mmm.' His lids fluttered, the dark lashes tickling her cheek, then he was still again.

Isobel tugged the greatcoat more securely over them, curled her arms around him and lay, cheek to cheek, thinking. Nothing lasted for ever. She had him now and for a few days and precious nights even though she did not have his words of love. She would not waste those moments by anticipating the inevitable parting; she would live them and revel in them and then do her best to live without him. *I will not pine. I will find some purpose, some joy in life. I will not allow something so precious to destroy me.* In the distance thunder rumbled.

An HOUR LATER they approached the house from different directions, Giles from the western drive, Isobel retracing her route, bringing Firefly across the wide sweep of gravel before the house to the stables. They met, as if by chance, outside the stable arch.

'Mr Harker! Good morning.' Isobel let the groom help her dismount and waited while Giles swung down from the grey. The sound of bustling activity made her look through into the inner yard where the back of a chaise was just visible.

'Visitors,' Giles observed. 'Have you had a pleasant ride, Lady Isobel?'

'Very stimulating, thank you. But I fear it is about to rain.' She caught up the long skirt of her habit and walked with him across to the front door. Benson opened it as they approached and Isobel stepped into the hall to find the callers had only just been admitted. A grey-haired man of medium height with a commanding nose turned at the sound of their entrance, leaning heavily on a stick. Beside him a thin lady in an exquisitely fashionable bonnet started forwards.

'Isobel, my darling! What good news! We had to come at once even if it did mean travelling on a Sunday.'

She stopped dead on the threshold. 'Mama. Papa.' Her mother caught her in her arms as Isobel felt the room begin to spin. There was a crash of thunder and behind her the footman slammed the door closed on the downpour. *No escape.*

'Darling! Are you ill? You have gone so pale—sit down immediately.'

'I… I am all right. It was just the shock of seeing you, Mama. Thank you, Mr Harker.'

Giles slid a hall chair behind her knees and Isobel sat down with an undignified thump. 'Lord Bythorn, Lady

Bythorn.' He bowed and stepped away towards the foot of the steps.

'Wait—you are Harker?'

'My lord.' Giles turned. His face had gone pale and the bruises stood out in painful contrast.

'Lord James Albright tells me that you were injured standing with him to bring to account those scum who compromised my daughter. And I hear from her own letters that you rescued Isobel and young Lizzie from the lake.'

'The lake was nothing—anyone passing would have done the same. And Lord James is an old friend, my lord. I merely did what I could to assist him.' Giles made no move to offer his hand or to come closer. Isobel realised her mother had not addressed him and she was looking a trifle flustered now. Of course, they knew who he was, what he was, and Giles had expected that, should he ever meet them, he would receive this reaction.

'You have my heartfelt thanks.' The earl paused, a frown creasing his brow. 'You are a resident in this house?'

'I am undertaking architectural work for the earl. Excuse me, my lord. Ladies.' He bowed and was gone.

'Well, I'm glad to have the opportunity to thank the fellow in person,' her father said, wincing from his gout as he shifted back to face her. 'But I must say I'm surprised to find him a guest in the house.'

'Lady Hardwicke always gives rooms to the architects and landscape designers,' Isobel said indifferently. 'The earl works so closely with them, I believe he finds it more convenient. I met Mr Soane when I arrived, but I have not yet met Mr Repton.'

'Soane? Well, he's a gentleman, at least. I hear rumours of a knighthood,' her father said. Isobel opened her mouth to retort that Giles was a gentleman, and a brave and gallant one at that, then shut it with a snap. To defend him would only arouse suspicion.

'The man looks a complete brigand with his face in that state,' her mother remarked with distaste.

'He was injured in the fight defending Lord James and, by extension, me.'

'Well, he might be less of a menace to women now he has lost his looks. The man was a positive Adonis, so I hear—and there are enough foolish ladies with the instincts of lightskirts to encourage men like that,' Lady Bythorn added with a sniff.

'Perhaps he is only a menace to married ladies,' Isobel said sweetly, her hands clenched so tightly that a seam in her glove split. 'Cousin Elizabeth has no qualms about allowing him to socialise with her daughters or myself. Suitably chaperoned, of course.'

'I am glad to hear about the chaperonage, at least! But that is all academic—I expect your woman can have your things all packed by the time we have finished luncheon.'

'Packed?

'Well, of course.' Her mother beamed at her fondly. 'Now everyone knows the truth of what happened, there is no reason for you to be hiding in the country. You can come home and do the Season just as we planned.'

'But—' Isobel could hear Cousin Elizabeth's voice coming closer. And the butler and footmen were still standing in the background, having stood to attention with blank faces throughout Lady Bythorn's opinions on Giles's morals. This was no place to start arguing with her parents about her future.

'Margaret! Bythorn! What a pleasant surprise.' The countess sailed into the hall, beaming. 'You've come to collect dear Isobel, of course. We are going to miss her sadly.' She ushered them towards the Yellow Drawing

Room. 'Margaret, would you like to go up with Isobel to her room? I will ring for her woman to bring you whatever you need after your journey. You must have set out at the crack of dawn to make such good time.'

'I will go up in a moment, Elizabeth—it is so good just to see Isobel again! We left as soon as we received Lord James's letter and put up overnight at the Bell at Buntingford. I could not wait to get my dear girl home again. Thank heavens we have not missed anything of the Season.'

'I imagine Isobel is more glad about the restoration of her reputation than the opportunity to take part in social events,' Cousin Elizabeth said with a glance at Isobel. There was understanding in the look and a kind of rueful sympathy. She, at least, had some inkling of how reluctant Isobel was to plunge back into the social whirl that she so disliked and the imagination to understand what gossip and snide remarks would still follow her.

'I would prefer to stay here, Mama,' Isobel said. She folded her hands on her lap and sat up straight, as though perfect deportment would somehow be a barricade against this disaster. If she let her shoulders droop, if she relaxed in the slightest, she did not think she would be able to stop herself either sobbing in despair or running to find Giles.

CHAPTER SIXTEEN

'Stay here?' said Lady Bythorn, turning her gaze on Isobel. For a moment she thought there was hope, then her mother shook her head. 'But you cannot impose on Lady Hardwicke's hospitality now it is not necessary. Really, Isobel, it is about time you shook off this pose of indifference to society. We should never have allowed you to stay with Mrs Needham for over a year in that remote place as we did. I declare you came back a positive stranger to us.'

'I am sorry, Mama.'

'It would be best for you to go back to London, Isobel,' Cousin Elizabeth said. 'We will miss you, but there is the risk that rumours may begin again if you do not make an appearance. It might seem that you have something to hide after all.'

So there was no help there. Where else could she go? If she ran away to Jane and Annabelle, then Papa would fetch her back and she did not think she could face him meeting his granddaughter all unawares. Without her allowance she had no money. To throw herself into Giles's arms would be to embroil him in a scandal that might wreck his career.

It seemed very hard to think coherently. Isobel felt she was running through a darkened house, banging on doors that all proved to be locked, twisting and turning in a maze of corridors.

She had thought she had a few more precious days with Giles—now those had been snatched away from her. She had to speak to him. When he left the hall he had turned towards the stairs. He must have gone up to his chamber to change.

'Mama, shall I show you to my rooms? I can set Dorothy to packing.' From somewhere she dredged up the courage to smile and stand and pretend composure.

'Of course.' Her mother linked arms with her as they went up the stairs. 'Now, you only have to overcome this indifferent shyness you seem to feel and all will be well. The country air has done you good—your cheeks are rosy, your lips look fuller and there is such a sparkle in your eyes.'

All the consequence of Giles's lovemaking, if her mother did but know it. It seemed she had no suspicion that anything untoward had occurred, even though they had entered the house together. Perhaps it seemed impossible to Mama that her daughter would even think of flirting with someone in his position, let alone anything else.

'Here we are. It is a lovely view, is it not? Dorothy, please can you pack all my things as soon as possible— I am sure you can ask for help if you need it. We will be leaving after luncheon, so do not neglect your own meal. But first, please fetch hot water for her ladyship.'

'Yes, my lady.' The maid bobbed a curtsy to the countess. 'I am so glad Lady Isobel is going home, my lady, if I may be so bold.'

'Thank you, Dorothy. We are all delighted,' Lady Bythorn said and the maid hurried out.

'Mama, would you excuse me while I run up to the nursery and schoolroom and say goodbye to the children? I have become very fond of them.'

'Of course. I will just sit here and admire the prospect from the window and rest a little.'

Isobel dropped a kiss on her mother's cheek and went out of the door leading to the back stairs. As soon as she was out of sight she ran up to the attics and into the school-room.

'Cousin Isobel!' Lizzie jumped up beaming from her seat beside Caroline, who had her head wrapped in a shawl and was looking very woebegone.

'Excuse me, Miss Henderson, for interrupting your lesson, but I have to say goodbye to the children. My mama and papa have come to collect me, Lizzie.'

'Oh.' Her face fell. 'Can you not stay a little longer?'

'No, I am sorry. I promise I will write to you all. Is Charles in the nursery? I must kiss him as well,' she said as she disentangled herself from the children's hugs.

'If you are all very good, we will wrap up warmly and go out on the leads to wave Lady Isobel goodbye,' the governess suggested.

'That will be lovely. Thank you. Now, I will be going to London, so I will send you all a present. Would you like that?'

She left them agog at the thought of gifts arriving when it was not even their birthdays or Christmas and whisked down the stairs and along the passage leading to Giles's bedchamber. There would be just time, if he was only still there.

Isobel pressed her ear to the panels, but she could hear no voices, so the valet was not with him. Without knocking she opened the door and slipped inside.

'Isobel!' Giles strode out of his dressing room and shut the door behind her.

'Your face—why have you taken the dressing off? The doctor hasn't even removed the stitches. Oh, it looks so sore!'

'It looks thoroughly unsightly and will, I hope, convince your parents that no daughter of theirs would look twice at its owner.' He gave her a little shake. 'What on earth are you doing here? There will be hell to pay if you are found with me.'

'I had to talk to you,' she protested. 'And I do not know when we could have snatched even a moment alone. Papa intends to return home immediately after luncheon. Giles, what are we going to do?'

'Nothing, except come to our senses,' he said, his face harsh. 'This is a blessing in disguise—the longer we were together, the more chance there was of this being discovered.'

'But we have no chance to plan now—'

'There is nothing to plan for. You are not a romantic young girl, Isobel. You knew this was hopeless, just as I did, but we let ourselves daydream and now it is time to wake up.'

'Just like that?' She stared at him. The cold, aloof man of their first meeting was back and her tender lover was quite vanished. 'No regrets, no sadness, just a *blessing in disguise*? I love you, Giles.'

'And I let myself think I could dally with an earl's daughter.' He cupped his hand around her cheek. 'Sunshine in February. I should have known there would be a frost to follow. *Wake up*, Isobel—it is over.'

'So you really do not love me?' she asked painfully. He thought of what had happened as just a dalliance? The rain drumming on the window echoed the frantic beating of her heart.

'I told you that. And you have not fallen in love with me, if you will only be honest with yourself. You had been hurt and rejected by people you thought were your friends. You wanted affection and you wanted to rebel, too.'

'You think so? After we made love as we have, you can still say it was all a delusion, an act of rebellion? It must have been, because I thought I knew you and now I do not think I do, not at all.'

She turned away, unable to bear his touch any longer, then swung back. 'Why did you fight for me if I was not important to you?'

'It was the right thing to do, for my friends and for any lady who had been betrayed in that way.'

'Gallantry, in effect. Just like rescuing two drowning people from the lake. I thought I was your friend.' It sounded forlorn, but however much it hurt her pride, she could not help herself. 'You said I belonged to you.'

'It was wrong of me to think I could make a friend of an unmarried lady and what I said about you being mine was foolish sentimentality.'

'So there is nothing between us?' It was like sticking pins into her flesh, but she had to have the truth from him. 'You were gallant and then deluded. We made love, but that was merely lust.'

'I admire your courage and your generosity, your wit and your elegance. I was privileged to share your bed, and my lips will be for ever sealed about that. You need have no fear I would ever give the slightest hint that so much as a kiss had passed between us.'

Isobel stared up at the scarred, battered face and tried to find her friend, her lover, her love, somewhere behind the hard mask. But there was nothing, just a faint pity, the hint of a smile. 'I trusted you, Giles.'

'I never lied to you. I never told you I loved you. I am sorry it went as far as it did.'

'But not as sorry as I am, Giles.' Isobel turned on her heel and walked out. She wanted to hesitate at the threshold, to stand there a moment, for surely he would call her back, but she made her feet keep walking, closed the door behind her with care and went back to her own room. He did not speak.

HER MOTHER, HAIR tidied and complexion restored with the judicious use of rice powder, was sitting with her feet on a stool while Dorothy bustled about packing.

'Isobel dear—have you been crying?' Her mother sat up straighter and stared at her.

'No… Well, a little. I was upset at leaving the children, they are very sweet. I suppose it has made my eyes a trifle watery, that is all. There is the gong—shall we go down?'

They descended the stairs arm in arm again. Her mother had relaxed now, Isobel sensed. Her unaccountable daughter had yielded, the Season could be exploited in every possible way and, by the end of it she, Isobel, would have come to her senses and be betrothed to a well-connected, wealthy man who would father a brood of admirable children. All would be well.

Cousin Elizabeth and her three eldest children were already in the dining room. Lord Hardwicke and her father followed them in and then, on their heels, Giles entered.

Lady Bythorn took one look at his face, gasped audibly and plunged into conversation with Lady Anne. Cousin Elizabeth frowned, more in anxiety about the effects of leaving off the dressing than from any revulsion at the scar, Isobel thought. Her father stared, then resumed his discussion of tenancy issues with the earl. Giles, apparently oblivious, thanked Lady Caroline for the bread, passed her the butter and addressed himself to his meal.

'Some brawn, my lady?' Benson produced the platter. Isobel stared at it quivering gently in its jelly and lost what little appetite she had left.

'Thank you, no, Benson. Just some bread and butter, if you please.'

It was strange, she thought as she nibbled stoically through two slices of bread and butter and, to stem her mother's urgings, a sliver of cheese. She had not expected a broken heart to feel like this. She was numb, almost as if she no longer cared. Perhaps it was shock; they said that people in shock did not feel pain despite dreadful injuries.

Over the rim of her glass she watched Giles and felt nothing, just a huge emptiness where only a few hours ago there had been a turmoil of feelings and emotions. Hope, love, desire, fear, uncertainty, happiness, confusion, tenderness, worry—they had all been there. Now, nothing.

She found she could smile, shake her head over Cousin Elizabeth's praise of her courage in rescuing Lizzie, tell her mother of the interesting recipe for plum jam the vicar's wife had given her. When her eyes met Giles's down the length of the table she could keep her expression politely neutral, even smile a bright, social smile.

It was only as they were gathered in the formal elegance of the Yellow Drawing Room to make their final farewells that Isobel realised what she felt like. She had visited Merlin's Mechanical Museum in Princes Street once and had marvelled over the automata jerkily going about their business with every appearance of life and yet with nothing inside them but cogs and wheels where there should have been a brain and a heart and soul.

She shook hands, and exchanged kisses, and smiled and said everything that was proper in thanks and when she saw a shadow fall across the threshold, and Giles stood there for a moment looking in, she inclined her head graciously. 'Goodbye, Mr Harker.'

But when her parents turned to look he was gone. Like a dream, she thought. Just like a daydream. Not a memory at all.

CHAPTER SEVENTEEN

'I have absolutely no expectation of finding anyone I wish to marry, Mama,' Isobel said, striving for an acceptable mixture of firmness and reasonableness in her tone. 'I fear it is a sad waste of money to equip me for yet another Season.' For four days she had tacitly accepted all her mother's plans, now she felt she had to say something to make her understand how she really felt.

Lady Bythorn turned back from her scrutiny of Old Bond Street as the carriage made its slow way past the shops. 'Why ever not?' she demanded with what Isobel knew was quite justified annoyance. She was doing her best to see her second daughter suitably established and any dutiful daughter would be co-operating to the full and be suitably grateful. 'You are not, surely, still pining for young Needham?'

'No, Mama.'

'Then there is no reason in the world—' She broke off and eyed Isobel closely. 'You have not lost your heart to someone unsuitable, have you?'

'Mama—'

'Never tell me that frightful Harker man has inveigled his way into your affections!'

'Very well, Mama.'

'Very well what?'

'I will not tell you that Mr Harker has inveigled in any way.'

'Do not be pert, Isobel. It ill becomes a young woman of your age.'

'Yes, Mama. There is no illicit romance for you to worry about.' *Not now.*

'We are at Madame le Clare's. Now kindly do not make an exhibition of yourself complaining about fittings.'

'No, Mama. I will co-operate and I will enter into this Season, fully. But this is the last time. After this summer, if I am not betrothed, I will not undertake another.'

'Oh!' Lady Bythorn threw up her hands in exasperation. 'Ungrateful girl! Do you expect me to wait for grandchildren until Frederick is finally old enough to marry?'

The guilt clutched like a hand around her heart. Mama would be a perfect grandmother, she loved small children. She would adore Annabelle and Annabelle would love her. 'I am afraid so, Mama. Thank you, Travis,' she added to the groom who was putting the steps down and remaining impassive in the face of his mistress's indiscreet complaints.

Isobel followed her mother into the dress shop, sat down and proceeded to show every interest in the fashion plates laid out in front of her, the swatches fanned out on the table and the lists of essential gowns her mother had drawn up.

'You have lost weight, my lady,' Madame declared with the licence of someone who had been measuring the Jarvis ladies for almost ten years.

'Then make everything with ample seams and I will do my best to eat my fill at all the dinner parties,' Isobel said lightly. 'Do you think three is a sufficient number of ballgowns, Mama?'

'I thought you were not—that is, order more if you like,

my dear.' Her mother blinked at her, obviously confused by this sudden change of heart.

One way or another it would be her last Season—either a miracle would occur and she would be courted by a man who proved to be outstandingly tolerant, deeply understanding *and* eligible enough to please her parents or she would be lying in a stock of gowns she could adapt for the years of spinsterhood to come.

'Aha! All is explained! Lady Isobel is in love,' the Frenchwoman cried, delighted with this deduction.

Isobel simply said, 'And two riding habits.' She felt empty of emotion. That had to be a good thing. It meant she could lead a hollow life and indulge in all its superficial pleasures for a few months: clothes, entertainment, flirtation. It would satisfy Mama, at least for a while, and it would be something to do, something to fill the void that opened in front of her.

'I AM NOT certain I quite approve of Lady Leamington,' Lady Bythorn remarked two weeks later as the queue of carriages inched a few feet closer to the red carpet on the pavement outside the large mansion in Cavendish Square. 'She strikes me as being altogether too lax in the people she invites to her balls, but, on the other hand, there is no doubt it will be a squeeze and all the most fashionable gentlemen will be there.'

Isobel contented herself with smoothing the silver net that draped her pale blue silk skirts. A shocking squeeze would mean plenty of partners to dance with, many fleeting opportunities for superficial, meaningless flirtation to give the illusion of obedience to her mother. In large, crowded events she felt safe, hidden in the multitude like one minnow in a school of fish.

Following the scandal of Lord Andrew's arrest and sub-

sequent disappearance to his country estates, she found
herself of interest to virtually everyone she met. Men she
had snubbed before seemed eager to try their luck with
her again, young ladies gasped and fluttered and wanted
to know all about how *ghastly* it had been. The matrons
nodded wisely over the sins of modern young men and
how well dear Lady Isobel was bearing up.

'I DO NOT care any more, so I have suddenly become attractive,' she said wryly to Pamela Monsom who stopped for a
gossip when they met in the ladies' retiring room. Pamela
had been one of the few friends who had stood by her in
the aftermath of the scandal, writing fiercely to say that
she did not believe a word of it and that men were beasts.

'It is not just that,' Pamela said as she studied her,
head on one side. 'Although you are thinner you also look
more… I don't know. More grown up. Sophisticated.'

'Older,' Isobel countered.

'Oh, look.' Pamela dropped her voice to a whisper. 'See
who has just come in!'

'Who?' Isobel pretended to check her hem so she could
turn a little and observe the doorway. 'Who is that?'

The lady who had just entered was exceedingly beautiful in a manner that Isobel could only describe as *well
preserved*. She might have been any age above thirty-five
at that distance—tall, magnificently proportioned, with a
mass of golden-brown hair caught up with diamond pins to
match the necklace that lay on her creamy bosom.

She swept round, catching up the skirts of her black
gown, and surveyed the room. The colour was funereal,
but Isobel had never seen anything less like mourning. The
satin was figured with a subtle pattern and shimmered like
the night sky with the diamonds its stars.

'That, my dear, is the Scarlet Widow,' Miss Monsom

hissed. 'I have never been this close before—Mama always rushes off in the opposite direction whenever she is sighted. I think she must have had a fling with Papa at some point.' She narrowed her eyes speculatively. 'One can quite see what he saw in her.'

For the first time in days Isobel felt something: recognition, apprehension and a flutter very like fear. The wide green eyes found her and she knew Pamela was right: this was the Dowager Marchioness of Faversham, Giles's mother.

The lush crimson lips set into a hard line and the Widow stalked into the room.

'She is coming over here!' Pamela squeaked. 'Mama will have kittens!'

Isobel found she was on her feet. Her own mother would be the one needing the smelling bottle when she heard about this. 'Lady Faversham.' She dropped a curtsy suitable for the widow's rank.

'Are you Lady Isobel Jarvis?' The older woman kept her voice low. It throbbed with emotion and Isobel felt every eye in the retiring room turn in their direction as ladies strained to hear.

'I am.'

'Then you are the little hussy responsible for the damage to my son's face.'

'I shall ignore your insulting words, ma'am,' Isobel said, clasping her hands together tightly so they could not shake. 'But Mr Harker was injured in the course of assisting Lord James Albright to deal with his sister's errant fiancé who had assaulted me.'

'You got your claws into him, you convinced him that he must defend your honour and look what happened!' The Widow leaned closer, the magnificent green eyes so like Giles's that a stab of longing for him lanced through

Isobel. 'He was *beautiful* and you have scarred him. You
foolish little virgin—you are playing with fire and I'll
not have him embroiled in some scandal because of you.'

No, I do not want to feel, I do not want to remember...
'I should imagine that Mr Harker has far more likelihood
of encountering scandal in your company than in mine,
ma'am,' Isobel said, putting up her chin. 'If a gentleman
obeys an honourable impulse on my behalf I am very grateful, but as I did not request that he act for me, I fail to see
how I am responsible.'

'You scheming jade—'

'The pot calling the kettle black,' Isobel murmured. Her
knees were knocking, but at least her voice was steady.
She had never been so rude to anyone in her entire life.

'I am warning you—keep your hands off my son.' By
a miracle the Widow was still hissing her insults; except
for Pamela beside her, no one else could hear what they
were talking about.

'I have no intention of so much as setting eyes on your
son, ma'am, let alone laying a finger on him,' Isobel retorted.

'See that is the truth or I can assure you, you will suffer
for it.' Lady Faversham swept round and out of the room,
leaving a stunned silence behind her.

'What dramatics,' Isobel said with a light laugh. 'I have
never met Lady Faversham before and I cannot say I wish
to keep up the acquaintance!'

That produced a ripple of amusement from the handful
of ladies who had been staring agog from the other end
of the room. 'What on earth is the matter with her?' Lady
Mountstead demanded as she came across to join them.

'Her son was injured assisting Lord James Albright to
put right an unpleasant situation—I am sure you know to

what I refer. The Dowager blames me for some reason.'
But not as much as she blamed herself.

Isobel lingered, working to dampen down the speculation, turn it towards gossip about the scandalous Widow
and away from her own affairs. She felt reasonably confident she had succeeded when she left the retiring room,
but her mother would be aghast, she knew it.

'I had best go and find Mama and warn her of that little
incident,' she said to Pamela. 'If we do not see each other
again tonight, you must call, very soon.'

'I will most certainly do that.' Pamela was still wide-
eyed with speculation. 'And I expect to hear all about the
shocking Mr Harker. But now I suppose I had better go
and rejoin my party in the supper room.' She hurried off.

Thoroughly flustered, Isobel took the other right-hand
corridor. It was deserted, badly lit, but she thought it might
lead to the end of the ballroom where she had last seen
her mother. The temptation to tell her nothing at all was
strong, but the gossip would be certain to reach her ears,
so she had no choice but to warn her.

She hurried on, head down, trying to think of a way
to break the news that she had been accosted, in public,
by the Scarlet Widow. 'Ough!' The man she had walked
right into caught her by both arms to steady her, then, as
she looked up, the grip tightened. 'You!'

'Me,' Giles agreed. He did not release her and she stood
still in his grasp, not knowing whether that was because
she wanted to have his hands on her or because struggling
would be undignified.

'Your face is healing well.' It was the first thing that
came into her head that she dared say out loud. *I love you*
or *You abandoned me* or *Take me away with you* or *I hate
you* were all impossible. 'How long have the stitches been

out?' The scars were still red, but the swelling and bruising had gone—soon they would begin to fade.

'Two weeks.'

'You look…it makes you look dangerous.'

'So I have been told.' Something in his tone suggested that whoever had said so had been female. 'You appear to be enjoying yourself, Isobel.'

'Do I? You have been watching me?'

'You are hard to miss in that gown and when you are so ubiquitous. Dancing every dance, flirting with so many gentlemen. Your heart has quite recovered, I see.'

'And also whatever of yours was engaged.' Isobel twisted her right hand out of his light grip and flicked at the trace of face powder on his lapel. 'The lady favours Attar of Roses, I think.'

'One of them, as I recall, yes.' He sounded bored, like a tomcat who could hardly be bothered with the hunt. With his newly broken nose and the scars above the immaculate white linen and complicated neckcloth, he looked like a pirate playing at being a gentleman.

'Such a bore for you, all these women throwing themselves at you,' Isobel said, her voice dripping with false sympathy. 'Still, I suppose you can hardly afford to neglect your admirers—who knows, one of them might be about to persuade her complaisant spouse that she needs her boudoir remodelled.'

'The lady with the Attar of Roses wants a new library as a present for her husband.'

'And I am sure she will be at home the entire time to supervise.'

'Probably.' He was angry at her jibes. The colour was touching his cheekbones and the green eyes were cold, but the drawl was as casual and as insolent as before. 'What are you doing in town, Isobel?'

'The Season. What else?' She shrugged.

'I thought that was the last thing you wanted.'

'That was before a certain gentleman reminded me about the pleasures of the flesh,' she said, smiling at him when his brows snapped together in a frown. A demon seemed to have taken control of her tongue. 'I thought perhaps I might be…entertained if I came to London.'

'And I thought you did not want to marry again.'

'Were we discussing marriage, Giles?'

'You little witch. If it is fleshly pleasure you want—' He tugged on the wrist he still held captive, pulling her against his exquisite silk waistcoat. The lingering scent of roses warred with his citrus cologne in her nostrils and under it was the faint musk of a man who was hot with temper.

And lust, she realised as his mouth came down and his hands trapped her and his lips punished her for defiance. She knew his body and he knew hers. She found she had clenched one hand on his buttock, holding him tight against her. The pressure of his erection sent tongues of flame to the core of her as his mouth left hers and he began to pull at the neckline of her gown, his lips seeking the nipple, his tongue and teeth wreaking havoc with her senses.

They were crushed into a corner now, his hand under her skirts as she lifted her leg to hook it around his hip to give him access. It was mad, insane, they were both so angry, both so—

The sharp clip of heels on marble was like a bucket of cold water thrown in her face. Isobel gasped, found her feet, pushed at Giles even as he spun round instinctively to shield her.

'Geraldine,' Giles said. His mother.

From behind him Isobel could see the dark sheen of black satin, the glitter of diamonds. She pushed her way free to stand at his side and confront the other woman, her chin up.

'You little fool,' the Dowager hissed. 'So you lied to me. You will be sorry for this. Very sorry.'

Isobel simply turned on her heel and walked away. Neither of them made the slightest attempt to stop her.

The passage turned and she jumped at the sight of someone coming towards her, then she saw it was her own reflection in a long glass. Her bodice was awry, her hair half-down, her skirts crumpled. With hands that shook Isobel righted her gown, twisted the loose ringlets back into order, fanned her face with her hands until the hectic colour began to subside, then went out into the ballroom before she had time to think about what had just happened.

'Mama.' Lady Bythorn was deep in conversation with the Dowager Lady Darvil, but she turned with a smile that became rigid when she saw Isobel's face.

'Are you unwell, my dear? You look quite—'

'Flustered,' Isobel hissed. 'I know. Mama, I must speak with you alone. Urgently.'

'You have the migraine?' Lady Bythorn said clearly as she got to her feet. 'Do excuse us, Georgiana, I fear Isobel is suffering from the heat—we had best go home. Come, dear.'

With a suitably wan smile for Lady Darvil, Isobel let herself be led to the hallway and fanned while their cloaks were found and the carriage called.

'What is it?' her mother demanded the moment they were inside. 'Has someone been referring to the scandal?'

'No. Mama, the Dowager Lady Faversham found me in the retiring room and said the most horrible things. She blames me for the injuries Mr Harker suffered.'

'Oh, my heavens! That frightful creature. I knew Frederica Leamington could not be trusted not to invite the wrong sort of people. Did anyone hear her?'

'Only Pamela Monsom and she is very discreet. There were other people in the room, but they did not hear exactly what she said and when she left I explained that she was upset about Mr Harker's scars and they were very sympathetic. But they are sure to gossip.'

'And now your name will be linked with his,' her mother observed grimly. 'There is nothing to be done but brazen it out—thank goodness he was not there tonight!'

Isobel bit her lower lip. She did not feel capable of confessing to her mother that Giles Harker had indeed been at the ball. Her body still quivered from his touch and from the anger that had flashed between them.

'There, there.' Her mother leaned over in the shadowed interior to pat her hand. 'It will be all right. That woman has such a dreadful reputation that no respectable person would believe a word she has to say.'

But I do. She said I would be sorry, and she meant it.

CHAPTER EIGHTEEN

'What the devil are you about?' Giles planted himself squarely in the corridor to block his mother's furious, impetuous path. She was quite capable of sweeping out into the ballroom on Isobel's heels and continuing this scene there.

'You fool,' she snapped at him, eyes flashing. 'You aren't content with having your face ruined for the sake of that little madam, but now you are getting yourself entangled with her. She'll be the ruin of you! She's an earl's daughter—Bythorn won't stand for it and he has influence.'

'And he never slept with you, so you can't play that card,' Giles drawled, hanging on to his temper by a hair's breadth. 'I am not entangled with Isobel Jarvis—'

'Hah!'

'We were merely continuing an argument.'

'An argument? I have heard it called many things, Giles, but never that!'

'I am not having an affair with the girl.'

'No,' the Widow said grimly. 'You fancy yourself in love with her.'

'I am not in love with her. I am considering strangling her.'

'Listen to me! I have found you the perfect wife, Giles,' she said as he turned on his heel.

'Really?' he threw back over his shoulder. 'Some plain daughter of a Cit?'

'No. Caroline Holt, the daughter of Sir Joshua Holt.'

'And what is wrong with her? Or the family, that they should consider allying themselves with us?'

'There is absolutely nothing wrong with Miss Holt who is tolerably pretty, intelligent and twenty-three years old. What is wrong with her father is a series of investments that have gone badly wrong, an estate mortgaged to the hilt and four unmarried daughters on his hands.'

Giles turned round fully to face his mother. 'So Caroline is the sacrificial lamb. You buy her for me, Holt pays off the debts and the other girls can enter the Marriage Mart with some hope of attracting respectable husbands. Provided they aren't seen with their brother-in law, that is.'

'Exactly. And you get a well-bred wife who will be grateful for all we have done for her family.'

'How did you find her?' he asked even as he wondered how he was managing to keep his temper, and the urge to storm into the ballroom and drag Isobel out of it, under control.

'I have excellent enquiry agents.'

Of course, Geraldine had always prided herself on being able to find out anything about anyone. It was how she made such good choices in her lovers, avoided blackmailers, kept away from men with wives who had connections that would be dangerous to her and always found the right place to invest her money.

'I hope you have not made the Holts any promises.' His body was throbbing with frustrated desire. He felt as though he had been kicked in the gut and he had an overwhelming need to break something. 'Because I am not marrying the girl, for which she should be profoundly grateful. I have told you before, there is nothing you can buy me, least of all a wife.'

A dismissive flick of Geraldine's hand was all the acknowledgement she gave that she had heard him. 'Caroline Holt is not going anywhere far from her home in the wilds of Suffolk,' the Widow said with a thin smile. 'She will wait until you come to your senses about the Jervis chit.'

'My senses are perfectly in order, ma'am. My refusal to marry Miss Holt has nothing to do with Lady Isobel.'

'Liar!' she threw at him. 'She ruined your looks and yet you lust after her like a—'

'Mother,' Giles said. It stopped her in midrant. He never called her that unless he was deeply angered and she knew it. 'I have it on good authority that a broken nose and a couple of scars gives me an interesting air of danger. Really, I should thank Lady Isobel.'

The Widow took a deep breath. 'I would sacrifice everything for you, Giles. I would do anything to ensure your future.'

It was guilt, he knew, although she would never admit it, or probably even recognise it. Her actions had made him a bastard—now she would fight tooth and nail to force society to accept him.

'I can look after my own future,' he said, not unkindly. He hated it when her voice shook like that. 'Society accepts me for who I am and I make my own way in it. Go back to Carstairs and stop plotting: I'll not have Lady Isobel insulted.' Knowing Jack Carstairs, her current youthful lover, he would be scouring the house trying to discover where Geraldine had got to, well aware that he would probably have to extricate her from some scrape or another when he did find her.

Giles walked away with the firm intention of getting drunk. Behind him he thought he heard Geraldine repeat,

'Anything,' but he was not certain. Besides, there was no need to worry—there was nothing that she could do to harm Isobel. He was her only dark secret and Geraldine would not risk involving him in further scandal.

'Who is your letter from, Isobel?' Lady Bythorn glanced up from her own correspondence. 'You've been staring at the same page for minutes. Is the handwriting bad?'

'No. No it is from Jane Needham. I am just…thinking.'

We are all in the best of health and the children are flourishing despite being cooped up with the dreadful weather, Jane had written. *Nathaniel wants a puppy and Annabelle wants a kitten, so I foresee scratches all round before much longer. The oddest thing happened the other day: there was a stranger staying at the Needham Arms—we heard all about him because, as you know, we hardly ever get any strangers in the parish and the rumour was he looked like a Bow Street Runner. Which is pure fancy of course, because no one here has ever seen a Runner!*

But he came to the house asking for you and when I saw him and told him he was mistaken, that you do not live here, he just brushed it aside and said he's heard you stayed here sometimes. I demanded to know his business and he said he had been sent by a distant relative of yours, a sea captain, who was estranged from the family and was trying to make contact again, but who did not want to go directly to your parents. It sounded the most perfect non-sense to me and I said as much and he bowed himself off. But the thing that worries me is, when Molly went out for firewood yesterday afternoon she found him talking to the children in the yard—they had gone to look at the puppies.

She sent him about his business and I have had young Wally Hoskins go with them everywhere since then, just in case. But if he was intending to kidnap them—why these children? We are not wealthy, he must have realised that.

I thought I had better tell you—because of him asking for you by name. Perhaps I am worrying too much and he is just what he said. Or slightly mad. But I must confess to being anxious.

'Mama, do we have any relative who is, or was, a sea captain? Or any relative who is estranged from the family?'

'A sea captain? Or someone estranged? Goodness, no, I do not think so. In fact I am certain. Why?'

'Oh, Jane met someone who said something that puzzled her. She must have misunderstood.'

'No doubt she did. I cannot help but think that living so secluded as she does cannot be good for her.'

Isobel folded the letter, then opened it again. The mysterious man had been asking for her and then he was found with the children. *Annabelle.* Lady Faversham's words came back to her like a curse, even though it had been almost a month since they were uttered. *You will be sorry for this. Very sorry.*

She could not possibly know and Isobel had seen neither her nor Giles since that night. And yet Annabelle was Isobel's only weak spot, the only secret she was desperate to keep. She tried to tell herself it was pure fancy, yet she could not be easy in her mind.

THREE DAYS LATER there was another letter. It began, *Do not leave this lying around, for I cannot write in such a way that would disarm suspicion if your mother reads it and yet convey my anxiety adequately. The strange man is still hanging around the neighbourhood—and still asking questions about us. When you were here, how long you stayed, what happened to Ralph, how old the children are—he has looked at the parish registers, I am certain, for Mr Arnold found him right by the cupboard where they are stored and it was not locked.*

He is very subtle about it, which, I confess, worries me most of all, for it seems professional somehow. It is only by piecing together bits of gossip that I can see a pattern in his questions, for he never interrogates the same person for long. I have spoken to the few servants who were with us that year and who know the truth so they are on the alert. I cannot see how he would approach Dr Jameson, who, besides, would never say anything.

Can you make any sense of this, dearest Isobel? I vow I cannot. I have hired two of the Foster brothers—you recall what a size they are—and they patrol the house and yard at night and one of them is always with the children by day. It is doing dreadful things to Nathaniel's vocabulary!

It would not take much effort for anyone to find out where she had spent that year after Lucas's death—they had made no secret of it at the time, quite deliberately. Isobel's refusal to allow any friends or relatives to visit had been lamented by Lady Bythorn to all her circle and had been attributed to hysterical grief followed by a sad decline. The very openness of her mother's complaints seemed to disarm all suspicion that there was anything to hide and Isobel's reluctance to socialise since her return had contributed to the diagnosis of a melancholic temperament.

'Jane is unwell,' she said to her parents, the letter tight in her hand. 'I must go to Hereford.'

'Now?' Her father put down the copy of *The Times* he had been muttering over and frowned at her. 'In the middle of the Season? All that way?'

'It would take me only twenty-four hours, even if I go by the Mail, but if I might take a chaise, Papa, I could do it in less time and more comfortably.'

'Certainly not the Mail,' her mother said firmly. 'And a chaise? Oh, dear, you know how those things bring on my migraine and they do your father's gout no good at all.'

'I can go with Dorothy, Mama, there is no need for either of you to disturb yourselves. If we leave before luncheon and take a basket with some food we can go right through to Oxford for the night with only stops for changes—and there are any number of most respectable inns where I could find a private parlour.'

IT TOOK ALMOST an hour of wrangling to convince her parents that she could not possibly abandon her friend when she was unwell and worried about the children. That, yes, of course she would come home just as soon as she could and not miss the Lavenhams' ridotto which promised to be the event of the Season. And yes, she would take the greatest care on the road and not speak to anyone unless absolutely necessary and certainly no gentlemen.

It was only then, as she organised her packing, that the apprehension churning in her stomach turned to real fear. If she was ruined, then that was just too bad, although she was very sorry that the disgrace would distress her parents. But for Annabelle to be exposed as an illegitimate child would destroy all her prospects as well. And what of Jane? There might be penalties for allowing a false record to be entered in the registers. Would it even cast a shadow over little Nathaniel's legitimacy?

It had to be Lady Faversham behind this, for surely Giles would not do anything to hurt her, however angry she made him. It was only as she climbed into the chaise and waved goodbye that she realised she had no idea what she could do when she reached Hereford. But she could not sit in London while her child was in peril and leave Jane to face whatever this was alone.

'YOU WERE RIGHT—GERALDINE'S up to something and she's planning to go to Hereford of all places.'

'Are you certain?' *Hereford*. Giles put down his knife and fork and stared at Jack Carstairs over his half-eaten breakfast. His mother's lover had arrived at his Albany chambers without warning and seemed decidedly put out.

Since the confrontation at the Leamingtons' ball Giles had been at pains to avoid Isobel. It would do her reputation no good to be seen with him and it seemed he could not trust himself to keep his hands off her. There were two things he could do to protect her: stay out of her way and make certain his mother did her no harm.

Before Jack's arrival, it had occurred to him after a night of tossing and turning that the best way to circumvent Geraldine was to discover where Isobel was vulnerable. He was certain there was something, something more to her past than the simple loss of her virginity to her fiancé.

Unable to sleep, his remedies had been either a cold bath or distraction. Shrugging into his robe he had taken a candle and pulled the *Peerage* off the shelves. He might as well start by getting the family straight: Isobel's family, the Jervises—no, after ten minutes he could see nothing out of the ordinary there.

Then, on impulse, he looked under Needham. The current viscount was a half-brother of Lucas who had drowned in January 1797. He looked at the other entries for the same name. *The Hon. Ralph Needham decd.* Lucas's other half-brother, he worked out. And he had died on the same day as Lucas, Giles realised, flicking back to check. *Married Miss Jane Barrymore, by whom issue Nathaniel and Annabelle.* Twins born posthumously in September 1797. *Longmere Manor, Gaston, Hereford.*

Hereford rang a bell. Isobel had mentioned it with a note of longing in her voice and then, when he would have questioned her about it, for the area was unknown to him, she had abruptly changed the subject.

Giles had stared at the entry, working out the relationships. Ralph was Lucas's younger half-brother. That was a close connection to Isobel, but what did it signify and how could it harm her? *Lucas and I were lovers*, she had confessed. But what of it? She had been betrothed to the man. He ran a finger over the close-packed black lines of type, half-formed ideas worrying at the edges of his mind.

GILES DRAGGED HIMSELF back to the present and the other man. He had taken Carstairs into his confidence to a degree, putting it to him that it was in Geraldine's interests if they could stop her embarking on a destructive feud with Lady Isobel.

'I'm certain. But I've no idea why, she won't tell me. Threw the coffee pot at my head when I wouldn't go with her. Damn it, Harker,' Carstairs said, pulling out a chair and sitting down, 'I'm not trailing half across the country in support of one of her vendettas and I told her so. Told her you wouldn't like it, either. Is there any fresh coffee?'

'Hicks! Coffee for Mr Carstairs.' Giles picked up his own cup and frowned into the dregs. They held no answers. 'Any more letters?'

The other man nodded. 'She's been getting letters daily that have been pleasing her inordinately, as I told you, and then this one arrived and she said, *Hah! I've got the little hussy now* and ordered her woman to pack and sent her footman out to hire a chaise.

'Thought you ought to know, because I'm pretty certain it has some connection with Lady Isobel. Or, at least, something to do with you. When she got these letters she'd stare at that portrait of you over the fireplace with such a look in her eyes. Brrr.' He shuddered theatrically and peered at Giles more closely.

'How's the face? Looks as though it is healing well. Thought they'd carved half of it off, the way Geraldine was carrying on at first.'

Giles shrugged. 'Healing. There will always be scars. Geraldine attaches too much importance to looks.' What the devil had the woman discovered about Isobel?

He was prepared to go to any lengths to protect her, he realised, even though he was not willing to put a name to his feelings. Her hints at the ball that she might take a lover had made him jealous, furiously jealous, even while he knew she was deliberately provoking him and would no more do such a thing than fly. With disastrous honesty she had told him she loved him and she had meant it. His attempts to reject her for her own good had made her angry, but it had not changed her love for him, he sensed that.

'I'm going to Herefordshire to find out what is going on. But I'll see Geraldine first and make damned certain she stops this nonsense.'

'The best of luck, old chap,' Carstairs said with a rueful grin.

ISOBEL GOT DOWN from the chaise at the Bell in Oxford at seven in the evening, nine hours after she had finished reading Jane's letter at breakfast that morning. They had made better time than she had expected, but even so she felt exhausted already and there were another fourteen or fifteen hours travelling ahead of her.

'Looks a decent enough place,' Dorothy conceded with a sniff as one of the porters came forward, touched his forelock and took their bags.

'We will require two adjoining bedchambers and a private parlour,' Isobel said. 'The quieter the better.'

'Yes, ma'am, there's just the thing free, if you'll come this way.'

'And hot water and tea and a good supper,' Dorothy chimed in, clutching the dressing case that she insisted on keeping with her even though Isobel had brought no jewellery.

'We're famous for our suppers, at the Bell.' The man halted. 'Just mind this chaise coming in, ma'am.'

The vehicle with four horses sweating in the traces swept into the yard and pulled up in front of them. Isobel stepped back to take a new path to the inn entrance.

The door opened in her face, the porter hurried forwards. 'Here, mind the lady!' Dorothy took her arm and a tall figure dropped down onto the cobbles.

'Giles!'

'What the devil are you doing here?' He slammed the carriage door shut and confronted her, for all the world as if he had a right to know of her movements, she thought, feeding her temper to keep the treacherous delight at seeing him at bay.

'Never you mind my lady's business and watch your tongue, you rogue.' Dorothy planted her hands on her hips and confronted him, bristling. 'A respectable lady ought to be able to travel the country without being accosted in inn yards by the likes of you!'

Heads were turning, more carriages were pulling in. 'I think we would draw less attention if we go inside,' Isobel said, tugging at her stalwart defender's arm. 'Come, Dorothy.'

'I'll have them fetch the parish constable, I will,' the maid scolded as she marched into the inn on Isobel's heels. 'I told you he was no gentleman. What's he doing here, I'd like to know!'

CHAPTER NINETEEN

'I, too, would like to know what Giles Harker is doing in Oxford,' Isobel said with feeling. She felt queasy with surprise and nerves, her pulse was all over the place and her thoughts were in turmoil. After that initial shock, the delight of thinking that, somehow, he had come for her, common sense reasserted itself.

What *was* Giles doing here? It was too much of a coincidence that they should both find themselves in an Oxford inn. Had she been wrong and he was the one behind the mysterious stranger who was probing the secrets of Longmere? But if that was the case it could only be out of some twisted desire to hurt her, to expose her secrets, and surely she had done nothing to deserve that? It was hard to believe she had been so far awry in her assessment of his character.

'Welcome, my lady.' The landlord appeared and ushered them farther in. 'If a nice pair of rooms with a parlour on the quiet side of the house is what is wanted, we have just the thing. If you will follow me, ma'am.

'I'll have hot water sent up directly, my lady, and supper will be on the table within the half hour. Here you are, ma'am.'

'That looks very satisfactory, thank you.' He could have shown them into a prison cell for all Isobel cared, or no-

ticed. The man bowed himself out and Dorothy threw herself dramatically in front of the door, her back pressed to
the panels.

'He'll not get in here, the vile seducer!'

'Oh, for goodness' sake, Dorothy, Mr Harker is no such
thing, although what he is doing here I have no idea.' A
rap on the door made Dorothy jump. She emitted a small
scream and flung it open to reveal a startled maid with a
jug. 'Your hot water, ma'am.'

'Thank you.' Isobel waited until the girl had gone before
she turned back to Dorothy. 'There is no need for alarm.
Please be less melodramatic! There is absolutely no call
for all this shrieking—oh!' She pressed her hand to her
thudding heart as the door swung open on the knock and
Giles stepped into the room.

'Lady Isobel. Will you join me for supper?'

'Certainly not. I have no intention of dining with a man
in an inn, and most definitely not with you.' She looked
at him with painful intensity. The scars were paler and
thinner now. His expression was politely neutral, but his
eyes were wary. *As well they might be*, she thought as she
strove to settle her breathing.

'The middle of the Season seems an unusual time to be
taking a long coach journey, Lady Isobel,' Giles observed.
'Your admirers will be missing you.'

She did not attempt to cover her snort of derision. 'I
hardly think so. A friend needs me for a few days, then I
will be returning.'

'A friend in Oxford?' He leant a shoulder against the
door frame and frowned at her.

'No. If that was the case I would hardly be staying in
an inn.'

'Where my lady is going is none of your business,' Dorothy interjected. 'Shall I go and get a couple of pot boys and have him thrown out, ma'am?'

'I do not think that is necessary, thank you, Dorothy.' Isobel doubted two lads would be capable of ejecting Giles in any case. She knew he was strong and fit, but now he looked leaner—and tougher with those scars and his dark brows drawn together into a frown. 'Mr Harker will be leaving immediately, I am certain.'

'If I might have a word with you first—alone.' He straightened up and held the door open for Dorothy.

Isobel opened her mouth to protest, then thought better of it. If five minutes of painful intimacy meant she discovered what he was about, then it would be worth it. 'Dorothy, go downstairs, please. No,' she said as the maid began to launch into a protest. 'Either you go or Mr Harker and I will have to. I wish to speak to him confidentially.'

'But, my lady—'

Giles bundled the maid out of the room, closed the door and locked it before she could get another word out.

'It is a strange thing if a lady may not visit a friend without being waylaid and interrogated,' Isobel snapped.

'Yes. I wonder that you stand for it,' he said musingly, his eyes focused on her face. 'I would have expected a cool *good evening* on seeing me and then for you to refuse to receive me. It is very shocking for us to be alone like this.'

'I am well aware of that, Mr Harker! I want to know why you are here.'

'In Oxford? Why should I not be?'

'In Oxford, in this inn, at this time? I was foolish enough to fall in love with you, Giles Harker. Even more foolish to trust you. This is too much of a coincidence for my liking.'

'That trust certainly appears to have vanished. Isobel,

you know full well you could trust me to take only what was offered to me.'

'I am not talking about—' She could feel herself growing pink, whether from anger, embarrassment or sheer anxiety she could not tell.

'Sex?'

'Yes, *sex*.' She was blushing, she knew it, and it was more from desire and anger at herself than embarrassment. 'I am talking about the way you abandoned me, washed your hands of me the moment my parents appeared.'

His eyebrows rose. 'You wanted me to treat you as a friend in front of your parents? You wanted to risk your reputation by acknowledging a liaison with me?'

'No, I did not want that and you know it! But there was no word of affection or regret, no acknowledgement that I was distressed or of what we had shared. You had your amusement—and yes, I am aware of your self-control, I thank you—and then, when it all became difficult, you shrug me and my feelings aside.'

Giles pushed away from the door, all pretence of casualness gone. 'Isobel, I only did what was practical. It would not have helped to have drawn out our parting, merely added to your unhappiness.'

'Practical? Giles, there was nothing practical about my feelings for you.'

'Was? Past tense?' He came so close that the hem of her skirts brushed his boots, but she would not retreat. 'I thought that when you loved, you would love for ever.'

'Then I cannot have been in love with you, can I? Just another foolish woman fascinated by your handsome face.'

'We did not make love until after this.' He gestured towards his scarred cheek.

'Guilt, then. Gratitude. Lust. Call it what you like. It was certainly lust, those few mad moments in the passageway at the Leamingtons' ball!' Only her anxiety for Annabelle and Jane, only the price of misplaced trust, kept her from falling into his arms. 'What do my feelings for you matter? I want to know why you are here. Are you following me?'

'No,' Giles said. 'I am not following you and our meeting here is a genuine coincidence.' Truth? Lies? How could she tell? She had thought he had fallen in love with her and he had not. Obviously she could not understand him at all.

If she did not love him, he would not make her so angry. If she only dared trust him—but he would be disgusted when he realised she had given away her child, had not had the courage to raise her as his own mother had raised him. Whatever she thought of the Scarlet Widow, the woman's fierce love for her son could not be mistaken.

'You are very agitated for a woman who is merely going to visit a friend for a few days,' he remarked, cutting through her thoughts and sending her tumbling into unconsidered speech.

'If I am agitated, then it is because I cannot get free from you. It seems I cannot keep even my secrets—' She stumbled to a halt.

'So,' Giles said slowly, his eyes never leaving her face with its betraying colour, 'I am right. You have a secret, one greater than the loss of your virginity, one that you would not trust to me even though you tell me you loved me, even though then you had no reason to mistrust me. You are afraid. Is it a secret that lays you open to blackmail, perhaps?'

'Blackmail?' Isobel went cold. 'No, of course not.' Was that what the prying stranger was about? But who had sent him? 'You may leap to whatever conclusions you wish, Giles Harker. You have made me so angry I scarce know what I am saying.'

'No, you are not angry.' He caught her hands in his and

held them even when she tugged. 'Or, rather, anger is not the main emotion here. You are afraid.'

Unable to free herself without a struggle, Isobel turned her face away. What she was going to do when he left her alone—if he ever did—she had no idea. She dared not let him know where she was going or she might lead him to Annabelle. All she could do was to get to Jane and try, somehow, to work out how to protect her daughter and her friend.

'Of course I am afraid—I am locked in a room and being manhandled. Am I your prisoner while you interrogate me?' she demanded. Defiance was the only weapon she had against the fear and the awful weakness of her love for him. And that love would betray Annabelle.

Giles released her wrists and she stood rubbing them, although he had not held her tight enough to hurt. The touch of his hands, the fingers that had orchestrated such pleasure in her, seemed to burn like ice. 'This has gone too far for me to walk away from it now, Isobel, whether you want me or trust me or not. You are in trouble, more trouble than you know.'

He turned the key in the lock and walked out, letting the door slam behind him. Isobel sank down in the chair behind her, her knees suddenly like warm wax.

'My lady? I passed him on the stairs and he looked like thunder—are you all right, my lady? I should never have left you alone with him.'

'I am perfectly fine, Dorothy,' Isobel said with a calm that was intended to steady herself as much as the maid. 'Mr Harker and I had unfinished business, that is all. I did not have the opportunity to say everything I wanted to when we left Wimpole.'

She had not convinced her, but there was nothing to be

done about it now. 'Dinner will be here soon and neither of us have so much as washed our hands.'

But what had those parting words meant? How did he know she was in trouble?

'JUST YOU STOP right there, my bullies.'

The chaise juddered to a halt and Isobel let down the window. 'Ned! Ned Foster, it is I, Lady Isobel. Please open the gate.'

'Yes, my lady!' the big man called back and swung open the heavy gate that barred the entrance into the manor courtyard. Chickens ran flapping in panic as the postilions brought the chaise in and Isobel heard the clang of the gate thudding back into its catches. It felt as though she was in a besieged castle. Isobel fought back the melodramatic image and gathered her things.

She was paying off the men and Dorothy was carrying the bags around to the back entrance as Jane came running down the steps, a big shawl bundled around her shoulders against the raw air. 'Isobel! I did not dare hope you'd come. How long can you stay?'

'For as long as it takes,' Isobel said grimly as she hugged her friend. 'I am so glad to be here. The weather was bad after Oxford and there was a landslip about sixty miles from Oxford so we had to spend another day on the road. Oh, Jane,' she confessed as they entered the hallway, out of earshot of the servants. 'I do not know what is going on here, or who is to blame for it, but I have been so foolish. I fell in love with the most impossible man and I think this is a consequence. I am so sorry.'

'Foolish to fall in love?' Jane smiled. 'That is never foolish.'

'It is when the man in question is the illegitimate son of the Scarlet Widow.'

Her friend's eyes widened. 'Oh, my, I have heard of her. But how on earth did you meet him? Does he know you love him?'

'Unfortunately, yes. We made love, Jane,' she added as the drawing-room door shut safely behind them. Best to get the entire confession over as quickly as possible.

'You aren't—'

'No. But it all ended badly—I thought he felt the same for me, but it is quite obvious that he does not, and, in any case, there is no way we can ever be together. His mother sees me as a threat to him and I think she must be behind whatever is going on here. But how she ever found out, I do not know.'

'You did not tell him?'

'That I had a child? No. He knows that Lucas and I anticipated our marriage, but that is all.' Isobel paced to the window and stood staring out at the darkening gardens. 'Perhaps I am worrying unduly after all, for unless one of your people betrays us, there is no reason anyone might suspect Annabelle is not exactly who you say she is.'

'And I trust them implicitly,' Jane said, nodding. 'There might be a danger if she resembled you closely, but as it is, she is very obviously a Needham. It is seven months since you saw her, isn't it? She is growing.'

'Yes.' It seemed like seven years. 'May I see her now? I did not want to speak of this unless we were alone, but now, I cannot wait. Is she much changed?'

'I think she is perfect, but you will judge for yourself.' Her friend's smile was warm and once again Isobel was filled with gratitude that Jane had taken her child, loved her like her own and yet was prepared to share her so unselfishly. 'She is bright, quick and very lovely. Come and see—they are in the kitchen with old Rosemary, hindering her efforts to make cakes.'

Isobel almost ran down the stone-flagged passageway and into the kitchen. Two small children were perched on the edge of the big table, legs dangling, their eyes glued to the big bowl of fruit cake mixture the cook was stirring.

'More plums,' Nathanial demanded, but Isobel could only focus on the little girl.

She scooped her up, warm and sweet and slightly sticky around the mouth from stealing batter. 'Surprise!'

'Aunt Ishbel,' Annabelle said with a crow of delight and a kiss. She had never been able to get her tongue around Isobel's name.

'How pretty you look—and how sticky you are.' Isobel whirled her round in her arms and everything in the world was right again. Then she stopped at the sight of their reflection in the battered mirror propped at one end of the dresser. Annabelle, female to her chubby fingertips, examined her own image with interest. Two heads of tumbled hair, soft and slippery, sliding out of its pins, but Annabelle's was blonde while Isobel's was brown. Two rather determined little chins, but very different noses. Two pairs of wide grey eyes.

'Pretty,' Annabelle said with a crow of delight.

'Pretty,' Isobel agreed. *Oh, thank you, Lucas, for giving me this child.* And anyone who saw them together would not pick up any significant likeness, she was sure. She turned to see Jane smiling as she watched them.

'She grew so quickly,' Jane said. 'One minute she was still a chubby little baby and the next, there she is—a little girl. Now I think we can see what they will be like when they grow up. They are both going to have the Needham height, don't you think?'

'Yes,' Isobel agreed, swallowing the tears that threatened to well up. It was ridiculous to weep because she was

so happy to be here and it would frighten Annabelle. 'I
cannot believe how she has grown.'

She had dreamed of the experiences she and her 'niece'
would share as Annabelle grew up. They would go shopping together, she would be there at her first parties, her
first dance. She would hear her whispered confidences
about first love.

'Isn't it bath time?' she asked, grinning at little Nathaniel as he stuck out his lower lip mutinously. 'Come along,
I'll tell you stories about Wimpole Hall where I have been
staying and about London and I'll tuck you up in bed.'

'Cake,' Annabelle said. 'Cake and bath and stories and
bed.'

'Bath and bed and stories now, cake in the morning,'
Isobel countered, holding out her hand to the little boy.
'How many stairs is it up to bed? I'll wager you cannot
count them yet.'

'I can!' He was off at a run and Isobel followed him,
her cheek pressed against Annabelle's soft one. *Oh, Lucas,
what a lovely child we made. I'll protect her, I promise.*
Even if the danger was from the man she now loved.

'COME AND SEE the kittens.' Annabelle stood beside the
breakfast table and hopped from one foot to the other while
Isobel spread honey on her last piece of toast. 'Mama says
I may have a kitten.'

'A puppy,' Nathaniel contradicted.

'Both,' Jane said, rolling her eyes. 'But by the time they
decide which they are going to have they'll be grown cats
and dogs.'

'Shall I help choose?' Both heads nodded as one—this
was obviously the solution to an intractable problem.

'Come along, then.' Isobel put down her napkin. 'And
wrap up warmly.'

The farmyard was enclosed, with high arches in the walls to east and west. The walls kept out the wind and the stall-fed cattle and the horses kept the barns and stables surprisingly warm, so it was no hardship to sit on a bale outside the cowshed while the children brought out the kittens and puppies for inspection.

'I think the little boy with the white tip to his tail,' she said to Nathaniel. The pup was big and bold and looked as though he would cope well with the rough and tumble of life with Nathaniel. 'And the black-and-white kitten with the white tip for Annabelle—and then they will match.'

Delighted, the children reached for their new pets and Annabelle promptly had her knuckles swiped by the mother cat who had stalked out to see what was going on. Isobel hauled the crying child onto her lap and hugged her and the kitten equally while she wrapped a handkerchief around the scratched hand. 'It is all right, she was only cross because—'

'What a charming picture. Maternal love. I thought that must be the secret, from the timing of things.' The deep, familiar voice cut through the sounds of the farmyard, the child's sobs, the barking of the sheepdog on its chain.

CHAPTER TWENTY

Isobel froze and Annabelle stopped wailing to inspect the new arrival.

'Go—' With an effort Isobel moderated her tone so as not to frighten the children. 'Nathaniel, Annabelle, go inside and ask Cook to find a proper bandage for Annabelle's hand and tell her I said you may have a slice of cake each.'

They ran, tears and strange men forgotten, before she changed her mind about cake directly after breakfast. Isobel stood up, the kitten unregarded in her hands. 'You are not welcome here, Giles. How did you get in?'

'The brawny yokel outside is guarding the front gate, but he does not appear to have the wit to work out that there is a perfectly obvious track leading to this one.' Giles strode across the straw-strewn yard and stopped by the mounting block.

'What do you want?' Isobel demanded.

'To discover if what I suspect, what my mother believes she has discovered, is true.'

'Your mother discovered? So this is blackmail?' *Is it a secret that lays you open to blackmail, perhaps?* Giles had asked. *He knows*, she thought, a sort of bleak misery settling over her, eclipsing even the fear.

'It would have been if I had not caught Geraldine in time and made her tell me exactly what she had discovered about you. She's as protective as that mother cat and has about as many scruples.'

'What do you think you know?' Isobel asked. Her lips felt stiff, the question almost choked her, but she had to know what she was fighting.

'That you have a love child whom you gave away to your friend to raise as her own.'

'I did not want to let her go!' The kitten gave a squeak of protest and Isobel set it down next to its mother who promptly began to wash it. 'It was the only thing to do. I suppose you think I have no courage because your mother kept you.'

'I have to thank her for that,' Giles said.

'It seems she had no scruples about shaming her family or taking you from your grandfather's care. You grew up with a mother who had a scandalous reputation, and, apparently, she had no concerns about bringing you up to have to fight every day of your life because of who you are.'

'She gave me life and she gave me, I hope, some of her courage. But she had to fight for so long that she does not know how to stop. When I discovered that she had found out something to your detriment and was coming here to threaten you with it, I stopped her.'

'How? Are you telling me you can control that woman?'

'Oh, yes. She believed me when I told her that if she tried to hurt you I would take her back to the Dower House, lock her in and keep the key. I have done it before when she went beyond the limit and I'll do it again if I have to.'

'Then I must thank you for that, at least,' she threw at him. 'But if you have the situation under control, what are you doing here?'

'I wanted to make sure you were safe here, that her

agents had gone. I knew you had a secret before she discovered what it was.'

'How?' She had been so careful...

'Just putting together things that you said. I realised it was something here, in Herefordshire, something to do with Needham.' He took a step towards her, then shook his head and turned back to hitch one hip on the mounting block. 'I must have gone over every word you have said to me, Isobel. Every silence, every moment when there was such sadness in your eyes. Until I realised she was on your trail all I wanted to do was protect you by keeping away.'

'Why, Giles? Why did you care so much? Are you—?' Isobel broke off, her courage almost failing. But she had to know. 'Are you telling me you love me after all?' she asked flatly.

'No,' he said, his face tight and stark. 'Nothing has changed, Isobel. I care for you, I want to keep you safe. And I am every bit as ineligible for you as I ever was.'

Her pride would not let her weep or plead. 'What a good thing,' she said. 'Of course, I have realised that I do not love you—it was a foolish infatuation when I was lonely and miserable. Now I am doing the Season and looking for a husband—I will be delighted if I never see you again.'

'I was a foolish infatuation, was I, Isobel? In that case either your acting skill is incredible or you have equally good powers of self-deception. You fell in love with me and I believe your current protestations as much as I did those at Oxford or at the ball.'

'I am not a good actress, merely someone telling the truth,' she said forcing the words out between numb lips. 'I needed what you could give me at Wimpole. I needed heat and warmth and...affection.' One brow slanted up satirically at the euphemism. She felt her cheeks burn red.

'You do not care for me now, so why are you concerning yourself? I told you at Oxford that I did not want you.'

'On the contrary, at Oxford you told me I had betrayed your trust and your feelings.' He stood up and took one step towards her before her upflung hand stopped him.

'I would say anything to get rid of you,' she threw at him, desperate to hang on to the last shreds of her self-control. 'I do not want you, I do not need you—all I need is your silence and for you to keep your blackmailing mother silent also.'

'So the little girl is your daughter and your friend is raising her as the twin of her son.' He glanced down at the Border Collie puppy that was attempting to chew the heel of his boot, picked it up by the scruff and handed it to Isobel. She caught it up without taking her eyes from his face and clutched the warm squirming bundle to her bosom like a shield. 'She has your eyes. May I see her?'

'No! I have told you, I do not want anything more to do with you. Go back to London and marry a wife your mama will buy you. She will purchase your heirs in the same way as she bought your accent and your education and your smooth society manners.'

'No one controls my life.' There was anger in his voice. 'Not since I was a child. Do you condemn my mother for wanting the best upbringing she could get for me? What do you buy for your child, Isobel? Do you pay for her clothes and her nurse? Will you pay for her governess? Will you search for the right husband for her when she is old enough to make her come-out, even if you do it from behind the walls of your own home? Or will you wash your hands of her and leave it all to Mrs Needham so you can walk away and find this husband you seek?'

'Between us Jane and I will do everything we can for

the children. I thought this would be best for Annabelle. I did not want her to grow up as…'

'A bastard?' Giles enquired in a tone that made her wince. 'I manage.'

'I do not want her to have to *manage*. And it is different for a woman and you know it,' she threw at him.

'Isobel, are you all right?' She turned and there was Jane, a shotgun in the crook of her arm. 'Don't you dare lay a finger on her,' she said fiercely to Giles.

Giles took a reckless step towards the woman with the gun. A woman who Isobel knew was perfectly capable of taking a shot at a cattle thief. And now it was the children under threat. 'There is no call to shoot anyone.'

'None at all if you leave,' Jane agreed. 'And are silent about this.'

'I will tell no one,' Giles said. Then, ignoring both Jane and the gun, he went to stand in front of Isobel. He lifted the puppy from her arms and set it down before catching her hands in his. 'Isobel, I thought you loved me.' He spoke directly to her as though they were alone, so close she could feel his warmth, smell his familiar scent of clean linen and citrus and something that was simply Giles.

'I—' She stared into the green eyes and the farmyard seemed to vanish. Jane, the animals, everything faded away and there was only the two of them, handfast. She could not lie to him, not about this. 'Yes, I love you. I try not to, but I cannot lie to you about it.' And in his eyes she thought she read an answering love and all the doubt and fear vanished. 'I love you, I trust you and I am sorry that my faith in you wavered for a while.'

She waited for the words, but they did not come, only a shadow that clouded the clear green eyes and a twist of the mouth that she so much wanted to kiss. 'Do you truly

not love me?' she had to ask at last when he did not speak.
'Can I be so wrong in what I feel from you?'

'I cannot allow myself to love you, Isobel. There is no
future for us. Nothing has changed except that now I know
you are too vulnerable with this secret to risk the slightest breath of scandal. The secret is safe, I promise you.
There will be no risk, Isobel, because this ends here. This
is where we part.'

'I know.' She had faced that finally on the long drive.
There had never been any hope because a scandal would
ruin him, would break her parents' hearts, might even compromise Annabelle's future in ways she could not foresee.
'I know that. I give up.' Her voice cracked and she controlled it somehow. 'I just need you to tell me how you
feel, Giles.'

'No.' His face was stark as he bent his head. 'No, I will
not say I love you, Isobel. Only that I care too much to
make this worse than it already is.' The kiss was gentle,
achingly tender. His lips lingered on hers and she could
taste the heat and the passion that he was holding in check,
feel the tremor that ran through him when she raised her
arms and curled them around his neck to hold him for just
a moment longer.

'Goodbye, Isobel.' He turned and strode out of the yard
and when she sank down onto the bale, her legs too weak
to hold her, and looked around, she was alone. Jane had
gone. Distantly there was the sound of carriage wheels,
then silence.

Something wet touched her hand and she looked down.
The puppy that had been chewing Giles's boot was lick-
ing her hand. It wasn't the pup Nathaniel had chosen, but
a skinny little female with a comical white patch over one
eye. Isobel scooped her up and the puppy licked her nose.

'Hello,' Isobel said, her voice sounding thready in her

own ears. Then she got up and walked inside with the dog in her arms. 'One more day and then we are going to London,' she said to it as it wriggled.

'Isobel.' Jane stood just inside the empty kitchen and hugged her and the pup together. 'Oh, my dear.' When Isobel just shook her head she said, 'I would not have shot him, you know. Not the man you love.'

'Thank you,' Isobel said, her smile hurting. 'I will go home tomorrow. May I take the puppy? I don't expect trying to housetrain a dog in a post-chaise is easy, but I will manage. We will be fine.'

'Of course you will,' Jane said and her face showed that she knew it was not the puppy that Isobel was talking about. 'Come and let Annabelle choose a name for it.'

A PUPPY IN a post-chaise was certainly an excellent distraction. Maude, as Annabelle inexplicably named the black-and-white bundle, proved to be ravenously hungry and ate and drank everything put in the dishes on the floor for her—with inevitable consequences. Jane had the foresight to give them a small sack of sawdust and a large roasting dish, so Dorothy climbed out to empty it at every stop, complaining vociferously.

But Isobel would not let her chastise Maude, even when she started to chew shoes and the edge of the carriage rug. 'She's only a baby, Dorothy,' she said, picking up the puppy and receiving a wet slurp on the nose for her pains. With a contented sigh the little dog went to sleep on her lap, worn out by her adventure.

Which left all the stages from Gloucester still to sit through. They would not arrive in London until past ten that night after a six o'clock start in the morning. Dorothy started to doze, wedged in one corner against the jolting, but Isobel sat upright, cradled the puppy on her lap and let her mind wander where it might. She was too tired and too hurt to try to think sensibly. And besides, what was there to think about?

Other than Annabelle, she realised with a smile that faded as the guilt took over once more. Her parents would adore her and yet they would never know they had a grand-daughter.

She realised she was about to drift off, and did not fight it. It would bring dreams, she supposed, but dreams were all she had left now.

Trust... I trust you. The words she had said to Giles. But it was not his face in the dream, it was her parents, watching her anxiously. She woke, but the image did not fade. They had trusted her when she had fled to Hereford, loved her enough to leave her there a year when she wrote and begged not to be asked to come home. They had believed her when she was sent home in disgrace after the house party when virtually no one else had. If she could trust anyone, she could trust her parents, she realised. Perhaps, after all, some good could come of this unhappiness.

Isobel curled into the corner of the chaise and went back to sleep.

'GOD, SHE HAS courage, my Isobel,' Giles said to himself as he sat at the writing table in his inn bedchamber.

Isobel, so frank, so brave, so direct with the truth and with her love. She had known he would never act on his true feelings, never show her what was in his heart. The most she could hope for was his flirtation and his idle, thoughtless kisses. So she had shown him what love was.

He screwed up what he had been writing and threw the paper on the fire. A letter would only do more damage. He had written the words he had wanted to say, the true

words. But they were better as ashes—it would do Isobel
no good to tell her he loved her.

What was he going to do now? He was not going to
marry Miss Holt, that was certain. Somehow he would
have to make Geraldine accept that. She only wanted him
to be happy and she found his independence infuriating.
She wanted to arrange everything to her satisfaction, including his happiness.

He would be happy again, one day, he supposed. One day.

CHAPTER TWENTY-ONE

'Mama. Papa. May I speak with you?'

'We have been speaking to each other for the last half hour,' Lord Bythorn pointed out. But he folded his copy of the *Morning Chronicle*, laid it beside his breakfast plate and waited.

'I mean, in private. In your study.' Isobel's chest felt tight, her breakfast—what little of it she had managed to eat—was sitting uneasily in her stomach and she was all too aware of her parents' anxious attention.

'Very well, if you can keep that confounded puppy of yours out of it. It has already destroyed my slippers and it has only been in the house twelve hours.'

'Thank you, Papa.' He was making a joke out of it, bless him.

'Now, WHAT IS this about, eh, Isobel?' He sat behind his big desk, Isobel and her mother in the two wing chairs in front of it. 'This looks uncommonly like a confession.'

'It is.' *Trust*, she reminded herself. *Too late to back out now. Just trust them, they love you.* 'In the last few weeks before Lucas was killed, we were lovers.'

She heard her mother's sharply indrawn breath. Her father's face went blank, then, to her surprise, he said, 'Shocking, but not so very unusual.' There was the very faintest suspicion of a smile in the fleeting look he sent her mother. Isobel opened her mouth to blurt out a question and shut it hurriedly.

'After he died, I discovered I was pregnant.' This time the breath was a gasp and her father's face lost its smile as the colour ebbed out of his cheeks. 'That was why I stayed with Jane. She is not the mother of twins: her daughter is mine. Your grandchild.'

The silence was broken only by her mother's sob, quickly stifled with her hand. Isobel reached out her own hand, hesitated, then withdrew it.

'You could not trust us to look after you?' her father asked with a gentleness that warned her he was keeping a tight rein on his emotions.

'No,' Isobel admitted. Only the truth would serve now. 'I was not thinking very clearly. I wanted Lucas and he was gone—I was frightened that the child would be taken from me. I could not trust anyone except Jane.' The tears were running down her mother's face now. This was as bad as she feared it would be—she had hurt them dreadfully. 'I am so sorry. I did it for the best.'

She turned and this time took her mother's hand. It stayed in hers and, after a moment, the fingers curled around her own. 'Her name is Annabelle.' It was her grandmother's name.

'Why now? Why are you telling us now? Is something wrong with her?' Her mother clutched her hand with a desperate urgency.

'She is perfect and she is well. No, it is not that. I realised I am never going to marry and have a family. And I saw that I was depriving you of your grandchild and that was wrong. And I have been thinking a lot about trust, these past few days—and I knew I should have trusted you from the beginning.'

'Who knows about the child?' her father asked.

'Jane's old family retainers, but they would never betray her secrets and they adore Annabelle. The doctor, and he is a family friend.' She saw their relief and knew she had to shatter it. 'And the Dowager Marchioness of Faversham and her son, Giles Harker.'

'What! That wanton creature? How in blazes did she discover this?'

'She feared I would marry Giles and that there would be a great scandal which would harm him. She uses enquiry agents all the time, it seems, so she set a man to find what secrets I might have. Her intention was to blackmail me into giving up Giles.'

'Marry him? Give him up?' Her mother stared, aghast. 'You are not having a liaison with that man?'

'I am in love with that man,' Isobel corrected gently. 'But, no, we are not lovers and I will not marry him—she is quite right, the scandal would ruin him. He will not admit he loves me because he thinks it would ruin *me*.'

'You love him? He is a—'

'So is our granddaughter,' Lord Bythorn said and her mother gave a gasp of dismay. 'Will he and that woman hold their tongues?'

'Oh, yes. She had no other motive than to protect her son, she will wish me no harm once Giles has convinced her I am no threat to his standing or his career.'

'Hah!' Lady Bythorn said, swiping ineffectually at her eyes with a tiny scrap of lace.

'Mama, he saved my life when I would have drowned. He was scarred defending my honour.'

'True enough,' her father admitted. 'Can we see Annabelle? Or must you keep her from us?'

'No! Of course I will not. But we cannot acknowledge who she is, you must see that. Her prospects are good now—her birth seems perfectly respectable, she will grow up without any stain, a Needham. And her supposed father was Lucas's half-brother, after all.

'But we can visit. She calls me "Aunt," so it is only natural that you should take an interest in her. Jane can visit us here and bring the children.'

'Oh, yes.' Lady Bythorn brightened, sat up and rubbed her palms over her wet cheeks. 'My *granddaughter*! Oh, my goodness.'

'And what of you, Isobel?' her father asked.

She shook her head. 'I cannot marry. I cannot hide this from my husband and even if I did find someone, I dare not risk Annabelle's reputation by telling him before I am wed.' She added, 'I will finish this Season, I do not wish to cause any further talk.'

'Oh, my dear.' He sighed and shook his head, but when he looked at her there was a smile lurking under the heavy dark brows. 'But thank you for my grandchild.' As she got up he rose too and came round the desk to embrace her. 'I had hoped, after Needham's death, you could have found a good man who would love you.'

'I did, Papa,' she said. 'But it seems I cannot have him. I must write to Jane.'

The Season was in full swing now. Isobel hurled herself into it as though the sea of frivolity and pleasure could wash away the pain and the longing. Only her parents' delight in hearing about Annabelle kept her spirits up and the arrival of some portrait sketches that Jane had asked the village schoolmaster to make had them in a frenzy of planning for a visit just as soon as the summer came.

Taking tea after dinner a week after her return, Isobel overheard her father in conversation with their host. '...remodelling the entire West Wing of the Priory,' Lord

Roehampton said. 'Got a very promising young architect working on it—Harker. But I was forgetting,' he added, lowering his voice. 'He's the man who stood up for Albright over that wretched business your daughter fell victim to. Good show, that. His mother's a menace in society, but he can't help that and, to do him credit, he stands by her. Loyal, as I said to Lady Roehampton when she was cavilling about employing him. The man's got the instincts of a gentleman.'

'Yes,' Lord Bythorn said slowly. 'It seems he has.'

Isobel stared at her father, a hope forming in her mind so improbable, she hardly dared try to think it through. As the three of them sat in the carriage on the short ride home through the streets of Mayfair she said abruptly, before she could give herself time to lose courage, 'Papa, if Giles Harker came to you now and asked for my hand in marriage, what would you say?'

'My love, he would not do such a thing. He knows it would cause a scandal. I think I've discovered enough about the man by now to know he won't hurt you,' her father said gruffly.

'But if he did, would it cause a scandal if you said *yes*?' she asked. 'I know it would if you forbade the match and we ran away together. But if it was seen that you approved, would that not make all the difference?'

'Isobel!' her mother interjected. 'You cannot marry a man born out of wedlock.'

'Why not? I am not going to marry any other man and it seems to me that if it does not hurt anyone else, then I may as well be happy as not! It is not as though I wish to be received at court again or spend my time at Almack's. Papa—if you gave us your blessing, *would* there be a scandal? One that would hurt you and Mama, be difficult for Frederick at school? One that would ruin Giles's business?'

Her mother moaned again at the word *business*, but her father said, after a pause, 'You heard me talking to Roehampton? I must confess, I see Harker in a different light now, with all that has happened. No, I do not think it would cause more than a seven-day wonder, not if I gave it my blessing and your mother received him. You have enough of a reputation for eccentricity already, my dear.'

'Oh, Papa!' She launched herself across the carriage and hugged him, squashing his silk hat. 'Thank you!'

'But he will not ask me, will he?' Lord Bythorn said gently, setting her back on her seat. 'The more he cares for you, the less likely he is to approach you again.'

'No,' Isobel agreed. 'So I will just have to ask him.'

Her mother subsided against the squabs with a moan. 'I knew I should have brought my smelling bottle!'

THE FIRST THING was to find out where Giles was, Isobel decided as she sat up in bed the next morning nursing a cup of chocolate in her hands. The work at Wimpole could not have been completed yet, but she assumed that, like Mr Soane, he would have several commissions in hand at any one time. Some she knew about, such as Lord Roehampton's West Wing, but Giles could be anywhere.

There was only one person in London who might know, and Mama would have the vapours if she thought her daughter was going anywhere near her. It did not seem to have occurred to her parents that if she married Giles then the Scarlet Widow would be her mother-in-law, which was probably a sign that they believed there was little chance that such a thing would ever happen. Well, time to worry about that later, she thought philosophically. Just at the moment it was the least of her worries.

'Will you fetch me a London directory please, Dorothy?' she called.

'Yes, my lady. Just one moment. This dratted dog has chewed the tassel on the curtain tie.' The maid sounded exasperated, but Isobel knew full well that she doted on Maude and sneaked biscuits to her in her basket.

'Here we are.' Dorothy bustled out of the dressing room with the book in her hands. 'Heard about an interesting shop, have you, my lady?'

'Er...no. I am just looking up the address of a new acquaintance.'

Lady Faversham lived not so very far away in Bruton Street. Close enough, in fact, not to need the carriage. 'My blue walking dress and the dark blue pelisse and the velvet hat this morning, Dorothy. I have some calls to make, but I can take one of the footmen with me, so you can carry on with those alterations.'

AN HOUR AND a half later, at an unconscionably early hour to be making a call, Isobel was admitted to Lady Faversham's elegant hall by her equally elegant butler.

'I am sure that if it is a matter concerning Mr Harker her ladyship will wish to receive you,' he said, admirably concealing any trace of speculation. 'If you would care to wait in here, my lady, I will enquire.'

Giles's name did indeed open doors. Isobel was received by her ladyship who was reclining on a chaise in her boudoir in a confection of lace and sea-green gauze that roused a pang of envy in Isobel's breast.

'What do you want with my son now?' the Widow demanded, narrowing ice-green eyes at her.

There did not seem to be any point beating about the bush. Isobel took a deep breath and said, 'To tell him that if he asks for my hand my father will give it to him willingly. There will be no scandal, he will be welcomed into the family.'

'What?' The Widow stared at her.

'My parents have accepted that I will never marry anyone else. They are grateful to Giles for what he has done for me. And,' she added as the Widow opened her mouth, 'they know about my daughter.

'And also—' she slipped in before Lady Faversham could speak. 'I am well dowered, well connected and perfectly placed to help Giles's career. All I need to know is where he is and I will go and propose to him.'

'Propose? You have courage, I will say that for you. And if I object?'

'Why should you be so spiteful?' A hint of colour touched the older woman's cheekbones under the powder. 'If he does not want me, he can always refuse. If this is some sort of trick, you have the instrument of revenge in your own hands.'

'I only want him to be happy,' Lady Faversham said and to her horror Isobel saw one tear roll down her cheek. 'And he is so stubbornly independent. Will you make him happy?'

'Oh, yes,' Isobel said. 'I promise.'

'Excellent.' With a dab of lace the tear was gone, taking the momentary weakness with it, and the green eyes defied Isobel to ever recall she had seen it. 'He is at Wimpole Hall.'

'Thank you.' She turned to go, then on an impulse swung round. 'Where did you purchase that exquisite robe?'

'Mirabelle's,' the Widow said and, to her amazement, smiled. 'Buy blue, not green. Blue and silver.'

GILES FLOATED ON his back in the plunge pool, ears below water, the steam coiling and rising around him. It had been a long, hard, damp day up at the Hill House supervising the demolition and the salvaging of the best stone and he had become chilled to the marrow.

The heat soothed his body, but the more he relaxed physically, the more his imagination could work and the worse the pain in his heart was. The gentle lap of the water made him think of Isobel's caressing fingers, the silence gave her voice space to echo in his mind. *I love you, Giles.*

He had done the only thing he could for her and her daughter, he told himself for the thousandth time. He had left her, he had silenced his mother and he had refused to tell Isobel what was in his heart. *Cruel to be kind.* The easy cliché mocked him. Cruel to be perhaps less cruel in the long run, that was the best he could hope for.

Before Isobel had come into his life he had never felt lonely. Now he ached with it. Here at Wimpole, as the bustle of the family's preparations for their departure to Ireland gathered momentum, he could have company every hour of the day and evening if he chose. But he knew he would feel this alone in the midst of thousands without Isobel.

It seemed that to deny love, the emotion he had never believed he could feel, required as much courage and resolution as facing a fellow duellist. The pain certainly lasted longer, bad enough to force him to admit that the emotion was true and would never leave him. He loved her. He could admit it now he was no longer a danger to her, now he would never see her again, except, perhaps, across a crowded ballroom.

He wanted to write to her, tell her how he felt, tell her why this was so impossible. He wrote the letters every night and every morning burned them. How long was it going to be before he could shake off this sensation that without her he was merely a hollow shell, going through the actions of life? Or perhaps he never would be free of it. Perhaps the heart could not heal as the body did.

But doing the honourable thing, the right thing, was never going to be easy. He was not a gentleman, but, for Isobel's sake, he was going to behave like one. He could cope with physical pain, he just had to learn to deal with mental torment, too, or go mad.

A ripple of water splashed his face and his floating body rocked. Someone else had got into the pool. Lord Hardwicke or young Philip, he supposed, opening his eyes and staring up at the vault of the ceiling, wishing they would go away. The other bather said nothing. Giles raised his head and saw something on the curving edge at the end of the pool.

A small black-and-white puppy was sitting on its haunches watching him. Its tongue lolled out, its tail thrashed back and forth—it was obviously delighted to see him. A long blue leash curled onto the damp brown marble where it had been dropped.

Giles surged to his feet, turned and found Isobel, as naked as a water nymph, her wet hair on her shoulders, standing behind him.

'Isobel.' She smiled, that warm, open trusting smile. 'No! No, go away, damn it! I do not want you.' And he turned to forge his way through the water to the steps.

CHAPTER TWENTY-TWO

'Giles.' Her voice stopped him for a second, two, three, then he summoned up all his will and began to walk away again. 'Giles. Please. If you feel anything at all for me, answer one question.'

He should keep going, deny his feelings for her sake, but he found he could not lie to her. 'What is it?' He did not turn around: to see her face, those wide eyes, would be too much to bear.

'If you had not only my father's agreement, but his blessing, his public acceptance, would you marry me?'

'If wishes were horses, beggars might ride,' he said, still looking at the steps that rose out of the water, then twisted steeply to the changing area. Escape. His voice was choked in his throat.

'It is not a wish, it is a fact.'

It could not be. It was impossible. He was dreaming.

'Giles,' the voice from his dreams persisted, 'I wish you would turn around. I am trying to propose to you and it is very difficult talking to the back of your head.'

That brought him round in a spin that created waves. The puppy retreated with a yap of alarm as water sloshed over the sides. The naked nymph was still there, her wet hair almost black, plastered over the curves of her breast. Not a dream, not an hallucination. The real woman.

'Isobel…' He sank his pride and tried an appeal. 'This is not fair. Not to you, not to me, to pretend this is possible.'

'I have only ever lied to you to protect my daughter,' she said, her gaze locked with his. 'I swear on her life that I am not lying to you now. I am not delusional. My father accepts I will marry no one else, ever. I told my parents all about Annabelle, you see, so finally they understand. And once my father thought about it, once he began to hear about you from other people, he realised that he respected you.'

She made no move to come closer to him, only waited patiently, watching his face as he worked painfully through what she was telling him. 'You told them about Annabelle—risked that, for me?'

'No.' She shook her head, painfully honest as ever. 'But it is because of you that I told them. You made me think about trust and honour and what I was withholding from them because I dared not take a chance on their love. So I told them. It was later that I realised that, now they have given up all hope of me making a conventional match, they might consent if they thought you would make me happy.'

'There is a lesson for me in that, you do not have to spell it out,' Giles said. *Trust and the withholding of love.* He had not trusted her to be strong enough to cope with his impossible love as well as her own. 'I thought I was doing the right thing, making the right sacrifice.'

'So it was a sacrifice?' For the first time he saw her fear and her uncertainty in the wide grey eyes and the way she had caught her lower lip between her teeth.

Still the words would not come. How could he risk her regretting it as soon as the knot was tied? So much of her life that she took completely for granted would be lost to her. But if Isobel could trust him, then he must trust her. 'Yes, it was a sacrifice,' Giles admitted.

Her smile was radiant. 'Oh, thank goodness.' It was an ungainly business, splashing towards each other through water that was more than waist-deep. Giles found he was laughing when he finally had Isobel in his arms and so was she, and crying, and the puppy was yapping.

'This is so bizarre it has to be true,' Giles said, his arms full of wet woman. His pulse was racing, he felt dizzy. 'I thought I was dreaming. How on earth did you get here?'

'Never mind that! Will you marry me?' Isobel demanded, her arms twined round his waist.

'Are you sure?' This time he knew she saw his hesitation clearly, realised he had not said those words that mattered to her so much.

'Not if you are not.' All the animation drained away, leaving her naked and vulnerable. 'I am sorry if I misunderstood. I thought it was only the fear of scandal that stopped you and if that was no longer there, it would be all right.' Isobel pushed away from him and splashed to the steps. She climbed out, dripping and naked, the puppy gambolling around her feet until it sensed her unhappiness and crouched, whining.

'Isobel!' Giles took three long strokes and climbed the steps beside her. 'You do not realise what it would mean to be married to me.' He caught her, blocked her escape up the narrow twist of steps that led to the changing area.

'You are used to a great house, a London home, dozens of servants. You are received at Court, you are invited to the most fashionable functions.

'I cannot give you that. You won't be received at Court any longer, there will be people who will snub us, my country home is a tenth the size of this and if we want to live in London we must rent, at least at first. I don't own a carriage. I—'

'Is that all?' she demanded. 'What do you think I want,

Giles?' When he just stood and looked at her, she prodded him in the ribs.

'Me?' Isobel nodded. 'Our children?' Another nod.

'That is all and that is everything. I have a perfectly good dowry which will keep me in all the fashionable frivolity I want—if I want it. The rest can go to the children if you are too stiff-necked to take it to buy a town house or a carriage or whatever you want to improve the estate.'

'Truly?'

'Truly. Now, tell me why you will not marry me, because the only reason that I am prepared to accept is that you do not love me.'

It was like shackles breaking or a dam bursting inside. There was only one thing between him and having the woman he loved and that was his stubborn fear of believing what Isobel was telling him.

Giles took a deep breath. 'I love you.' He found he was grinning. 'I love you. I never thought I would be able to say it to you.' He picked her up, slippery as a fish, and started to climb as she wrapped her arms around his neck and buried her face against him. Apparently his love had run out of words.

Giles stood her on her feet when they reached the little changing room. His brocade robe hung neatly on one of the hooks on the wall that was warmed by the boiler. His slippers equally tidy below. 'My dear love,' he said mildly as he surveyed the scattered feminine clothing that strewed the floor. 'Am I to expect our home to be in this much of a muddle?'

'I was in a hurry,' Isobel said with dignity. She ran her hands over his body. 'I still am. You love me,' she murmured, as if she could still not quite believe it.

Giles caught her wrists as her fingers descended lower. 'And I will prove it to you. But I refuse to make love to you on the floor.' *Not here and not now, anyway.* There was a large bearskin rug in front of his dressing-room fire at home that had fed a particularly delicious and tormenting fantasy about Isobel.

'In my bedchamber, then. Or yours?'

'Neither.' Reluctantly he let her go and pulled on his robe, stuffed his feet into his slippers. There was something respectable about slippers. Wicked rakes did not make passionate love in slippers.

'Why not? You want me.' She slanted a look that was pure provocation from beneath her wet lashes.

'Of course I want you, you witch. I love you. But I am going to marry you.' *Marry you.* He repeated the words in his head, trying to convince himself that this was really going to happen. 'So I am going to do this properly. Respectably.' Isobel opened her mouth to protest. 'I am going to go and get dressed. So are you and you will then find Lady Hardwicke.

'I will ask the earl if he can spare me for a few days. We will drive back to London, in separate chaises, where I will formally ask your father for your hand. We will then proceed to do whatever it is that respectable people do for the duration of a respectable betrothal before they are respectably married.'

'Giles, that will take *weeks*.' Isobel rescued a stocking from the puppy and began to pull it on. Giles studied the way the walls had been painted with minute attention while the rustling and flapping of her dressing went on.

'Precisely. Our wedding is going to be the exact opposite of an elopement.'

'I am dressed. You may stop looking at the architraves or whatever it is you are pretending such interest in.'

'Soffits,' he said vaguely. 'God, you are beautiful.'

'No, I am not. I am—'

'Beautiful. I love you.'

'Then kiss me, Giles. You haven't kissed me since you told me you loved me.'

'Not here.' He watched as she wrapped her wet hair into a towel. 'I will walk you to your room and I will kiss you at your door because I cannot trust myself to touch you here.' He looked down. 'Why is there a puppy chewing my slipper?'

'It is the same one from the farmyard. You gave her to me to hold. She is the only thing you ever gave me—except my life and my honour and a broken heart—so I had to keep her.'

'Oh, hell,' he said, appalled to find his vision blurring. 'Come here.'

Isobel melted into his arms and Giles wondered why he had not realised from the first moment that he touched her that this was where she belonged. Her body was slender and strong in his embrace and her mouth hesitant, soft, as though she was shy and this was the first time.

So he kissed her as though it was, as though this was new for both of them. And it was true, he realised, because this was love and he had never loved before. So he did not demand or plunder, only explored and tasted gently, leisurely, until she was sighing, melting in his arms and he realised that he was more simply happy than he had ever been in his life.

'WHAT WAS YOUR favourite thing about the wedding breakfast?' Giles asked Isobel as she curled up against him on the wide and opulent seat of the carriage that had been his mother's wedding present to them.

'My father plotting a new shrubbery with your grandfather's advice and your mother and mine circling each other like wary cats and then deciding their mutual curiosity about each other's gowns was too much to resist. I have to say, it does help that Papa never had an affaire with her. Did you notice Pamela Monsom's father dodging about the room to avoid her? Pamela is convinced there was something between them.'

'Oh, Lord,' Giles groaned.

'It doesn't matter. Or rather, it does to Lady Monsom, of course, but we can't help that now. I like your mama— she says what she thinks and she is very kind to me now she doesn't regard me as a menace to your well-being.'

'She has had eight weeks to get used to the fact,' Giles said.

'And we have had eight weeks of blameless respectability.' She snuggled closer and nibbled his earlobe.

'I am not going to make love to you in the carriage,' he ground out. 'There is a big bed waiting for us. After that you may assault me where and when you please.' She curled her tongue-tip into his ear. 'Within reason!'

'Very well.' With an effort Isobel stopped teasing him, sat back and watched the countryside rolling past in the sunshine of the late afternoon. 'Wasn't Annabelle lovely? The children were so well behaved. I am so glad Jane brought them down.'

'We will have them to stay whenever she can come,' Giles promised. Isobel had watched him, seen how he was with both the children, how careful he was not to single Annabelle out. He would make a wonderful father.

'We are here.'

She craned to look at the grounds as they rolled up the carriage drive. The house when they reached it was perfect, the brick and dressed stone still crisp with newness, but the garden already embraced it, softened it. 'I love it,' she said and felt his pleasure at hers. 'Where is the room with the big bed?'

'At the back, overlooking the lake. Don't you want to eat first?'

'No, I want to make love,' she whispered in his ear as he swung her down from the carriage. 'Where is everyone?'

'I told them you would meet them in the morning. You see, I guessed you might want to inspect the bedchamber first—there should be a cold meal laid out.'

The front door opened as if by magic as he swept her up into his arms and carried her up the steps, but there was no one to be seen in the hall with its wide staircase. Giles carried on up to the first floor to where double doors stood open on to a room decorated all in palest grey and in blue silk with a wide Venetian window framing the landscape and, as he had promised her, a very big bed.

'Lady Isobel Harker,' Giles said as he set her on her feet. 'There is something in the marriage service about worshipping you with my body and I take promises very seriously.'

'I hope so, Mr Harker,' she murmured as he began to unfasten her gown. Silk and lawn whispered to the ground, her stays followed with a facility that she would tease him about later. But now this felt too important for levity, only for deep happiness.

Giles carried her to the bed and stripped off his own clothing. 'I have never seen you without all those bruises,' she murmured, running her hands over the flat planes of his chest, the ridged muscle of his stomach. 'I was too nervous to notice in the pool that they had gone.'

He lowered himself over her, his scarred cheek resting next to her smooth one and she twisted so she could kiss it, then his nose with its new bump.

'I love you,' he told her as his hands began to caress her. Every time he said the words it seemed to her that it was never just a phrase. Each time he seemed to find it wonderful and new, a surprise to love and be loved.

'Show me,' she whispered back, curling her legs around his waist, cradling him between her thighs where she had wanted him for so long.

'Eight weeks of respectability is all very well,' Giles said, his voice husky. 'But it makes a man very, very impatient.'

'So am I,' Isobel told him, and lifted her hips to press against him, took his mouth and thrust with her tongue to tell him it was all right to be urgent, to take her. It had been a long time since Lucas, but for all his scarce-controlled desire Giles was gentle. She opened to him when he entered her, as he slid home deep and sure to make her his, and then she lost every trace of apprehension in the heat and the joy of their merging and the pleasure that he spun out of caresses and kisses to send her wild and desperate for release.

They cried out together and sank into sleep together. When she woke Giles was watching her and lifted his hand to trace where his eyes had been roaming, across her brow, down her cheek, softly over her lips.

'You were meant for me,' Isobel told him.

'I know. I think I knew from the moment I caught your hand in the lake and feared I was too late. Mine,' Giles said. 'Mine for ever.' And he began to prove it all over again.

* * * * *

Subscribe and fall in love with a Mills & Boon series today!

You'll be among the first to read stories delivered to your door monthly and enjoy great savings.

MILLS & BOON